The First Gentleman

The First Gentleman

Kristina Bachman

iUniverse, Inc.
New York Lincoln Shanghai

The First Gentleman

iUniverse, Inc.

For information address:
iUniverse, Inc.
2021 Pine Lake Road, Suite 100
Lincoln, NE 68512
www.iuniverse.com

ISBN: 0-595-33193-9 (pbk)
ISBN: 0-595-66765-1 (cloth)

Printed in the United States of America

For Mark, my love, my life, my "First Gentleman"

It's dangerous to be right when the government is wrong.

—Voltaire

**Special thanks to Geoff, Alex, Jane, Michael, Nancy and Donna for their expertise and support.
And to everyone else for their humor, understanding, and patience.**

Prologue

Milton's wife had a knack for making him uneasy. Mind you, she wasn't manipulative, just never went for the idea of a quiet, simple life somewhere raising their children and crops, having less to worry about, fewer challenges, no lust for power. Crammed into the immense cavity of The Kennedy Performance Center, he imagined the fans rushing the stage, trampling him underfoot. The crowd was a pulsating mass oozing forward, desperate for their tireless leader's attention. Ecstatic political hounds, just one rung above the group of kids that had been arrested at Woodstock 3, commemorating the 35th anniversary of the original rockfest. Had the authorities been wrong to bring a traditional celebration inside for security purposes? Milton stood beside his wife, his palm sweating in hers, as he tried to remember just when things had become so crazy.

He did his best to ignore Bonnie Sinclair, persistently urging him to wave. He and his wife's assistant had never meshed, and now that Meredith had won, Bonnie would be bothering him for another four years. He didn't care what her sexual preference was and decided that he had defended himself for the last time. She knew how to get people elected and enjoyed treating men like dog shit on the bottom of her shoe on a sweltering August afternoon. The most important thing was his marriage and family; if nothing else he would enjoy that every moment. People envied him. With a plastered smile he waved, imagining he looked like the silly Margaret Thatcher sticker he had in his old college Subaru. Darryl Rodriguez, his wife's campaign manager, pounded him on the back and whispered,

"Hey Milton. Hey buddy, perk up. You look like you've seen a ghost. It's a happy day, one for the history books."

Darryl's irrepressible charm radiated as he went back to teasing the crowd into pandemonium. Through the streamers in the front row, Milton caught a glimpse of his mother with Meredith's parents and brothers, surrounded by heavily armed police officers. The spotlight blinded him, another balloon bounced off his head, and the pavilion rocked as the Marine Corps Band played "Hail to the Chief."

"I now introduce you to President Meredith Nicholson!"

Milton steadied himself. Even now, as she took center stage, he was amazed that he was the one that she'd chosen to spend her life with. He had watched her shower and dress for over 20 years. He knew where she kept her vibrator and that she actually *had* inhaled in high school. He reached over and took her hand gently, reassuring himself that everything was real and all right. She smiled at him and he fell in love with her for the millionth time. She put the "lime" in limelight and if he could change anything about her it would be that, but at the moment here they stood, the world watching.

She began to speak. He knew every pause, every affirmation. He had heard it a hundred times. He felt like a buffoon, but a proud one. She had wanted this so badly. Her passion was so strong even he could taste it. After all the chaos, for better or for worse, Milton knew this was all that mattered now. His eyes burned from salty sweat. He steadied himself as he reached into his pocket, brushing the note as if it would burn his flesh. It materialized right before ascending the stage stairs, although Bonnie insisted that pockets were never for hands. He pulled his hand out quickly, glancing down as if he could read it through the gabardine: "I know what you did." How could anyone know? All right it was possible, but who? He relaxed his shoulders. Anyone who could know was just as guilty and if he had it to do over again he would. After all what were husbands—"First Gentlemen"—good for if they didn't go above and beyond for the ones they loved. How often was murder justified? He smiled at his children and their hands rose in unison, cut-out dolls clinging, bowing reverence to their country.

The inaugural ball was about to begin and an army of agents and officers led them off the stage. The array of armor made the jubilant event seem more like a prison rally. Milton caught a glimpse of one officer swiftly approaching their entourage, his loaded machine gun glistening. Milton mopped his forehead, adamant that the geriatric crowd not compare him to Nixon and the excruciating Kennedy debate in the `60s. He inhaled deeply. He needed to enjoy. He needed to forget. He would focus on the ideal and think more like a superhero than a criminal. He was directly behind Meredith when the "gun-toting officer" brushed passed him and jumped headfirst into the confetti-covered floor, extracting two inebriated feminists brawling over an autographed picture of his wife. He followed the familiar Secret Service figures, his family ahead oblivious of the skirmish.

He swallowed hard, as the bitter, dry taste of truth was forced down his throat. *Everything's going to be fine*, he thought. "For now," he whispered as he glanced one last time over his shoulder, bending low to the chauffeur's umbrella, as he slid into the backseat of the limousine.

PART I

CHAPTER 1

In the beginning

"It's a girl," the candy striper screamed through the fogged window of the labor room, her facial features exaggerated as she pressed her smile against the glass. Sam Nicholson, on his second pot of coffee, jumped nervously to his feet.

"A girl!" he repeated as he hugged the only person left in the waiting room, crushing the cheap cigars he had hurriedly bought when he had received the call more than 24 hours before.

Meredith Nicholson came into the world like the majority, head first. Gertrude stroked her daughter's damp hair, smiling at the doctor and nurses, repeating it over and over, "It's a girl."

"But Dad, I don't want to give her anything!" Sam had his youngest son on the phone encouraging him to do as his mother asked and make something nice for his new sister when they came home.

Why don't you draw a nice card or make something for Meredith, Charlie. She's a little baby, but even babies like presents."

"But Dad, I don't want to."

"Now Charlie, stop that. It's been a long night and your mom just worked harder than any soldier I've known. Do as you mother wishes young man. OK?"

The mention of his mother again was enough to send Charlie back to his room for construction paper, leaving the phone dangling.

"It's a girl?" David mumbled as he picked up the phone, rocking his weight back and forth, poking his toe through the worn canvas of his sneaker.

"Yes David, you and Charlie have a new sister. A beautiful new sister." Samuel rocked back and forth, not having seen her yet, but undeniably knowing that she was beautiful. *A daughter*, he thought, *my goodness was that a good thing*?

"When is Mom coming home?"

"Your mom and baby sister will be home in a few days. Now, mind Mrs. Deering and when I get home we can work on that fast-ball. You like the Deerings' baby girl. Now you have one of your own to love. Keep an eye on your brother, OK, David?"

"OK, Dad." The unconvinced seven-year-old climbed up the stepstool to replace the receiver. "Dammit!" he stammered, mimicking what his best friend Tommy said in big guy situations, "I can't believe Mommy had a girl baby."

Samuel called their parents and then the doctor escorted him to his wife cuddling the tiny pink bundle. She smiled and all of his worries vanished. The gentle, cautious, keeper of the peace held his daughter for the first time and wiped his eyes with his handkerchief, holding back tears.

"Welcome to the world, Meredith Nicholson," he whispered. He took his wife's hand with his free hand and mouthed the words "I love you."

It was the fall of 1958, and Amherst, Massachusetts was as pleasant as Thanksgiving dinner. The anticipated traditional longing set taste buds watering while the whitewashed town exploded in autumn colors. Settled in the 1600s, the town was the epitome of old New England with its white clapboard and weathered cedar shingles. Nantucket blue shutters hung proudly on ancient brownstones. The City Hall and Catholic Church nestled in the town's square, the aroma of potluck supper rising from the latter's basement. The '50s were almost a memory, yet Amherst was slow to give up its wicked witch bicycles or Buddy Holly dreams. Simplicity was sacred. The residents of Maple, Elm, Spruce, and Adams streets were all arranged and ready to welcome their newest member as she settled into her well worn, freshly painted crib. Ignorance was bliss.

She would remain pink and clean for almost five years before her brothers would enlist and train her for their elite neighborhood battalion. Of course, her responsibilities were small at first, yet the cops, robbers, Indians, and cowboys of their world now had another Nicholson to contend with. This was where Meredith would first taste, and revel in, power. She struggled relentlessly on the male-dominated block, but served as fort leader when her brothers were out foraging and never once allowed the "enemy" to penetrate her defense. Her brothers kept a close eye on her, Charlie more so than David. He knew the "enemy" could devour his sister if left unattended too long and he did it for his mother. He watched and worried and wished his mother would forbid her from their games, but his mother thought it was cute and relished her children's love for each other. These were the times of *Leave it to Beaver*, and Gertrude let her children roam. Charlie rarely had fun once his sister had been brought home. He was torn between hating every cute thing about her and a devout, intense feeling of responsibility and love. Either way, Meredith grew up thinking her brothers were the toughest kids on the block. At such a young age her devotion and love added another dimension to the entire family. It was impossible for any of them to remember a time before she arrived.

"Daddy, what's a jockstrap?"

Samuel Nicholson set down his coffee cup and peered down over his reading glasses at his almost-school-aged daughter. Her frayed dungarees and tousled curls were a front and his first thought was to dodge the question and bend the truth. He knew the complications of trying to ignore her were impossible since she was four going on forty.

"Well, my little princess, a jockstrap is a strap jocks wear." He held his breath, hoping he was in the clear.

"Well I want to wear a jockstrap, Daddy. I'm a jock." Her tiny hands were secured to her hips. The cherub face that made the captain of Amhert's police melt peered up at him with supreme authority.

"Well, my little one," he reached over and scooped her onto his lap, "I'm not sure they make jockstraps for women."

"Jockstraps? What are you two talking about?" Gertrude asked, as she came into the kitchen with yet another load of dirty laundry, the revolving pile her children and husband perpetuated daily.

"Daddy is not sure if they make jockstraps for women, Mommy, but if they do, I want one OK? Even if they don't, I think I need one because they said…" and she pointed out the window, "they said if Tommy Towson had been wearing his jockstrap, he would be feeling a whole lot better right now."

Samuel and Gertrude exchanged glances, stifling their laughter. They both hugged their daughter and promised her that if they ever saw a jockstrap for women that she would be the first one in Amherst to have one.

"Now Mommy, I doubt that if they make jockstraps for women that I will be the first, but I still want one all right?" She jumped off her father's lap, satisfied she'd made her point and skipped across the pale yellow linoleum to the door, eager to get back out to the gender heavy world. She turned and smiled at her parents, revealing a few gaps awaiting grownup teeth.

"Gert," Samuel sighed, "I think we may have created something bigger than ourselves."

She placed the laundry down and wrapped her arms around his neck, tenderly stroking the badge he had worn almost every day of their lives together.

"Not us darling, let's blame this one on God."

He smiled and kissed her.

Late that evening, Samuel was mindfully overwhelmed with love as he bent over his sleeping daughter, her arm wrapped tightly around a disheveled Raggedy Andy doll. He brushed a tiny curl from her face and thanked God that his family was healthy and safe. His day had started with an innocent question from this tiny creature and ended with delusion and sadness. Amherst, along with the country, had been shaken and shocked with the afternoon's news that their country's young President from Massachusetts had been assassinated. He kissed her gently and made his way quietly out, lest he disturb her.

The decade of peace, love and understanding barreled into Amherst like a gutter ball. The state's university brought thousands of new and some lifelong students to the area, and world issues were thrown on the town's table. Everything from apartheid to animal rights got its due, made its way and faded slowly. Powerful pictures of the Vietnam War gave a naive country a look at hell that few could've imagined until that moment. Samuel's memories of World War II were revived and his demeanor swayed each time he had to keep angry protestors for peace at bay. His promotion to chief kept him away from home more than usual and Gertrude watched her husband struggle with the changes. Her love and understanding kept him sane and together they were determined to keep their children grounded, even shielded from the harsh realities that loomed.

David dreamed of being a soldier; Charlie, the Lone Ranger; and Meredith, at ten, wanted to be the leader of their dwindling neighborhood gang. She had become fast friends with Amy Deering, who was six months older than Meredith and frequently reminded her of that fact. Theirs was a forced courtship, having shared the same playpen many times as babies, but inevitably friendship endured. Because of their acknowledged age difference and the only other "girl" to be reckoned with, Amy had a slight edge and dared to bring Meredith to a more realistic level.

Amy stood five-foot seven inches, well above her peers. Her golden blonde hair hung just below her waist, a few perfectly placed freckled on her nose. Meredith had freckles as well, but this was the only physical similarity they shared. Gertrude insisted they were "beauty spots," but Meredith's were not nearly as subtle as her best friend's.

"A connect-the-dots game with your splotches could last forever," Amy teased as they walked toward the center of town. Meredith shoved her horn-rimmed glasses back where they worked best and tightened the daily newspaper's elastic around her frazzled ponytail. On the fringe of five feet, she forced two steps to Amy's one.

"So really, Amy, what do you think about us starting our own gang? We can call ourselves, hmmm, what can we call ourselves Amy?"

"Mere Nicholson, are you crazy? Start our own gang? The two of us? Our own gang? That has got to be the dumbest thing you've ever said. What's wrong with the gang we're in? That Tommy Towson is scrumptious!"

Meredith frowned. She had no interest in boys the way Amy did. She relentlessly reminded her that boys were dumb and a dime a dozen. She insisted that women were the reason for their survival and why they were all here to begin with.

"Tommy Towson is a screwball, Amy. Gosh, what is it with you and Tommy Towson?"

Amy just smiled. Meredith knew, Amy had told her a thousand times before. She just wished her friend would be more like herself than the silly girls that looked for the boys' attention.

"Amy, Tommy is a drip. A complete nincompoop, and I believe that we have to stand up and be heard," consciously repeating what her history teacher had just said.

Amy looked at Meredith in that familiar way only best friends understood, but the shorter firecracker was determined.

"I mean it, Amy, why can't we just start our own gang? Something new. We could be the envy of the neighborhood. We could!"

Amy's final look would end of the gang topic for the day.

"Meredith, I'm thinking Butterfinger!" She focused on the corner store where their sweet teeth were known on a first name basis. "Oh and look there's Tommy and his friends now. Gosh, your brother David is with him. They drive now. Oh I wish I could drive. This kid stuff sucks."

Amy waved and Meredith glared at the passing car, her brother and Tommy completely ignoring them.

"Oh Mere, you've got to make sure next time Tommy is at your house, you call me, OK? Please! OK?"

"Yeah, I'll call," she said, disgusted.

With their allowance they paid for candy and sodas, and Amy expertly pocketed two packets of matches as they walked out. They went behind the store and down a makeshift pathway to the camouflaged opening of their secret hideaway. Amy pulled out two non-filter cigarettes, carefully wrapped in tissue, that she had taken from her father's uniform pocket. She lit the match and inhaled.

"Oh it's so much fun being an adult." She coughed, waving her arms as she tried to make her point.

Meredith nodded, the nauseous feeling happening once again, clouding her answer. She watched as her beautiful friend flicked her ashes daintily, while flipping her hair seductively from her face. Meredith tried doing the same but her cigarette had gone out and her matted ponytail was far from seductive. Shifting, she spilled her soda.

Amy fell backward holding her side in laughter. "Mere, we have got to teach you again how to keep that lit!"

Meredith kept her head barely between her knees, focusing on the tiny carbonated streams making their way through the trampled weeds. Today she would succeed and not upchuck. Today she was determined to keep the cigarette lit and become a lot more cool. She barely turned to see her friend giggling on her back and without another moment's notice, her stomach gave back all of her allowance and then some.

Chapter 2

David's head swayed low as his father paced behind him in the kitchen. He caught a glimpse of the impeccably shined shoes as they made their way back toward him. He saw tiny pieces of confetti from his graduation party tucked inconspicuously under the edge of the cabinet, a fond reminder of how his childhood ended. The same kitchen floor that he had taken his first steps on. He hated it. He would talk to Mr. Towson when he got back and surprise his mother with one of those new ceramic tiled floors. Gertrude absently wrung her hands as she sat beside him with a maternal urge to run her fingers through her oldest boy's dark curls. He had grown almost five inches in the last year; his now six-foot frame seemed uncomfortable in the old wooden chair. His mother instinctively looked at the timer on the stove as she leaned into the kitchen table. Breakfast was getting cold.

"It's not that I think you shouldn't be in the service, Son. It's just wartime and a terrible war. Your mother and I think you're too young to make this kind of decision." Samuel looked strained, feeling much older than his 47 years.

"Too young? Dad, I'm the same age as you were when you served!"

"I know, Son. I know. What I meant was, well, I meant they haven't even drafted you and you don't know the first thing about combat. It's horrible. I regret the stories I've told your brother and you, I mean, I regret the way I told you. I saved my friends by doing something I am not proud of. I wasn't brave. I was scared to death and I ended another man's life with my rifle. I filled him with bullets." He stopped. He had sworn he would never completely account to his children what had happened that day. The soldier's head had fallen off in front of him. He touched his wife's shoulder. He continued softly, feeling her tremble.

"I will never forget that day, nor should any forget that war, any war. It was horrible and, like Vietnam there is nothing glamorous about it. I don't think you need to see that, Son. Please rethink this. Please."

David turned 18 the summer of 1970. The Vietnam War had gained the illustrious reputation that the great America was overpowered. Protests grew. They were solemn reminders that the United States involvement continued to be questionable. David's best friend Tommy had been drafted a month before and David waited anxiously for his call to duty. Impatience to be with his comrade and help the cause moved the volunteer issue to a moot point. He had vowed to be a soldier for as long as they could remember. He felt like a man, except when his uniformed father loomed over him. From an honored soldier to a respected police officer, his father had always been his idol. He wanted to revel in his pride. He felt perversely blessed that it was wartime and the possibilities were endless.

"Dad, I can't believe that you're upset with me. You alone saved seven of your friends in France. I know I may have to kill someone and I know all wars are terrible. It's not that I don't care about the danger, but I'm not afraid. It's my duty to my country. I want to be a soldier and this is my chance. I want to go and I want to go now."

Samuel closed his eyes, hearing his own determination 30 years before. Yet he had memories he couldn't bear to pass on to his children. David would return with the same memories.

"David, please rethink this. I can't bear to think that you may never come home." Gertrude's eyes filled with tears, begging him to stay. The thought of losing him, any of her children, was inconceivable.

"Mom, please don't cry. I'm planning on coming home. I promise." He avoided her embrace. She was the only one that could sway his decision. She was the voice of reason that could change his mind. As children, she had stood by all of them, healed their wounds and wiped away their tears. She had always been in the bunker with them. He loved her dearly. He would come home alive for her, if for nothing else.

He stood, adamant, finished with his explanation. He didn't look back at his parents as he left the room. Gertrude wiped her eyes with the dishtowel as Samuel sat down beside her. She couldn't make him stay, neither of them could. The army was accepting recruits daily with volunteers and draftees alike, parents attached to their limbs, begging them not to go and pleading that the government not take them. David passed his eavesdropping brother and sister at the bottom of the front stairs and he smiled. Meredith reached out her hand and he messed her hair before he closed the front door. The muffled engine coughed then faded.

"Shouldn't you two be off to school?" Samuel's voice called out. Charlie and Meredith looked at each other guiltily then quickly picked up their books and left without a word.

A week later they stood alongside the runway at Camp Edwards, just shy of the bridge that welcomed tourists to Cape Cod. Meredith looked toward the island, itching for sand between her toes and inhaling the salty air. She listened for the ocean then shaded her eyes, admiring the handsome soldier approaching them. In just a week he seemed a foot taller and 10 years older. She watched as he bent to kiss their mother and not until he leaned toward her was she completely convinced that he was really saying goodbye. She buried her face in his neck. He stood back and smiled, then he saluted his family, his first battalion. Meredith, Charlie and Samuel did the same. Gertrude closed her eyes.

He tipped his hat revealing the freshly cropped head and then was lifted out of their sight by the Air Force helicopter. They watched until it disappeared into the early morning fog, unforgiving most mornings near the ocean. Meredith looked at her mother, a tired unfamiliar face focused on the asphalt cracks. Meredith reached for her hand and saw the corner of Gertrude's mouth curl slightly.

"Mom, he'll be back. He'll come home soon."

Charlie and Meredith held her hands as they walked slowly back to their car. Samuel brought up the rear, quiet in his own thoughts. Meredith stayed in the middle of the backseat, never a cherished position, and Charlie did not object. They wanted to leave David's spot vacant. Two hours later they arrived home in Amherst, less one soldier.

"I cannot believe your brother volunteered. That is just so friggin amazing!" Amy's hair was piled high on her head, a few wisps hanging alongside her face as she twisted one end deliberately. She and Meredith sat side by side in math class and while Meredith always was intent on learning, Amy aspired to talk about anything else but math. It had been almost a year since David had left, yet Amy mentioned her brother's decision and heroism everyday as if he had volunteered ten minutes before.

"Is there something you would like to share with the class, Miss Deering?" The teacher's voice echoed across the room.

"Um well I, I'm sorry Miss Bushnell, it's just Meredith's brother is in Vietnam and, occasionally, well, it's just too much for her. She's just having a bad day and I was just trying to help." Meredith stared in disbelief.

Miss Bushnell gazed sympathetically at her best student. Many of the children had a sibling or family member involved with the war and so many had experienced heartache from it.

"Meredith, are you all right? Have you had any update about your brother?"

"Ma'am," Meredith stumbled, embarrassed. "I just miss him. We all do," and she glanced with hatred at Amy. "We haven't heard from him in over, well…."

"Three months," Amy chimed in.

"Oh dear, I see. This is a hard time for us all. Meredith, maybe you should go home early today and tomorrow will be a better day, all right? Let me know if there is anything I can do or if you ever want to talk about it."

Meredith stood dumbfounded, too shy to question her. It was easier to just leave the classroom, all eyes more jealous than sympathetic. Amy stood to collect her things as well.

"Miss Deering, where are you going?"

"Oh, well Miss Bushnell, I need to go with her. You see what a state she's in. I can't let her be alone right now. I'll bring her home and collect her homework for tomorrow. Thank you so much for being such an understanding teacher." Amy shuffled Meredith through the door before anyone else could object.

"Wow Mere, that was awesome. We have the afternoon off. This is really cool!"

Meredith just shook her head and Amy wrapped her arm around her.

"Come on girlfriend, let's do something fun. Anything will be more fun than Math!"

"Amy, you don't care the least bit about David or what I'm going through?" Amy's face grew pale, and Meredith immediately felt badly for saying such a thing.

"Of course I care about David and you and your whole family. I can't believe you could say such a thing." She pulled her wrapped arm away as if she had been pushed.

"Gosh, Amy I'm so sorry. It's just I was so embarrassed. We could've stayed in class. We could've talked about it later. I'm sorry. You are part of our family too and my mom has been so worried and my Dad so frustrated with the news. Don't be angry with me, Amy. OK?"

Amy's frown turned upward. She prided herself on her ability to convince anyone of almost anything, Meredith included. She smirked at how she had played Miss Bushnell, getting permission to leave school early. Another one for the diary. She would have to use it on a few other teachers sometime. She wrapped her arm back around Meredith. Poor little Meredith.

"Come on little sister, let's go to our spot. We can hold a vigil for your brother and Tommy and all the soldiers. Pray for their safe, gorgeous return." Meredith smiled in agreement, not quite feeling the little sister comfort she hoped for, but bewitched by the only friend she had. Amy was only an inch taller since they had started their freshman year, but Meredith was awkward in so many ways that the golden blonde still appeared to tower over her. She thought about her mother as they quietly left the school grounds. She didn't want to upset her anymore than she was, the past year like a never-ending nightmare. Amy walked with purpose, Meredith with trepidation, not looking forward to the same old cigarette scenario.

They picked up their candy bars, potato chips and sodas with their lunch money and Amy predictably swiped the matches before they left the store. The early spring had brought wildflowers and knee-high weeds to their trail, inching their way past the wild rosebush thorns. They sat on their slickers and Meredith waited sulking.

"Amy do you steal cigarettes from your father everyday?"

Amy just looked at her humorously.

"I mean we were going to be in school all day today until you decided otherwise. When were you going to smoke them?"

"Oh Mere, Mere, Mere. Do you really think I only smoke here, with you? I've got friends who smoke and there's even a guy who buys me cigarettes. I don't need my father's stupid cigarettes now."

Meredith bowed her head to nibble at a cuticle, so sure that she was Amy's only friend too. It hurt to think that Amy had gone off and made other friends without her.

"What other friends, Amy? How come I haven't met them?"

"Oh lordy, Meredith. I can't introduce you to everyone I meet and besides you wouldn't like them much anyway." Meredith instantly thought it must be the other way around. Amy's new friends wouldn't like her.

"Who's the guy who bought you the cigarettes?"

"Mere, I told you, you wouldn't like him and besides he's gone off and volunteered just like your brother. He gave me a little present though before he left and I haven't shown anyone," she lied with finesse. "I want to show you though because you're my oldest and dearest friend." Sometimes appeasing Meredith's feelings was enough to make them both queasy.

Amy reached into her book bag and proudly showed the crinkled cellophane wrapped around the carved wooden box. She placed it carefully on her coat and released the barrette that held her hair, allowing it to fall across her shoulders and back. She had watched the older girls do just the same thing and wanted so much to be like them. She rolled her eyes at Meredith who had opened the chips, chomping loudly, anticipating the gift. Amy cradled it like a baby in her palm displaying the tiny meerschaum pipe that she had discovered and "borrowed" from her grandfather's desk.

"He gave you a pipe?"

"Ugh, Mere, no, this is from my grandfather. He has loads of them. He's very proud of his collection." Meredith looked bewildered.

"Your grandfather gave you a pipe?"

"Oh Mere, grow up. I borrowed it. I'm going to give it back. Now do you want to see the surprise or should I just save it for one of my other friends?" Slap! That one would sting for a bit.

"No, no, I just meant I want to see the surprise. Was he like your boyfriend, Amy?"

Amy blushed. She wasn't about to tell everything.

"I guess you could call him that. He was a boy and a friend." She enjoyed her jests.

"What was his name, Amy?"

"First of all, his name is the same that it was last week. He's just not in this rotten stinking town with us to share it. Second, forget the guy Mere, it's time to smoke!"

"Fine, fine, I'll take a cigarette please.

Another smirk before she handed Meredith the pipe.

"I'm not going to smoke out of a pipe, Amy. Why? We have cigarettes."

"Just inhale when I light it and you'll see. It tastes better."

Meredith shrugged and inhaled slowly, knowing full well if she refused Amy would patronize her for the rest of the day. Her lungs filled with smoke and she coughed so harshly that even Amy thought maybe she had made a mistake. She rolled back on her jacket gasping for clean air, her eyes watering.

"Are you OK, Meredith?" Amy asked, remotely concerned.

"I'm OK," she whispered, "That tobacco sure hurts without the paper."

Amy started giggling, which turned into convulsions as she rolled beside her sickly looking friend. She smiled into her face and whispered back,

"That wasn't tobacco, Meredith. That was marijuana!"

Meredith's eyes looked back, horrified at the criminal lying beside her.

"What?" she sprung back up dizzily.

"That was marijuana, my dear little friend. You just had your first of what I hope is many puffs of marijuana. You just graduated to bigger and better things."

"Marijuana? Amy, oh my God, that is an illegal drug. I can't believe you tricked me into smoking marijuana! You are a terrible person, Amy Deering, just terrible. I never want to do drugs! I never want to get arrested! I thought we were going to come here and smoke cigarettes and talk about David. You lied to me, Amy."

"I never want to do drugs! I never want to get arrested!" Amy mimicked her blubbering friend, repulsed. "Give me a break, Meredith Nicholson. You're such a baby. Really, everybody's doing it, getting high, loving each other and you're in this stupid innocent world. My God, I don't even know why I hang out with you. That's it! I can't hang out with you anymore. I can't believe I shared my secret with you!"

Meredith's crying only angered her more as she gathered her things, careful as she packed the pipe back into its case. Just as she was about to slip it into her book bag, the smell of cologne made her hesitate. She glanced up, the first to see their visitor. She reached over and squeezed Meredith's arm, causing her to cry louder.

"Stop it, that hurts, Amy!" She stopped squeezing but kept her hand on her arm, frozen while Meredith inspected the mark she had left.

"Is that what marijuana does to you Amy, makes you mean?"

"Shush, Mere, be quiet. Damn it, be quiet!"

"Well, well, well, what do we have here?"

Both girls looked at the young police office, horrified.

He scratched his forehead just underneath the band of the new regulation hat. Meredith blinked, hoping the hallucination would disappear. Amy moved her knee to hide the box, but it was the first thing he had seen. He leaned over to pick it up and inspect the contents. Fresh out of the academy and on his first day, he was about to make a drug bust.

"It looks like you two are having a real nice party here for yourselves." He looked around, suddenly concerned there might be more hoodlums in the woods.

"Is it just the two of you?" he asked with a slight hesitation.

"Yes, officer, just the two of us. We were just having a picnic, a little fun. We weren't doing anything wrong." Amy stumbled over the last few words.

"Really? I guess college hasn't taught you that marijuana is illegal?" He would have a little fun before he handcuffed them.

"Um, college, sir? We're in high school. We're freshman in high school. Please officer we won't do anything wrong ever again." Meredith eyes burned, the words actually throbbing in her ears.

"What? High school?" he said in disbelief. His first bust and it was two juveniles. Two freshman juveniles! He could've sworn they were nearly twenty.

"What are your names? Both of you."

Amy trembled as she stood up, straightening her skirt, pushing her hair behind her ears.

"My name is Amy Deering. Officer please, really, we were only having a little fun. Please don't arrest us." She said this in her most seductive voice and for a brief moment Officer O'Malley was caught off guard. But work was work and he needed to get back to his work. He would confiscate the paraphernalia and bring both juveniles in so their parents could collect them. He was sure their fathers would take care of the rest.

"And you Miss, what's your name?" He looked down at the blubbering one, conscious of the blonde stepping closer.

"Her name is Meredith Nicholson, Officer, and she's thirteen going on fourteen. Really we were just having a little fun, please don't arrest us." She laid on the charm and eased herself even closer. Once beside him she let him have it.

"Meredith Nicholson, Officer, the daughter of Captain Nicholson. I'm really not sure even your boss would want to hear that you terrified two young girls in the woods while they were having a picnic."

O'Malley looked right into the pretty blonde's eyes, but spoke to the terrified child still sitting. "Is that true young lady? Is your father Captain Nicholson?" His voice wavered and Meredith's whole body trembled.

"Um, Miss, please stand up. I'm taking the two of you to the precinct and we can call your parents." He wasn't going to be fooled by another pretty blonde, ever.

Amy helped Meredith stand and the sense of urgency in her face caused her to react.

"Um, Officer, my name is Meredith Nicholson. I live at 1019 Elm Street and my father is the captain of the police."

A slow tick started in his left eye as he surveyed the disheveled teenager and the situation in front of him.

"Jeez Louise, the captain's daughter? What the hell are you doing out here smoking dope? Oh my God, my first day and I'm about to arrest the captain's thirteen-year-old daughter. Goddamn it!" He cussed sharply. The girls looked at each other not sure what to do.

"I've got to tell their parents, I've got to do the right thing," he mumbled. "Get the hell out of here! Right now!"

He waved angrily. "I better never see the two of you here again, ever! Don't you think I won't be checking! Do you hear me?" Amy and Meredith were already at the front of the candy store by the time his last question hit the air. The acid burned in their legs, but it wasn't until Meredith's house was almost in sight before they stopped, ready to collapse.

"Oh my God, Mere, do you think he'll tell our parents? He wrote my name down. Oh my God, if he tells my parents they'll kill me. My father's not the captain of any police force, he lays floors! Oh my God, he's going to kill me!"

Amy feared nothing, ever. Meredith was hunched over, catching her breath. The tears had stopped and her swollen face expanded each time she gasped. She had to be brave.

Amy leaned into her, "Mere, I can't go home!" Amy's edge softened, tears appearing in the corner of her eyes.

"Listen to me Amy. We have to go home, like that officer told us to and we have to pray really hard that he won't tell a soul. I don't think he was excited about telling our parents. Now let this be a lesson to us both," Meredith preached, "drugs are bad, illegal, and we don't need them!" Amy nodded, hugging her comrade, wiping her face on her coat sleeve.

"I know, Mere, I'm so sorry. Please make sure you call me if I don't call you by eight tonight. We just need to check on each other, make sure no one has been told." Meredith squeezed her hand in reassurance. That was their plan.

"If I'm not at the bus stop tomorrow, Mere, promise me you'll come looking for me."

Meredith shook her head, not sure whether Amy was joking or not. She watched as she walked away.

"God will watch over us, Amy, pray really hard!"

Amy continued on sluggishly, knowing full well that God had nothing to do with it, nor would he fix a damn thing. Her fingers were crossed tightly.

Meredith walked up to her own house, exhausted and numb. She was her family's biggest disappointment. She walked beside the black Oldsmobile parked behind her father's squad car, oblivious, then shocked, as the extended bumper caught her pant leg. She ignored the tear, instead horrified as she noticed the dormant lights atop her father's car. Her father was home from work early.

"Damn you, Officer O'Malley. That didn't take you long," she whispered as she opened the front door.

CHAPTER 3

The plan was to sneak upstairs even if it allowed her only a few more minutes of immunity. A barely audible sniffle rose from a pile of clothes on the sofa and she squinted toward the dimly lit room. She spotted her brother's sneakers protruding from the pile and was curiously confused. Charlie was her favorite brother. She had no intention of ever saying this to anyone since David was a close second, but she silently deemed Charlie her hero ten years earlier. He was kind to her, truly concerned about her well-being. If she were to ever get into trouble, even though the occurrence proved rare, he would be on her side. There wasn't a time that she could remember where he treated her like a nuisance. There was just something special about him. Something she couldn't put her finger on, but it was calming. She needed him the most when her parents got the call.

He was still in his letterman jacket, his face hidden under a blanket. There was mumbling coming from somewhere near the kitchen and the hair stood on the back of her neck. She was sure the officer was telling her parents the story, each detail of their only daughter's crime. Charlie was banished to the living room until the story was spilled.

"Charlie, I can explain."

He looked up and covered her mouth, gesturing her to be quiet. He pointed towards the kitchen and went back to concentrated eavesdropping.

"Please Charlie, let me explain!" she whispered, but his look of disappointment made her cower. He was afraid for her. Charlie had to be there for her. He would make her prison sentence tolerable, sneak her snacks and magazines, and slip coded notes underneath her door. He would ask his parents daily if this were the day his beautiful sister would be released. He would consistently remind them that she was an almost perfect daughter and be committed to hush the enormity of the mistake, whittling them down and finally convincing them that the punishment was sufficient and that her own disappointment in herself was enough to scare her straight. He would support her effort to being once again the best daughter in Amherst. She could only hope.

He leaned over and wrapped an arm around her, whispering into her ear, "Oh Mere, Mere, David's dead."

Meredith's heart stopped. She could barely feel her brother's embrace or see the grandfather clock's face bathed in the orange glow from the stained glass atrium. The mumbling grew louder, unbearable and she lurched towards the kitchen calling for her mom.

"Meredith? Children? Meredith, where is Charlie? Oh there you are. Have you two been outside this door long?"

Samuel's staunch voice cracked. Charlie glanced up at his father and looked past him at the two uniformed soldiers at ease. Meredith's heart sank, realizing that Officer O'Malley was not the one talking in her kitchen. The soldiers shook Samuel's hand and saluted after he led them to the door. His shoulders hunched, a powerful man broken. He turned toward his children and Meredith clung to him.

"Daddy, Daddy, please Daddy, no, it can't be. No!" He kept his composure and held his daughter.

"I'm sorry, princess, it is true. It's true, I'm so sorry it's true."

Charlie stared in disbelief. How could this have happened? David promised he would come home alive.

"It can't be true. David's smart. He promised he would come home alive." The tears streamed down his cheeks, "He's smarter than any war, Dad. I don't believe he's dead. I just don't believe it. Why Dad? How could this have happened? Why?"

"Oh children, no, no, your brother's not dead. Oh my goodness, no. He's wounded, terribly hurt, but he's alive. He's alive and he's coming home."

The siblings looked at each other in disbelief, a moment they would forever share. David was dead and now he was alive. His life had been spared. He was coming home alive. Gertrude came from the kitchen visibly shaken and Samuel reached for her.

"He's alive, darling, and he's coming home."

Charlie hugged his sister, remembering the draft notice folded neatly in his back pocket.

The servicemen that had brought the news of David had also warned it could be several weeks before he was able to be back in the states. His extensive wounds prevented him from immediate travel, and Gertrude insisted daily they go to him, while Samuel reminded her of the impossibility of such an idea. Their only consolation was that he was coming home. They would follow protocol and wait.

Meredith forgot her perilous life of crime, now trivialized by the news, and she forgot to call Amy that evening. Not until she encountered Amy's fury did she remember the promise.

"Amy, really, I'm sorry but we received news about David and I just, I just forgot.

Amy knew what selfish sentiment was and the news about David would have been sufficient any other time, but the evening before had been terrifying for her and when she hadn't heard from Meredith she had determined their fate. Meredith shook her head amazed that Amy didn't understand. Their lifetime friendship was permanently marred.

"Meredith?"

She was out in the garden helping her mother, trying anything to keep her mind busy. David and Amy consumed her. During the day she went to school and rarely talked to anyone. She existed through classes, no one to share her apprehension or loneliness with. She silently thanked God when the last bell rang and released her to summer vacation. David would be home any day now. That was all that mattered.

She whistled as she plunged the hoe with her dirty sneaker back into the flowerbed.

"Meredith?"

She looked up and smiled, "Yes, Charlie, I'm out back." Charlie was her only confidant now and she welcomed his company. He turned nineteen the week before and had numerous disagreements with his parents finally persuading them that taking six months off before starting college was not the end of the world. How different things would be if he had only done what they had wanted. It seemed that working at McDonald's and volunteering at the church could not keep you from strapping on a rifle and slaughtering innocent people.

"Hi, Charlie."

"Hey there, Sis, I was just looking for you, I wanted to…" He glanced at her gloved hands darkened with soil, her stained knees and pale freckled skin. He saw for the first time that she wasn't a child anymore. Even in the Bermuda shorts and baggy tee shirt, the subtle curves of a woman could be seen. He was feeling melancholy and he wished he had said goodbye to the sweet little girl that had shadowed him for years. The young woman in front of him now, she didn't need him anymore. She smiled again, "Charlie, what?"

"I need to talk with you about something. Something I don't want Mom and Dad to know about."

She exaggerated a look around the yard, "Just little old me. Dad's at the station and he's picking mom up from church on his way back."

"Mom's not around, are you sure?" he asked apprehensively.

"Yes Charlie, she's at the church helping with the bake sale, what's wrong?"

He could barely see the top of her head. She had always been so small, even petite, the baby. He would miss her the most because she would change the most. He would miss her prom and her graduation. He would miss her first date. He didn't know how long he'd be gone but he knew that he would miss enough.

He handed her the draft notice.

"What's this?"

"It's a draft notice."

"A what? A draft notice?"

"Yes, Meredith, they sent me a draft notice."

Meredith sat down in the dirt. Charlie walked over and sat down beside her.

"But Charlie, no they can't. They already got David, why, how can this happen?"

"David volunteered," his eyes filled, "and I'm not a student anymore and, well, I'm not sure why, but it's a draft notice."

"Oh Charlie, this just can't be. You can't leave now, oh my God, this just isn't happening."

"Meredith, when Mom gets home she's going to be very upset. I just heard the news from Mr. Deering that they found Tommy Towson's body. He was killed, Meredith, killed!" He barely could say the words, his speech slurred with emotion.

Meredith hung her head and prayed for her brother's childhood friend. A senseless death. David would be devastated. She hugged her knees and cursed silently.

"I'm not going to fight in this war, Mere. I'm not going to go over and get my head blown off for something I don't believe in. I'm not going to die far away from home, from mom and Dad, from you. I'm not!" He covered his face with his hands, desperate and afraid. He had made his decision and he was leaving that night.

"Charlie, can you do that? Can you go down to the draft office and say you don't want to go?"

"No, I wish, but no. I'm leaving. I'm leaving tonight so I don't have to go down to the draft office ever!"

"Leaving? Charlie, you can't leave. Oh my God, please Charlie, I know what happens to draft dodgers Charlie. There has to be another way."

"I'm not a draft dodger Mere, I'm a conscientious objector and I'm not going to fight in this war?"

"Charlie, where are you going?"

"Meredith, I can't tell you, but I promise I will be safe."

"Oh my God, this is horrible, Charlie. Mom will just die. She's already lost one son."

"David is alive and coming home. I'll be safe. It's better than me going to Vietnam and coming back in a body bag. Mom will know that I'm safe. I'm sure she'll understand."

"Why can't we tell them Charlie?"

"The less people that know, the better. Please understand. I've written them a letter. Poor Tommy. Damn the war. Damn it!"

She held him tightly, digesting the idea that he wouldn't be around anymore.

"What about me, Charlie? What about me?"

"I'm so sorry, Meredith. There's nothing else I can do. I'm so sorry."

They cried until there were no more tears. No one could force someone to fight for a cause they didn't believe in.

"Charlie, I don't want you to go to jail. Don't they arrest people who dodge the draft? I hear stories all the time. Isn't there another way?" She couldn't give him up.

"I'm telling you because I'm leaving tonight. I will be back, I promise. When the war is over and our government has realized the terrible mistakes they've made."

"Won't they arrest you when you get back?"

"Mere, I don't know. They say it's illegal, I say it's my right of freedom. They can't take that away from me."

Meredith struggled in the soft dirt to stand, eyeing her mother coming out the back door. She wiped her face, leaving dirt across her forehead. Charlie watched their mother cross the yard.

"Not a word, Sis. I love you. I always will."

"I love you so much Charlie."

"Hello darling," Gertrude leaned down and kissed the top of her son's head, "have you come to help your sister and me out with this disheveled garden. My my, my youngest seems to have more dirt *on* her than under her," she tenderly teased her daughter.

"Mom, did you hear about Tommy?"

"Yes darling, what a terrible tragedy." Her mother's reaction was far less dramatic than they had anticipated.

"We should pray for the family, all of the families who have lost someone. I can only say that I am forever thankful that David is coming home, alive."

Charlie and Meredith glanced at each other and realized their mother's solemn outlook bolstered by the fact that God had spared her own child. It had only been minutes since Charlie's confession and Meredith felt the weight of his secret, the future of their family and the void left by Amy, overwhelming. She leaned into her mother's shoulder and cried again.

"Mere, oh dear, I know everything seems so out of place. Everything will be all right darling."

Meredith said nothing. She couldn't, afraid that anything she said would only cause her mother grief. Charlie gave her a quick hug, asking, "Is Dad home?"

"No Charlie," she answered, brushing her daughter's long hair with her fingers, "he's still at work. Father Dickens gave me a ride home. Dad should be home before dinner." Charlie looked directly at his mother, searching her eyes, wondering if they had told her.

"OK, then, I'll get to that lawn mower so I can have it done before he gets home."

Charlie's nonchalant stagger went only noticed by his sister. As he walked away, he knew that he had no other choice.

When Samuel opened the cruiser door, the smell of freshly cut grass filled his nostrils. The sweet aroma had an intoxicating, tranquil effect and he was transported back twenty years when he and his new bride had purchased the now beckoning home, bathed in shadows and warm light. He saw himself carry her over the threshold, and then later through the bay window, she watched their children playing in the front yard, running to greet him, his lovely bride smiling. The time was peaceful, not filled with the terrors of war. All of their times together, memories, all lingering here on Elm Street. David was coming home in a few days. He was more than just his oldest now, more than just his son. They would share a union, a combat bond, and he wanted nothing more than to have his son home. He had already spread the word and there was a position waiting for him at the newspaper, whenever daily rituals were comfortable. He could enroll in college or take some evening classes whenever he was ready to pursue his degree. He knew that the healing process had no time frame and that the visions of war only slowed that process. He wouldn't rush him. He would support him, be proud of him, and in time they would all be whole again. The thought of his son's body, less one leg, was haunting. Physically he would never be whole again but, God willing, his psyche would recover. God willing, his son would have the chance to create his own comforting memories.

In the early morning hours, while everyone slept, Charlie tossed a duffel bag out his bedroom window and eased himself down the trellis. He suddenly felt glib, wondering if his father would be perturbed at the discovery of the trampled rosebushes. The thought that his father would care more about flowers than about his son's well-being was manufactured. He was sure that his father, both his parents, David, and the rest of the town, would understand why he'd left. He had slipped a note under Meredith's door and left another one for his parents on the kitchen table. He was angry that he was forced to make such a decision. He hated the idea. He was about to take his existence into his own hands. They would grieve his absence and he theirs, but they would at least have the guarantee of his safety. He saw the car waiting on the corner and quickly made his way toward the passenger side. He wasn't a coward. All he wanted to do was live. He wondered naively, *Who would question that*?

Chapter 4

It was a warm, humid, April morning in Saigon when the country fell to Communism. The South Vietnamese surrendered, while the US enjoyed Jack Nicholson's *Cuckoo's Nest* and warned bathers to "stay out of the water." Fifty-eight thousand Americans died on Vietnam soil and Captain and Tennille crooned, "Love Will Keep Us Together." For ten years, men and women were murdered, families devastated, without apparent reason. With President Nixon's announcement to bring "peace and honor" to Vietnam and the official cease-fire that prevailed, the United States Army withdrew its forces, released its prisoners, and strived for reunification of North and South Vietnam. But the Vietnamese government condemned the idea. Less than three weeks after the Paris agreement was announced, the cease-fire was desecrated and the war resumed, another 80,000 lives lost. That same year, America's President resigned with impeachment assured, due to the Watergate scandal. The North Vietnamese General Colonel Bui Tin was quoted after the last Americans were airlifted out of the crumbled Saigon, "You have nothing to fear; between Vietnamese there are no victors and no vanquished. Only the Americans have been defeated." America desperately needed to heal and that sentiment was just as apparent on Elm Street.

David's homecoming was delayed almost six months. Charlie was gone. His secret departure brought angst and embarrassment to the family. After a sobering few months of being the only child, Meredith returned to school, happy to be out of the house. Their parents' reaction to Charlie's decision confused and alarmed her, and a day didn't go by without mention of their names. They were torn, Samuel almost reluctant to be happy for David's brush with death and Gertrude quiet and contrite, thankful that her youngest boy was alive as well. Just two months into her junior year of high school, Meredith coasted through reality, a victim of tragedy.

When he was first wheeled out of the van, neighbors and friends celebrated with cheers and tears. Immediately visible was David's composure and reluctant smile. He had been shot several times in the leg and an infection had festered, requiring amputation just above the knee. He had fallen in a remote jungle, unconscious from pain, and another platoon had discovered him almost dead, two days after the skirmish. He lost his left eye when maggots devoured part of his cornea. He struggled to his feet on crutches and Samuel cursed himself for not having a ramp installed. It was almost 24 hours before David asked of Charlie's whereabouts. When they told him, the disgusted look of their broken son was all that could be acknowledged.

"I guess it's better than ending up a cripple like me, huh Ma?" he said with more spite then he intended. "Maybe not. Who knows? One thing's for sure, I'm a cripple. People can't even look at me. Maybe I should've run, dumb fuck that I am. I must've had a death wish. Even better, maybe your God should've left me there to rot. I'd be better off a dead hero, don't you think?" His remarks were vile and he watched his mother's swollen eyes fill once again.

He had no interest in speaking with his father about honor or heroism and anything else that had been unjustly acquired. He had begged his transport to leave him at the airport, but their orders were to return him home and they turned a deaf ear on the grief of one more damaged soul. The scenario all too common, it was their only means of coping. Follow orders. Don't ask or answer any questions.

On the weekend that Samuel installed the second handicapped runway outside the backdoor, David threw a tray of food out his bedroom window and loudly instructed that he just wanted to be left alone. That was enough for Gertrude to seek help from the Veterans Association. Refusing physical therapy from anyone in Amherst and despising the neighborhood that gawked, David finally agreed that Boston would be a place to disappear in. He stared blankly at the television, watching President Nixon's resignation, avoiding impeachment for high crimes and abuse of power. Meredith watched him as he scoffed at Watergate's comparison to the Civil War but with no redeeming features like heroism or sacrifice. He wanted nothing to do with chaperones on the two-hour ride and he didn't look back as the van drove on. All they could do was pray.

"Meredith, would you have some spare time after school to assist me with grading papers?"

Meredith looked up at the English teacher not entirely convinced he was speaking to her.

"Can you spare the time?"

"Um, yeah, I guess so." She looked around wondering who else he might be addressing, but since she was always the first student to get to his class it could be no one else but her.

"That's great, I'm swamped and I could really use the help. Say around three-thirty?"

"Sure, Coach Murphy, three-thirty."

Her distorted reflection peered back from the beveled glass in the classroom door. She had her arms folded harshly around her books, her hair vigorously pulled back in a ponytail. The only physical changes since middle school were the six inches of gangly height and thicker lenses. She thought about Charlie everyday. No one had heard a thing from him in almost a year. She was disillusioned and exhausted. Making friends was a commitment she couldn't muster. When the last bell rang, it was an odd sensation that she had something to do, other than go home with homework and feel the despair the house held. She made her way back to Coach Murphy's classroom, relieved at the mindless work ahead of her.

"Um, I'm here. What would you like me to get started with?" She said this with slightly more enthusiasm than when originally asked, and Murphy smiled.

"Hey Meredith, did you know that I'm also coach of the debate team?"

Meredith looked disinterested, more impressed with the stack of papers he was handing to her. She was convinced that he might be on something more than caffeine. He had to be. Why would he have any interest in her at all? She shook her head.

"Well, I am and it's really a lot of fun. I was hoping you might be interested in trying out for the team this year."

Meredith looked up at him hoping for a punch line. The debate team? Did he think she was stupid? She was sure that in the entire school history, the debate team had always been comprised of geeky boys.

"Um, Coach Murphy are you kidding? I know you're the coach of the field hockey team too and I don't have any interest in either, thank you. I'm much too busy with other extracurricular activities, and besides isn't the debate team just boys?" She hoped that the part about her being busy would lay the subject to rest, but really who was she fooling anyway? Too busy? She'd fit right in with the geeks and freaks.

"Really? Oh I'm sorry. What team are you on?"

"Um, I'm not on any team. I go home after school to help my mother, since my brother, well since he came home from the war, it's been very hard on her." She swallowed hard. Lying was not her forte.

"Oh, yes I'm sorry, I heard about your brother. I know how hard it must be for your whole family. I just thought I'd ask you about the debate team. Since its conception there's never been a woman on the team and I thought you'd be a wonderful addition. You're one of the brightest students I've ever had the pleasure to teach."

Meredith blushed. It was rare that she received a compliment, even if it was for her brain.

"OK, well I just thought I'd ask. It would be great to integrate the team. Get a bright woman's perspective on the world. Add some pizzazz to our school. Will you think about it at least?"

"Sure, Coach Murphy, I'll think about it, but really I don't think I can."

"Tryouts are next month. If you change your mind, please let me know."

Meredith didn't look back at him but felt gratification as she marked a freshman's quiz with a bright red marker.

"Oh, and one more thing, Meredith. I really like my students to call me Mack. Mack Murphy."

"Um, OK, Mr. Murphy. I mean Mack."

He nodded and looked back down at his daily planner. He was getting through to her.

If someone had told her that the coach of field hockey and debate would change her life, she would've surely laughed for the first time in a long time. For the next two days, though no one noticed, Meredith pondered the possibilities. She absolutely had to find Amy, just this once, and see what she thought.

Amy looked at her approaching the lockers and felt sorry for her. It had been a long time since they had done anything together, and Meredith was nothing more than a loner. She was surprised when she stopped and smiled. Amy smiled back, embarrassed.

"Amy, I was wondering if I could ask a favor of you?"

"A favor?" she retorted, taken aback with the sudden communication.

"Well not really a favor, I just need your opinion on something and well, yes it would be a big favor to me!"

"Ha, well, OK. What opinion of mine do you need?"

Meredith hesitated than asked, "I was wondering what you'd think about me trying out for the debate team?"

"Hmmm," Amy smiled. "I was wondering why you don't buy some new clothes and stop wearing your older brother's shirts?"

"Amy, I'm not joking, really, I wanted to know what you think?"

"I'm not joking either, Meredith Nicholson. You really ought to look at yourself in the mirror."

Amy now sported a cropped haircut that stood up in frantically odd angles. Tiny lines carved deeply around her blue eyes and she smelled strangely of rose perfume and marijuana. Meredith couldn't fathom the bitter sarcasm that came from her old friend, who desperately needed to take a look in the mirror herself. Amy was embarrassed to be seen talking with the nerd another minute and switched on her small radio in an effort to send her away. The Sex Pistols pounded the speaker and Amy's head nodded, mouthing the words, "And now the end is near, and so I face the final curtain..."

"Well I guess I'll be seeing you, Amy. I just thought I'd get someone's opinion that mattered."

Amy was startled, so with a bit of empathy she called quietly as Meredith turned to leave, "Hey, sure you should do it, I guess. I took it up and spit it out," the words of Sid Vicious finishing her thought. She watched as the baggy, flannel shirt disappeared into the fourth-period abyss. Two old friends that were, were absolutely no more.

Meredith walked towards the gymnasium offices and let Coach Murphy know her decision. She was convinced if she didn't say yes at that very moment, she would never have the nerve again.

"Hello, may I please speak with David Nicholson?" Meredith gripped the receiver tightly.

A gruff voice answered and then what sounded like a phone hitting the floor. Then silence. When the unfriendly voice reappeared it growled, "He doesn't want any."

"Oh, please can you tell him I'm not trying to sell anything. It's his sister, Meredith."

"Who?"

"His sister, Meredith. Please, can you tell him?"

"I didn't know old Davie had a sister, humph, well then all right, hold on."

Silence. Meredith was about to hang up when footsteps grew louder.

"Hello?"

"Hi David"

"Um, hi back. Are you all right, is everything all right?"

"Sure sure, everything and everyone's fine. We're fine. I just wanted to call and see how you're doing. We never hear from you. I just, well, I wanted to say hi."

Silence.

"David?"

"Uh, yeah, I'm here. I'm fine Sis just fine. Thanks for calling." He was about to hang up when she sputtered, "David I need your help!"

"What kind of help?" he asked cautiously.

"I'm going to try out for the debate team and you're the smartest person I know and, well, I was wondering what you thought of that and if you could help me?"

"Do you want to know what I think about being the smartest person, or what I think about you trying out for the debate team?"

"The debate team, David, what do you think?"

Silence.

"David?"

"Yeah, I'm here." She could hear someone coughing up a lung in the distance.

"Well?" Her effort seemed hopeless.

"Um, I don't know Meredith. I just don't know. How can I help?"

"Oh, well, I was wondering if I could come up and visit for a weekend and show you some of the literature that I need to read. Maybe get your perspective on some different issues and help me get ready for the tryouts. Or, of course, you could come here."

Silence.

"David?"

"Um, let me think about it. I'm really busy and not sure if this is a good time." He stuck a ruler into his prosthesis to scratch an imaginary itch on his imaginary leg. He glanced around at the filthy kitchen in the rooming house where he now lived in Somerville, a sloppy suburb of the city. He heard the toilet flush down the hall and watched one of the new borders sway back and forth to his room, clinging to a pint of gin.

"I'll call you back, OK? Meredith, OK?"

"OK David, please call. It was really nice talking with you. Thanks."

"Yeah and you too. Bye."

She looked at the receiver as if to fault it for the conversation.

"Goodbye," she whispered.

Two days later, trudging reluctantly home from school with yet another stack of references to study, she expected the usual cold, dark house to greet her. Since David's return and Charlie's dishonor, their father kept late hours and their mother was always down at the church or the hospital volunteering. Always praying for a miracle, Meredith presumed. The homeless shelter saw more of her than Elm Street and the residents ate more of her meals than her family now. It was early November and she avoided the school bus habitually, the walk in early winter darkness made for lonely thoughts and ill feelings. She was alone and confused, convinced that this idea about the debate team was completely ludicrous, just another cause for embarrassment. She tugged at the flannel shirt bunched under her jacket, remembering the caustic words that her once-best friend said to her. Meredith squinted, startled to see her home luminous. The church was not one to send a ferocious activist home early to cook dinner for her only hungry child and loyal husband, but it appeared that Gertrude was home and had left a number of lights on.

Nice of Father Dennis to release her from her penance, Meredith thought. Their mother acted as if her sons' destinies were a fault of her own, and she was bound and determined to be forgiven, so her sons would be returned to her. She was patient and relentless, inadvertently neglecting her daughter. Meredith walked in the front door, half expecting the electricity to shut down and the welcome to vanish; but instead the pungent odor of garlic and onions simmering, made her dizzy and her belly growl. There were candles lit on the mantle and her mother was humming in the kitchen.

"Mom?" She poked her head into the kitchen, her senses and concerns on overload.

"Oh honey, I'm so glad you're home. Wonderful. Guess what?"

"Mom, are you all right?"

"Oh yes, yes, I'm fine, just fine. Your father is on his way home and guess what, darling?"

"What Mom, what?" She stared at her complexion, glowing from the steam and the smile that had been scarce for almost two years.

"David's coming to dinner!"

Meredith smiled and stepped towards her mother, whose gray curls came to just the top of her chin. She knew that she was growing out of her clothes—the "flood" remarks rampant at school—but possibly her mother was shrinking? She held her close. She wondered again what it would be like to be the first woman on the Amherst High School debate team. She focused on her disheveled hem, her ankles peeking just above the white socks. There would be no more "flood" retorts if she had anything to do with it.

"Mom, that's great. About David, I mean. I was wondering if maybe you could give me a ride to the mall after school tomorrow?"

Gertrude looked a bit bewildered but answered, "Of course, we can talk about it after dinner."

They were all waiting when David arrived. Samuel stood in the doorway anticipating the help he might need with his chair, the unused ramp now needing a new coat of paint. He held his breath as his son got out of the driver's side, maneuvering his way slowly to the front door, resting one side on a cane. The injuries now accustomed to prosthesis and an eye patch, David's proud grin replaced the menacing scowl. Samuel was overwrought with emotion.

"Hey Dad."

"Hello Son."

"You can get rid of the ramp now, Dad. I don't need it."

"All right," Samuel grinned at the handicapped rail, "I'll do that tomorrow, definitely tomorrow."

"Hi Mom."

Gertrude was crying and David winked at his sister as his mom reached for him. David was home.

"OK, Sis, now we need to get to work."

It had been two days since David's grand entrance back into their lives. He had settled back into his old room, despondent each time he passed his brother's bedroom door. Gertrude had talked of making it a sewing room but everyone knew that would never happen. Once a week the room was dusted, everything in its same place since the day he left. Gertrude would never give up hope.

David made it their "war room." He brought up all of the encyclopedias he'd found on the shelves downstairs and covered the trophies and pictures, all reminders of Charlie. Sitting there he wondered which one of them really was the hero, when all was said and done. He tapped on his hollow reminder. He believed he had done the right thing, but just couldn't point the finger at his brother for not putting his own life in danger. Survival of the fittest, and Charlie still had all his limbs and senses. He looked at his sister buried in the *Britannica* Bs and smiled.

"OK, now, first things first, is that one of my old shirts you're wearing?"

Chapter 5

"Nobody cares for eyes more than Pearle," David crooned as his sister approached him, without the horn-rimmed spectacle's she had worn since elementary school.

"What do you think, David?"

"Well, well, I always knew you were beautiful, but it sure makes a difference seeing those eyes the way they should be seen."

Meredith smiled, glancing into the compact the store had given her. She didn't remember a day that she had not worn glasses and now she looked at herself for the first time without blur and blushed.

"Put that money in your pocket and look at me." David was sitting on the bench, just outside the store, his fake leg stretched out awkwardly. "Now that we can see the real you, here, sit down here." He patted the spot beside him and she sat.

"Mere, I know the last few years have been really hard on you, they have for all of us, but I am so sorry that you were caught up in everything that we were involved in. When I left for 'Nam, you were a sweet, innocent hellion but you've grown up and you're skinny as a flagpole and you don't seem to care about the way you look." Meredith gnawed on a fingernail nervously. "Listen, everyone loves you, and it's time to love yourself, don't you think?" It was an awkward scene in the middle of the mall, her brother chastising her.

"Pot calling the tea kettle black," Meredith snapped back.

David chortled, "It's pot calling the kettle black; not the 'tea kettle' you goof. Now you're right. Let's both stop feeling sorry for ourselves and get on with the renovations. If you're going to be the first female on the debate team, you have to look the part."

The makeover was remarkable. Meredith stopped fumbling with her money when the perfectly coifed Chanel assistant turned her toward the mirror to admire the results. Her hair was washed, cut and styled, the elastic band thrown away forever. The retail stores were on alert as the clothes came off the racks and into garment bags headed for Elm Street. She left David several times to relax in the food court. When she returned for her final display, David stared in disbelief at the beautiful woman fidgeting in front of him.

"Do my eyes deceive me? Is this my sister? Now that's more like it; a beauty with brains. A sight for sore eyes."

"David, shush. Thank you. I wonder what mom's going to think." David just shook his head in amazement, wondering what the world was going to think. Meredith hobbled in her new heels as they made their way to the car.

"Mom's not going to recognize you. No one is."

"Coach Murphy?" Meredith said sweetly, standing just inside his office. Mack Murphy was engrossed in the new budget, or lack thereof.

"Coach Murphy, excuse me, do you have a minute?"

He looked up at the stranger.

"Yes, yes, of course, how can I help you?"

"Well, um, I hope I'm not disturbing you. I just wanted to drop by and tell you that I think I'm ready for the big day."

He reached for his glasses and cleaned the lenses with his shirt hem. "Um, I'm sorry, I've just been busy with numbers, what big day are you referring too?"

"The debate tryouts, Coach Murphy. Remember, you thought I should try out? Well I've been working really hard and I think I'm ready."

Mack Murphy rubbed his temples trying to recall when he might've spoken with this student about the debate team.

"Coach Murphy, Mack, is everything all right?"

"Uh, oh sure everything is fine, forgive me, just focused elsewhere, please remind me, I've forgotten your name."

Meredith blushed. So far anyone that knew her before was reacting this way. Wow, she thought, I must've been a sight.

"It's Meredith Nicholson, Mack. I just wanted to drop by and let you know I think I'm ready for the tryouts. I'm ready!"

He stared in disbelief.

"Come on, that's enough for tonight, I'm whooped."

Meredith collected the books and notepads spread out on the bed and desk and yawned in agreement.

"See, you're tired too. We have two more days. I think you're a shoo-in for the part. You're gonna blow them all out of the water."

"Hmmm," she smiled, "I hope so. I told you about Coach Murphy didn't I?"

"Yes, twice. Now off to bed. I need my beauty sleep."

"Thanks David, for everything." She kissed his forehead and stepped into the hall.

"Hey, Meredith? I was wondering if you might want to talk about Charlie soon?"

She stopped and turned towards him, "Yes, I would love too." She stepped back toward him, but he waved her away.

"Not tonight, silly, it's late. But soon, OK?"

"Thanks David. I don't know how I could have done any of this without you."

"Oh, give me a break. You had it in you, you just needed a kick in the pants."

His heart and head were light, listening to her fuzzy slippers shuffle down the hall. It was nice to be home. He had only planned to stay a few days, but they had turned into a few weeks. That morning he had made the crucial, laboring trek to Tommy's parents' house and together they grieved their loss, and agreed on the brutality of war. The Towson family was grateful, and David realized how much he loved the town he had once abhorred. Everything still carried its comforts except for Charlie's absence and the dull sorrow that persisted. Where was Charlie? David knew that a successful avoidance of duty meant complete anonymity. There was no threat of combat anymore, just the threat of prison and a small price to pay for his parent's sanity. David longed for the sweet, simple lives they had shared, now shredded, irreparable until his brother returned. He decided he would wait until Thanksgiving, then return to Boston and take the starting position at the *Globe*. He needed to get out of the past and start life anew. His visit home had given him the strength to not only do it, but to want it.

Two days before the tryouts were to take place, the press came to Elm Street surprising Meredith. Mack Murphy had started an innocent rumor in the teacher's lounge that had spread, for lack of better news, to the local television station, which in turn encouraged the excitement. Taken aback and unprepared, she answered the last question with such certainty, such zeal, that her face made it on a Boston network as well.

"Why do you want to be the first female on the high school's debate team, Meredith?" She pondered the fact that she really had nothing better to do, but retorted, "Aren't male and female brains identical except for the skulls that house them? I was alarmed to find out that a woman had never tried out for the team. Why not? I encourage more women to try out. It's not a big deal, really."

The big deal was made. By the time her family drove up to the auditorium, her determination to win had tripled. It was the Saturday before Thanksgiving and the cars spilled across the street and into the library lot.

"Meredith, I think there are more cars out here than at the game last year, remember?" Her father looked back at her grinning.

He pulled up behind the stage door and they all turned toward her. David punched her shoulder lightly. "Break a leg!"

"I'll meet you in the lobby when it's over. Bye!" She hurried inside as some neighborhood fans apprehended her parents. She walked up the stairs and caught a glimpse of the hall through the opening in the drapes. The seats were almost full and suddenly anxiety consumed her. She walked into the room where everyone was waiting. Mack Murphy spotted her, first offering her a warm hand then a seat. His enthusiasm made her even more nervous and she quickly looked around at the other students ready for debate.

"There are twelve of you trying out for four seats," Coach Murphy addressed them. "This is the biggest turnout in my tenure. I just want to go over a few rules."

Eleven men and one woman, Meredith thought. *Please God, I know that I may not deserve this, but please help me through this.*

"Good luck to all of you," Coach Murphy winked, grinning from ear to ear. It was time to be seen. They were all seated according to the chart and the Coach fiddled with the tangled curtain, revealing 24 legs, only two in stockings.

How could I have agreed to this, she nodded as the packed auditorium welcomed them with applause? Everyone appeared to be looking at her.

The audience was welcomed, then addressed the rules. Each student would have three attempts, two minutes in length, at securing a position on the team. Their stance would be selected randomly from a hat, the topic selected randomly by Coach Murphy.

When Meredith was called for her first attempt, her knees buckled slightly, and there was commotion through the backdoors as several people came rushing back to their seats from the bathroom. As she approached her podium she was handed a cue card "Vietnam-pro" and underneath, "Why America's involvement was the right choice." She glanced up toward the lights, convinced it wasn't coincidence. Someone was watching over her. Herbie Ericksen was her opponent, and he was to start.

He spoke softly, hesitant, while Meredith mentally prepared. There are many sides to an idea, a subject. She remembered David's words and wondered what he would say if he were in her shoes. Today she had to be passionate about her side only.

She stood when called and held the podium for balance. Without hesitation she plunged into the Communist scare. "We were there for the innocent, not the evil. America was there to protect what we so greatly enjoy, even take for granted: freedom! We're not cowards nor will we ever allow evil to rule and destroy people's lives. If we're here to be judged, then let us be. For the good of all mankind we believe in life, liberty and the pursuit of happiness. No one should be allowed otherwise." David grinned, charmed that his sister would quote him almost word for word.

Her time was up. There was a roar of approval from the audience. Her second cue card read "Leniency of dress codes at school-con." She attempted to persuade that leniency was a broad idea. With the strange subject and after a lame attack, she sat down despondent.

The spectators were getting restless. Two hours had passed before the last and final debates were to begin. Meredith was convinced that she was not in the top four. She was second to the end and approached the podium for her last time. "Roe vs.Wade and abortion rights-pro". "Oh boy," she whispered. The microphone picked up her sigh and the crowd erupted with laughter. She glanced at her opponent. She had seen him before, but didn't know his name until he was introduced. Jerome Curtis began to speak. He was strong, articulate and the darkest black boy she had ever seen. The audience was mesmerized. She didn't quite hear everything that he said, but heard his tone, the pauses and then the silence when he finished. What was happening?

After ten seconds of silence, there was a single clap that turned into a thunderous applause. They were standing. A young Negro man had argued the con of abortion rights and had a small town on its feet? Meredith applauded.

She stepped close to the microphone and everyone settled.

"I feel a bit of an underdog after such an eloquent deliberation," she glanced toward Jerome. The crowd chuckled. "But I still have a job to do and the circumstances are not even close to the importance of the topic. Abortion rights! Finally the word 'rights' has true meaning. Because of the Supreme Court's decision in this case, finally women do have rights when it comes to decisions about their own bodies. I understand this is a sharply divided issue, but I have no qualms about the freedom of choice or the constitutional right to do so. What one decides to do with their life, with their mind or their bodies, no one should be able to take away. Giving a woman the right to choose motherhood is not acceptable. She already had that right, she is born with it, and our current government just concurred. The reason I can say this is not because it's the way I stand, which it is, but because I am a woman. I deserve, no, I *demand* the rights that every human on this planet deserves. This decision was not about abortion but about a woman's right to choose. We are free to choose our religion, our lifestyle, what we eat, where we sleep and what we want to do with our lives. A woman's body is her own; she has the right to life, liberty and the pursuit of happiness. It seems to be my quote of the afternoon, but deny it and you might as well live in a communist country. Thank goodness for our constitution and for our freedom. Thank God we have a right to choose."

The audience stood for her as well. Lightheaded, she paused before going back to her seat. If nothing else, she had accomplished a very difficult task. Putting her mind and body into the spotlight and addressing the task at hand, whether she believed in the subject or not. She closed her eyes and thanked God again for the nerve. Coach Murphy took the stage and announced that the esteemed academic judges would be taking twenty minutes or so to make their final decision, and that refreshments were being served in the lobby. Meredith smiled behind an open hand. The passion this man had for his team was obvious. He loved the attention and his team.

"Meredith, you were wonderful, just superb," her father boasted as he hugged his youngest. She smiled at David, who gave her thumbs up from across the room. He was standing near a table filled with punch, talking with a pretty brunette. She would've interrupted but her fans were relentless. The local news was close by and her mother was being interviewed, heard to say later "whether pro or con, good or bad, she is bright and smart and I am so proud to have her as my daughter." Meredith accepted outstretched hands and pats on the head but when she turned to figure David's whereabouts again, an open palm slapped her across the face.

"How dare you say it's a right to kill unborn babies, innocent children, just because it's not the best time to be a mother? How dare you!" Samuel took the angry woman by the arm and led her towards the entrance. Gertrude was beside Meredith before a tear had been shed and led her straight to the lavatory. Gertrude was appalled. The angry woman was the sister of their own Father Dennis.

She had always been a family friend and now she had raised a hand to one of her children? What was this world coming to?

"So this is what high school debate is like," Gertrude joked, as she patted her daughter's red cheeks with water. Meredith buckled with laughter and several heads peeked in to see what the commotion was. They embraced as the warning bell rang, "It's time to hear your name announced darling."

They returned to their seats.

"Anyone's name that is not called is also to be congratulated. You all did a remarkable job. Let's give them a hand shall we?" Coach Murphy was basking in the final moments. "What a pleasure to have so many of you here today, our biggest turnout ever. I hope we see you on the road this year while the 1978 Debate Team attempts to go for the gold. I now have the privilege to announce this year's debate team. Would you all please stand?"

The twelve stood.

"Chosen to represent Amherst High School are Daniel Zipper, Michael Sloan, Jerome Curtis, and, last but not least, Meredith Nicholson!"

The auditorium roared. Meredith looked over at her teammates and acknowledged the forlorn faces. She hugged Coach Murphy and shook Jerome's hand. He smiled at her and she realized they would be friends, relished the idea, as her parents and brother approached the stage. She looked for Jerome's family but he left the stage alone. She watched him as her father gave her an exuberant bear hug. She touched her cheek where Tammy Dennis's handprint had faded, even though the memory would last a lifetime.

CHAPTER 6

"Honey, I was wondering if we could talk just a minute about what you said up there today?" Gertrude beamed with pride as she asked, watching her daughter climb into the backseat beside David.

"Sure Mom, what can I help you with?" Her answer seemed smug and David punched her lightly in her side.

"Well I was…Samuel? Careful, please. These people are all trying to leave at the same time. I'm sorry, Meredith, anyway I was just wondering about the debate. Your debate. Do you believe everything that you said or should I find it compelling that you can argue a point so well, when it goes against your beliefs?"

Meredith looked at David's closed fist and knew exactly where this was going. It was not the time to debate her mother.

"Mom, they give us the topics and the pros and cons and our job is to argue the side as best we can! I won, Mom, I won!"

Gertrude smiled, not completely convinced, and looked at her husband's composed profile.

"Let's celebrate darling, where would you like to have dinner?"

Debate became Meredith's first love. She had found an avenue where she could not only be a hero, but also the gang leader and a star. Back at school she was unprepared for the celebrity status that came with her conquest. Her new look and new outlook with the students and teachers was soon recognized. The once-quiet, plain Jane learned quickly to bask in her found fame. She relished the attention.

It was several days before she and Amy crossed paths. Amy watched from a distance and was the first to crack a debate team joke if anyone was listening.

"Hello, Amy."

"Oh hey, Meredith."

"I was wondering if you went to the debate tryouts? I was hoping you did, since one of the reasons why I was there was because of you."

"Ugh, no Meredith, I don't come to school on Saturdays, no matter what great thing is going on. Sounds like you did well with the geeks and all. Um, I have to go, my friend Lisa is waiting."

"Oh, OK, well just wanted to say hi and thanks."

"Thanks for what, Meredith? Really not necessary."

Meredith watched her old friend walk away. Though they hadn't been close friends for several years now, she felt an overwhelming sadness. They would never be the same.

At lunchtime, many classmates said hello and even invited her to share their tables, but Meredith refused politely, looking for Amy, hoping that maybe if they had lunch together, she could smooth things between them. She passed the table of black students, always crowded and segregated, grinning when she saw Jerome looking at her.

"Hi Jerome, we did pretty great, huh?" He smiled and nodded.

"Yes Meredith, we did a great job. See you at practice then, OK?" Everyone else at the table was either gawking at him or the white girl, but Meredith reacted unknowingly.

"Sure, see you then. I really thought you were brilliant!"

"Yeehaw! Brilliant, buddy, she thought you were brilliant!!" One of Jerome's friends mimicked her and Jerome shot an angered look to stop the taunting.

"Meredith, thank you. You weren't so bad yourself."

The table snickered when Jerome looked around once again to silence them. Meredith smiled shyly, suddenly aware that she was embarrassing them both. Her sudden confidence evaporated. She was the girl who had never even considered approaching a boy in the cafeteria. She quickly continued her search for Amy, confused and hungry.

Winter in New England brings darkness before most have had time to enjoy the daylight. Debate practice would be two hours, twice a week and Mack Murphy was serious about getting down to the business at hand. When the first practice ended, the four new recruits were frazzled with information and all arrogance had dissipated. Mack wished them all a nice Thanksgiving and a reminder that the next Monday, their first meet, would be a difficult one. Meredith hurried to the payphone to call her mother for a ride. Since David's return her mother seemed alive and concerned again, insisting she call and never walk home in the dark.

"Are you heading home, Meredith?" Jerome awkwardly called out to her.

"Um, yes, I have to call for a ride, my mother insists." She was happy her mother was in better spirits although she sometimes still felt the forgotten child.

"Well, I was going to go to the library first, then head home. Maybe get a few books to help with the meet against Amherst. Would you like to come with me?"

"Uh, sure, yes I would very much. I'll call my mom from there."

"Hmmm, nice weather we're having," he joked as he wrapped his arms around his chest. They walked in silence, bearing the blustery north wind that had whipped through the town. He opened the library's large oak door for her as she shivered, a blast of warm air thawing her face. They shed their layers and proceeded to different shelves, both appearing with a stack of books, but once settled, never opened. They talked for two hours and could've continued all night if the librarian hadn't warned them that they would be closing in 5 minutes. Meredith reluctantly called her mother, and offered Jerome a ride home, which he hastily refused. He touched her hand before it slid back into its mitten and she watched as he disappeared into the night. She couldn't stop thinking about him and when sleep finally prevailed, she dreamt of him. When she woke she realized that maybe, just maybe, this was love.

"Amy, I was wondering if you had some time after school, could we talk?"

Amy looked at Meredith with glazed eyes, then down at the stack of papers that fell out of her locker.

Meredith bent to help her collect them adding, "I really would like to talk."

"Um, when?"

"Well, after school if you're not busy."

"Hmmm, I'm supposed to go to a friend's house after school, maybe some other time."

"Oh, O.K., when?"

"You know, I guess I could skip Lisa's, I'm so sick of her irritating voice. Meet me here at 3. All right Meredith, does that make you happy?"

"Sure that sounds great. Thanks Amy, have a great day at school!"

"Have a great day at school?" Amy mumbled under her breath, kicking her locker door closed.

Meredith's last class was study hall, allowing her to finish her homework and head straight to her locker for her coat. On the way, Mack Murphy stopped her, asking whether she was ready for the tournament on Monday and she smiled, replying wholeheartedly yes, then rushed upstairs to meet Amy. When she reached the top, her heart skipped a beat, seeing Jerome standing beside her locker. Was he waiting for her?

"Hello, Meredith."

"Hi, Jerome, how are you?" She fiddled with her combination steadying her nerves.

"I'm just fine, thank you. I haven't seen you all day so I thought I'd wait and see if you made it home safely last night?"

"Oh, yes, of course. I hope you did as well. It was so cold. We should've brought you home."

"No, I'm used to it. And that's not really why I'm here. I'm," he hesitated.

She noticed his foot tapping, his long lean body, and his beautiful smile. She leaned against her locker.

"I was just wondering if maybe you would like, I mean maybe we could go to a movie sometime?"

She smiled, her face like a steamed lobster. She was being asked out on a date for the first time in almost 16 years. Two days before her birthday, this would top all presents.

"Jerome, I think that would be grand!" *Grand* she thought, I sound like a moron.

He smiled, relieved with her response. "Great," his poise only slightly better, "we'll talk by Friday. I have your number from the debate letter. Hope you have a nice Thanksgiving if I don't see you before then"

"Oh, you too. I love Thanksgiving. It's my birthday too!"

"Your birthday! Well then, I'll have some candles when we get together. How old are you going to be?"

"Sixteen," she gushed.

"Wow, I would've guessed you for seventeen for sure."

She giggled then grabbed her coat and said, "Call me soon."

She was going on a date with Jerome Curtis. Now she had more than ever to talk about with Amy. "Wow, oh my God," she muttered as she bundled up, running a few minutes late.

Jerome walked away with his hands in his pockets, a bit more swagger in his step. He was going on a date with Meredith Nicholson, the most beautiful girl at Amherst High.

"I was just about to leave, damn it," Amy's said in a nasty tone.

"Gosh I'm sorry Amy, I ran into a couple of people, and hey, I'm only five minutes late, jeez."

"You and your newfound fame. Let's get out of here. I can't stand this place. Your new found fame. Bullshit it is." Amy swung her backpack over her arm and headed for the exit, Meredith dutifully following. Old habits never truly died. When they stepped outside, winter's woe instantly froze any exposed flesh.

"Where would you like to talk, Meredith?" Amy asked, thinking they would probably be off to the Nicholson house, which wasn't that bad, and was much better than going home. *Too bad it's so fucking cold,* Amy thought, *we could go to our spot behind the convenience store.*

"Oh, I was thinking the coffee shop, maybe we could get some coffee or hot chocolate, warm up a little."

"That's fine, whatever." Amy knew one thing. The thin, army coat she wore did very little to keep her warm, so she'd need a little help with that problem. Coffee wouldn't cut it.

It was an awkward reunion, having been almost two years since they had been alone together. Both were at a loss for small talk. When they reached the cafe Meredith, ever doting, asked Amy what she wanted as she stepped in line. Amy indifferently replied "whatever," before making her way to the ladies room. She emerged several minutes later and tossed her backpack on the floor as she pulled a seat up beside Meredith.

"OK Meredith, what is it that you're about to pee your pants about?"

"Um, well I wanted to talk with you about boys, I mean *a* boy."

"You're kidding right?" Amy chuckled, wiping her nose on the napkin in front of the hot chocolate.

"No, I'm not kidding at all. I really, well, I need your advice and just wanted to talk with a girlfriend about it."

"Meredith, it's been years since we've talked. You still think we're friends?" She paused, quickly regretting her thought, "I mean it's been almost two years, I just thought that, well, that you didn't care."

"I know, Amy, I tried, but you were just too busy and I've been through a lot at home and, well, you were the one who was angry."

"We've all been through hell at home Meredith, I guess I was just surprised you still thought we were friends. But here we are, just the two of us, having nice hot chocolates and catching up on old times. Right when you need something." Her sarcastic tone was intolerable.

"Amy, please stop acting that way. I've always cared about you and I'm really sorry that our friendship has suffered. I love you, I've always loved you and I care about what happens to you. I've missed you, but you just didn't seem interested and, well, you got all those new friends and anyway, something wonderful has happened to me and you were the first person I wanted to share it with."

Amy looked at Meredith. Sure she was angry at the geek for the last couple of years, but they had known each other since, well, forever and had some fun times. Maybe she could give it a chance?

"All right you win, Meredith. I'm all ears, what's up?" She leaned back on two legs of the chair, wiping her incessant runny nose, staring blankly at her long lost friend.

"Well, I've met a boy, a junior, and I really like him and I guess I'm not sure what to do. I mean I really like him."

"Oh jeez, yeah, the guy thing. Come on Meredith you know how to act with a guy!"

"Oh no I don't, Amy. I've never been on a date. I guess I'm just having these funny feelings and I'm not sure. I thought I would ask you since you're so popular and all."

Amy's laughter shook the table, disturbing the other customers. She rocked backwards and the chair slipped. Meredith reached, catching her before she fell. It took Amy a few minutes to compose herself, and even then, she let out a few more snorts.

"OK, OK, I'm all right now," she smirked, "OK, since you insist that I'm so popular, I will be the voice of reason. Let me go to the bathroom before I get hit with the questions. What are you all gawking at?" She perused the room as she stood, sending the curious back to their newspapers and boring lives.

"Amy, you just went to the bathroom!"

"Well, sorry, but I have to go again."

She grabbed her sack and disappeared back into the ladies room.

Meredith waited patiently then started to worry. When Amy appeared she swayed then sat carefully, clutching her seat.

"Are you all right, Amy?"

"Yeah, yeah, just great. OK now, where were we?"

"Well, I met this boy, a junior."

"Oh yes, the boy. Who is this lucky fellow?"

"His name is Jerome. Jerome Curtis. He's on the debate team."

"Hmmm, I know him. Cute nigger."

"What did you say?"

"I said 'cute nigger', Meredith, he's a cute nigger."

"Oh my gosh, Amy, how mean are you? That is a terrible word and well."

"Oh Jesus, Miss prissy pants, please. The guy is a spook, what else can I say? I said he was cute."

Meredith shook her head, while Amy grabbed another handful of napkins to wipe her nose.

"Amy, I really like him, I do. I just wanted to, oh I don't know what I wanted to do."

"You want to find out how to get in his pants?"

"Amy!"

"Well do you?"

"Amy, this is a big mistake. I thought you would be a little more sensitive but obviously I was wrong asking you to talk."

"Great Meredith, that's just great. You ask me to meet you after school, I cancel going to another friend's house where they serve a lot more than fucking hot chocolate, you're late because you're flirting with your new little nigger boyfriend and you sit here and accuse me of being rude?"

"Not only that, Amy, but if I didn't know better I would say you're doing drugs!"

"Fuck you, Meredith Nicholson!" Amy pushed the table, spilling the contents of her own mug all over the table. "You can't accuse me of anything. You don't know me!" She kicked her bag out from underneath her chair, spilling its contents on the tile, "And you can just go fuck yourself!" She grabbed at a pocket-knife and a glass straw rolling across the floor. It was too late; Meredith saw it.

"What the hell is that, Amy?"

"Oh fuck you, Meredith. And your little nigger too!"

Amy slammed the coffee shop door, rattling the windowpanes. The room was silent, shocked at the scene. Meredith collected her things and hurried home embarrassed but even more worried.

Meredith knew that something was wrong and that Amy was in trouble. She called her mother, than called Mrs. Deering, but there was no answer. She tried again when she got home.

"She said she was going over to your house after school. We were so happy that you two were talking again." Mrs. Deering's voice sounded worried.

"Oh, I'm sorry. I did see her after school, I was just wondering if she was home yet. I forgot to tell her something. When she gets in will you have her call me?"

"Absolutely, Meredith, I will. It's so nice to hear from you."

Meredith looked for Amy at school the next day, but couldn't find her. She finally called her house, hoping she'd answer. Mrs. Deering answered pleasantly, late in the afternoon

"Oh Meredith, I'm sorry. I told her you called last night. She said she would call. I saw her before she went to school, so I'm sure she's there."

"I'm sure she is. You're right. I must just keep missing her. I'm sorry to bother you again. Thanks and Happy Thanksgiving."

"Happy Thanksgiving to you too, Meredith."

Meredith assumed Amy was avoiding her and decided to stop worrying and keep an eye out for Jerome instead. After all, it was Amy who walked away again.

"Captain are you all right?" the female detective leaned over her superior.

Samuel closed his eyes, exhaled and went back to questioning the boys who had found the body, frozen; face down in a shallow, trash collected puddle. There was an empty bottle of bourbon and two prescription bottles strewn beside her. The child had been so high on pills and liquor she didn't know she was freezing to death. He cried as he drove home.

"Mere, do you want to talk?"

She'd had been in her room most of the day, Thanksgiving had been put on hold with the news of Amy's death, her birthday cake left in the box without candles.

"No, David, I don't." Her tone made him uncomfortable, so he sat on the corner of the bed, ready for the assault. His sister needed to get angry and if he was the target, then so be it. *She's been through so much*, he thought. .

"No, I'm not kidding Mere, I mean it. I know the news about Amy has everyone in shock, and I guess you've forgotten your own birthday. First I left, then Charlie and now Amy is gone. I just think we should talk."

"David, your timing sucks, you know that? You've been home a month. A month, David! I've been alone for so long. I'm just so sad for my friend," tears welled in her eyes. "my oldest friend killed herself. Damn her. I'm hurt and I don't care about my stupid birthday or Charlie right now. He isn't here to help. He doesn't care. He doesn't remember my birthday or Mom's or Dad's or anyone's, ever! I remember his but have nowhere to send a card. I remember everyone's and what do I get? My only friend is dead and I have a stupid crush on a boy that I'm a fool to think I even can have a chance with. What's wrong with me? How can I even think about him when Amy is gone? Damn, damn, damn. Why Amy? Why?"

David moved closer to her and said, hushed, "What do you mean you have a stupid crush? Meredith, I'm sorry but I'm confused. What are you talking about?"

Meredith gulped for air and shook her head. "It's just, well, Amy and I talked. I told you. There's this boy on my debate team that I really like and, well, Amy called him a nigger and I said she was rude and since Dad came home with the news I've been thinking, maybe she was right? I can't date a black boy in school, can I David?"

"Why the hell can't you date him? A black, yellow, red, or striped guy? Who's to say who you can and cannot date? Meredith, if you like him and he's a good person, of course you should go on a date with him. Amy was a sick, confused young girl and what she did is a terrible waste, but you can't waste your life because of something she said. You know that color is insignificant. I'm surprised at you. That you'd even let the thought fester. Go out with this guy. Go out and have fun. Charlie would say the same thing."

"Oh, fuck Charlie!"

"Meredith, Jesus! Coming from you, that language is detestable. Don't let Mom hear you. And remember, Charlie loves you and always will. I'm not angry with him anymore, Mere. We have to forgive him, try to find him; we have to get the pieces back together in the puzzle. Look at me now, you know he loves you?"

She leaned over and dried her eyes on his shoulder, knowing full well Charlie loved her and wondering whether Amy had loved her. If only she could see Charlie. She held onto to David and whispered, "Thank you, David."

"Happy 16th birthday, little sister!" David squeezed her gently.

"David, do you think I should tell Mom or Dad about Jerome?"

He thought about their parents, their possible prejudices, then quietly added, "I think I'd wait a bit on that. Mom and Dad have a lot on their minds and, well, let's not put worry where worry doesn't need to be put."

Jerome called as promised on Friday and Meredith told him about Amy. He listened through the tears and sniffles. Amy was buried on Saturday. Hundreds of students and teachers along with parents and friends attended. Jerome caught a glimpse of Meredith, and watched her from the back of the church. He'd never felt this way before. All he wanted to do was hold her.

CHAPTER 7

"Meredith, are you ready yet? Come on darling, you're going to be late and we want to see you before you leave." Gertrude's voice cracked with excitement.

"Ugh, this new look sure takes a whole lot longer," she mumbled as she fiddled with the zipper on her jacket. She glanced again in her full-length mirror. What used to be a clothes hanger, she now used much more for its original purpose. The picture of her and Amy, arms around each other's shoulders when they were just kids, faced her, and she smiled. "Oh Amy, I wish you were still here. I wish, God I wish. Do you think I look sixteen now?" She could distinctly hear her friend's snide, "You could probably pass for a freshman if you tried," as she grabbed her book bag, glancing one last time at the photo. "Amy, life was just beginning for us. Now I'm going it alone. I would very much appreciate it if you could give me your confidence. At least your blessing, OK?"

"Who are you talking to?" Gertrude's voice rose from the bottom of the stairs, "Come on now, you're going to be late."

Meredith bounded down the stairs and into the kitchen, grabbing her lunch and briskly kissed her mother and father. "Dad, what are you still doing home? You're going to be late too." She smiled as she messed his receding hair.

He smiled back, "We've been waiting for you, your mother and I. We wanted to give you something before you left for school.

"Cool. I guess I can be late for math," she snickered.

Gertrude and Samuel winked at each other and Gertrude came behind her daughter and tied a dishtowel around her eyes.

"Mom, what are you doing? That better be clean. I mean it," she giggled as her father took her elbow and steered her around.

"Where's David? He should be steering. I'm afraid, Dad, your driving, well, has a lot to be desired," she joked reaching to tickle his side.

"My driving? Well, missy, what I've seen of your driving in the past few weeks is nothing to boast about."

"Dad, where are you taking me? And about the driving, I think I'm getting pretty good. Mom even thinks so."

"Your mom thinks you do everything well, now hush. Just a few more steps."

Gertrude had opened the front door quietly and Samuel removed the towel, revealing to Meredith a bright yellow Volkswagen Beetle in the driveway with a large red bow tied around it. David stood to one side dangling the keys.

"What? Mom, Dad, is it mine?" She squeezed them in a group hug before they could answer, skipping down the front steps and grabbing at the keys while David dangled them out of reach. "Oh my God, it's beautiful!"

"Now you know you shouldn't take the Lord's name. Yes, it's yours. Of course it's yours." Gertrude was beaming.

"David, please!" He conceded, handing her the keys as she jumped into the driver's seat. She leaned over and rolled down the windows, the cold air rushing in, unable to control her excitement.

"This is incredible, I love it so much! Thank you, thank you! Oh my gosh, I can't wait to drive it to school."

"Now, young lady, you're running late and well, I think maybe we should take it for a test drive first when you get home?"

"No Dad, no way, I want to drive it today. I'm ready, I have my permit, come on Dad. Dad, it's less than 2 miles!" David was making his way back outside with her coat and books. There was no way his sister would go to school not driving her new car.

"Dad, let her go. She'll be fine. It's not far." Samuel smiled at his son. It was good to see his family smiling. He would do anything to keep them happy.

"Oh all right then, be very careful!" The engine turned on his last word and she grinned from ear to ear as she turned the radio up loudly, leaving the windows down while she backed down the driveway slowly. They could hear her singing off-key all the way down the street.

"You got a *what* for your birthday?"

"I know. I can't believe it either. It's the cutest little thing you've ever seen, I can't wait to show you."

Jerome just shook his head in disbelief. He got two books from his mother and a deck of cards with naked burlesque women from his uncle for his 16th birthday. Meredith got a car.

"Wow, that is something else," he said as he started to walk away, noticing the attention their conversation was generating.

"Hey, wait, really, I want you to see it. Are we still, well, going to the movies?"

Her leaned back toward her and whispered, "In style me lady. See you later."

She smiled. Her first date and she was driving her new car. She noticed a few girls giggling a few lockers down. *Who cares,* she thought, *my first date, a gorgeous guy, and my new car. Oh Amy, I wish you were here.*

They lost their first debate against Northampton High. Meredith had begged her family to let the first few go by without representation, so they could be at their best for the audience. Mack Murphy had driven them in a school van and coached them the short drive to the other school's campus. Meredith felt confident with her team, but with the crushing 10-4 loss, there was nothing left but disappointment. Winning was what they must be determined to do each time they set out and if they failed, they had to press harder, study longer, and surprise the enemy with their intelligence and savvy. It only took a grueling hour to be defeated and the ride home was quiet.

"Listen, you four were great. You have a lot of potential. I'll see you on Wednesday. This was our first time, and you did fine, really."

They walked away, each quiet in their own thoughts.

"Meredith, are you still up for a movie or something?" Jerome needed reassurance that the date was still reality.

She didn't turn around. He hurried to her side and saw she was crying.

"Meredith, it's OK. It's not that bad that we lost. We'll get it right and get them next time. We will."

She smiled wiping her eyes, trying to keep the mascara from running.

"I just hated the feeling. I hated losing."

"Now, now, hate is a very strong word. Dislike is so much better."

"Jerome, you sound like my mother," she giggled." OK, I disliked losing immensely. Come and see my car and let's go to a movie, or get something to eat, or just talk awhile."

Who kissed who first? Now that was a matter for debate. They were in the middle of talking about Amy and the team and Coach Murphy and the weather, and then it happened. They would tease each other later, arguing about who leaned in first and who stopped talking first. But both agreed it was the most wonderful kiss. The kiss that sealed the reality of their love. Now, neither had ever been in love, but even so, they were sure of the feelings they shared and nothing could be sweeter or more exciting. There was only one hurdle left for them. Telling the rest of the world.

David left the following weekend, his family excited for him, but anxious to see him leave. His return had brought life back to the family and the remaining three worried that it would leave with him for Boston.

"I love you, David. Gosh, I wish you weren't leaving, I have so much to tell you."

David smiled, recognizing the glow of his little sister, secretly yearning for a love of his own. "I hear you, Sis, but Boston is so close, and once I get settled you can visit all the time, bring your new friend maybe?"

"What new friend?" Gertrude cut in.

"Oh Mom, you know your daughter, new friends all over, everywhere. Just another admirer of the smartest, brightest gal in town." David pinched her cheek and kissed her goodbye. Boston wasn't far and she had Jerome.

"What new friend, Meredith?

Meredith busied herself towards the door, not answering.

"We would love to meet your new friends, darling. Know they are always welcome here." Samuel nodded in agreement, his eyes still focused on the horizon.

"Of course, Mom. You'll meet my new friends. They're really great. Oh, I wish that David could've stayed," she added, changing the subject quickly.

"We all do, darling, we all do." Thoughts of Charlie weighed heavy on their minds.

Spring came and went quickly. The summer of '74 was filled with part-time jobs, drive-in movies, and experimenting with first and second base. They talked on the phone for hours when their parents weren't home and when they were, they wrote love letters and planned their future. Jerome finally got the nerve to show Meredith his home, a simple ranch in a rumored rough area of town. She never judged him and found she liked the convenience of his mother working nights, allowing them to play like adults. They would sip from the liquor cabinet and replace the missing with water. They would dance to music that she had never heard, and she found herself humming the same songs over and over. On the night before the first day of their senior year, Barry White serenaded them down the hallway and into the bedroom. A tangle of hands and buttons and sweet kisses below her waist followed. She loved to touch his body and melt in his embrace.

He asked her tenderly and she wanted him so badly she could hardly answer. The sweet pain as he eased inside of her, overcome with emotion and lust. He held her tightly and she arched her body against him, clinging to his hips. They were one and no one would come between them, ever.

"Well, are you two in for another year of debate?" Mack Murphy grinned as his two senior hopefuls approached.

"Oh Mr. Murphy, of course, but we have to make the team first." Meredith grinned back knowing that she and Jerome had made a big difference in their second place finish in the finals.

"Now, you're right, somehow I'm sure you will by putting your best foot forward. We could use a few bright seniors on the team." He winked and watched as they made their way through the corridor. He could recognize young love from a mile away. Two bright kids with a very dim future together. "Good luck to you," he muttered entering the classroom full of wide-eyed freshman.

"Hello and welcome to Amherst High School and your first English class. My name is Mr. Murphy, but you can call me Mack. Also, if any of you're interested, I also coach field hockey and debate. Any takers? OK, think about it and let's get busy. Open your books to the table of contents."

The debate tryouts came and went, and, as predicted, both Meredith and Jerome made the team. There were several more female students that tried out, but they lacked confidence, and Meredith remained the lone female. It was also the one safe way for her and Jerome to spend time together, since they had kept their relationship secret from their families and friends. Meredith had only confessed her feelings to David a few weeks after his move, which in turn caused an argument between her and Jerome and a promise that if anyone were to be told, they would both have to agree to it. Needless to say, no one else was made privy to their love. Their classmates questioned their friendship and rumors flew and fizzled, but neither gave away the most important thing in their lives. They were apart for the holidays and when another harsh winter settled on their small town, they couldn't bear to be alone or stop the desire. They took precautions, agreeing that college, then marriage and family were the correct order.

One bitterly cold morning in early February, Meredith broke down. Her period was several days late and she was sure she was pregnant. After several lengthy and emotional discussions with Jerome, they decided together that they would tell their families and do the right thing, get married. When her period came the next day, they were more disappointed than relieved. They had made their first commitment to tell their families and now their secret would stay secret.

"I guess I just thought, well, the idea of telling the world and marrying you and having our child, it was a dream come true I guess."

Jerome touched under her chin gently and lifted her angelic face toward his own.

"Meredith, I love you, with all my heart. I know how you feel, because I feel the same way. Your heart beats with mine. I want to be with you forever. I want to be your husband and I want us to have many children. Will you marry me, please?"

She said, "Of course I'll marry you. Many children?"

They held each other tightly and laughed.

The two concocted an ingenious plan. Their class trip would be an early May visit to the Grand Canyon. Every team and committee sold candy bars and wrapping paper, had bake sales and carwashes, generating enough money to send the entire class of 100, along with 10 chaperones, to one of the seven natural wonders. The energy and excitement was hard to mask, and only when everyone finally boarded the plane, did Jerome and Meredith exchange looks. Glances that solidified they would be man and wife on their return.

The plan was simple. Distract the chaperones and board one of the many tour buses made available for those who desired to visit "Sin City". Las Vegas had dozens of chapels and would pay little attention to their IDs. A few scratches on her birth certificate changed the year 1958 to the year 1957, making her a few months older than her husband-to-be. They made one last promise that neither would tell their classmates until they told their parents and families. Once back in Amherst, they would go to their respective homes, tell everyone, then meet the next morning. Hopefully their families would join them to celebrate.

Their plane landed at home and they exchanged one last bit of intimacy. Jerome brushed her hand as she passed, approaching her parents. While waiting for her luggage and answering her parents' excited questions, Meredith strained head above the crowd, trying to catch a glimpse of him, her sweet love. He was nowhere in sight.

CHAPTER 8

"Mom, Dad? I have something I really need to talk with you about."

They had stopped for dinner and were home in the kitchen having tea when Meredith decided the time was right. Her father put his paper down and her mother smiled as she placed a cup in front of her husband.

"Sure, darling, what would you like to talk about?" She looked at her father lovingly, the sweet, calm, keeper of the peace, the best father anyone could ask for.

"Mom, please sit." She motioned to a chair, her mother wiping her hands on the dishtowel, smiling and taking her seat at the table. "It's so nice to have you home sweetheart. We missed you."

Meredith sat in her designated seat of the last seventeen years. The thoughts, emotions energizing the confidence to finally tell the two people, the world's best parents, what she had been dying to scream at the top of her lungs for over a year.

"Um, I really need to tell you both about the last year of my life."

The familiar kitchen table, where so much drama had transpired, was now in complete silence. Neither parent had even tried to interrupt. Meredith hoped for at least an understanding nod, but only got glossy stares. Finally her father spoke.

"Let me get this straight. You and this young man, Jerome Curtis, are married? Did I hear this correctly? Gertrude, remind me to call the doctor tomorrow to get fitted for a hearing aid, because I'm sure that I heard something wrong." A rage built inside him, his hands trembled. "Well?"

"Dad, please don't. Yes you heard it right; Jerome and I were married in Las Vegas. We're in love! We want to be together, forever!"

Samuel's cup rattled, spilling some of the tea. Meredith started crying and Samuel raised a hand to strike her. Gertrude jumped up and grabbed his opened palm, holding it to her chest. Samuel had never once raised a hand to any of his children. His reaction was caustic.

"Samuel, please calm down. It seems the deed is done. I'm not sure what we can do right now, but anger will solve nothing right now. Please, go for a walk. Please darling, right now!"

He stood, gripping the edge of the table, not looking at either his daughter or wife. Finally he moved out of the room, leaving the kitchen door swinging. Gertrude moved next to her daughter, her hands folded in front of her, eyes closed, praying.

"Mom?"

"Meredith, please I need a few minutes to think. This is not something that anyone could've been ready for. Your father is upset."

"Upset? He almost hit me, Mom."

"Meredith, please. Your father would've never hit you. I have never in my life been so surprised. No, shocked. Your father's reaction was just that, a reaction. He thought he knew his only daughter. You sit down and tell us that you have gone off and married a young black man from your debate team because it was the only way you two could proclaim your love to the world?"

"Mom, please don't. Don't patronize me. I thought you'd understand. I thought you'd both understand." Meredith started to cry.

"Meredith, who do you think you are?"

"No one, Mom, no one. Just like when David was hurt and Charlie left. I'm the kid that everyone forgot. The 'no one' in this family."

"You're telling me you did this because you're angry with us?"

"No, Mom, forget it. Neither of you get it. I was wrong to think you would."

"What do you mean that you're no one?"

"Just what I said, Mom, no one."

Tears streamed down her face as she brushed her teeth. She wanted to call him, to leave the house, but her father had taken her keys and she didn't dare leave until morning. She needed to talk with Jerome and make some arrangements.

Morning came after a sleepless night and she scrambled to pack a few things.

"Where do you think you're going?" Samuel stood in the doorway of his daughter's room in his uniform.

"I'm going out."

"Well, maybe we should talk about where you are going?"

"No Dad, we don't need to talk about anything. I am leaving."

"You are 17 until November 24th, remember? Until then you're not an adult, you are my daughter, and I will make the decisions as to where you're going."

She sat on the bed, shaking her head.

"I've already contacted the boy's mother and things are being taken care of right now." Meredith could see her mother's shadow outside the door.

"What have you done, Dad? What have you told them? You seem to forget that Jerome and I made this decision together. We are in love. I'm an adult and you can't do anything about this. I'm in love with Jerome Curtis and he's in love with me. We are M-A-R-R-I-E-D. Married, Dad, married!"

"Not if I have anything to say about it young lady. And I have a *lot* to say about it. You're seventeen. You're not an adult. The whole ludicrous ordeal is illegal and it will be taken care of."

"Illegal? Dad, we didn't do anything wrong. I'm sorry we didn't tell you or ask your permission, but I don't need your permission for anything, anymore, ever again!" Samuel kept still, his wife's presence tangible.

"Where did we go wrong, Meredith? Where did we go wrong?" He was shaking his head, confused and emotional.

She waited for him to turn, then jumped past them and ran out of the house and down Elm Street as fast as she could. She made it to the corner store and the payphone, before she turned, expecting them to pull up behind her. She dialed his number and a man answered.

"Yes, hello," she responded sadly, "may I speak with Jerome please?"

"I'm sorry, he's not here, may I take a message?"

"Please, please let him know Meredith is on the phone. I'm sure he'll want to know."

"I'm sorry, miss, he's not available right now, but I'd be happy to let him know."

"Please sir, I don't know who you are, please can you get him?" She started to cry again, but there was only silence on the other end.

"Sir, please," she begged.

"Miss, I'm sorry, but I can't. I'm sorry for everything. Please leave well enough alone."

"Who are you, Sir?" The other end clicked, leaving a dial tone humming in her ear.

She wasn't exactly sure what happened after that. Years later it would stay a blur. She started running, her heart aching and mind racing. She had clocked the miles too many times to count, always excited when the odometer turned to eight and she knew in less than a sixth of a mile she would be at her love's door. Sweat dripped into her eyes and she wiped back her tangled hair and tucked it behind her collar. When she turned the corner of his street, Sunday morning churchgoers were the first to notice her. She stopped at the end of his driveway, not recognizing the stranger's car parked where her little Volkswagen belonged. She tried to collect herself, straightening her pajama top, now soaked and clinging to her breasts. Before she even passed the first car, the front door opened and an elderly gentleman stepped onto the porch.

"Excuse me, Sir, please, may I talk with Jerome?"

"I'm sorry, miss, he isn't here."

"Please, please." She stared down at the cement, noticing the blood from one of her heels. She wasn't wearing any shoes. She had forgotten to put on shoes. Tears poured down her face.

"Miss, please don't, your father's on his way. Can I get you a glass of water?"

She shook her head and sat down in the driveway, unable to answer. He went back inside and reappeared with a glass of water and a towel. He walked up to her calmly and handed her the towel, which she refused, then asked her quietly, "Please, Miss Meredith, please drink the water." She reached cautiously and sipped it twice then handed it back to him.

Her father's cruiser pulled up behind them and her mother got out of the passenger side and helped her to her feet. She felt nothing as she hobbled to the open car door, a quiet criminal. She didn't look back at the house. Once at home she obediently followed her mother upstairs. She picked up the hall phone and dialed, both parents aware but not objecting. It rang three times, and then thankfully he answered.

"Hello!"

"David, I need to talk with you."

PART II

CHAPTER 9

In the middle

Milton Stafford was an emergency C-section on Christmas Eve. His mother Beth, not expecting for several weeks, was home with her feet up wrapping the last gifts of the evening, when her water broke. Her father-in-law, with whom they had been living since her husband Pete's mother had passed two years prior, reacted faster than most emergency doctors and had her on a gurney at the local hospital within 10 minutes, even though they lived almost twenty miles away. It would be an hour later, traveling in almost blizzard conditions, when Peter Stafford would arrive, leaving his staff to mind the last-minute shoppers at the grocery store. He was greeted by his father and given the news gently that emergency surgery could not have been delayed because his new son had decided that breach was a better way to enter the world.

"Dad, Dad, are they all right?"

"Yes Peter, they're both doing just fine. Beth lost a lot of blood but the doctor says that she'll be fine. She's a trouper, Son, a real trouper. And that little boy of yours, wow! Leave it to a Stafford boy to jump into the world feet first, or try to at least! He's small, just a dash over five pounds, but once we get him home, we'll fatten him up. They're both going to be fine, Son, just fine."

Peter wrapped his arms around his father's broad shoulders and wept. When he had received the page overhead at the store, he was in produce, trying to settle an argument between a customer and one of his employees over a package of kumquats. The clementines in 1958 were abnormally small, so it was easy to confuse them with the kumquats. He had run to the back of the store when he heard the page but the connection was bad due to the weather and the only thing he could decipher was, "He's almost here, Son!"

"Can I see them now?" he asked anxiously.

"Sure, sure Peter. The doc said as soon as you arrive to let him know. Come on, let's go meet your boy. My grandson. What was that name again? Milton? Hmmm, I think that'll suit the little guy just fine."

Beth was groggy when they entered the room. She arose enough to smile at her husband and father-in-law and glance over at the crib where their new baby lay sleeping.

"Oh Beth, I'm so sorry I…."

"Shhh." She put her finger to his lips, "It's all right. Everything's fine. Dad was amazing. Drove like we were in a flying sleigh. I wonder if Santa knows he has competition?" She smiled as she said this, but sleep was overpowering.

"Now, now Beth, you go to sleep. No need to talk right now." Harold Stafford smiled down at his daughter-in-law. The only daughter he ever had.

"Dad, what did she mean by that? How fast did you drive?" Peter turned toward his father now standing by the crib.

"Peter, aren't you going to hold your new baby boy?" He handed the small blue bundle to his son, who held his arms out nervously, and once cradled in an awkward stance, he sat down in the rocking chair and admired their miracle.

"My oh my, Milton, you sure got us in a scare. I'm so happy you're here and just hope you can promise that you won't ever scare us like that again."

"Peter, the child is a newborn. He can't promise anything right now. Just needs to eat, pee, poop, and be loved. That's all that's gonna happen for the meantime."

"I know Dad, I know. Just hoping, that's all. Just hoping."

"Can't wait to get him home and show him my new invention!"

"Dad, I think Beth may want to keep him inside for a bit. At least until the springtime and, well, you know some of your inventions can be kind of, well, I guess I can just say, dangerous."

"Nonsense, Peter. He needs to get out in the lab as soon as possible. He needs to see what his future may hold."

"Dad, you just said that peeing and pooping and loving were all he needed right now."

"You're right, you're right, but a man can hope, can't he?"

They both smiled.

Wolfeboro, New Hampshire has the distinction of being known as "The Oldest Summer Resort in America." Well over 200 Years old, the summer months burst with tourists and water lovers, anxious to squelch the New England summer heat in the cool water of Lake Winnipesaukee. Spectacular charm, surrounded by the White Mountains and the largest lake in the state. Peter's parents had brought him every summer to their camp, where he fondly remembered learning to swim and fish and enjoy what God gave everyone to appreciate. After his father retired from the manufacturing mill in Lawrence, Massachusetts, he sold their original camp and built a much larger cabin on the lake. Harold designed and foresaw construction of his wife's last home. When Peter's mother, Sara, was diagnosed with cancer, everyone's first reaction was to get her back to a civilized hospital area where she could receive the best care. But she always seemed to fare better in their log cabin on the water, where the cancer finally took her last breath.

Peter had met Beth at the state university, and after several years of courting, they married at the small Catholic Church just off the main street of his parents' summer home. She fell in love with the town and like her new husband, felt a sense of peace and rebirth away from the hustle and bustle of city life. They traveled the three hours every Friday night for several months to be with his mother in her last days of life. Peter didn't want to leave her side and there was no debate when they decided to move permanently to the resort town. Peter grieved, but worried even more for his father. A few months after his mother's death all three of them took up residence together in the house that his father had built. With his father's help, Peter started a small grocery store just off the main street. Summer months proved lucrative enough that the slow winter months were exactly what the people that lived in the town wanted. Everything peaceful, quiet and just enough to get by. When Beth announced to the two men in her life that she was pregnant, the marriage of the three was forged.

"I swear darling, only one week a year do we carry kumquats and by golly, that was what they were arguing about."

Beth looked at her husband and broke out in laughter, sure that the kumquat story would be passed on for generations. The baby at her breast jiggled up and down as she tried to control the hiccups that came with the belly laugh. Peter brushed her hair back from her head and kissed her gently as he left the room to give them a bit of quiet.

"Oh Milton Stafford, you're a hungry boy, you are. You'll grow up to be big and strong like your father and grandfather. Much taller than all of us, I'm sure. I know one thing. You will grow up and do something important. Something for the history books. I just have this feeling. Well, I can hope, right?" She giggled again carefully as she cuddled her baby boy, wondering what he would grow up to be.

The grocery store flourished, being one of the first full-service stores open year round within fifty miles. His father and mother were kept busy while his grandfather took daycare responsibilities to the fullest extent. It was a Norman Rockwell childhood with a bit of Picasso thrown in. Harold Stafford jumped headfirst into raising his grandson and teaching him the ways of the land—and the garage—as efficiently as possible. Milton learned to love the earth and the makeshift invention center. His grandfather dabbled in everything from ways to melt the snow on the driveway to a no-nonsense cure for poison ivy, based primarily on honey and turpentine. None of inventions came to fruition but he took his young grandson aside on his 7th birthday to reveal his largest plan thus far.

"I'm going to be the one to find the cure for cancer Milton."

Milton's eyes were wide with wonder and he nodded, knowing full well his grandmother had perished from the disease and that a cure would be good for so many.

"Pop, really? But how?"

"I know what you're thinking. So many big scientists are trying to do the same thing, but I have an idea that no one seems to be trying yet and I know that if I have the time, God willing, and the energy, I'm sure that I'll find a cure for that awful killer."

"Pop, what is it?"

"In time, Son. In time, I'll tell you all my secrets. I promise. When that time comes you'll be the one privy to the greatest cure of all and if for some reason I'm not here to finish it, you'll be the one who can."

"Pop? You'll be here for a really long time and I can't wait for you to cure the world."

Harold Stafford smiled at his toothless, freckled grandson and knew at that moment that he would not be the one, but possibly he was looking at the one who would. Two years later, just after Milton's 9th birthday, cancer took the life of Milton's hero. The death took a toll on everyone, but especially the young protégé who was sure cancer would be abolished by this birthday. Instead, cancer won again and this time took the best chance of ridding the world of the menace. Milton made a promise to his grandfather just before he died.

"Pop?"

"Oh, come closer, Son, my eyes are getting old."

Milton sat gently beside his grandfather and ached inside, feeling his hero's pain.

"Pop, I want to make a promise to you now."

"A promise? Son, you don't need to promise me anything. You've been the apple of my eye, ever since the day you were born. No old man could have requested or received a better gift than you. You're my grandson, and that's all I've ever needed from you."

"But Pop, I'm going to make a promise either way. I'm going to find a cure for cancer. I am."

"Oh child, I believe you, I do. But what I really want to hear is that you'll be a good man, a strong man, and you'll aspire on whatever road you travel."

"Pop, I promise. I'll be a good man and I'll be strong. I will aspire on whatever road I travel but I'm also serious about my other promise. I mean it. I'm going to continue your research and find the cure for cancer."

Harold Stafford clasped his grandson's hand and smiled.

"I believe you, Milton. I believe you will. One can only hope right?"

"Right, Pop. One can only hope. I love you."

"Oh Son, I love you too, with all of my heart. It's time for me to see your Nanna. I'm sorry you never met her in this life, but sometime 80 or 90 years from now, we'll both be waiting for you and you can tell us all about it."

At first Milton mourned with his parents. Harold Stafford was missed dearly. But soon Milton turned his grief to what he and his grandfather had best, science. He studied hard and entered into the private Brewster Academy several years before his peers. Life was lonely, with few friends, but when his science fare project brought interest from elder colleagues from all over the United States, his parents were convinced that their child had a gift that needed more nourishment. A cloning idea that he developed using plants originally derived from one of the Indian lore tribes of the area, brought him to the SAT tables at the tender age of fifteen and into the University of Massachusetts prodigy program the summer of his junior year in high school. He had no fear of the unknown and Boston was just another exciting discovery. By his 17th birthday, he was enrolled in college full-time and could barely get enough of what college and city life offered. Everything delighted him and suddenly, without warning, for the first time in his pubescent life he was discovering the female side of humanity. He looked in the mirror and asked out loud, "Will any of these beautiful creatures ever find me beautiful?"

"Well, that's to be determined, young Milt. You see, you need to look at more than a test tube or a microscope. You need to pay more attention to your hair and your clothes and your breath before any one of those beauties you mention will be interested in you."

Milton turned to see his roommate jesting in a vulgar way.

"Brandon, you say it like it's so easy. Look at you. Born handsome. I need a lot more miracles than just using what I was born with."

"Oh that's crap, Milt, just crap. You need to start seeing you, seeing what other people see. Sorry to say, but people don't see the brains before the beauty, even though wed like to believe they do. In a perfect world!" He said the latter as he glanced in the mirror carefully placing the blond lock that had fallen in an unfortunate way on his forehead.

"OK, I get your drift, Brandon. I do. Just need some time to figure out how to do that."

"Time is of the essence, young Milt. What are you, 17? Lord, Jesus you're almost at your prime. If you blink, you'll miss it. Tomorrow, we start with the clothes and the hair and lord you need to whiten those teeth. Don't they have fluoride in New Hampshire? You'll see Milt. In just a few short days, you could be scoring with the best of us."

"For your information, I'll be 18 in December."

"Oh my, Milton, 18? Then we have less time than I thought. Now listen very closely, because this might be some of the best advice you'll ever receive."

Milton doubted it, but clung to every word. He could only hope that it would work. Some unforeseen power had overtaken him and he knew that he had to make himself more desirable to the opposite sex.

Milton did exactly as he was told. He had his hair cut in a more popular style that within hours had turned into his own interesting mix of old and new. Clothing was not as easy, since his budget proved that you can only get what you pay for, but thrift shops and the Army-Navy store helped cover up a few of the noticeable flaws. The teeth required a good cleaning from the dentist and focusing less on coffee and more on water. Milton would never have a movie-star smile. The breath part was easy. Brushing and flossing and a good Binaca blast lasted for several hours. Brandon stood and eyed his young roommate, almost admiring his reflection in the bureau mirror.

"Well I say, dear Watson, I think you have something. I do."

"Brandon, shut up and pass me that hair stuff you insist that I wear."

"It's not just any hair stuff, young Milt. It's what Tony wears. You know Tony?

Saturday Night Fever? The biggest and best movie ever"

"Yes, Brandon, I know Tony. He's an Italian from Brooklyn. I'm an immigrant from the very cold island off of England and lord if we were born with color in our skin and dance in our bones, the world would be a very different place."

Brandon laughed and slapped him on the back, wishing him luck. The night proved interesting. The opportunity to talk with a pretty piano major from Berklee until the bar closed was his coup de grace. He kissed her hand goodnight, not able to get the nerve to ask her for her number.

Brandon left school the next semester for a modeling contract in Atlanta. Milton helped him pack, bound and determined that he would try to stay cool. At least an eighth as cool as Brandon.

"Brandon do you really think it's wise to leave school your last year for a modeling contract? I mean, jeez, you could go in a year, have your degree and still have your looks to kick about and make money on."

"Milt, Milt, Milt. You just have no idea what it's like to be me. This gig is exactly what I've always dreamed about. And who knows what I might look like in a year?"

"But Brandon, Atlanta? I thought all the big modeling 'gigs' were in New York or Europe?"

"Atlanta is big too. Real big. I'm off, buddy. It's been nice knowing you and good luck with the chicks."

"You too, Brandon. Thanks for everything and good luck with, hmm, the camera!"

Milton Stafford was on his own. He was ready to make his dreams come true. Cure cancer and find his soul mate. Modeling seemed a whole lot easier.

CHAPTER 10

Meredith tapped lightly on the glass, her hand tucked inside the unzipped carry on. The decision had been an easy one, yet the arguments fierce. Two weeks after the ordeal, she stepped aboard a Greyhound bus; one foot still bandaged, in sandals, adamant she would never return. The picture of Amy clinked lightly under her nails, as she recalled the horrible things she had said. Vicious words, hateful thoughts, the look of her mother's face when she told her father to "go fuck himself". A rift built in just a few sentences, deemed impenetrable, eternal. Amherst High would send her diploma. She watched as the rolling countryside emerged into a city sprawl. David was there to give her a hug.

"Do you want to get some lunch?" David attempted to keep the situation light.

"No, I'm really not that hungry."

"But I am, so if you don't mind I'll stop for sandwiches before we get to my apartment." He looked at her gaunt profile, concerned.

"Oh, sure, that's fine, it's just I'm not that hungry." She lazily marveled at the downtown location of the bus station, the heavy traffic, the curious characters seemingly attracted to such a location. They said nothing more except for the intermittent road rage that David nonchalantly threw out about pokey rental vehicles or disorderly pedestrians.

"Ugh, move it, you idiot! It's true what they say about New England drivers." Meredith smiled lightly, not acknowledging aloud that her brother was one as well.

After a quick stop at a sub shop and a hugely celebrated on-street parking find by her brother, Meredith followed David, dragging what was left of her belongings, up the stairs to a fourth-floor walk-up in an elaborate, cramped building in Beacon Hill. He had rented a car for the day because his sister was bringing "everything she cared about," his usual transportation being the oldest subway system in the United States. It was an annoyingly hot and humid day at the end of June. They were sweating and aggravated by the time they reached the top, shoving the duffels wherever there was open space. Meredith's face gave way to worry.

"Hey Sis, it's going to be fine. It's only a few months and then off to the dormitory for you. What happened to your feet?"

"But David, you're already jammed in here like a sardine. I'm sorry. I had no idea I was going to be such a nuisance." She ignored the latter.

"Oh please, nuisance? It'll be fun and, like I said, a few months, then off to the dorms for you."

"I feel like I am intruding on your life. What about if you have a date or…or…."

"Well's been dry for some time, sister. So don't you worry. Maybe you'll bring me better luck. The neighbors have spotted a beautiful divorcee in and out of my building." He smiled.

"Hmm, well I hope I bring you better luck than I brought myself."

"Do you want to talk, Mere?"

"No, not right now. I'm just tired. Go on now, eat your lunch. I'll try to find a spot for some of these things."

"I'm not eating unless you join me. No fun eating alone if you don't have to."

"Oh all right, jeez you'd think I brought Mom with me."

"Or Dad?"

"Yeah, right. Dad never cared if we ate or were even alive."

"Meredith, now come on. Of course he did."

"Nah, I don't think so. I think he left all the caring to Mom. Really, I think he was the sperm donor and that's about it."

"All right, eat!"

Meredith picked out the onions and nibbled the salami as her eyes glazed and her stomach growled.

They made room for her things, piling each piece atop another. On their way back to the car rental office, she admired the gold dome of the state building and the Faneuil Hall Marketplace. The city was rich in history and she felt like she was in a completely different world from just that morning. She looked forward to the smells and the pulse of the old brick walls that seemed to be at every turn. She thanked David numerous times for letting her crash his world for awhile.

"Listen, you're not invading my space. The company is great and you were there for me when I needed it. Blood is thick Meredith, don't you forget that."

They boarded the orange line at the subway station back to the downtown area and changed to a red line heading south exiting at the JFK Library and University of Massachusetts stop. It was just a short walk to the *Boston Globe* building where David worked, but he hustled her past since he had called in sick, so he could be there to collect her at the bus station. It wasn't a very important job, but as assistant to the assistant of the editorial department, he had his foot in the door at least. Of course, the pay was nothing to write home about, so he didn't, thus the tiny apartment and no car. He did stick to the exclusive area, the political heart of the city, hoping one day his choice would not only introduce him to the world of political news, but a world of beautiful women. That was one thing David had determined long ago: where there was money and power, beautiful intelligent women tended to gravitate. Like working in a fine restaurant over a diner—the tips are always better at the finer. He took evening classes at the University and cowered a bit when he found out Meredith would be attending the same school. Of course, she would be in class during the day full-time while, no one had brought up how she would be surviving whilst being a student. He suspected it had been taken care of earlier in the year.

"Here it is, the grand dame of state schools!"

Meredith absorbed the campus, the students and the ocean smells. This was where her new life would begin.

"So I know it's a sore spot bringing up Dad and all, but Meredith, are you all set with tuition and, well, living money?" She looked at him blankly not sure how to respond. Unless her father had cancelled the checks sent earlier, she was set for a semester and that was it.

"Um, Dad paid for the first semester a few months ago, to get me settled into my dormitory, but after that I guess I'm on my own."

"Really? That's not going to be easy, you know? It's hard enough being a student, let alone working and studying and eating enough."

"I'll be fine, David. I can fend for myself."

"Hmm, you've never had to before, how can you be so sure that you can handle this?"

"I'm sure, David. Trust me."

The next day at work, David called the apartment to check on her but the phone rang incessantly. She was out doing the last and only thing that her mother had instructed her to do once she got to Boston. Her father had an attorney friend downtown that had received some papers regarding the marriage and divorce and all they needed was her John Hancock. The divorce had been illegal, the papers doctored. There wasn't anything else she could say. She thought that love prevailed but she was wrong. The nauseous feeling returned as she entered the office only after taking the wrong bus twice, stumbling along the way into a not-so-friendly indigent preaching the end of the world was upon them. Jerome never called back. Her mother wanted to get her to the emergency room for her feet, and she refused. Her world had been transformed in a matter of days and the hardest part was the emptiness that she was left with. How could he never have contacted her? Had his family sent him away? He could've tried calling, a payphone, anything but nothing. She was sure she would never see nor hear from him again. When Amy had died she realized her mortality. When Jerome disappeared she realized reality. There were no guarantees. She would have to do things on her own and not depend on anyone. She had lost the war on love and was determined to never lose again. As she left the office, she decided that to win, she would never partake in the war, that way she would never be in jeopardy of injury or pain again. She wandered aimlessly down the Cambridge Street, staring at the billboards for Diet Pepsi, "Say NO to Drugs," and "Connie King for State Selectmen." Meredith stared into the bleach blonde, middle-aged woman's eyes, then focused on the word "Selectmen". Why not "Selectwoman"? Sure "men" was used at the end of words to cover the gambit of civilization but why not be a bit brazen and write "woman"? She wandered aimlessly down the busy street, not nearly as shaken when another beggar approached her for bus fare. She reached in her pocket for loose change sparing a few quarters for the musician's guitar case that she stepped over. She was startled as a horn blared while she was crossing the street, and turned back to see the double-sided advertisement of Connie King staring back at her.

"Connie, Connie, Connie, you must really want to win. Hmm I wonder if you've thought about the word "selectwoman"? She waved at the poster as her bus pulled away from the curb. It was a strange moment, a growing pain. Her life with Jerome and Amherst and all she knew was over. She would begin again in Boston. She would be a student, an adult, avoiding wasted love, leader of her own gang. She laughed at herself quietly in her bag, afraid she might appear as odd as some of the others on board. "If I were running for that office, I'd insist on Selectwoman."

"You what?" David looked at her, tired. He had left the house before eight that morning to catch the bus, then the train; worked all day, then headed off to school for two classes. By the time he reached the top of the building where he lived, he looked like he might collapse. His prosthesis ached and his back needed an adjustment, but at the moment, he was greedily eyeing the velvety macaroni and cheese and pulled-pork-sloppy-Joe dinner his sister had made.

"I signed the papers today, so I can be completely rid of that nuisance, went for a walk in Cambridge, spotted a billboard that made me cringe, contacted the delegate for the "Selectwoman" position, shopped for groceries, met most of your neighbors, watched Phil Donahue, made dinner, took a nap, and read the *Globe* front to back." David hung his head snorting into his napkin.

"Well you did ask me what I did today!"

"I did, Meredith, you're right. Now come on, let's talk while I eat this wonderful looking meal. Thank goodness you learned to cook, because I know I suck at boiling water and I bet Charlie doesn't know how to either." His name always drew a quiet lull. Meredith hadn't thought about him in the last few weeks. Ghosts weren't reliable. She refused to miss him anymore.

"Anyway, I got a job today too!" David's eyes grew wide, his mouth full. "Oh, I guess I neglected to tell you that. Save the best for last."

"And where will you be working until school starts?"

"With that Selectwoman I told you about. She says that most people volunteer for these positions, but I told her that's impossible, I would need to work at a restaurant or grocery store before I volunteered for someone. She laughed; she asked me why I was there, what I thought I could do for her in the campaign. I told her the first thing I would do is change all of her mailers, fliers and billboards to reflect exactly who she was and what she wanted. You should've seen her smile. They had a position in public relations that they thought I might be good at. It pays only minimum wage, but it's better than nothing and, well, I really think I'll like it."

"Hmm, PR, huh? Does that mean you'll be going around soliciting this woman's ability to be a good Selectman?"

"Select*woman* David. She's running for Selectwoman."

"Meredith, don't get me wrong, I think it's great that you went out and got all of this accomplished today, but do you even know what a Selectman-*woman* does?"

She was quiet for a moment as she cleared the table, fully aware with the traps scattered that David's apartment had unwanted, filthy visitors, "That is what I'm going to get done tomorrow, David." He smiled and leaned back in his chair. It was nice having her around and whatever she got involved with, he knew she would give it her all, learn every aspect.

"I don't doubt that for a minute. I have to crash, up and at it early tomorrow. Ugh my damn leg!" She helped him toward his room then kissed his cheek adding, "I love you David."

"I love you too, Sis. It's nice to have you here." He didn't tell her that their parents had called him at the office. She wished him a good sleep and went back to the "other" room, her bedroom/living room/dining room/kitchen and settled in to read the literature Connie had given her.

"Damn if I'm going to wait until tomorrow to find out what a Selectwoman's responsibilities are. Connie is going to be second first leader of my gang!"

CHAPTER 11

"Well, well, seems here you've done your homework, Ms. Nicholson."

Meredith smiled. She'd been going to the campaign headquarters' dull, drab building for almost three weeks and had already been promoted to Public Relations Vice President.

"Well, it seems Mr. King, that someone had to buckle down and focus on getting Connie elected. A Selectwoman has a very important job. I'm just here to make sure that anyone unclear on that, gets clear on it." She smiled again, not looking nearly as tough as she sounded.

"You're right, Ms. Nicholson, so very right. Now be a good girl and get the boss lady's husband a cup of coffee." She looked at him cross-eyed and he held his stomach in laughter.

Connie's husband knew what his wife was capable of and was impressed that this new, young accomplice felt as fervently about her decision to be part of Massachusetts's politics. They'd been married for seven years and each year he had fallen more madly in love with her. She put her legal career on the back burner when their fourth child arrived. She was even outspoken about wanting at least one or two more, but she wanted to wait until after the election, afraid of nausea or public scrutiny. She didn't want anything as ridiculous as breast-feeding in public to be the reason for a loss. She was determined, and knew she had the wits, guts, and stamina to be a great representative of the people along with her innate talent to rear a family. "Phooey," Meredith had gingerly added, knowing that Connie was probably right, but that the truth wasn't easy to swallow. Connie was an exceptional mother and wife and if she decided that she could be the Selectwoman too, then so be it. She would. Meredith hoped secretly for an easy campaign, a strong sense of not wanting to lose heavy on her mind. Connie would split the jobs equally, the latter brought to life by the desire for her sons and their friends to have a skateboard park behind their middle school. It had amazed Connie all the tension and conspiracy that something so innocent had spawned, and she had taken the road of decision very personally. The best way to get the job done, to make this world a better place for her family, was to be part of the decision making process. Of course she did not expect that it would be that easy in most cases, but in regards to the skateboard park, it would be one of the first "menial" things discussed. She kept it under her hat and grinned at the photograph of her four boys. They were why she was here. The pay was minimal, the hours grueling and the appreciation of others almost nil, but she did it for them, her family, and for herself. Meredith learned the true meaning of self-preservation and a strength that few women experienced in their lifetime. She adored Connie and her family and concluded that true love was possible for some.

"Hey there, Missy. You're off to college in just a few weeks?"

"Yes Mr. King, the same day of the early election is the same day I sign up for classes and pick up my books."

"Ready to vote?"

"Ugh, Mr. King. Please don't rub it in. I'm not registered to vote, yet. I can't. The law says 18 and I'm only 17."

"Come on, I'm kidding, kiddo. You'll have plenty of time to vote. A lifetime. Good for you about school," he changed the subject. "You'll do well at the university; knock'em dead I'm sure. Lots of nice-looking boys will be dying to win your approval."

"I'm not interested in boys, Mr. King."

"Oh, forgive me. I just assumed…well."

"Mr. King! I'm not interested in dating anyone. I'm just too busy to waste my time with immature boys right now. I'm determined to see Connie win this election and get on figuring out what I want to do with my life. Boys just seem useless right now."

"Useless, hmm. One day you'll feel differently, I'm sure of it."

"Differently about what?" Connie breezed into the room, her body tightly squeezed into a lavender suit, her freshly bleached hair pulled up into a French twist. Meredith smiled, thinking that beauty was in the eye of the beholder, but Connie's confidence made her even more so.

"Oh nothing, Mrs. King, nothing important," Meredith quickly retorted, diving back into her project.

"Hehe. It seems, Con, that our Ms. Nicholson has no interest in boys right now. Seems she is more preoccupied with you winning and what she wants to be when she grows up."

Connie, enveloped in rosewater, leaned across her desk and whispered in Meredith's ear, "You dear, will be anything that you want to be and have been an angel in my quest. Boys can wait. You continue on just as you are. "And," she leered playfully at her husband, "Our dear Meredith is already very much grown up." She touched the top of her head lightly and Meredith felt like her mother was consoling her, encouraging her. She missed her mother.

The sky opened up on the morning of the election. Meredith watched the small television as she hurriedly dressed. The weatherman had predicted that rain would prevail most of the day, dampening everyone's Tuesday. New England was used to inclement weather, but on this day, this one day, Meredith had prayed for glorious sunshine and a huge turnout at the polls. Her prayer went unanswered and she failed to locate an umbrella. David had called and said he would be staying at a friend's house. The thought weighed heavily on her mind, as well as the fact that she had absolutely no idea what she was in for on her first day of college. Tears started to well as she stepped out into the downpour, a blue plastic garbage bag tied around her head.

There was no available seat on the bus or on the train when she transferred, and by the time she opened the doors to the administration building she looked like she had run alongside the public transportation instead of in it. She drew in a dry breath as she glanced over hundreds, maybe thousands, of students, scurrying from table to table, like rats in a maze.

"Hello, welcome to the University of Massachusetts, you look like you could use a little help." The woman on the other end of the voice was elderly, dressed in a very dapper light tweed suit; her shoes matching perfectly, her lipstick flawless upon the once-plump lips.

"Um, yes please. I'm here to sign up for fall classes and get the books I'll need for the semester."

"Of course you are dear. First let me show you to the restrooms so you can freshen up a bit. You must feel terrible with this weather today." Meredith smiled, knowing full well how terrible she must look compared to this prim and proper academic.

"Yes, thank you, that's a good idea."

"It's right over there to your right, down that first hall. Once you're done you need to go over to the main desk to register as a freshman—a freshman right?"

"Yes, I'm a freshman."

"Of course you are, dear. Once you've done that you can proceed to signing up for your classes. Of course you'll need the prerequisites and be careful of the scheduling. All too often on the first day, new students sign themselves up for classes that are at the same time as another, and then they end up in a class they have no interest or desire to be in. It's all a little complicated, but I'm sure you'll do fine. Now go on, so you don't get shut out of something you might absolutely need to learn."

"Thank you," Meredith glanced at her nametag, "thank you Mrs. Bidlack. You've been very kind."

"You're welcome dear, good luck."

She found the restroom crowded with young women, desperately trying to get a feel for college along with appearing incredible on their first day. *First impression bullshit,* Meredith thought as she found an empty stall and sat surveying her drowned leather loafers. She found half a mirror to apply lip gloss and wrapped her wet hair up in a knot securing it with bobby pins. She didn't look much better, but decided at least she wouldn't be dripping on the paperwork. She waited in the registrar's line, catching pieces of excited conversation, childish drama, and full-fledged pursuits of the perfect class schedule. The prerequisites were easiest and then she was caught in the dilemma of what she had dreaded for weeks. What additional classes did she really want? She studied the signs above each table. Legal, medical, liberal arts. But when her eyes reached the table labeled "political science" her body moved in that direction. She would take political science classes and if nothing else she would learn more than she knew now and transfer the second semester to something else. She envisioned Connie, her family and all the volunteers voting and waiting. She was anxious to be part of that frenzy. She recalled dreaming of college life and now couldn't wait to get her first day behind her.

"Hello."

Meredith didn't respond, quite unaware of anyone around wanting to speak with her.

"Um, hello, can I help you with anything?"

Meredith looked up from her schedule to a tall, awkward-looking boy squinting at her.

"Um, sorry, are you talking to me?"

"Yes, I am. Hi. You looked a bit, well, befuddled and I thought maybe I could help you with something."

"No, thank you, I'm fine really. Are you all right?"

"Oh, yes, yes. I guess I should be wearing my glasses. I just, well, feel kind of geeky when I wear them." He slipped the wire spectacles back from his pocket and placed them on his nose. "OK then. Anyway, my name is Milton, Milton Stafford."

Meredith smiled uninterested, "Hi Milton. Nice to meet you. I'm Meredith. Meredith Nicholson. I know the feeling. I used to wear glasses myself."

"Yeah? I mean, really? What happened? I mean, where are they, your glasses, now?"

"Contacts," she pointed to one eye and giggled, happy that someone was talking with her.

"Well very nice to meet you Meredith Nicholson. Is this your first year?"

"Uh, yes, I'm a freshman. It's been a bit hectic this morning, I'm sorry. It was nice meeting you, but I've got to sign up for this class."

"Oh sure, sure, political science. There are some great teachers in that department. Mr. Lipshitz—I know the name is horrible—but he's a wonderful teacher. Really enjoyed his class. I think you would too."

She looked at him awkwardly, "You've taken them? I'm sorry. I thought you were a freshman too."

"Well, no, not really. I've been taking courses here for a couple of years. I'm, well, never mind, really I'm a freshman at heart."

"What do you mean at heart? You've been taking classes for a couple of years and you're still a freshman?"

"Well, I guess you can say I'm the pain in most of my professors' asses. It's a long story but to make it short, I've been taking classes since I was fifteen. My parents had me test out of high school and go right on to bigger and better things."

"Really? Wow. So how old are you now?"

"Eighteen. Just like the rest of this group I guess."

"Are you taking political science classes too?"

"No, no, not this year. This year I'm going to focus on science alone. I enjoy it the most and, well, I've taken almost all the other classes and repeating isn't good for the resume." He laughed at his own remark and Meredith found herself giggling.

She reached the table to register and excused herself.

"Oh sure, sure, good luck with your classes. I guess I should be getting to mine. It was really nice to meet you, Meredith Nicholson. I hope to run into you again."

She glanced back quickly and smiled, watching him wave as he disappeared into the crowd.

Her schedule was set, her Fridays afternoons quiet, leaving her plenty of time to work for Connie during long weekends ahead. She waited in another endless line to get her books, quietly thanking God that her father had paid for the semester in advance as she watched a few students counting out singles and change, some not able to afford all the required reading. With her backpack stuffed, hair almost dry and a voracious appetite, she slowly made her way to the exit. Mrs. Bidlack was at the top of the stairs where she had first greeted Meredith and her perfectly coifed lips smiled as she watched another frazzled freshman begin their adult voyage. Milton also watched Meredith from a distance, as she lugged her backpack up the stairs and outside, braving once again the torrential weather. He watched and he smiled. Today he had met an angel. He couldn't wait to see her again. Next time he would be much more charming. "*Much* more charming," he said quietly to himself. He looked down to see that another pen, this time red, had sprung a leak in his shirt pocket and he sighed as he rushed to the restroom to salvage his shirt.

"Well?"

"Well, what?"

David grinned at the receiver. He knew what his sister was thinking.

"Well, Meredith, how was the first day?"

"Oh, that. It was OK, the weather just charming. I signed up for all of my classes and got my books. I can move into the dorms anytime this week."

"Gosh, yeah, I was thinking about that. Too bad the rules state all freshmen have to live on campus. It sure has been nice having you around."

"Is that sarcasm I hear, big brother? Hmm, seems you've had other places to crash."

"Sarcasm, back at you. Yes, well what are you up to tonight? I would love to catch up. I've met someone, Meredith. She, well, she makes my heart go pitter patter." Meredith felt a pang in her chest. She was happy for him but sad for herself.

"Sis?" He knew it was hard for her.

"Oh, yeah, I'm, well, I'm going over to the campaign office now and should be back around dinnertime. Maybe we can have dinner then go back to the office together. I really want to be there when the tally comes in."

"All right then. Don't make dinner. I'm dying for Thai food so I'll pick it up on the way home. Sounds like you've had a hectic day. Did you meet anyone nice when you were registering?"

Why is it when someone is happily dating or in a relationship, they want the whole world to be happy too? She held the thought to herself.

"Well as a matter of fact I met grandma's clone in tweed and an idiot savant." She felt awful as soon as she said it.

"Nice, Sis. Real nice. Take a load off. I'll see you tonight."

"Bye David."

"Bye grumpy."

She sat down at the kitchen table, an enormous pile of textbooks, notebooks and papers staring back at her. She picked up the phone again and called down to headquarters, a busy signal answering back. She grabbed her raincoat and a new garbage bag for her head, excited to show Connie her class schedule.

Oh my, Meredith contemplated, *Mr. King is going to tease me about Wednesday morning's Lipshitz class. Hmm, what was his name again? Milton something. The only Milton I've ever heard of is Milton Berle. Mom would like that.* She laughed at herself in the mirror, this time a yellow bag bonnet tied snugly under her chin. She could never be in a bad mood for too long. There were just too many funny things to think about. All the bad stuff could always be worse. Her name could be Lipshitz or she could be married to Milton somebody someday.

CHAPTER 12

A gust of windswept rain helped her through the door of Connie King's campaign office, interrupting what appeared to be a meditation meeting. Connie was on the phone, her husband leaning against the desk beside her and a dozen or so employees and volunteers sat spellbound waiting for their leader to speak.

"Dan, oh I know, it's just, well we've never been in this situation before and we're all a bit anxious...Absolutely!...OK, then when do you think I should check back with you?...Oh no, I don't want to be a pest, hehehehe...Yes, yes he's here...Of course I will...Thank you Dan, really. Thank you very much for everything...All right...Yes...All right...I'll talk with you soon...Ta-ta...."

"Well?" Joe King asked, slightly confused.

"Well darling, all of you, it seems it's a bit early and the polls don't close for another four hours, but as it stands right now, you are looking at the next Selectwoman of Cambridge."

A huge cheer rang out, whistling and laughter, and the oldest recruit grabbed his cane and swung a drenched Meredith around the room. An elated Selectwoman made her way around the room, hugging each individual who had helped her cause. When she reached Meredith both women were crying.

"You, my angel, have been my guardian angel. Less than two months ago you appeared out of nowhere and your zealous charm and candid intelligence, really, truly were essential in getting the people out there to vote for me. Thank you, Meredith Nicholson. You are wonderful!"

Meredith was speechless. She hadn't felt this way since she had won her seat on the debate team. It was intoxicating and she was determined to keep it. She kissed Connie on the cheek and got a bear hug from Joe and headed home for dinner, promising to be back before the polls closed.

"I'm home, David. David, are you home? I can't believe..." Meredith almost knocked over the pretty blond stranger in the hallway. Behind her stood a slightly flushed big brother.

"Oh hello. Um, I'm Meredith."

"I figured," the vixen flashed a blinding white set of teeth.

"Meredith, this is Katherine. Katherine, Meredith. I thought we could all have dinner tonight, and, well, I brought home Thai."

"Great, sure," Meredith reacted coolly. "I didn't know we were having company. I would've cooked."

"Nonsense, I told you I was craving Thai and it seems Katherine loves Asian food too, so there. Now let's eat."

"David, guess what?"

"What, Sis?" he answered as he set the tiny table for three.

"Connie won. Well, almost won. The polls will be closed soon and it seems she has won."

"Wow, that's really great Meredith. You worked really hard, good for you and for her."

"What did she win?" the bombshell asked innocently.

"Oh, um, she won the Selectwoman position in her district in Cambridge. Do you know anything about politics?" Meredith had a way with sarcasm. David winced.

Katherine smiled sweetly, placing the napkins under the forks and pulling a chair out for herself, "Hmm, I know a little bit. Connie? That wouldn't be Connie King you're talking about?"

Meredith sat across from her, purposely leaving the cramped chair to her brother.

"As a matter of fact it is. Did you see the billboard or something?"

"Well what I meant was, that's not how I know her. I work in Cambridge and, well, my boss is her attorney—her's and her husband's."

"Oh, I see. Are you a secretary there?"

Katherine helped herself to a heaping portion of pad thai and Meredith wondered if she might be purging it later, assuming her goddess figure couldn't take much food.

With her mouth full she answered, "No, I'm a partner there. My name is Katherine Kaziwalski, of Sherman, Reiser, and Kaziwalski. Do you know where the courthouse is?"

David smiled at Meredith and thought, *she's got you now, doesn't she?*

"I do. Wow, a partner and you know Connie. Wow, how old are you, 30?'

Katherine smiled again, inhaling another large mouthful. Meredith thought for sure she would choke. "Nope, I'm 25, like your brother, David. We met at school. UMass, I hear you registered today?" She said all of this with a mouthful and sparkle in her eye. Meredith was stumped.

"Yep, I did. All set for freshman year. You two are in the same class?"

David and Katherine looked at each other and he winked. He looked delirious.

"You could say that, Sis. She's my teacher."

Meredith threw in the towel. She could see that David was perfectly engrossed with this beauty with brains; Meredith knew she had lost the battle. Katherine passed all the tests and then some and Meredith felt a bit of a fool. Katherine seemed amused and used to the scrutiny and complimented Meredith more than once, earning extra points. The rest of the dinner conversation became a vivid description of the rain's abuse of hairstyles and the lack of female politicians in the nation. David leaned back in his chair and inhaled deeply. He was in love. There were things he had to do before he could admit it to anyone but himself, like graduate with honors and snag a column of his own at work, but he was reveling in the feeling. He wasn't going to let this one get away.

"I have to get going, back down to the office. I really want to be there when the polls close."

"Can we join you?" Katherine asked while wiping her plate clean with the last piece of fried bread. David looked away, hoping to have a little quiet time with her. He was dying to hold her again.

"Oh yes, I would love that and, well, you already know Connie. The more the merrier."

Two hours later it was official, Connie King had won with 61percent of the vote. Of course, it was an early election and the turnout slim, but either way, she had attained her goal and title. Meredith could not decipher the feelings she had as the last newscast reported the winners and losers. She was mesmerized with the numbers, the anticipation. She didn't hear her name being called. "Hey you, we should get going, Connie and Joe are tired."

"I guess I'm a bit tired," Connie yawned, "I would love to drink more champagne, but tomorrow, well, the boys will be up early and lord almighty, it's my first day on the new job." Connie was rambling as her husband helped her into her Burberry raincoat.

"Meredith?" David touched her shoulder.

"Yes?" she kept her eyes on the television.

Joe came over and turned it off. "Time to go little lady, don't you have a busy day tomorrow too?"

"Oh yeah. I'm sorry, I was just...."

"No need to explain honey, now you go home with your brother and his darling girlfriend. We don't plan to see you until Saturday, now scoot." Connie gave her a tender push.

"Oh all right. Saturday? I can be here tomorrow. I can put off my move into the dorms."

"No, no, no. You need to get your things situated in your dorm so you can start your pursuit."

"My pursuit?" she asked as she collected a few pieces of memorabilia and pulled her raincoat over her debate team T-shirt.

"Yes, dear, your pursuit."

"Hmm, I wish I knew what that was."

"Oh, I think you know. You just need to open your eyes." Connie smiled, her eyes drooping from exhaustion. She hugged her goodnight and shut the lights off. Joe made sure everything was locked and they said their goodbyes again.

"Congratulations Connie," Meredith yelled as she crossed the street with her brother and Katherine.

"Yeehaw!" she responded back.

"Well, goodnight you two," Katherine smiled as she pulled up in front of their apartment building.

"Goodnight?" David asked disappointed.

"Yes, handsome man, goodnight. I'll see you tomorrow. Meredith, it was a pleasure meeting you and your friends. I had lots of fun."

"Yes, Katherine, great to meet you. Hope to see you again soon, maybe without this wise guy?" She knew she was cramping his style.

"Oh, I think we'll let him hang around. He's kind of cute." Katherine leaned over and kissed David on the lips. He reluctantly got out of the car.

David walked slowly up the four flights, so Meredith lagged behind with him.

"Sorry if you and Katherine, well I mean, sorry if I'm in the way."

"Oh nonsense. Sure I would've loved—oh you never mind. So you liked her huh?"

"Yes," she nudged him lightly, "I liked her very much."

"I do too."

"Ugh, duh, who couldn't tell? You were drooling like a puppy."

"Oh boy, here we go. What time can I help you get your things out of here tomorrow morning?"

She didn't answer.

"Hey, I'm sorry. I was just kidding."

They got to the door and she used her key to let them in.

"Really I was just kidding. Are you all right?"

"I am. Just thinking. Tomorrow I start my third life and, well, I guess I'm a little nervous. It's been really nice here David, thank you so much for saving me from the depths of Amherst."

He chuckled, "Sure, anytime. Now listen, tomorrow is the beginning of some of the best times of your life. I am positive you will love college!"

"Oh God, I hope so. No other choices out there, so I better."

"Good, there now, goodnight, sweet dreams, see you in the morning."

She heard his bedroom door click and the quiet conversation going on over the phone. David had met a wonderful woman. *Good for him,* she thought. He deserved to be loved and to love. Nothing that she needed, but she was sure that it would be good for her brother.

When she walked down the corridor of the three-story building, her home for the next year, she wondered what she was getting into. Doors were open, displaying decorated rooms with Jim Morrison and Einstein posters, Union Jack flags and lava lamps. She reached room 13—lucky 13—and knocked.

"Who is it?"

"Um, your new roommate."

The door swung open and a pint sized girl in a fluorescent pink teddy and a towel wrapped around her head stood before her.

"Candace, Candace Baylor?"

"Yes, yes, are you Meredith? Oh come in, come in, I'm so excited to meet you. I guess that won't be the last time you'll have to knock!" Candace giggled while Meredith stared at the room.

The entire room was pink. Pillows, blankets, posters, clothes. Even the hairbrush on the dresser.

"Oh, I'm sorry. I'll move some stuff. I haven't had a roommate all summer and kind of took over the room." She rushed around grabbing every combination of pink God created and tossed everything on her bed.

"You've been here all summer?" Meredith asked as she dragged her things through the door, thankful that David was able to help her get them into the building. He had offered her a hand up to the room, but Meredith had refused. She had to move in on her own.

"Yep. Summer school I guess you would say. I did pretty bad in a couple of classes the first few months—I mean, semester. It's not that I'm not smart. I am, really, it's just that, well, I had a pregnancy scare. You know what I mean, and, well, anyway I had to stay the summer to make up some lost time and get my one point nine grade point average up. I feel like I've been on probation my whole life. English and math are hard! Anyway, so what's your major? Ow!" she yelped as she worked through a knot of tangled her. Meredith had never known anyone who could talk so much or had so much hair!

"Um, well I guess political science."

"Oh wow, a brainiac. Great! I could use some help with studying."

Meredith considered her new roommate as she applied an additional hair product while plucking her eyebrows. At least should could multitask.

"Oh no, I'm not a brainiac. Just a regular brain, Candace."

"Oh Meredith, pleeeez call me Candy. All my friends do."

Meredith smiled, "Oh, OK then, Candy it is. And you can call me Meredith."

Candy burst into laughter and stepped over hugging her tightly.

"I'm so excited to have a new roommate. We're going to have so much fun."

Meredith just nodded and smiled. *Beggars can't be choosers,* she thought. Candy was going to be her new friend and she absolutely could use one of those. She stood up and gave the bubbly cheerleader a squeeze back.

"I'm sure we will, Candy."

By the fourth week of September, Candy was truly pregnant—with twins no less—and she had to leave UMass forever. Meredith had mixed feelings about her departure. Even though their work ethics and lust for partying were opposite, she would miss what friendship they had.

"If one of them is a girl, I'm going to name her Meredith, "Candy whispered as she put her pink pillow in her father's car. "There now. All packed for the long ride back to Kansas."

"Oh gosh, Candy that is so sweet. You take care of yourself and keep in touch OK?"

"Of course, Meredith. I'll write you all the time."

Meredith put in for a single room in the hopes the RA would make a freshman exception due to the sad circumstances and a superior debate. Surprisingly, there was room available, the exception made, and Meredith got the peace and quiet that she was sure she wanted. She dropped two postcards in the mail a few weeks later but she never heard from Candy again. Another comrade lost.

She studied day and night, ignoring most of her classmates. She spent her free time visiting Connie at the office or David, who had since moved in with Katherine in Charlestown. Each morning she constructed a list of things to do, read the paper, grabbed a coffee on the corner, and headed off to class. She kept to herself except when debating a professor. She had had no contact with her parents since she had left and fun was staying glued to the television to watch Carter's victory over Ford, and her party's return to the White House. She watched the televised version of *Gone With The Wind* and wept for Scarlett and then for Jerome. A few weeks later, she celebrated her 18th birthday alone with a bowl of fettuccini, a slice of chocolate cake, and a split of Asti Spumanti. She didn't notice her admirer. She was too busy perfecting lonely.

CHAPTER 13

"Meredith?"

"Hey, what's up?"

"I'm taking Katherine home to meet Mom and Dad over the holidays. Seems they really want you to join us. What do you think?"

"I think you're right. It would be nice for them to meet Katherine. She's awesome. I'm sure they'll approve. I've already made plans to stay in the city for the holidays. Spend time with some friends."

He was somber; familiar with the feelings she was having, reliving his own return after the war.

"Please think about it. Katherine and I would love you there."

"Thanks, maybe next year. Plus I have to work at the bookstore. Got to make the money for next semester. Who was it that first warned me?"

"Yeah, I guess it was me, but I'm sure Dad would help you, and the bookstore isn't open Christmas day."

"And pigs have wings. I'm not about to ask or do I expect anything from him. I know the store is closed that day. Come on, enough on the subject. You can't change my mind. Got anything new and interesting, maybe funny to talk about?"

"Well, hmm, I was wondering if you had put any thought into my aspirations to be Liz Taylor's seventh husband. Do you think it's a bit far-fetched?"

She laughed loudly in his ear and hung up. *Christmas*, she thought, *Bah humbug. To hell with Christmas this year.*

She had started work at the Harvard Bookstore Café right after the election. With the campaign over, Connie insisted, "It might be nice to have a real money job." Meredith did love Newbury Street, dotted with expensive boutiques and restaurants, and her job offered the occasional chance to see a celebrity or be privy to Boston's elite gossip. But what she loved most were the books and the coffee, which she now mixed with hot chocolate on her breaks and after her shift. She would adopt one of the outdoor, sun-drenched tables; something that took merit and skill in the fall, and insanity in the winter. It was the time to fantasize with whatever title or headline grabbed her. The weather became cold quickly and by early December most of the staff labeled her as a hardcore bookworm loon, especially when she swore it would have to be blizzard conditions before she was driven inside to read. The second week of December the temperature dipped into the low twenties. She bundled up on what was sure to be her last time that year, and headed out with the extra-large version *of The Complete Book of U.S. Presidents*. She donned her Jackie O sunglasses and settled into the Harlequin Romance stuffed in the middle of the book.

"Hello, Meredith?"

She glanced over her sunglasses, interrupted, completely content to be the only person outside for several blocks other than the shoppers running between heated shops.

"Meredith?"

"Yes, that's me."

"Oh, I thought so. God, it's cold out here! Do you come here often?"

She suddenly felt as peculiar as she looked and started to get her things together.

"No, gosh, no, I didn't want to disturb you, I just wanted to say hello, that's all."

She didn't recognize him.

"Oh that's all right, I guess I do look a bit odd out here."

"No, not at all. It's a great place to read and outside is always the nicest place, as long as you have mittens." She smiled still with no recollection of who he was. "Anyway, I was going to grab a coffee, would you mind if I joined you?"

"Um, well, no. Sure that will be fine."

"Great book by the way."

"You think so?" she looked surprised.

"You don't remember me do you?"

She shook her head, "I'm sorry I don't."

"Milton Stafford. I met you the first day of registration. You were a bit frazzled; anyway, it's a good book. A really good book. I've never read the whole thing, maybe you can give me some insight? I would hate to be missing something." She smiled awkwardly now, remembering his name yet misunderstanding what he was referring too.

"What I mean is, I've never read it upside down." He leaned over the table, turning the outside book right side up. Smiling sweetly, he went inside for coffee. She stuffed the Harlequin into her pocketbook, her crimson face she could blame on the cold.

They talked for two hours, indulging in several half-and-halfs. He was nothing like she remembered, and she was everything he had. They talked about school and politics and even dipped into the family album. He made her laugh and she made him nervous. It was an instantaneous friendship. After that meeting, they talked or saw each other every day, Milton more determined for the latter. Each time he saw her or spoke on the phone with her, his heart ached and yet she seemed oblivious to his true feelings.

A few days before Christmas, Milton was packing his bag to go home when she called.

"Hey, I just wanted to wish you a safe trip home and Merry Christmas. When you get back I have a little something for you."

"Oh, well thank you. What are you up to? I don't have to leave for a few hours, let's go get a little hot toddy. I think Santa left a little something here for you too."

"Hehehe. Just what I was thinking. See you downstairs?"

"You're downstairs?" He dropped the phone and was two floors down before she could respond.

They settled into one of the dark booths at the local college pub, known for its cheap beer and strong buttered rum. Milton ordered two and asked Meredith to close her eyes. He pulled out the thin tube stuffed inside his coat and handed it to her. She opened her eyes and smiled as she pulled out the copy of the Presidential poster for John F. Kennedy.

"Oh my, Milton, this is unbelievable. Really you spent way too much money."

"Oh now, what is money for but to lavish it on friends, right?" She blushed, embarrassed about her gift for him.

"Um, Mere, OK, I'm ready for mine."

"Isn't it better to give than to receive?"

"Sure but you said…."

"I know. I'm just taken aback by your gift. All right then, sorry, close your eyes."

She had bought a hard copy of *The Complete Book of U.S. Presidents* and had taken the inside out of the binder. Then she had turned it over and glued it, making it an upside-down reader. She had stuffed a Harlequin romance in the middle. Milton opened his eyes and almost spit his rum out laughing.

"Do you like it?"

"Mere, it's the best Christmas present I've ever received. Thank you so much."

"Really?"

He reached over and squeezed her hand. "Really," he answered quietly.

"When do you leave for New Hampshire?"

"The bus leaves in about an hour or so, how about you? Are you excited to get home?"

She hesitated just a second before answering, "Yep, psyched to see the folks and, well, all my friends at home. I'll miss Boston though. And you."

"Sure, sure, same old, same old. A turkey, the tree, Aunt Betty, but we'll be gone for just a few weeks. We can plan lots of fun stuff this winter to stay warm."

"Milton!"

"I mean, skiing, snowshoeing, and hot chocolate with peppermint schnapps," he lifted his glass. "What were you thinking?"

"Oh you, never mind."

"Merry Christmas, Milton. I hope Santa brings you everything you want."

"You too, Meredith, you too!"

She watched as the snow fell serenely outside her dorm room window. She hadn't seen nor heard another soul in her building since the early morning and for a moment she wondered what the Elm Street clan was doing. There were few headlights that passed twinkling between flakes. She knew she had to end the pity party, but the hurt that lingered toward Jerome and her father was still very real. She heard church bells ringing and pictured the children's choir singing carols. She had always loved mass on Christmas Eve. She would wish baby Jesus happy birthday while looking up at the sky for Rudolph's red nose. This was her first Christmas alone. She looked at herself in the mirror and scolded, "Now get yourself up and get something done. Write or read something. Sure it's not the best thing in the world being alone on Christmas Eve, but think of all the lonely souls that have no choice. No, it won't be a tradition, just something that is this year. You wanted this, now make the best of it." It was usually easy talking herself out of the doom and gloom, but when she heard the tinkling of "Silent Night," somewhere in the distance, she sat on her bed and started to cry.

She didn't hear the light tapping on her door, her head buried in a pillow. She hadn't bothered to lock the door, since everyone else couldn't wait to leave. She didn't see Santa Clause standing in the doorway, didn't even peek to see why the music had grown so much louder. She was convinced her imagination was playing tricks on her, making her homesick.

"Ho ho ho," Santa said tentatively, placing the radio down beside him.

Meredith didn't look, sure that madness and hallucinations were equivocal to misery.

"Meredith?"

Oh great. Now I'm in my own Dickens novel and I'm about to meet three ghosts. She pulled the pillow away from her bloodshot eyes and blinked, focusing on the large, red velvet suit standing in her doorway. She bolted, grabbing the lamp next to her bed.

"Wait, Jesus Christ, Meredith wait. It's me! Don't you recognize me?"

"Yeah, you're the big fat guy that brings presents to all the good little girls and boys and you're here to show me all the terrible things I've done so far in my life. Well I'm not buying that. Get the hell out of my room or I'll bash your bearded face in."

He pulled his hat off and the beard below his chin and she stared.

"Milton Stafford, how dare you scare me like that? Who do you think you are and where did you get that ridiculous costume?" He was quiet, shocked that he had provoked such anger.

"Well, what do you have to say for yourself?" She stood beside him now, shaking, the lamp still secure in her swinging arm.

"I, um. I am so sorry I scared you. I just figured I would come and bring some Christmas cheer, since you were here alone. I didn't mean to alarm you or make you angry. Please can you put the lamp down?" She placed it recklessly on the nightstand and glared back at him.

"Really, Mere, I'm so sorry. I had no intention of scaring you."

"Well you did, "her voice softened a decimeter, "And I thought you were in New Hampshire. What are you doing here?"

"I did go home, but couldn't stand the idea that you were here alone. I talked to my folks and they understood. Mom even made the bird early and sent me back with turkey sandwiches. I just, well, I just wanted to spend my birthday and Christmas with you."

Meredith looked down at his shiny black boots and the overstuffed bag and wanted to laugh and cry at the same time.

"Your birthday? You mean you were born on Christmas Eve? Goddamn it Milton Stafford, you should've told me. How did you know I was here?" She didn't look up when she asked.

"Hey now, no need to swear. I, um, well I just had a feeling. I wasn't totally sure."

"What if you'd been wrong?"

"Well, it wouldn't be the first time Santa has made a lonely trip on his own. I guess I would've wandered the streets, looking for a sleigh." She giggled.

"I really am sorry, Meredith. I really am."

"I forgive you, you big lug. And thank you. I really am happy to see you."

"Really?"

"Yes, now don't push it, but yes." She leaned towards him kissing him sweetly on the lips. She wrapped her arms around his waist and whispered in his ear, "what do you have in your big duffel bag Santa?"

He pulled her close and buried his head into her hair. All he wanted for Christmas was Meredith Nicholson and all she wanted was him.

"Merry Christmas, Meredith."

"Merry Christmas and happy birthday Milton Stafford. Ooh I'm so mad at you!" She squeezed him tightly.

David called Christmas Day and was happy to hear his sister cheerful. They made plans to meet New Year's Eve at Katherine's apartment where they would watch the ball drop and ring in 1979. That evening, David discovered the reason for Meredith's cheer. He grasped the outstretched hand of Milton Stafford and breathed a sigh of relief. Katherine proudly showed the diamond engagement ring that David had surprised her with on their way home to the city. He had told his parents and called her father for permission, but had not decided on when until they had stopped for gasoline and in the midst of a heated discussion about Sylvester Stallone's height, David opened the passenger side door, got down slowly on his good knee and proposed. Katherine had cried and repeated yes, several times, adding that even *Rocky* couldn't have been more romantic.

CHAPTER 14

"Hello, this is David Nicholson."

"David?"

"Yes, how can I help you?"

"David, it's Charlie."

Silence. He hadn't recognized his only brother's voice.

"David?"

"Yes, yes, I'm here. My God, Charlie, how are you? Where are you?"

"I'm in Nova Scotia. Um, I'm sorry I haven't been in touch."

"Uh, that's an understatement. My God, Charlie, I can't believe it's you. What have you been doing little brother? It's been, Jesus, four years. We need to see you."

"Five years. We?"

"Yes! Meredith's here. She's at UMass, studying everything she can get her hands on. My God, Charlie, I just don't believe it. Meredith is going to need a shot of whiskey when she hears this."

"I didn't plan on shocking anyone. It all just worked out this way. I'm sorry it's been so long, the months and years just slipped away. I guess I've been scared since the day I left. I'm sorry David, I was just scared."

David wiped the tears from his eyes, "It's OK Charlie, and damn it, I just can't believe it. Anyway when can I—we—see you? Can we come up there?"

"No, no, that's not necessary. I think it's my responsibility to get down to see you both. I haven't talked to Mom yet, I'm not quite sure how to go about that but Dad told me where you were working. It's strange he didn't mention a thing about Meredith in school there?"

"Oh man, we have so much to catch up on. When can you be here?"

"I have a few things I need to finish here and I can be there by the end of the week. Friday or Saturday. I'll let you know as soon as I do David I really need to tell you something before that happens."

"OK, don't leave me hanging here. Charlie, what"

"Actually David, it's Father Charles. I'm a Catholic priest."

Silence.

"David?"

"Yeah, I'm here. God, I don't know what to say. I guess I have something to tell you too."

"What David?"

"Uh, I lost a leg and an eye in the war. I'm a bit different now too."

On January 21st, nineteen hundred and seventy seven, President Jimmy Carter, in his first act as President, pardoned close to ten thousand civilians who peacefully opposed the Vietnam War and evaded the draft. This act caused nationwide controversy, with some elated and others insulted. Millions had honored the draft and fought and many died in the war. Yet thousands had avoided combat all together. David heard and read the opinions over and over. Reminiscing always brought back the pain in his invisible leg. Phrases like "class distinction" and "moral dimensions of the war" were bantered and, though well intentioned, President Carter's infant presidency was shrouded in naivety.

David walked to the train that night, telling Katherine that one of his interns would give him a ride, knowing she would object otherwise. His handicap was always noticeable but tolerable. He didn't want her to feel sorry for him and he hated to lie, but he needed to be alone, to think, even though the wind-chill dipped below zero and icy sidewalks made for a dangerous stroll. Charlie was coming home. So many years had passed since he had seen his little brother, now almost 24 years old. Five years since he had hugged him goodbye at the Air Force base. He himself had gone off to war and lost a leg and an eye and his desire to live, but had been reborn in the innocence of his sister and the tender love of Katherine. Of course he could forgive Charlie. He had pardoned him almost two years before. He needed to get home and hold his fiancée. He had to tell his sister in person and hoped his father had prepared his mother. Maybe Charlie's return would help heal the family. Maybe.

"So, I hope you both like Italian?"

Meredith and Milton giggled, ready to admit they liked liver and onions for a home cooked meal.

Katherine smiled back at them from her small galley kitchen.

"I like Italian, sweetheart!" David wrapped his arms around her from behind.

"I wasn't asking you. I know you like Italian. 'Love,' I should say. You like anything if I'm cooking."

"You are cooking, good looking."

"Now, get out of here, silly. Careful. Ouch, oooh, that's hot."

"Stop bragging, beautiful!"

"Oh, I said that's hot, not I'm hot."

"But you are gorgeous. You're hot!"

Meredith and Milton smiled at each other. The apartment was bursting with love. Grabbing a cold beer, David took a seat beside his sister. He tapped the table with his fork, tracing the lines of the ceramic tiles.

"Hi David."

"Hi Mere."

"So, we're both psyched that Katherine is cooking, but you sounded like you had something to tell me when you called."

"I did?"

"Yes David, and we've seen the shiny diamond on her finger, that can't be it. When is that wedding going to be anyway?"

Katherine leaned back and gave Meredith the middle finger then said sweetly, "Darn, we shouldn't ruin a good thing."

David smiled, "Yeah, why ruin a good thing?" He winked and Milton nudged her.

"Hmm. Well you're right, I do have something to talk with you about, but I thought it could wait until after dinner."

"Oh dinner, sure, come on now. Cough it up, what is it?"

"Well,…We both know that President Carter pardoned all the draft dodgers or conscientious evaders just a few days ago."

"Yes."

"Well that means Charlie has been pardoned."

Meredith was silent then snapped, "Of course I know that. I'm not an imbecile."

"Now, don't get angry, I just wanted to preface it because Charlie called me yesterday."

No one spoke. Meredith started tapping the table with her own fork. David waited patiently. Finally she sputtered, "Well, what did he have to say?"

David smiled and touched her hand to stop the tapping.

"He said hello to everyone and of course the whole thing was a bit uncomfortable but he's in Canada and wants to see us."

"David, I prayed for his safety all of these years and now I don't know what to say to him. When can we see him?"

"Soon. He said he would call back this week."

"Is he going to come here?"

"Yes, of course. Go see Mom and Dad too."

"Sure, of course. Gosh I'm just, well, I knew this would happen. I just don't know what to say."

"I was the same way, Mere, the same way. But I can't wait to see him, to hug him. He's our brother, our only brother. Now for the really big news!"

"What do you mean big news? What could be bigger than Charlie coming home?"

"Well, little sister, lower your voice and try to be calm. He's gone off and become a Catholic priest."

Meredith dropped her fork, "A priest?"

"Yep, that's what he said."

"Oh, well, a priest. That'll make Mom happy and I guess he might even pass you for the favorite." She started to giggle, shaking the table, causing a chain reaction. All four of them were laughing when the phone rang.

"Hello," David answered trying to compose himself.

"David, it's Mom."

"Oh hi, Mom." Meredith gave him the evil eye. Milton and Katherine held their breaths for the fill of Nicholson dysfunction.

"Hi David. David, Charlie he called, he's all right." She was sobbing on the other end.

"I know Mm, he called me too. He said he spoke with Dad and, well, I guess we should all be happy, thrilled. The President has allowed him to come home."

"Do you think he'll come home for good David?"

"I don't know, Mom. I only spoke with him a few minutes at work, but I'm sure we'll see him soon."

"Does Meredith know?"

"Yes, I told her. She's excited. The best news is that he's healthy and it sounds like he's taken care of himself in Canada."

"Your father is torn, you know, just torn."

"I didn't expect Dad to be any other way. I know it's hard for him, but he must be thrilled about his vocation?"

"I didn't get that far with him David. He just went back to work mumbling. I know your father, David. He's still brooding about Meredith. He really feels like he failed."

"Mom, bad time to talk about this. I'm about to sit down to dinner. I'll give you a call as soon as I hear back from him and we can make some plans, OK?"

"Yes David, all right. David?"

"Yes Mom?"

"Please tell Meredith hello and that we love her. We miss her so much"

"I will. I'll tell her, Mom."

"It's just, well, I just love all of you so much."

"We know Mom. You have a good night and I'll talk with you tomorrow."

"Goodbye David. I love you."

"Bye Mom, love ya too."

Meredith focused on the bent tine of her fork while Milton's hand stroked her back. Everything was happening so fast. She had told him just the other day about Jerome. The shock was starting to wear off about her high school sweetheart and their marriage. He didn't like it, but the past was the past and Meredith loved him now and that was plenty enough for him. Now Charlie was coming home.

"Everything all right in here?" Katherine asked as she placed a large bowl of pasta in the middle of the table.

"Everything's just fine, "David added as he stood to pull out her chair.

The train ride back to their dorms was silent. Meredith had a lot on her mind and Milton took care not to interrupt her thoughts, avoiding confrontation. He just snuggled around her, and when they reached their stop, he walked her to her dorm and kissed her goodnight. He walked back to his own building thinking only of her. Meredith was thinking about Charlie.

Father Charles Nicholson arrived the next Saturday. They all gathered in Charlestown and when Meredith saw her first favorite brother, she broke down. He was nobler, even more handsome than Meredith had pictured he would look in his vestments. They held each other tightly for a few minutes, and then she collected herself, wiped her eyes with her sleeve, and tapped his clerical collar.

"So Charlie, where the hell have you been?"

They all laughed and Charlie sat to tell them the story. He left Amherst with their church's help. He was put on a train ride to Canada and given documents to cross the border. His first thoughts were of becoming a fisherman, but after staying in the monastery for a while, he couldn't imagine life any other way. He was determined to pay God back for all the love and guidance he had received so far in his life and a priest's life was the answer.

"Oh my God, Father, and the others were the ones who helped you?"

"Yes. They were the ones I turned to and they asked no questions, just seemed to understand my fear." David's head bowed in agreement.

"But Charlie, what about girls?" coming from his not-so-baby sister anymore.

"Women are not really of any consequence right now Meredith. Everyone is God's child and, well, I'm now married to God."

"Wow," David responded, arm wrapped tightly around Katherine on the sofa.

"I know it's hard to understand, but please know I am happy. I have missed all of you terribly. The only thing that kept me sane was the church and knowing this moment would come soon. David, I'm so sorry I couldn't wait for your return. That was probably the worst time for me."

David's eyes filled and he leaned over and put his hand on his brother's shoulder.

"Me too, Charlie, me too. No more needs to be said about that. I'm just so relieved you are safe and home. We've missed you more than you know. Gosh, and who would've thought Mom and Dad could rear such gorgeous kids?"

They were back together and Father Charles had already put in for a transfer to any of the Boston churches, with the hope he would be stationed there by early spring. He leaned back in his chair, as if a weight had been lifted from his whole being. His prayers were being answered, one by one.

"OK, so Meredith what's going on with you? When I talked to Dad he didn't mention anything about you being in Boston."

She shifted uncomfortably in her chair, "Charlie, let's not talk about that right now. It's a long, torrid affair and, well, I'd much rather talk about happier things."

"All right then, who is this nice young man who keeps stroking your hair?"

"Hello, I'm Milton Stafford, Father Nicholson." Milton removed his hand as if reprimanded and hurriedly stood to shake what he considered his future brother-in-law's hand. He had fantasized that Father Charles, Charlie, would marry them in Wolfeboro, New Hampshire, near his family's house. He saw it all in the light caught in the strands of his sweet-smelling angel's hair.

Meredith giggled, bending over to pick up the napkin Milton had lost on the way.

"Charlie, Father Charles, this is Milton. He's at UMass too. He's a scientist, and well, quite an admirer of mine."

"Well, it's very nice to meet you Milton. Very nice to see someone has taken a liking to such a wonderful girl—oops, I mean *woman* that my sister has turned into. Meredith, I missed you so much. It was so hard, knowing that I'd miss so much in your life and you're all grown up now. I'm so sorry."

She went over to him, Milton still standing beside him, and she hugged them both, then walked over and gave David and Katherine the same treatment.

In her best dramatic flair she added, "Oh brother. I am just out of sorts. I haven't been this happy in so long. I think we need to celebrate."

"Here, here!" they cheered.

"All right then," Charlie added, "but before the champagne, let's call Mom and Dad and include them in all right?"

David laughed and Meredith groaned.

Chapter 15

Although the 39th President had a fan in Meredith, the southern farmer and brilliant businessman had his hands full trying to convince even his own party of his worth. A high point in his presidency was the signing of the peace treaty between the Israeli Premier and the Egyptian President, but the highlight quickly faded with the handling and considered fumbling of the hostage crisis in Tehran. When the 1980 election came to fruition, Meredith and Milton were about to graduate with honors and the Democrats were about to lose the presidency for a long twelve years. Both brothers and Katherine helped with their big move to the top of the rehabbed brownstone. Fifty-two steps to their door. David remarked that no Nicholson could live on the first floor, while Milton joked lightly to David that it would keep him in shape and give Meredith time to cool down from each day, before she reached the top. They were one step closer to his dream.

"He should just stay put in acting. Oh that's right, he was a terrible actor too!"

"Oh darling, you are such a Democrat!"

"What? Is that bad?" she asked grinning from ear to ear as she tackled him to the floor of their new apartment.

"Ow, ow, hey there, be careful of the family jewels and ouch, this wood is hard."

"Oh, I'm sorry, let me see those jewels."

She grabbed for his pants and he protected himself, rolling over into the leg of a dining room chair.

"Mere, Mere, please, ow."

"Oh, all right then my sweet scientist. Thank God you're not a politician. You would never survive."

"Thank God is right," he said as he stood then helped her to his feet.

"I love our new home, Milton."

"I love you, Meredith"

Milton had learned early on of her passions, and to argue politics with her was suicide. She never stepped in with an opinion on how to cure cancer, so he found her obsession tolerable. She had a way about her and she bewitched him. They knew what they knew best and respected each other. At times he would agree that she was unbearable in the birth of the Mondale campaign. With graduate school and full-time jobs, quality time together was at a minimum. Working countless volunteer hours on top of it all, Meredith's vision caused the worst argument they had ever had and his quote to "just sleep at headquarters, but just make sure you're sleeping alone," became a private joke for years to come. She had just recently fashioned a steady but still cool relationship with her mother since David and Charlie had given her the scare about her Mother's age and health, but nothing would change between her and Samuel. She had thanked her parents each year with a thousand-dollar check and no card, a reimbursement for school loans. She didn't want to owe them anything. The checks were never cashed. Numerous conversations and plans to unite the two proved fruitless. Daughter and father did not budge. Samuel had only Sons, and politics was her papa.

"Hey Milt, what do you think of this one?"

Milton leaned back into the aisle as David traipsed by in a candy-apple red tuxedo jacket.

"I, um," he smiled. "I really don't think Katherine will approve of the color, David. I think she'd blame me for the choice, so please, how about this nice gray one?"

David waltzed by again, this time cavorting in a powder-pink number, laughing at himself as he glided past the mirror.

"David, come on buddy, I've got to get back to school and we promised Katherine we would have this one thing done today."

"You're right, "David appeared, much more solemn in a white dinner jacket. "I'm just so excited, Milt. Just so fucking happy she said yes."

"I know, David, I know. You've only been saying that for four years. She said yes and yes she means, even if it only took you forever to pick a date. If we end up at the altar in a Caribbean blue ensemble, I'm afraid she might change her mind."

"You think?"

"Yeah, I think she would change her mind."

"Oh man, she loves me so much Milt, loves me more than I can explain and I love her. I am the luckiest man in the world!"

"One of the luckiest, bud. Remember I've got one of the best too!"

David smiled, fully aware at how much his sister's boyfriend, and now his best man, loved her. He had seen it from the first day he had met him and finally stopped worrying that his sister would devour him. He had something about him that calmed her, made her more rational and thank goodness for that, because she was on a mission to save the human race from everything but a true, fair democratic society and she appeared sometimes to only be able to care about her cause. Milton's patience was admirable and brave. He was the one man for her. He was the only man for her.

"Hey, that one's nice. You look great. Very debonair." He added with sarcasm, "We should go with that and if all else fails, we'll wear the same ones to my wedding."

"What?" David retorted as he narcissistically admired the jacket in the mirror.

"You heard me. I'm going to marry your sister."

"When?"

"Just as soon as you two get back from your honeymoon, I'm going to ask her. And please don't say anything to Katherine until you're away. I really want to surprise Meredith."

"Wow, congratulations! I'm thrilled for my sister, that's for sure. But Milt, this political stuff, won't it drive you bonkers for a lifetime?"

"Nah. She loves it so I tolerate it and I know you're her brother, but she's one hot tamale!"

David punched him lightly adding, "She's a firecracker, that's for sure. Hmm come to think of it, Katherine loves me and is going to marry me!"

"Yep, you're a lucky guy." They both smiled.

"So, what do you think Meredith? Meredith?" Katherine turned on the pedestal grasping the long train of the gown in her free hand. "Meredith?"

"I'm here, I'm here. Sorry, I was, wow!" Meredith stood in the doorway of the dressing room her hand to her mouth and tears in her eyes. "Katherine," she almost whispered, "you look like an angel."

"Oh Mere, that is so sweet. You really like it?"

"Like it?" She gathered the train in her arms and allowed Katherine to face back towards the mirror, "You look absolutely breathtaking!"

Katherine smiled and squeezed her maid of honor's hand. "That was a whole lot easier than I thought it would be. Now we have plenty of time to find a dress for you."

Meredith just gazed at her best friend and her brother's wife-to-be and wondered what the feeling would be like. To be someone's bride, someone's wife.

"What on earth is on your mind today? Is everything all right?"

It was just like Katherine to be concerned for others first, even on this special day.

"I'm sorry, I was just imagining what it must be like to be in your shoes. Shoes I could never fit into. I was just wondering that's all."

"Here, help me with this, silly," Katherine mumbled as she struggled to get the hoop over her head. "Listen my dear friend, you'll fill my shoes and go three sizes bigger I'm sure. You're an amazing, compelling, intelligent woman and about the prettiest girl in Boston."

"Except for you, of course?" Meredith added as she clumsily hung the yards of satin.

"I said 'about', didn't I?" Katherine giggled, "Now come on, let's go find a dress for you, so we can get back to our mothers and let them know what color not to wear!"

"Oh Katherine, I dread seeing him you know."

"Meredith, you really need to relax. Your father is a sweet, gentle man and I bet you every gift David and I get, he's as nervous as you are. He's getting older, Meredith. You really ought to think about talking with him. Your life has completely changed. The past is the past. You and Milton are starting a life together and you're still hung up on something that happened eons ago. Your Dad made a mistake, I guarantee he regrets it, but honestly if he hadn't made that mistake, you wouldn't be standing here today with me and contemplating a life with the darling Milton Stafford."

"Katherine, I know you're right, really I do. I just can't deny that I still harbor hateful feelings toward him and Jerome. I know it was eons ago. I will try. I promise to be cordial. He's not that old, he's only 54."

"Hmm, I guess it's just a coincidence that you know that this second."

"Oh hush now, what do you think of this Caribbean blue gown?" They both giggled and embraced. They were two of the happiest women in Boston.

David and Katherine were married in a small Catholic Church in the North End, Italian section of the city. Charlie's homily wove together love, family, and overall happiness, leaving the intimate gathering scrambling for tissues. Milton would admit later that the bride and groom were glowing, but he could hardly remember anyone but Meredith. He watched her walk down the aisle in step to Pachelbel's Canon and he inhaled deeply as she passed. He watched as she leaned over gracefully to help Katherine with her train, just a trace of cleavage showing, her smooth freckled skin familiar and beckoning. He watched at the reception in one of the oldest Italian restaurants, how his beautiful Meredith danced across the room as she greeted old friends and family and how she came to reach her father and hugged him briskly, but still hugged. He smiled and knew at that very moment that as soon as the plane took off to the Caribbean with David and Katherine in tow, he was going to ask Meredith to be his wife. He couldn't wait a second longer.

"Really?"

"Yes, Meredith, really! Will you be my wife?"

"Of course I'll be your wife!"

She ran toward his outstretched arm, letting her towel from the shower fall to the ground. They lay on the bed giggling as she admired the beautiful ruby ring and he traced the tiny hairs around her belly button. They made love and called for takeout, vowing to stay in bed until the sun set and rose again. In the morning Milton woke, reaching for her and finding an empty space, he sat up and catching a glimpse of her through the crack of the bathroom door.

"Meredith?"

She looked up from the side of the bathtub, playing with her ring, her face tear stained.

"What's wrong, Mere?" He knelt down beside her, grasping her hands.

"I'm sorry Milton, I'm not sad. I've just been thinking about the past and the future and I'm so happy, just a little overwhelmed."

"It's OK, everything is going to be all right, I promise."

"I know, I know. I just thought I'd never be this happy again and, well, you've made me so happy, so completely happy. Thank you Milton. I love you."

She cried in his shoulder as he held her.

"Now young lady, enough tears, let's talk about when."

"When what?"

"When we're going to get married, silly. I was thinking maybe this fall or we could have a beautiful winter wedding. Gosh, even spring, but that seems so far away."

"Milton, can we hold off just a bit? I'm taking the bar exam in the fall and you're about to decide on which company offer you're going to take. Let's decide on a date once the dust settles a little. That will be all right won't it?" She looked into his eyes and all he could say was, "Of course that will be all right."

Two years later at the age of 24, Meredith was working at one of the top firms in Boston with whispers that partnership was not only in the near future but a party to celebrate the firm's youngest was in the works. Milton had accepted a mediocre job with a Brockton pharmaceutical firm, instead of the lucrative offer from the mid-Atlantic company, to counter the promises of Meredith's career choice and to enable them to stay within the city for her political fix. They were still engaged with no wedding date in sight. On a humid, summer evening, their lives would change forever.

"Meredith, please will you sit, so we can nail down a date?"

Drenched in perspiration, she wandered aimlessly around the apartment, collecting laundry and busying herself with unnecessary chores. She longed for central air conditioning.

"Please."

She looked at Milton, and sat, with a look of uncertainty, on the floor.

"Well?"

"Well, I guess we can…."

"Here, look at the calendar. What do you think about October?"

"Um, hmm, well I think that might be a bit too late."

"Too late? What on earth are you talking about? We've already waited over two years."

"Um, it's just, I'm not sure what I'll look like in October."

"You'll look beautiful as always, sweetheart. Are you all right?"

"Um, no. Yes, um, I don't know. Honey, have you ever seen a bride in a maternity dress?"

Milton blinked. "You mean we're? Oh my God, Meredith, why didn't you tell me?"

"I just found out today and, yep, seems that October may be a little too late."

Three days later the justice at the courthouse married them, with Katherine and David as witnesses and Charlie as God's representative. There was no time to wait for a date with the church, even though Milton pleaded, and a few minutes before the ceremony, both Milton and Meredith called their parents, promising that in the future they would have a big affair and a church wedding. They of course had the little miracle, a grandchild to look forward to. Milton's parents were about to embark on a 25th anniversary cruise, so they locked up the grocery store, stocked their home with everything any young couple could desire, and offered the lovely setting for the honeymoon. They graciously accepted. For two weeks they gorged themselves on gourmet foods and sparkling cider. They sailed and sunned and made love under the moonlight on the dock. When the moon refused to shine, they made love in the rain. Lake Winnipesaukee would be the place to reminisce and remember how young and innocent life was. The place where their unborn child would hear its first music, be read its first book.

Connor Harold Stafford would be born on Valentine's Day 1984. Milton could sense his grandfather smiling down on them as the priest baptized his son. That same year Meredith would become partner at her law firm, George Orwell's book would be dissected, and Walter Mondale would lose a grueling campaign with his "running mate" Geraldine Ferraro and her husband's financial woes. The actor turned governor turned President, would start a second term even after an assassination attempt and concern that his age had already exceeded Eisenhower's after he'd left office. Reaganomics, The Iran-Contra Scandal, Nicaragua, the Oliver North scandal, the Grenada invasion, and the effects of the Cold War were just a few choice subjects Connor would hear about in his first four years of life. During the year Reagan was to retire as the most popular outgoing President since Eisenhower, the 4-year-old could be heard quoting his mother, "How can anyone have taken this man seriously and who's the biggest liar of all time?" Meredith's least favorite President stepped down and her next-to-least favorite succeeded him. Connor turned 5 years old, when Meredith decided that she would run for City Council. Not just any seat, but the President's seat. With Milton's trepidatious encouragement in the midst of her first campaign, the stress of her career and family were the least of Meredith's concerns. She was about to find out another big surprise. Connor was going to have a sibling.

CHAPTER 16

Poised as a rookie legislator, just shy of age 32, Meredith pounced on her advocates with knowledge backed by pure ardor and zeal for every office. From the day she'd met Connie, she'd been developing the knowledge and nerve that most elective officials would envy. With seven years as one of the city's most recognized attorneys, the second pregnancy proved to be more help than a hindrance. David's support with articles titled "Woman on the Move" and "Having a Family and Wanting it All" added to her popularity, but the resistance toward her age and lack of political standing loomed heavily in the local papers as well. She responded with a campaign that set the council's community and economic development, making them priorities independent of the Mayor's agenda. She was attractive, but prided herself on intellect and sensitivity. Men and women liked her. Some would say it was her idea of rehabilitating low-income housing or her tiresome efforts to raise the school drop-out age as the reasons. Others would blame the lack of a better choice, but either way, the end created one of the most historical and publicized races for City Council President in Boston. In 1990, Meredith Nicholson had won her election. For the first time, she had also been seen in the political world and would leave a lasting impression.

Connor was waiting for Santa and his 7th birthday when his mother and father lifted him clumsily in celebration. Santa came that year with a special gift for them all. Emily Deborah Stafford was born on Christmas Day, 1990, just seven weeks after her mother's triumph. This time the entire family celebrated in one of Boston's largest maternity wards, the press outside ready for a quick photo opportunity or impromptu interview. Meredith held her little girl for the first time, kissing her forehead, then passed her over to her proud father and brother.

She watched as they fondled the tiny bundle and peered out the door as it swung open, noticing the press pushing forward. She felt powerful and fulfilled. She was a mother now of a beautiful daughter, an adoring son and the wife of a kind, caring husband. She was also a politician. She felt complete.

"You old dog, you!"

"Connie, that's not nice."

"I'm just kidding darling, you are a top dog though, a top dog! And on top of all that you had yourself a baby girl! I tried for a girl for 10 long years. Finally gave up!"

Meredith smiled as Emily breast fed, something she swore silently she would be able to do for only a few days.

"So, President of the City Council, huh?"

"Connie, I can't believe it either. The past few weeks have been a whirlwind and, well, with Emily coming a little early, I'm just without words."

"I doubt that entirely, my sweet Meredith. I told you you'd go places and by golly you did just that. Joe and I are so proud of you, just so proud. We talk about you all the time. Do your ears ring?"

"As a matter of fact, I was just about to ask if they could check the contact ringing in my ears," she grinned. "Thank you for telling me. You saved my doctors some time and poor Milton more worries. Oh Connie, I miss you. How are Joe and the boys?"

"Oh, they're all doing well. Joe's as sweet as ever. I'm still getting over those four years as selectwoman. Man, that was something. I'd reconsider now, if I could."

"Oh no, Connie, really?"

"Darn tootin, Meredith. Politics, phooey! There was so much hush-hush and favoritism, it was rare that anything got done. And when it did, it wasn't anything good."

"Connie, that's not like you. What about your dreams to make the world better for your boys?"

"The best thing I could've done was stay home with them more Meredith. They needed me more and sometimes I was just too darn busy to notice. They're all doing well now, I promise. Can you believe Eric is about to start his second semester at Dartmouth? They grow up so fast. Oh I wish I could do that again."

"What Connie?"

"The baby thing. Once they're gone, you can't get them back. The baby years I mean. Enjoy motherhood, Meredith. Enjoy it to the fullest. Now, Missy, you get back to that baby and keep in touch. All right?"

"I will, Connie. Hugs and kisses to all of you. Thanks for calling."

Meredith leaned back on her pillow as Emily's hand brushed hers. She would balance motherhood with politics and she would make it work. Connor would be a focus, a main focus, since she hadn't perfected the duel role when he arrived. He would go without nothing, including her time and love.

"And you, little one, you are my second angel." She closed her eyes and ignored the ringing phone.

On January 2, 1991, she found herself sitting behind her new desk, in her new office chair, ignoring her secretary's urge to get back home to the little ones. She inhaled the new leather and office supply smells and collected her calendar for the next month. She smiled as she passed Harmony, her exclusive assistant, feeling very important as she exited the old government building. This was where is it all happened. She looked back at the gold dome she had admired her first day in Boston. She was 33 and at the top of her game. She had made the decision to take on this role and the public had seen fit to elect her the seat. She was determined to be the absolute best. Completely determined.

Milton dreamed that he was in a voter's box and the ballot in front of him was in hieroglyphics. He couldn't decipher what he needed to do and how he needed to do it and the anxiety caused him to sweat and stand in his draped cube, dazed and confused. He didn't dare just pick anyone, because it was better not to vote for anyone than choose between nationality, lucky numbers, or a name that struck him funny, and in his circumstance a symbol that he was drawn too. He was so afraid that an apathetic vote might be the sole reason an imbecile would be in charge of his tax money or children's welfare. Somehow he had to decipher the city council's names and make sure he at least selected his wife's name. When he stepped out of the box he was alone, until his wife stepped out of the one beside his. She smiled and he read her mind that she was impressed with his speed and confidence, but warned that hastiness sometimes made for mistakes. He walked a few paces behind her as they left what appeared to be a school cafeteria. The sun glared down upon them as he pondered his stupidity and plain lack of knowledge of the candidates that were served to him, the ones that would make or break so many things in his and his family's lives. He vowed never again step into a voter's booth without doing his homework. He watched his wife disappear, thankful his limitations were still secret. He suddenly bent down, telling his son truthfully that he had no idea if the Red Sox should build a new stadium or if free agents would finally start signing to Boston.

"Dad?"

"Hmmm."

"Dad?"

"Yes, Connor."

"Dad, Emily's crying and I can't sleep."

"Hmm, OK Connor. I'm getting up."

He looked at the digital clock beside the bed, 11:33 flashed. They must have lost power for a short time, and the thunder woke them up. He planted his feet in slippers beside the bed and let his wiry Son help him to his feet. They walked down the hall to his daughter's room and without turning on the lights, he made his way to the crib, the tiny pink cherub, clinging to the sidebars, tears streaming down her face.

"Now, now sweet girl, it's going to be all right. Connor, get me one of her binkies and let's see if we can get her back to sleep."

Connor headed for the kitchen as Milton tenderly snuggled his daughter in the rocking chair.

"Peeyuu, missy, I think you need more than a binky. I guess we need a little light to help me get through this." He switched the tiny lamp on just above her changing table as he placed her down gently. She had stopped crying the minute he had lifted her into his arms and now he held his hand to her belly as he fiddled to get the wipes and diapers out of the drawers.

"Here you go, Dad."

"Thanks Connor. You're such a good brother."

"Dad, can I go watch TV for a little while?"

"Connor, it's almost midnight. Go into your room and get one of your favorite books and I'll be in there in a few minutes to read it with you."

"OK," he said disheartened but hurried to scour the wall of reading he treasured.

"Now, now pretty girl, does that feel better?" Milton looked down at his baby daughter, now 3 months old, and waited for her ever-present smile. She stared at the glowing light and grinned from ear to ear, but something seemed different, wrong? He lifted her in a sitting position, and talked directly to her, but she focused more on the light than on his face. Nothing very strange about that, just something babies were attracted to? He placed her back in her crib and played peek-a-boo a couple of times, then he bent down to the carpet and popped his head up and said "cheese" as he appeared. She smiled as usual, but then it happened. He crouched down and popped his head up but didn't say a word as he peered down at her. This time she did not react, as if waiting for the words instead of his face. He brushed his fingers within inches of her eyes and she grinned, but he was sure it was from the smell of him and not the sight. He picked up her favorite stuffed toy and did the same thing, and she grinned again. He reached over to a large shelf where there was an excess of stuffed animals, and he picked one that he was sure she had probably never played with, and placed it within inches of her face. She did not react. He went back and forth with the favorite and the unknown and each time she responded positively with the familiar and without response to the unfamiliar. Her eyes started to quiver and he swooped her into his arms, where she fell asleep as he read his son the first few chapters of a Hardy Boys mystery before he too fell asleep. The storm had subsided but Milton's mind raced with fear. When Meredith came in from another late committee meeting she found him sleeping in their son's room, both children asleep on his chest.

The next morning at the pediatrician's office, Meredith and Milton held hands when the doctor informed them of the congenital disease that he feared, but he noted that more tests needed to come back before he was certain.

"You mean she may never see again, Dr. Adachi?"

"What I mean, Meredith, is that there is a chance she has never seen, since birth. It is so hard when infants are developing, to determine what they can and cannot do. I am sure with Emily's capabilities, she became instantly accustomed to being in the dark and using her other senses, making it even more difficult to diagnose. The results should be back later today and I will call you as soon as I get them. Please, I need you to both listen to me and do not let this overwhelm you right now. Emily is a beautiful, healthy baby. We will deal with this one step at a time, all right?"

"All right," Milton answered quietly as he scooped his daughter up into his arms. Meredith stroked her back, not able to respond. How could this have happened? What had they done wrong? Milton tried to take her hand as they left the office, but she had withdrawn into herself. On the ride home, she sat in the back with Emily. He watched them both in the rearview mirror and he wondered the same things that Meredith had, but he also wondered what this meant for them as a family. Who would take care of Emily?

"Darling, it's been almost a week since we found out. We need to make a choice. Neither of us can afford to miss another day of work. We need to make a decision so Emily can start getting used to someone now."

"I just don't know Milton. I'm just not sure about her."

"Meredith, she was a lovely woman and had the background of handicapped children all over her resume. She's even been a nanny for a blind child before. I'm not sure what you want, but I'm afraid we're running out of choices."

"Oh I just don't know. Maybe I should...what I mean is, I'm considering a sabbatical. You know, stay home with her. I'm not sure what to do Milton." She shook her head then put her fingers to her temples and closed her eyes.

Milton stared at his wife in disbelief. That she had even considered for even a moment setting aside her career for their daughter, touched him deeply. He knew the woman he'd fallen so deeply in love with and this surprised him. The doctor had barely severed Emily's umbilical cord before Meredith was back to work. Now she was considering a sabbatical? He also knew that she was not as qualified as Beatrice O'Reilly, and their daughter would have only the best care until she was old enough for the best school.

"Meredith," he said as he moved closer to her on the couch and wrapped his arm awkwardly around her. It was a strange feeling, feeling distraught about himself instead of the matter at hand. He watched as his wife stroked their baby daughter's golden curls and he wanted to take Meredith into his own arms. He wanted to stroke her hair and kiss her cheeks. He wanted to make everything better.

"Meredith, I love you so much more everyday."

"I love you too, Milton, I do." She put her head alongside his shoulder and together they nuzzled their baby daughter.

CHAPTER 17

"The Mayor's decided to do what?" Milton asked, placing his fork prudently alongside his untouched, sizzling steak. Both children faced their father. Connor saw a hint of worry in his eyes. Emily, now 2 years, sensed his concern.

"Milton, I'm sorry. I know it's a shock. But we talked about it and, well, yes, it's happened." Meredith was home for dinner. Something she had been trying to do at least two times a week since Emily's diagnosis. She had even prepared his favorite meal, which coincided nicely since it was Connor's favorite meal, always trying to imitate his father.

"Connor, please pass me the sour cream."

Connor reached over and passed his father a dollop of sour cream instead of the whole tureen. Milton looked down at his son's cowlicked bangs and the front gap in his teeth. He leaned over and squeezed his small shoulder gently. He would not make this a big deal.

"So, well, great! The Mayor has decided to run for governor. When will that be announced?"

Meredith looked across at her husband. She adored him most of the time and loathed him only when their children seemed much more convinced that he was the caregiver, the mommy. It was almost like having a relationship with someone who already had a dog. Of course the dog loved you and recognized you, but when the two of you were around, the dog had a tendency to ignore you. Meredith wiped the strained carrots from her daughter's rosy cheeks. Emily knew her mommy would be the feeder when she was home at dinnertime. Not as often as anyone liked. Meredith was working twelve-hour days and still juggling some pro bono for the office. She was tired. What they really needed was a vacation.

With the Mayor's decision to run for governor, Meredith automatically would be sworn in as the Mayor of Boston. Vacation or sleep, both were out of the question. She leaned over and kissed her daughter, keeping an eye on her ravenous husband as he picked at his dinner. Both of them knew this was something very, very big.

"Dad?'

"Yes, Connor?" Milton tucked the blankets around his son as he bent down to kiss him goodnight.

"Dad, does this mean that Mom's going to be the Mayor?"

Milton looked down at Connor, smiled, then kissed him lightly on his forehead, predicting his son's nightly ritual to wipe away the kiss from his cowlick as soon as it was complete.

"Um, that's a possibility. We need to wait and see what happens. You need to go to sleep now. School tomorrow, remember?"

"I know, but Dad, when Mom is Mayor will everything else stay the same?"

"Of course it will. Mom will just be in a different position that's all. Everything will be fine and yes, it will all stay the same."

"Even school, Dad? Will I stay in the same school?"

Milton took his turn to brush the cowlick back from his son's head.

"Connor, we need to wait and see what happens all right? This is nothing for you to worry about right now. Go to sleep now, all right?"

He answered unconvinced. "I'll miss my friends and I really want to be in the science show this year."

Milton turned as he shut the light and pulled the door, "Connor, you will be in the science show this year, I promise."

"OK Dad, thanks."

"I love you, Connor."

"I love you, Dad."

Milton peeked into their daughter's room. She was already asleep, her arms tightly clutching her freckled baby doll. He smiled, always in awe of her ability to pick out the one with the freckles. She was growing like a weed and was smarter than most 5 year olds, but there had been no improvement from the last operation. He prayed every day for his daughter to have sight. He could imagine the smile on her face if suddenly she could see her baby doll. Everyone in the family, including his parents and Connor, had learned to read Braille and everyone prayed the same prayer, that one day Emily would be able to see. The doctors remained cautious. Milton would keep praying for his miracle. An overwhelming feeling of love came over him, as he pulled the door gently, checking the monitor on the dresser as he did.

Meredith put her book down when Milton came into their room. The rest of their evening, after her announcement, had been tense. She was prepared for a "discussion." Milton, still melancholy over his sleeping daughter, said nothing as he brushed his teeth, turned out the rest of the lights and crawled in beside her.

"Do you want to talk darling?"

"Not really, Meredith. I'm tired and, well, not really sure what I want or what can be said now."

"Are you angry?"

He looked up at her, still perched against her pillows under the reading lamp. The light was low and her hair fell around her shoulders. She was wearing his Red Sox T-shirt and a pair of boxer shorts. His favorite lingerie.

"Meredith, I just don't know. This all happened so fast and I guess I just didn't believe that the Mayor would jump into the gubernatorial race. Or at least not so quickly. Maybe I was just hoping he wouldn't jump and thought maybe City Council would appease you. Be enough for you, I mean."

"Is it enough for you?" She asked, as she cuddled up beside him.

"I don't know, Meredith. I need to think about this. I guess I kind of feel left out and this is one of those things that I think I absolutely should have been included in."

She wrapped her arm lightly around over his chest.

"Milton, I've included you in everything, always. Every decision, every option that has ever come my way. I've hidden nothing from you and never intend to. I told you before this was possible and I have no choice now in the matter. You are my husband, my confidant, and I need to know that you support me on this. We talked about it many times and I was hoping that out of everyone, you would be excited for me."

"Meredith?" He turned on his side, their faces only inches apart. "You are one of the biggest reasons why I love to wake up in the morning. One of the reasons I smile at every snowstorm. You're my life and I love you and support you in whatever you accomplish or wish to do. I guess I was just hoping that City Council would be it. I don't know. Emily's going to be three in a few months and…."

"And I know one big guy that's going to be 34 the day before."

"Yeah, Yeah, don't push it. You're going to be 33 this year. Wow, 33! I wonder if you'll be the youngest Mayor in the history of this city?"

"Oh sweet husband, I love you with all my heart. You're one of the biggest reasons I exist as well, but you know City Council is not the end of the line for me. The feeling I felt when I was told about the Mayor stepping down—I just can't explain it. It was electrifying. I felt the blood rushing through my body. I was expecting it, even predicted the very week it would happen, but when it did, it was overpowering. I've felt it before Milton and I want to feel it again. I want to make a difference."

"But Meredith, you do make a difference. Every day you make a difference here at home."

She smiled at him. He was always there for that reassurance, even though she was not always convinced.

"You know what I mean, darling. Your work, your ideas. When something comes to fruition, don't you feel the power?"

He rolled back on his back and looked up at the ceiling.

"I haven't felt that in years, Meredith."

"But you know what I'm talking about. I'm sure that you feel it again."

"I hope so, Meredith. I hope so."

"Milton, please, I just need to know that you're with me on this?"

"On the Mayor thing? Yes, of course I am. I'm not going to say that I really don't have a choice, because I don't want to appear selfish now. I sure would like to be the first reason you feel electrified though." He smiled as his hand reached under the sheet to touch her.

"You are the least selfish person I know in the world darling." Her body arched as his fingers explored.

"Well, that's nice to hear. Now how about that electrifying feeling? Think I can match it?" He found a spot that made her squirm.

"Milton, there may be more."

"Of course there's more my beautiful wife." His head was now buried beneath the covers.

"I mean Milton—Oh yes, that feels so nice. I mean there may be more than being Mayor. I'll only have a year to make some decisions about the future."

"Of course there's more," he whispered.

"I'll be the first female Mayor."

"Finally," he whispered again.

"I mean, I would like to be Governor some day as well." She sighed.

He paused for only a moment, but she knew he had heard.

The next morning was rushed, both Meredith and Milton up later than usual, but smiling. Meredith thanked Beatrice for a second time, kissed her children, and then reached for her husband as she grabbed her briefcase.

"I'll call you as soon as they tell me how they're going to announce it."

"OK Mere, go, go. You're going to be late."

She kissed his lips then was gone. Milton reached for his daughter from Beatrice, nuzzling her curls, then double-checked Connor's lunchbox and book bag and shuffled his son out the door.

He walked him to the corner, where the crossing guard and several children were already waiting, marching in place to keep warm.

"You all set, Son?"

"Yes, Dad," he answered, a little embarrassed.

"OK, call me when you get home, all right?"

"Dad? Did you talk with Mom about the…."

"Yes, I did, and when I get home tonight we'll talk some more, OK?"

"OK, Dad. Bye."

"Love ya."

Connor blushed as he turned to see his school bus approaching. He waved to his father as he disappeared inside.

"This traffic is frightful, don't you think?"

Milton turned and saw his grandfather, sitting in the passenger seat, shaking his head in disgust.

"Grandpa! You really need to give me fair warning when you decide to make an appearance. I spilled my coffee."

"Oh Milton, here," he handed him his handkerchief. "I didn't mean to startle you, Son, and when did you start calling me Grandpa? I just thought it might be a nice time for us to chat again, since it takes you almost an hour to go less than ten miles every day. This city life is for the birds"

Milton smirked. He half expected to see him today, even willed it a little. The hallucinations had been frequent as of late and he had convinced himself that it was harmless to speak with his grandfather about certain things that he might not be able to talk with anyone else about. Of course he was dead and there were no such things as ghosts, but it was nice to work things through with someone that he respected so much as a child. He missed him.

"No Pop, I don't want to get your handkerchief all full of coffee stains. No big deal. Just try to give me a little warning all right?" He waved away the offer as his grandfather wiped the drops on the console himself. He looked over at the elderly man, his idol.

"All right then. Maybe I should whistle or something?" A sly, dentured smile grinned back.

"We'll think of something, Pop. It's Connor and Emily, calling Dad, Grandpa. I guess it's just in my head. Now what can I do for you?" Milton looked over at the car stopped beside him as he inched his car close to the bumper ahead of him and realized how silly he must look talking to himself.

"Hmm, Son, there's nothing you can do for me. I'm dead. I'm here to help you. Call me Pop, OK? I like that. We need to talk, don't you think?"

Milton tried to ignore the carpool alongside him.

"Pop, maybe we should wait until later?"

"Nonsense Son, no time like the present and, well, you've got another 45 minutes of this mess ahead of you. Don't you want to talk about Meredith's big job, Son?"

Milton smiled, remembering the evening before, then glanced at his grandfather with one eye and a nod. After he and Meredith had made love, Milton had stayed awake for an hour after, listening to her breathe. Yes, he needed to talk with someone.

"Pop, I'm worried."

"Good. Here we go. So what are you worried about?"

"I guess I'm worried that Meredith may be in over her head."

"Really? That's what you think? Hmm. I don't think Meredith's in over her head at all. I think she's a bull in the ring and she's beaten every matador. She can handle this new post just fine."

"You think?" Milton asked, still not facing his grandfather, hoping that his lips moving appeared like he was singing along with the radio. He shook his head clumsily, from side to side.

"Son, stop that. Who cares what they think about you out there. They're nothing to you but a car full of strangers. You will never see them again. Look at me please, Son."

Milton did what he was told after he moved the car several more feet with the flow of traffic.

"I'm sorry, Pop, you're right."

"Of course, I'm right, Son. Where would I have been if I had cared what every Tom, Dick, and Harry thought of me? I never did things by the book and I don't expect you to either. You have a gift and I think it's time you start focusing on that and not using your wonderful wife's dream as a crutch."

"A crutch?"

"You heard me. A crutch!" There was silence and Milton raised himself in his seat, peering over the dashboard, looking for the favorite landmark that meant he was halfway there.

They both admired the gigantic man's profile, painted by Sister Carita, across the enormous oil tank. The sun placed just behind it, inching its way into the morning sky.

"I wish I had seen the nun paint that."

"Me too, Grandpa—oops, sorry Pop. Me too."

"Now, back to business. It's time, Milton."

"I know it's time. I need to get on that cure for cancer."

They were silent for a while, relishing the thought.

Finally, his grandfather turned and smiled. "You do that, Son. But remember, there are a lot of good things you can be working on right now. A mind is a terrible thing to waste."

"I want to feel that electricity Meredith mentioned, Pop. I really do." He pulled into the enormous parking lot of the pharmaceutical firm.

"Milton, I felt that electricity every day that your grandmother was alive and every day now that I'm with her. That electricity you're looking for needs to come from within." Milton watched as he faded away.

Walking through the parking lot briskly, the frigid air revived Milton from the cramped, long commute. He turned back hoping to catch a glimpse of him again, but no one was there.

CHAPTER 18

From August 1990 to March 1991, the United States found itself once again a major contender in a military conflict. The Persian Gulf War was a fast and furious force of power and duly took on the title of Operation Desert Storm. The war seemed to lift the American people's self-consciousness post-Vietnam, and the swift, televised victory proved to be a winning combination for the ruling Republican party and an intended end to an evil Iraqi dictatorship.

Twenty thousand Iraqi soldiers were killed in action, along with an estimated 3000 civilians. The United States lost 148 soldiers in action and another 121 died in non-combat incidents. 458 American soldiers were wounded and returned to their homes.

It was to be a short celebration. Despite the cease-fire, Saddam's government retained an iron grip in Iraq. The Iraqi and Kurdish people sustained great hardship and starvation, due to the economic and trade sanctions that followed. Their fear stemmed from the cruelty and torturous ways of their self-proclaimed leader. The Iraqi government showed no mercy with its own people, and the American soldiers, who believed they had proudly succeeded, would soon be privy to the legacy of war when the Persian Gulf War Syndrome would rear its ugly head.

Gerald Revo was born in a small town in Mississippi. He was raised by a strict, prejudiced father and a timid, walk-ten-steps-behind-your-man," mother. He was bright. And in his town in the 1950s, smart kids with strict parents or bad kids with rich parents, went to military school.

From the age of seven he could clean and dismantle a rifle. Difficult homework for most second graders, but a mandatory requirement in the creation of an exceptional soldier. His father, a retired Marine, expected only perfection. Gerald graduated with honors and was immediately deployed to Guantanamo Bay where he quickly adapted to the ins and outs of the few and the proud.

He was already a decorated officer when he received the call and hailed the chance to see action in the Persian Gulf. While he didn't notch his rifle for each "enemy" he killed, there was an ongoing joke in his battalion that he himself killed half of Iraq's Republican Guard. One night raid, bringing over a thousand American soldiers into a small village, Revo would earn his first of three Purple Hearts. Set up on the front line, he himself took aim and sprayed the oncoming enemies with bullets. He had no fear and even directed the tanks to arsenals that had not been detected by the radars. The village was obliterated and the enemies in hiding, massacred, their arsenals disintegrated. Only the American soldiers made it out alive. Revo would be commended and revered after that. Several comrades would pass on the victory story, remembering the cloud of sand and smoke that billowed over them when the battle was over, and Revo atop a small dune, smiling. Those who knew him dared never antagonize him. Those who didn't were quick to learn. A smart man with a weapon was a soldier's worst fear.

When "Gerry" returned home, the town threw a hero's parade for him. His father was pleased and suggested strongly that he boost his career by feeding off the patriotic frenzy. Notoriety in their small town was nice, but not even close to what Gerry's father intended. A one-time loser in a run for Governor, he was about to introduce the State of Mississippi to his namesake. With several notable connections, his father's clout, and an unlimited amount of donations, Gerald Revo entered the Senate race in 1992 and won. He took 70 percent of the vote, having no previous political experience. It was a strong year for the Democratic Party, who held the White House and Congress after a long twelve years, but Gerald Revo, a devout Republican and Presbyterian, watched and listened quietly. There would be a time to be heard, but patience was the first thing a soldier learned. He preferred bloodshed, but Gerald practiced patience.

CHAPTER 19

In 1992, Meredith Nicholson became both Boston's first female mayor and its youngest-ever-mayor. Because her predecessor stepped down seeking the Governor's title, Meredith's position as City Council President automatically placed her in the hottest seat in town. The city reacted with interested shock. How exactly did this happen? Explanation followed speculation and littered the local news. The press gobbled it up. David was kept busy at the newspaper, not only writing, but dodging family questions and ridiculous notions that there was foul play involved. Meredith made her first public appearance at a press conference the day after the announcement. With dignity and maturity she handled each concern. Even sexist questions about her qualifications were dutifully noted and addressed. She appeared capable and intelligent, tactfully winning a majority of the public over with a firm conviction of herself and the city's status. She ended the press conference with a promise that, if the city was not happy with her abilities in the next year, she would gladly step down and go back to practicing law. Of course, there would be an official election after her first year, and the voters would choose, but Meredith stood firm that she would not run for reelection if she proved incapable. The city and the nation eagerly watched, predicting an embarrassing fall, but in a very short time she was able to earn substantial recognition for a revived city. She was confident in a man's world, and though she received a fair amount of criticism, she stood firm in her conclusions. She raised more than a few eyebrows when she defended the new President's healthcare reform and foreign policy. Not only was she a big fan of the Oval Office's new resident, but she praised his wife as well. When the opportunity came to step into the shoes of the existing Mayor, the stage was set and the play had begun. But as history has proven over and over again, the political head of the moment is the one who receives the positive reinforcement or downright degradation depending on what script they are handed. Meredith was handed a winning script and never looked back. Even the stodgy, elite politicians of Massachusetts were taking notice. They grumbled that she only had eleven months to cause chaos and straightening out the mess would be unpleasant, but they didn't lose sleep thinking about reelection. They just wouldn't permit that.

"Meredith?"

"Yes, hello, Beth? I'm so sorry to keep you waiting."

"Meredith, I'm so sorry, I know how busy you are. We're so proud of you. I just thought we could talk for a minute. It's Pete. Well, it's not good."

Meredith was quiet on the other end, perusing another newspaper headline, when her mother-in-law told her the news. She laid the paper beside the stack of folders on her desk and sat far back in her chair.

"Is it?"

"Yes, Meredith. It's cancer. The tests came back positive and today they found two more tumors that they want to remove. He's being very stubborn. I'm not sure how long he has."

"We need to tell him, Beth."

"I know. It's just so discouraging. We were sure that the first results would be better and well you know, we always try to think on the bright side."

Meredith listened and smiled. The woman on the other end of the phone had stepped in where Meredith had left her own mother off. Even after Meredith had rekindled the relationship with her mother, Beth had proven a much more nurturing element. She had no history with her, so no bad feelings could prevail. Even now, as Mayor of Boston, Meredith still did not speak with her father, and the possibility that her gentle, sweet father-in-law could be dying made her strangely uncomfortable. Milton's and her own father were the same age.

"When do you want to tell him, Beth?"

"I was hoping you would, Meredith. I just don't know if I can keep myself together right now and I know that you're his rock."

Meredith winced at this metaphor. She sometimes felt like she was adrift and it was always he and the children fishing her out of the deep end, breathing reality back into her. How could she be his rock? She had to be the city's rock right now.

"Oh Beth, I don't know. He's going to want to talk with you, see you both right away. Are you sure?"

"Yes, Meredith, I'm sure. We're back in Wolfeboro and I expect that you will all be here this weekend?"

"Of course we will. Of course. Beth?"

"Yes, Meredith."

"We love you so much, Beth. I am so sorry."

"We love you all too, Meredith and I know. I'm so sorry too."

Meredith placed the phone silently on the cradle. Milton's parents had just celebrated their thirty-fifth wedding anniversary and now this. She handled crisis after crisis everyday. Murder, poverty, and crime were a part of her city and a part of her daily focus. Why did this news seem so much harder?

"You're going where?"

Bonnie knew it was a waste of positive energy to despise Milton Stafford, even though he was an albatross around her boss's neck. Of course his father's illness wasn't his fault, but when it came to winning in politics, illness and emotions needed to be set aside. Family had to come second, sometimes third. Especially the albatross.

"I'm going to Wolfeboro, Bonnie. I already told you. Milton's father is very ill."

Bonnie watched as her boss shuffled through a desk drawer. She reached over to the top of the filing cabinet and handed her the file that she was scrambling for.

"Oh, thanks Bonnie. I'm not sure what I'd be able to do without you."

Bonnie smiled, knowing full well her boss would be just fine without her, but she'd never let her in on that secret. She had all intentions of following her all the way to the Governor's mansion. *Oops, not "mansion"*, she corrected her thought. *Governor's Office.* The mansion, of course, was the residence. She and Karol might be invited every so often on special occasions, but it also would be where Meredith would reside with her ball-a-d chain of a husband. *Oh,* Bonnie thought devilishly, *the things she could teach her.* Even her sweet partner Karol admitted that Meredith appeared so incredibly independent and perfect, until she introduced the world to her Milton. He ruined the faultless image.

"Meredith, I'm sorry, yes you did tell me about your father-in-law and Wolfeboro. I'm so sorry about his condition. I'm sure it's very hard for all of you. I don't need to remind you though that I'm here to remind you of everything else that needs to be addressed right now. What I mean is, when will you be back?"

Meredith was still flustered, filling her briefcase and signing a few last documents. She looked up at her assistant and smiled, her mind cluttered with much more than her assistant's concerns.

"What's happening?"

Both Meredith and Bonnie glanced up at the opened door, where Darryl Rodriguez leaned casually against the door jamb. Bonnie turned toward Meredith, hoping for a response. Darryl had the ability to look seethingly handsome, even in ridiculous poses. Bonnie cared little for the look, but knew he might get through to her.

"Uh, Darryl, hi. I was just filling Bonnie in that I have to go to Wolfeboro for a few days to be with my in-laws. My father…."

"Say no more. I'm so sorry, Meredith. I know how close you are to him. Please send our prayers and love to them and Milton and the kids."

Bonnie would have preferred it less thick, but she knew that, together, she and Darryl would be running the show and he was best at setting the scene.

"Meredith, I know this is a tough time. Just need to get an idea of when…."

"Bonnie, I'm not sure. I think by Sunday evening we should be back. I know we have the budget crunch on Monday and the school board's decision should be in by Wednesday. I don't plan to miss any of that, unless…." Her voice trailed off. She hated putting work thoughts first when her father-in-law's health was so poor.

Bonnie walked up to her boss, stood beside her, and put a firm hand on her shoulder.

"Meredith, we understand. We are so sorry. We're here if you need us. Call us when you get there."

"Of course. I will. I'm just…."

"Meredith, go!" Darryl gently took her elbow and turned her toward the door glancing at Bonnie concerned.

"OK, OK, I'm going. Thank you, both of you. I'll talk with you soon and…."

"Harmony? Hi there. Make sure the driver is downstairs for Meredith. We're coming down." Darryl smiled sweetly at his boss's administrative assistant. She was efficient enough, and with everything so new, it was nice that Meredith could bring one familiar thing with her as she tackled mayoral life. He was still out on Meredith's innate ability, but he was damn sure that he would do his best, and either way, she or whomever filled her shoes next would be a fool not to keep him on. He had what it took to run the show and he did admire the attention Meredith drew. Anyone in politics knew that money couldn't buy that attention. He would ride this wave as long as he could. He liked the sudden change of events and he saw something in his new boss that few were privy to, yet. She just possibly had what this country needed right now. "TAB". Tits, Ass, and Brains.

He waved Bonnie back as the elevator opened. There was plenty to do and Meredith didn't need two chaperones to escort her down to the lobby. Bonnie didn't object, knowing full well that her roll was to get back in the office and keep things running. The admiration that she had for her boss mellowed her absent concerns, but she sometimes wished Meredith would respond to her as she did with Darryl. He was able to nurture her more. She, after all, was heterosexual and Bonnie knew there was no changing that, but she couldn't dismiss that sometimes the sight of her new boss made her quiver. Nothing ever made her unstable and this passing infatuation would disappear quickly. Bonnie Sinclair had overcome too many obstacles to let a fleeting fantasy foul up her plans. She knew Meredith Nicholson's history and there was something there that she had never encountered in her foraging career. A female politician with brass balls. There was no doubt in Bonnie's mind that Meredith Nicholson was something special. Even a fool like Milton Stafford couldn't miss seeing that.

Meredith stared out the tinted windows of the sedan as the driver inched the vehicle through the congested city traffic. She thought how easy it would've been to commute to their old home from the capital, but of course there was no choice but to move into the Mayor's mansion on the south side of the city. Connor had been so worried about changing schools, but now only whined about the hour earlier he had to wake to be driven to his old school. Being Mayor had its advantages, but since the announcement, things just weren't quite right between the two of them. She knew how hard change was and having a very public parent didn't make it any easier. Of course Mayor was a little different than police chief, but even so she felt that she could relate and had tried numerous times since the move to talk with her oldest. If anything at school was wrong, he just denied it. She had to trust that Milton would talk with him. The thought of her husband and her own father brought on the melancholy and she quickly diverted her attention to the winter scene of the Boston Public Gardens.

"It's a terrible time to be sick!"

Bonnie didn't look up. His cologne always reached his destination before him.

"I know, but what can we do?"

"We can run this place, like she's here, and when anyone calls, we can be her. I know your voice is much lower, Bon, but we need to practice."

She finally looked at him and cracked a smile.

"Hmmm, it's nice to see that beautiful smile. You look so much more beautiful when...."

"OK, that's enough. We have a lot of work to do and I don't want Meredith to be overwhelmed when she gets back."

"Did you go over the campaign agenda yet with her?"

"No, I didn't. The call from her mother-in-law had interrupted the meeting.

"All right. Then that's the first thing we need to do—start the analysis and polling and see exactly where we are so far."

"Start without Meredith?"

"Yes. Aren't you interested in the polls?"

"Of course I am, but I just thought maybe Meredith...."

"Meredith's the Mayor of this fine city and it's our job to get her reelected, correct?"

"Of course."

"Any other questions?" Darryl smiled at her.

"Hmm, just one. Exactly how big is your prick again?"

CHAPTER 20

"Yes, yes. I understand. We need to set up a meeting as soon as I get back. I know...Yes...Well, I'll have to get back to you on that...No...We should be there shortly and...." Meredith glanced over at Milton who had not looked at her—at anyone—since they had started for New Hampshire. "Yes, Bonnie, yes I know...Good, then I will see you when I get back and...Bonnie, thank you...Yes of course I will tell him...all right."

The large SUV made its way confidently on the single-lane highway. The road was covered with fresh snow, keeping the rest of the residents of New Hampshire inside.

"Bonnie sends her prayers," Meredith said quietly as she disconnected the call.

Milton stayed motionless, ignoring the comment.

"Milton?"

He turned toward his wife, his eyes still swollen from the night before.

"Milton?" Meredith asked again more quietly, touching his hand when she did.

"Yes, Meredith."

"Bonnie sends her prayers."

"I heard you, Meredith. Please tell Bonnie thank you. I'm sure she can't wait for this all to be over so she can get you back where you belong."

"Milton, please!"

"Never mind, Meredith. Please, can we just be quiet? We're less than an hour away and I really don't have anything to say right now."

"Of course, darling. I love you."

"I love you too, Meredith."

Connor and Emily were in the vehicle just ahead of theirs. It was common now to separate them from the children, especially on road trips, since Meredith, though surprisingly popular, also had a few enemies that had made themselves very clear when she was handed the keys to the city. She watched the vehicle ahead, bobbing through the unplowed slow, looking for a sign of one of her children. She knew Milton would much prefer to be with them right now, while her cell phone persisted on ringing. They made him smile, and in this sad time, it was very hard to see him distraught, knowing that she could do nothing but wait. She held his hand lightly and closed her eyes.

When they arrived, Beth was waiting outside, tackling the snow that kept piling up in the driveway.

"Mom."

"Oh Milton, I'm so glad you're here."

He reached over to hug her and whispered, "Can't we get a plow service, or someone to help you with this?"

She smiled. "It's really not that bad and it's good to get some fresh air. Plus I knew that I would have strong men here shortly to help me with this task." She lifted Connor's ski cap and messed his hair as she reached for a hug.

"Where is my little girl?"

Meredith walked around the other side of the sedan with Emily in her arms and for a second, hoped that Beth meant her and not her grandchild. She needed a mom hug herself right now.

"There she is. Oh Emily, you're getting so big."

Emily smiled and reached for her grandmother. Milton smiled as his mother nuzzled in his baby girl's neck. "Aren't you a sight for sore eyes!"

Meredith kicked at a piece of ice, always uncomfortable when people mentioned sight in front of her daughter. Of course there was no malice and Emily didn't understand, but Meredith hated the fact that her daughter could not see everything she saw. Milton always reminded her that blind people could see, just not in the conventional way. Meredith wanted to believe that, but it didn't make it any easier.

Milton wrapped his arm around Meredith, maneuvering her around the snow pile.

"Hi, Meredith." Beth said sweetly, winking to thank her.

"Hi, Beth." Meredith stopped and kissed her on the cheek, Emily's hand reaching for her lips as she giggled.

"Come on now, everyone inside. Grandpa has been waiting for you and he gets grumpy if we make him wait too long."

Meredith looked back at both the drivers and smiled. In doing so, they smiled back and each grabbed a shovel to finish the driveway.

"Well, well. What do we have here?"

Connor ran towards his grandfather, wrapped tightly in an afghan on the couch, and pounced on his lap.

"Connor! Be careful!" Meredith called from the kitchen.

"Oh it's all right. My goodness. You're getting quite big. Maybe a little too big to sit on my lap. How old are you now?" he asked. A little joke they always shared.

"Grandpa, you know. I'm 8. I was here for my birthday, remember?"

"Oh yes, that's right. Not really on your birthday though. Seems you had bigger plans with all your friends in the city."

"Oh Grandpa, we had so much fun. We went to the science museum and we saw them operate on a frog."

"Really? A frog? Hmmm, that must've been something." He gently nudged his grandson a few inches over, relieving some of the pressure.

Milton and Meredith stood in the kitchen doorway, Emily still in her grandmother's arms.

"Well, well, seems I must be quite popular today. Everyone's here to see me?'

They all smiled.

"Hello Meredith. It's good to see you Mrs. Mayor. Where's my granddaughter?"

"Hi Dad. She's right here." Meredith reached for Emily and placed her on his lap. Emily smiled again, pulling at his short white beard."

"My goodness, little one. You look like an angel."

Milton stepped towards his father.

"Hello Son."

"Hi Dad."

"I'm glad you're here."

"Me too, Dad. Me too."

An hour later, with the women in the kitchen and Connor outside making a snowman, Milton pulled a chair beside his father, Emily asleep in his arms.

"Do you want to put her down, Son?"

"No Dad, I'm fine. She hardly ever falls asleep in my arms anymore. It's nice. I miss it."

Pete Stafford smiled at his son then down at his granddaughter. He understood all too well the joys of fatherhood.

"I remember when you were that little."

"Long time ago now, huh?"

"Not that long ago. Your mother, grandfather and I used to argue on whose turn it was to rock you to sleep or read you a book. It really was funny. Three grownups just craving your attention."

"I remember, Dad."

"You remember when you were her size, Milton?" His father teased.

"I think I do Dad. Really, I think I do."

They both smiled at the sleeping baby.

"Dad?"

"Son, we really don't have to talk about it."

"I know Dad. I just want you to know how much I love you."

"Milton, you're the best son anyone could dream of having. You've been the light of our lives. Your mother and I are so proud of you. Your grandfather would be so proud of you."

Milton glanced around the living room, wondering if maybe he would appear.

"Dad, I wish I had been the one to cure what is making you sick."

"I know, Son. Boy do I know. Your grandfather wanted to do the same for your grandmother, and I'm sure so many people want to do it for someone that they love. It's all right, Son. It's just my time."

"Dad, you're young."

"Young at heart maybe, but this body has decided that it's seen enough and, well, I have to go with that I guess."

"Dad, would you reconsider the options?"

"Milton, no. I am through with the chemo and through with the radiation. I remember how much better my mother felt when she was here at her home in Wolfeboro. That was her best medicine. I'm sorry, Son. I know it's very hard. I'm going to miss all of you so much. I'm going to miss your mother the most. You need to take care of her Milton. You need to be here for her."

"Of course, Dad, of course. I hate talking about this like it's over. Maybe, just maybe?"

"No, Milton. It's just a matter of time. I love you. I love you so much."

Milton got down on the floor beside the couch, still clutching Emily, and laid his head on his father's chest. They both cried quietly, watching the snow disappear as it hit the tiny ripples on the lake.

Milton inched along the expressway with the thousands of other commuters trying to make it to work. He looked at the decorated oil tank and his eyes filled. A week before, with his mother on one side and Meredith and the children on the other, they buried his father on a hill overlooking Lake Winnipesaukee. Milton spent several more days with his mother after the funeral while Meredith needed to get back to the city. He watched as she and the children were driven away and wondered what life would be like now. He felt sure that something had changed and he was not exactly sure how he was going to cope. He remembered his father's words and minded his mother, who, in grief, was remarkably strong and positive. He wandered the snowmobile trails in the woods, asking over and over for his grandfather to please show himself. No one answered back.

"Goddamn it, Pop. I really need to talk with you!" He slammed the steering wheel with both hands, then roughly put the car in park in a space several hundred yards from the entrance to his building. He sat with the car idling, wondering how he was going to get through the day, any day, with the sadness he was feeling. He reached for his open briefcase and was about to open the door when he heard, "Aren't you going to turn off the car, Son?"

He looked in the rearview mirror, his grandfather smiling back at him.

"Oh yes, sure, I was going to turn it off. I was just…."

"Leave it on for a few seconds. Don't want it to get too cold in here." His grandfather was now sitting in the passenger seat where his open briefcase had lain.

"Pop, where have you been?"

"I've been here all the time, Son."

"But, I was looking for you, calling for you, I really needed you. Dad's dead."

"Now Milton, don't you know that I know that? Of course I know that. It's an amazing thing having your grandmother and your father with me now. I know it's hard, but Son, you have to get moving. You have to remember; now we're both with you. We'll always be with you."

"Dad's with you right now, Pop?"

"Not at this very minute, Son. It's hard to explain. You just need to know that we're here and that we'll always be with you."

"I don't know, Pop. I'm so overwhelmed right now."

His grandfather's hand touched his arm.

"Milton. Please, Son. You're needed here on this earth and it's time to get back to your life. No one will ever understand death and it'll never be easy, but you're lucky. You have me to tell you that."

Milton smiled. He felt the touch of his hand. Maybe his way of coping was better than some.

"Pop, what's next?"

"Oh boy, here we go again. You know I can't tell you that, but listen. Listen to your heart, Son Big things are coming your way."

"Please tell Dad I said hello and I love him."

"You just did, Son."

Then he was gone. Milton turned the engine off and walked inside, smiling.

CHAPTER 21

Meredith was about to embark on her most challenging voyage yet. Granted the Mayor's seat by default, she was now engulfed in a full fledge reelection campaign. Her staff, Bonnie and Darryl included, worked endless hours to keep their Democrat in control. Not only did they have to consider the Republican Party beating down the door, but contingents from their own party were hungry for the power.

Victor Floramo was the ex-police commissioner of Boston and her strongest opponent. He had been a Democrat and a decent man when he had run the department, but several years before, in his second term, he had resigned mid-stream, due to personal reasons. Speculations ran wild, despite rumors of marriage problems and a cancer scare that never surfaced. He disappeared, only to resurface still married and apparently cancer-free, ready for another fight. He had opened a popular Italian restaurant on the city's revamped waterfront, which in turn reestablished him in his community and in the hearts of the many that felt a man needed to run the city. He was suddenly a born-again Republican and a menace to Meredith's staff. After ten months in office Meredith felt her political world capsizing.

Floramo's tactics were dirty, but not below the belt. He denounced Meredith for being soft on criminals with her strong opposition to the death penalty and he charged her with a lackluster record for the homeless in the city, and claimed she was more concerned with potholes in the road than with potheads in the schools. He threw fury again and again over the hand slaps the Catholic priests accused of sexual misconduct were being given. It didn't help that her own brother was a fervent priest in the city's Irish section of town.

Floramo had the support of the police association and a not-so-surprising majority of the male vote. Meredith held her ground with the minority population and the environmental groups but it didn't prove enough. Floramo won the Mayor's seat with 64percent of the vote and Meredith stepped down quietly and gracefully. Hundreds of supporters were outside her office as she left for the last time. She could barely wave as she walked the steps of her City Hall one last time.

Charlie and David sat in the sun-drenched living room of Meredith and Milton's new home in Falmouth. Milton had been eyeing it for months and Meredith agreed hastily when they had no choice but to move from the Mayor's mansion. Meredith came in with a pot of coffee and mugs and a small pitcher of orange juice. She was dressed in tight Levi's and a white V-neck T-shirt, her hair pulled back in a ponytail with the elastic from the morning paper. Charlie and David both smiled. She looked ten tears younger and they agreed with a look, that maybe politics was not the best thing for her.

"Meredith, you look wonderful!" Charlie stood to help her with the tray, then grabbed her and gave her a loving hug.

"You do, Meredith. My goodness, you look like our kid sister again."

"All right you two. That's enough. It's been almost a year since my fiasco and I have to say I've been somewhat of a selfish homebody ever since. Anybody for a mimosa?"

"Meredith?" David leaned forward and took her hands in his. "You are an incredible woman, and you deserved some 'you' time. The past three years have been, well, for lack of a better term, chaotic. I don't mean that in a bad way, just the last 3 are a bit of a blur."

Meredith eyed her oldest brother and didn't respond. She knew he only had good intentions and he'd been an asset and advisor so many times in her life. She wasn't about to argue with him. She remembered every moment of the last 3 years and was finding the past one the most challenging. She was finding the sabbatical draining. She poured herself a glass of champagne; double-checking the clock to make sure it was past noon.

"Meredith? Merree?" Charlie smiled sweetly as he teased his sister out of her fog. "Isn't it a little early for that?" She giggled, predicting which brother would react first, then sighed when David helped himself to a small glass of bubbly as well.

Charlie continued, less concerned. "I'm glad you called, Meredith. Your home looks beautiful. You've done a wonderful job." He stood to admire the view, holding his coffee close. Charlie's past year had been full of sadness and torment.

The pastor of his own church, and Charlie's mentor, was now on trial for heinous crimes against children and he was barely able to work, due to the ongoing investigation and heartache for his friend. Meredith had been so caught up in her own turmoil, that she had found it difficult to address her brother's grief. For one, she had denounced the church so long ago, a victim of her own parents' guilt, and as a mother she found it very difficult not to feel rage against the crime and the criminal. Her feelings about the death penalty were far less stringent.

"Thank you, Charlie. I'm so glad you could come too." She stood and put her arm around his shoulder, following his gaze towards the bay. "I'm sorry about everything Charlie. I know the past year has been terrible for you."

He looked down at his sister and smiled. "Hush now. God works in mysterious ways and I plan to make things right at my church, for the parishioners and the good of the Catholic religion. I know this city has been traumatized. There's no time for me to be that way. All right then? Is there any champagne left?" Meredith looked back at David, hoping to see him smile, but he was staring off, in his own world.

"David?" She motioned for him to join them.

"How are you, big brother?" she asked as she extended her free arm around his shoulders.

"I'm fine, little sister. Just fine."

"How's Katherine?" It had been two months since Meredith had spoken with her sister-in-law, who was struggling with a bout of depression, unable to become pregnant.

"She's all right Mere. She's, well really, she's so sad."

"David, you'll be parents, I just know it. Have you done any more investigating on the adoption end?"

"She just can't stop thinking that if we only had our own. I would love to adopt and Charlie has offered his guidance through their charity, but she just is deaf to the idea. I wish you'd come see her Mere. She would love to see you."

Meredith winced slightly. The thought of crossing the bridge back to the mainland brought an anxiety that she continued to avoid.

"I will, David. I will. Or she can come here. Stay a few days. We can walk the beach and talk girl-talk, hmm?"

"I'll ask her, Meredith, but call her OK?"

"Of course I will. I'll call her later today."

The three smiled as they saw the remaining clan approaching the house. Milton lugging a soft cooler in one arm, Emily, now three, in his other arm, and Connor running ten steps ahead with a fishing pole.

"Mere, we need to talk about Dad."

"I know, Charlie. I know."

David shifted his weight and finished his champagne, leaving the begging to his brother.

"His condition is worse. The diabetes has really taken a toll on his legs. Since he retired, he's been really depressed and Mom is so frustrated with him. Prayers aren't the only thing they need right now. Meredith, he needs to see you."

Meredith watched as Milton placed Emily on the grass and unloaded the cooler into the garage. Connor had positioned himself on the other side of the open door, where he safely could practice casting. She watched as Emily made her way, with no fear, around the yard, her mouth moving, presumably singing one of the songs Beatrice had taught her. She saw her husband smile and swoop his little girl up onto his shoulders, calling for Connor who came quickly, when his father pointed to his Uncle's cars in the driveway.

"Charlie, David, I'm so sorry I have caused you both so much pain with my relationship with Dad. I miss our childhood. I miss him coming home and Mom cooking and our fort. I miss Tommy and Amy and Jerome. I've been so stubborn and because of that have missed almost two decades of Mom and Dad's life and they of mine…I'll go…I'll go."

"We can go with you. You're not alone here."

"No, I know that, but I'll go and I'll do it by myself. I have to do that."

Connor came barreling into the house and was only stopped by a bear hug from David. Milton came in with Emily who reached for her Uncle Charlie and tugged at his collar. Milton reached for his wife and instinctively knew that something wonderful had just happened. She clung to him, as he wiped the last tear from her eye.

CHAPTER 22

Gerald Revo was becoming a dynamo. The Senate had tagged him as an anonymous fledgling at first, but as 1995 quickly approached, he was getting more than his feet wet in politics. With a seemingly mild demeanor and a passion unparalleled, he was focused and precise with his work. When the bill to punish drunk drivers more frequently and swiftly was introduced, he pounced and it was passed. He abhorred alcohol and, though prevalent among his peers, he never indulged and believed ones who broke the law should pay. Alcohol disabled one's ability to think clearly and a soldier needed to always be in control. He never indulged and soon made it clear that he didn't appreciate those who could not control it. Mothers Against Drunk Driving named him their unofficial spokesperson.

He was also outspoken in his support of the bill that passed transferring certain juvenile procedures to criminal jurisdiction. Another deliberate motion, strongly enhanced by his own upbringing. He didn't believe a juvenile's thoughts to be any different than an adult's. If he had murdered someone intentionally at the age of fifteen, he would've expected a lifetime of incarceration or even the penalty of death as just punishment. He believed that the death penalty, strongly enforced, would eliminate most crime. This was only the beginning.

Under the wing of the Speaker of the House, he presided as the Budget Committee Chairman and was commended when the Republicans muscled a sweeping balanced budget through the Senate, disregarding the President's threat of veto. It was an important day for the Republicans. It was an even more important day for Gerald Revo.

He stood five-foot-seven, but even the salty Democrats seemed to bend a knee when he passed. He was a closed book, and for many that meant secrets needed to be revealed, to admonish his ego. But as a decorated officer and one with little time to create scandal, he remained respected and a very bright light for the Republican Party. He was encouraged to marry and several times was photographed with a special lady from his home state, who always appeared to be hiding behind him. She was a blonde southern belle, with three inches on him, but he declined to speak of his personal life and after a few exploits in the tabloids, she was never seen again. He would do anything for his party and for power, but if he had the choice, he would remain single. The thought of marriage repulsed him almost as much as the current President, but he spoke of neither. Gerald Revo was a bright bigot, like his father, and there were few quiet, obedient women like his mother, left in the world. He understood that if it became necessary, he would indulge.

His good looks and celebrity status intrigued both women and men. The camera helped enhance his height and charisma and he was considered a very eligible bachelor. He was tactful where and when he was seen and prudently enjoyed his rising fame. It was rare that a politician evoked such charm and, in the months to follow, Gerald Revo evoked a perfect balance between religion and state, Hollywood glitz and the capital dome. Good versus evil.

"Gerald? Gerald, over here. I want you to meet a friend of mine."

Gerald excused himself from the boring conversation the Prince of Saudi Arabia had dragged him into and walked over to what he was sure was another ridiculous brand of morons. He despised these state dinners, but respectfully attended every one that he was invited to, and they were adding up monthly.

The Democratic Senator that had interrupted was now waving foolishly, acting as if they were old friends. Gerald took every step when he could to avoid Southern Democrats, afraid he might not be able to hold his tongue. This one in particular took every occasion to slap him on the back or introduce him to someone new, with the hopes that a little of his popularity would rub off on him. He clenched his teeth as he approached.

"Gerald! Hello! Great to see you big guy." He grasped the unwelcoming hand by his side and slapped him heartily on the back.

Gerald smiled. "Nice to see you too, Frank. You're looking good. Been working out there, huh big guy?" He pointed to his portly middle and Frank crossed his arms around himself, embarrassed.

"Yeah, right! Anyway, Gerald, I want you to meet a friend of mine. Damion, Damion Desmond. Damion is from the south like us, Gerry, and, well, he wanted to meet you."

"Mr. Desmond." Gerald acknowledged with a slight tilt of his head.

"Yes, Mr. Revo. It's a pleasure to meet you. Frank was telling me all about you."

"Really? I hope all good?"

"Of course." Frank turned, laughing into his cocktail napkin as he slugged back the rest of his martini.

"Hmm, have you known Frank long, Mr. Desmond?"

"Please call me Damion."

"Of course, Damion. Have you known our friend Frank here long?"

"No, Senator. May I call you Gerald?"

"Of course."

"Gerald. No. I've known Frank here for less than ten minutes."

"Oh, really? Frank? I thought you said Mr. Desmond was your friend."

Frank's face was flushed. "Oh Gerry, I meant, well, he introduced himself and wanted to meet you and, well, since I know you so well, I thought you wouldn't mind."

"Not at all, Frank. That's fine. Mr. Desmond, was there something I could do for you?" Gerald's sarcastic tone was more to embarrass Frank, than to offend this admirer.

"As a matter of fact if you don't mind, Frank?" Damion Desmond looked at Frank in a way, that anyone with a little common sense would understand he was not welcome anymore. Frank had little common sense.

"Yes?" Frank asked, hoping to get into a good old southern discussion.

"Frank. I was wondering if you could give Mr. Revo and myself a moment alone."

"Oh yeah, sure. I, well, I guess I'll get another drink. Can I get you fellas anything?"

Both declined and Frank sauntered off to the closest bar so he could keep tabs on his friends.

"That is the sort of thing we hunt for sport, where I'm from." Damion glanced casually towards the bar and Gerald snickered lightly.

"Exactly where is that, Mr. Desmond?"

"Damion, please. That would be Texas, Gerald. Houston, Texas to be exact."

"Oh, I see." Gerald glanced around the room for better company. He'd never met a Texan he liked.

"Have you ever been to Texas, Gerald?"

"Um, yes. A few times as a youngster. Big state. Yep, big damn state. Damion, right? I'm sorry. I have obligations I need to attend to. Was there anything else?" Gerald's pompous yet polite attitude amused Damion Desmond. He had known men like this before and he was sure even this one had obvious weaknesses. He had been hired to do a job and he always followed through with commitments.

"Gerald, I'm sorry. I know you're very busy so I'll get right to the point. I'm a Texan, and as I stated before and I have a great interest in your future."

"Really?" Gerald was getting irritated.

"Yes. I'm in oil down in Texas, and well I think that we may have a few things in common."

"Really? And how is that Mr. Desmond?"

"Well, I have lots of money and I think you might be needing lots of money in the near future?"

Gerald looked directly into the stranger's eyes, waiting for the sign. The flicker of someone's eye, right before the lie. He saw it all the time, from everyone he met, and he found humor in detecting the bullshit before it was thrown. Desmond's eyes were black. All Gerald could see was his own reflection.

"What exactly are you getting at, Mr. Desmond?"

"I think you might be interested in running for President, Gerald and I'm interested in helping you attain that goal."

Gerald turned away, once again scanning the ballroom for better company, but he turned back smiling wide, "What makes you think I want to run for President, Mr. Desmond?"

"It's just a hunch, Gerald, and please call me Damion. And, in case you're interested, I would be your Chief of Staff."

CHAPTER 23

"Milton?" Dick Salinger's puckered face was mouthing through the window.

Milton lifted his goggles and looked at his boss perplexed. He opened the door and asked, "Yes Professor?"

Salinger slipped inside uncomfortably.

"Milton, I'm sorry to interrupt your work, but did you receive my memo?"

Milton fidgeted as he took off his gloves. He received memos everyday and they never pertained to him. He even asked himself on a daily basis, as he tossed each one in the basket or folded it up as a coaster, why they persisted on sending the whole company a memo when it was in regards to quarterly sales or the new IS project. There were plenty of trees worth saving.

"Milton, did you hear me?"

His lab was as quiet as a funeral home, so the sarcastic question annoyed him, persuading him to lie. "Yes, I think so, Professor. Which one are you referring too?"

"Milton, it was the one I addressed, about a meeting I wanted to set up with you."

Milton stood motionless. He was stuck.

"I'm sorry Professor. I've been so busy and I haven't had time to contact you in regards to that."

Salinger buttoned his lab coat and shook his head. "Milton, I'm not sure you understand the importance of this project"

"Professor Salinger, of course I understand the importance of this project. I've understood and been reliable on the hundreds of projects. I'm not sure what you're referring to, or what action of mine states that I don't understand."

"Milton?" Salinger moved closer and said quietly, "I'm sorry, I've been under a lot of pressure lately. I really need to speak with you in private."

Milton glanced around the lab. In the adjacent room, through the glass panels, there were two techs prepping for a case. But in the immediate area, there were Salinger, Milton, and two lab rats spinning on their wheels.

"Of course, Professor. Is this not private enough?"

"No, Milton. I'd rather meet in my office."

"Now?" Milton asked. The table was covered with specimens he was about to review.

"No, no. Not now. When you're done here. How about lunch?"

Milton had been working for the company and Professor Salinger for more than 10 years and had never been asked nor wanted to have lunch with his boss.

"Lunch? Uh, sure. Lunch would be fine. I usually take lunch at, ugh, well, I usually don't have a lunchtime."

"Lunchtime it is then. How about one o'clock in my office?"

"One sounds fine, sir."

"Good. I'll see you then and keep up the good work." Salinger left through the side door and gave an awkward salute as he passed the glass window.

Milton waved back uncomfortably. Anytime a scientist was asked to have lunch with the boss, someone got fired. Salinger had started with the company at the same level that Milton was now. He had never excelled, being a mediocre scientist, yet had wowed the hierarchy by ass-kissing and taking credit for other people's work and climbed swiftly up the corporate ladder. He still donned a lab coat as if he was a player-coach, but everyone on Milton's team knew otherwise. He was neither respected nor liked, yet he was the one in charge and letting people go was what he did best. Milton worried about what Meredith would say when he came home with a pink slip and the contents of his desk in one box. Two at home unemployed was going to be very difficult

Finding it impossible to concentrate, he looked more at his wristwatch then at the specimens he was testing. At 12:30 he assembled and stored what he was working on and filed the data entry. He washed his hands and made his way to his cramped, closet-sized office. He replaced his lab coat with a blazer, straightened a few tidy piles of memos and research statistical books and sat down to wait. He contemplated calling Meredith but decided against it. For the last year she had spent most of her waking hours with Emily or Connor when he came home from school and he didn't need to ruin their lunchtime. At precisely 12:59 he made his way down the hall and took the stairs two flights up to the executive offices. As the clock struck one, Salinger's secretary was announcing over the speakerphone that he had arrived.

"Don't keep him waiting, Marjorie. Send him in."

Marjorie looked at Milton without emotion, signaling to him that it was all right to enter. Milton was convinced she had seen the scenario so many times, and just had to separate herself from the axes that fell behind her.

"Hello, Milton. Please come in. Marjorie?" He was on the speakerphone, even though her desk was three feet from the open door, "can you please make sure that those sandwiches and sodas are delivered and after that, we are not to be disturbed?"

"Yes, Professor. Of course."

It pained Milton to hear her call him professor. He'd been instructed when he started at the company to call him professor, and he was acutely aware of the status. Salinger had received the title through speaking engagements. An invite from Milton's own alma mater to address the graduates of the class of 1980 solidified the label. Milton had thought it a desperate act by the school but ignored his own angst, calling him by his title. When he heard Salinger's slave saluting him, he cursed the hypocrisy. Salinger was a professor as much as Milton was tight end for the Patriots.

"Milton, please have a seat."

As Milton settled into the leather chair there was a slight knock at the door and Marjorie entered with his last meal. She declined to look his way. Milton felt badly for her, even with his own state of affairs. He would have to let Beatrice go. Emily would be crushed.

"Thank you, Marjorie. Remember what I said?"

"Yes. Of course Professor." She closed the door firmly behind her.

"There now, let's see what the kitchen whipped up for us." Salinger unwrapped a few packages, exposing New York, deli-style sandwiches on freshly baked rye bread. There were containers of cole slaw and baked beans and enormous barrel pickles. He even exposed two large slices of apple pie. Milton was impressed and knew immediately that the lunch had not come from the employee cafeteria. The food confirmed the rumors, that the bosses upstairs had their own chef. At least Salinger was treating him to a good meal before he escorted him to his car.

Milton did not hesitate, suddenly voracious. All the years of service and this is what he was offered? He would've requested wine if they had offered.

"Not bad huh?" Salinger smiled as he caught Milton's approval on his face. "Here you go Mr. Stafford. Wouldn't want you to have to work all day with mustard on your face." Milton accepted the napkin and declined to blush. *Fuck you, too,* Milton thought as he wiped his mouth

"So, Milton, how's everything going?" Milton eyed his boss through the massive second half of his sandwich.

"Fine, Professor Salinger. Just fine, thank you." He bit down hard on a crisp, dill pickle.

"Good. That's good to hear. I'll let you finish. You seem to be enjoying the lunch." Milton dared at that moment to tell his boss just how terrible the food was downstairs and how inappropriate it was to have such decadence upstairs, but the baked beans were still steaming. It would be a shame to let them get cold.

The next ten minutes were a quiet gluttony, mostly by the shameless scientist. When all but a spoonful of coleslaw had been consumed, Salinger whisked the plates and forks from the side table and handed Milton a fresh-brewed-cup of coffee. Milton knew Marjorie probably spent half her day fetching it for him. Bastard.

"Cream and sugar?"

"No. No thank you. I take it black." He watched as his boss added heavy cream and five cubes of sugar to his own cup. Then he started to stir. Nothing could sweeten this asshole.

"Well, then. I'm glad you enjoyed the lunch. We should do this more often."

Milton almost choked on his coffee thinking, *that might be hard with you here and me in my kitchen on the cape, Sir.* Instead he garbled, "That would be very nice, Mr. Salinger."

"Dick. Please call me Dick, Milton."

Milton closed his eyes, not allowing the burning liquid to cool in his mouth, and swallowed it and his laughter in a scalding gulp. He breathed in deeply. "OK then. Dick, yes we should do this more often."

"Great, then, anyways. I wanted to speak with you in private about a few matters of importance that I don't care to share with your team right now." He continued to stir his coffee, clanking the side of his cup. Milton wanted to break his hand.

Here it is, Milton thought. "Yes and what might those be, Professor?" he answered.

"Dick. Please, Milton. We've known each other a long time."

"I'm sorry. Dick. What might those be?" Milton was feeling nauseous.

"Well you know the quarter numbers are down and how important it is for us to remain one of the leaders in the science world?"

"Sure. Um, yes, of course, Dick." Milton leaned back, bracing himself for the inevitable, loosening his tie. He wished he had read more of the damn memos.

"You've proven your worth, all these years with the company, and I think it might be time for a change."

"A change, Dick?"

"Yes, Milton. A change. We've become affiliated with a controversial, highly important grant and are looking for a manager to head up project."

Milton looked perplexed.

"And Milton, we've made the decision that you're the perfect candidate for the role."

Milton continued to stare.

"Well, how does that sound to you?"

"Uh, it sounds fine, sir. I'm just surprised. I guess I wasn't completely sure why I was here to begin with."

"You mean here in my office?"

"Yes sir."

"Well, I'm here to make you an offer and hope that you'll accept."

"I'm all ears sir."

"The project, as I said, is highly sensitive."

"Yes sir. You did. May I ask what it pertains to?"

"Of course. It has come straight from the capital. We've been hired to help find an antidote or cure for the Persian Gulf War Syndrome."

"I see." Milton breathed deeply. He wasn't going to be fired today. He was being promoted.

"Are you familiar with the syndrome?" Salinger leaned toward Milton as he said this, whispering the last word.

"Yes, of course I am, sir. I've read numerous accounts on the fallout from the war. I understand it starts as a flu-like symptom and has been known to progress to aches and pains, comparable to arthritis. I believe lesions and simultaneous rashes run rampant?"

"Yes, yes, those are the most common side effects, but it's becoming an epidemic and the government is stepping up the studies to make sure that we nip this one in the bud."

"Really? I thought our government denied its existence?"

Salinger now stared at Milton, hoping to make him nervous. Milton wanted to laugh.

"There are many questions in regards to the aftermath of that war. Bio-chemical weapons were used by the enemy! It's imperative that everything be done to contain and control the syndrome. We need to help our sick soldiers. But it must be kept confidential, until it's clear that we've succeeded and the FDA can approve it. It must be kept confidential from our enemies!"

"I see." Milton nodded.

"Good. Are you interested?"

"In what? Sir? The project? Will I be able to handpick my own team?"

"Milton. I'm sorry, my fault. This would be a solo project. You would have no team."

Confused, Milton blurted, "No team, Dickey?"

Salinger smiled. "It's all right, my family calls me that. Dick is fine, and I'm sorry, no team, Milton. This is something that needs to be done as a solo project and we believe you're brilliant enough to do this on your own."

"But what about my other projects?"

Salinger's hand waved as if he had dismissed him. "Those will be taken care of."

"But I'm in the middle of several very important projects that I've been working on for almost a year."

"Yes, Milton, I'm very aware of that. This is the most important one now and I understand and commend the loyalty to your work. That is why I asked you here today. If you're not interested…."

"Dick. Professor Salinger. I've been working on a chromosome match for pancreatic cancer. I've made enormous strides since I've started. I think that it's very important too and…

"Milton Stafford, of course I understand the important decision this is. Why do you think we hired those three new, very promising techs from the other company? They're very willing and able to take on where you'll leave off. They're excited about your work and are anxious to be a part of your legacy. Nothing will be left alone."

Milton contemplated this. His boss had already hired people to take over his work. It was like leaving his children with Beatrice. Of course they would be all right, but they were his children.

"What else does this exactly entail, Dick?"

"We can get to the logistics next time Milton. I just wanted to give you a chance to roll it around and see what you thought. Of course, there would be a lucrative raise."

Milton now focused at his scuffed shoes. A raise? He hadn't thought of a raise. He didn't care about new shoes, but a raise would be nice. Indeed.

"We would give you 20 percent on top of your salary starting tomorrow and give you a month or so to transfer your current work over to highly capable hands. Each quarter, we would evaluate where you are with the project and after certain stipulations are met, you'd be in line for a $25,000 bonus per quarter."

"Per quarter?" Milton asked, eyes wide.

"Yes, per quarter. That's how important this is to our company, Milton, our country. So, what do you think?"

"Of course, it sounds wonderful, sir. I just need this evening to think about it, talk about it with my wife. I can get back with you in the morning."

Salinger walked around the table and sat in the chair adjacent to Milton. Leaning forward, his breath smelling of Bermuda onions, he said quietly "Milton. Maybe I didn't make myself clear and I apologize. This cannot go any further than this room. Neither your wife, your friends, nor your colleagues can be made privy to this information. Ever. I'm sure your wife will be happy about the salary adjustment?"

Milton leaned as far into the chair as he could to avoid the revolting breath. He knew that it was common knowledge that his wife was still not working after the election, but he disliked his boss referring to her at all.

"Hmm. I suppose she would Dick. In that case may I take the evening to think about it on my own?"

"I'm sorry Milton, but I can only give you the afternoon. You can back with me by five. All right then?"

"Yes, sir. Five."

Salinger looked as his watch and added. "I'll hear from you then?"

"Uh, yes sir." Milton stood and shook Salinger's outstretched hand.

Milton let himself out as Salinger reached for the phone. This time Marjorie smiled at him and he casually smiled back. The lack of yelling or crying behind closed doors must have alerted her to be cordial. Not only had he not been fired (thank goodness he had not called Meredith first), but he had left his boss's office extremely full and a whole lot richer. His whistling echoed in the stairwell, as he descended back to reality.

"I think we got him," Salinger said confidently into the phone, "Yes sir...No...I'm sure it will work out, sir...No, I mean I know it will work out sir...Yes, I know sir...You can depend on me sir...Of course. I'll take care of everything...Yes sir. I understand...."

Salinger hung up the phone as Milton began to scrutinize the first of thousands of internet files on the Gulf War Syndrome. Both men were smiling.

CHAPTER 24

When Milton arrived home, dinner was waiting but his wife wasn't. She had left instructions with Beatrice, who was watching over the stove, while Emily drew elaborate crayon drawings at the table.

"Hello, my princess!" Milton bent down to kiss his daughter's head

Emily beamed. "Hi, Daddy, Mommy's not home. But, she has a shur-rrrrprize."

"A surprise? Hmm, I wonder what that might be?" He tousled her hair and smiled at Beatrice, "Any idea?'

"No, Mr. Stafford. I'm sorry, I have no idea?"

"Beatrice, it's been four years. Think it's time now that you can call me Milton?"

"No, Mr. Stafford. I like 'Mr. Stafford' just fine. Ms. Nicholson said she would be back by eight and not to hold dinner. Would you like a glass of wine before dinner?" Beatrice said this, already opening a bottle from the refrigerator.

"Hmm. Mom will be home after dinner, now what's she up to?"

"A shurrrprize, Daddy. She has a shurrprize."

"OK then, a shurrprize. When are those big teeth coming in young lady? I think I will have a glass of wine, thank you Beatrice. Emily, where's your brother?" She pointed toward the family room and frowned. Connor had little patience for her these days. He was much more interested in video games.

"Oh…In the video dungeon, huh?"

Emily smiled and nodded.

Milton took his wine and walked into the dimly lit room, eyeing his son, stretched out on the floor in front of the screen.

"Hey there, buddy?" He was ignored. "Hey there, Connor?"

"Oh, hey Dad." He rolled onto his side and squinted up at his father.

"Hey, Connor. How about taking a break and talking to your old Dad?"

"Uh, Dad, I'm in the middle of a game."

"I know, Son. But I'm home a bit early and I thought we could hang out for awhile together."

"Can we take the boat out?"

"No, not tonight. It's getting late and dinner is almost ready."

"Oh. Hmm."

"Connor, we could talk, maybe about your day?"

"Oh, OK Dad, but this was a really important game."

"I know. I'm sorry, Son. Didn't mean to interrupt, but gosh I haven't talked with you since, hmm, I don't know…since yesterday?"

Connor smiled and turned off the television and turned on a light on the end table. He picked up a comic book and sat down on the other end of the couch.

"So, how was your day?" Milton asked, amused.

Connor smiled into the cartoons and said, "Fine."

"Wow, that's a whole lot of info, buddy. What else did you do today?"

"Dad, it's the same every day. You know I don't like the school. I miss my friends in the city and, oh I don't know."

"Hey, in just a few months you've got a big birthday coming up. Want to plan something in the city?"

Connor contemplated the idea and said, "Maybe."

"Maybe? What do you mean, maybe?" Milton jabbed him lightly in the side.

"I mean we have Christmas and Emily's birthday and, well, I don't know." He frowned when he said his sister's name.

"Hey buddy, you forgot Mom's birthday and Thanksgiving and my birthday. Yikes, that's a lot of stuff before the big 12 for you."

"Yeah, I know."

"Would you like to go into the city before all those special days happen?"

Connor smiled, "Can we, Dad?"

"Sure we can. How about this? I'll talk with your mother and we can set something up for this weekend.

Connor frowned.

"What? What's wrong with that?"

"Oh, Dad. It's just she'll say yes and want to plan a big day with the whole family and I really don't want all of you hanging out with all of us."

Now Milton frowned.

"Sorry, Dad."

"Nah. Don't worry about it. Go give your friends a call and see if they're around this weekend. If they are, you can have the whole afternoon at the museum of science. Just the guys, OK?"

"Thanks, Dad." He leaned in and jabbed his father a little rougher. Milton flinched then smiled.

"Go, get out of this room. It smells of video neutrons!" Milton watched as he ran upstairs to use the hall phone. His son was definitely growing up. He remembered those growing pains vividly.

After dinner, Milton took Emily upstairs, gave her a quick bath, and the two of them settled into a Winnie the Pooh story before bedtime. Just before he covered her with the blanket she whispered, "I want to stay up for the shurrprize."

"Hush now, little girl. You get some sleep and when you wake up we can get the surprise together, OK?"

"OK Daddy. Daddy? Tell Mommy night night, OK?"

"OK, my sweet girl." Milton kissed her cheek and flicked on the night-light. He had confessed to Meredith when he had come home with it, that he hoped one day she would enjoy the comforting glow as much as him. Her last doctor's appointment had stated just the opposite. There was no improvement with her sight. The tiny light glowed and he could see her smiling in her sleep. He tiptoed out.

"So, buddy, all set for this weekend?" He leaned into to his Son's room.

Connor removed one side of his headphones, "No. Forget about it, Dad."

"What do you mean, forget about it? I thought…."

"No one's gonna be around, Dad. Gosh, it's been a year since we lived there. I don't think anyone cares that I'm gone."

"Oh buddy, that's not true. What about Frank?"

"Nah. Frank is off camping with his troop this weekend. Just forget it, Dad."

"I'm sorry, buddy. Maybe another weekend, OK?"

"Yeah, maybe."

"Well, we got lots to do to the boat before we winterize it. Maybe we can take it on a race around the sound this weekend before we do that?"

Connor smiled. "Yeah. Let's do that." Milton tousled his hair and went downstairs to wait for his wife. Beatrice was just finishing up with the kitchen.

"Can I get ya anything before I leave, Mr. Stafford?" When Beatrice was tired, her accent won over her struggle to sound like a local.

Milton joked "Naa, Mrs. O'Reilly. I tink dat I'm good fer now, but tank you." Beatrice gave him a look of disdain, then smiled.

"I'm sorry, Beatrice. I couldn't help meself."

"Dats quite olrite, Mr. Stafford. Iz there anything else I can git fer ya?"

Milton smiled and shook his head. "No, no, really. Thank you for everything, Beatrice. You are just a godsend, I tell ya."

"Mr. Stafford, the kids are angels. I thank god everyday that we found each other."

"Back at you, Beatrice. Now what time did Ms. Nicholson say…." At that moment they both heard the front door open. He was anxious to see her and tell her the good news.

"Well, hello you two." Meredith leaned toward her husband and gave him a peck on the lips.

"Well, well, look what we have here. A mom late for dinner, just like old times." He regretted it as soon as he said it. Meredith and Beatrice shot him a glare.

"Ms. Nicholson, can I get you anything before I leave?"

"No. Thank you, Beatrice, for everything today. I know it was short notice and, well, thank you."

"I'll see you in the morning then."

"Goodnight, Beatrice." They said in unison.

"Now was that called for?" Meredith asked as she sat down, nibbling a cold piece of chicken from a plate Beatrice had handed her.

"No. I'm sorry. Just had so much to tell you about today and well, I guess a bit disappointed you didn't call me to tell me you wouldn't be home."

Meredith, content she had cleaned the first piece, looked across the table at he husband.

"I'm sorry, darling. It was last minute and, well, Beatrice had everything covered here. I wanted to surprise you."

"I guess I had a surprise for you too." Milton offered

"Really?" Meredith smiled as she started in on the mash potatoes. "Well? Tell me then. I'm starving."

"I got a huge raise today!"

Meredith put down her fork and smirked.

"Finally," she said with little enthusiasm.

"Mere. I mean it. Huge!"

"Milton. You've been with the company for 11 years and they've given you one raise. You deserve a huge raise."

"Mere, it's over a hundred thousand dollars."

Her eyes widened and she smiled again. "Darling, that is wonderful. You really deserve it. My goodness, that is a lot." She got up and walked over to him and snuggled in on his lap.

"Now, what are they going to require of you for this extra hundred thousand? A limb or two? One of our children?"

"No, Mere, please. This is real. It's finally appreciation for my work. They hand picked me for a special project and if goals are met, I could be making almost two hundred thousand more in a year."

"My goodness. My talented, rich scientist." She snuggled into his neck and he could smell the remainder of her perfume on her hair. "What's the project?" She whispered as she nibbled on his earlobe.

"Um, just some medical project. Not a big deal. Nothing you would be interested in."

Meredith looked up, into his eyes, "Of course I'm interested."

Milton ignored her question by asking the obvious, "Well, what is your shurrrprize?"

"Hmm," she giggled, "Seems our little one has almost spilt the beans?'

"Mere?"

"OK, OK. Let me get my potatoes and I'll tell you."

"The potatoes can wait, good looking. What is it?" He held her closely on his lap.

"All right, all right. Well Connie—remember Connie?"

"Of course, Mere, what about Connie?"

"Well she and I have been talking, quite a lot lately, and she and a group she works with have made me a job offer!"

"Really?" Milton let his arms loosen and his wife jumped up quickly to retrieve her dinner. She came back and sat beside him, playing with her food as she contemplated how to tell him the rest.

"Meredith, please, I'm waiting so patiently."

"I'm sorry. It's just so new for me too."

"What's so new? Will you please tell me what the job is?"

She put her fork down and took his hand. "It's a talk show and I'll be the host."

Milton eyed her suspiciously and asked, "A what?"

"It's a talk show. It'll be on every Sunday morning at eight and I'll be the host."

"The host of a talk show? What kind of talk show? One of those ridiculous...."

"No, no, no. It's a slot for the League of Women Voters and it's to get me back in the public eye, mixing a little of my legal background in, while encouraging more people to get out and vote."

Milton stared at his wife in disbelief. "I thought you never wanted to get back into the 'limelight' and all that mess? I thought the league *was* non-partisan?"

Meredith stared down at her empty plate, disturbed at her husband's remark and visualizing a new mound of potatoes would appear. She hadn't had an appetite like this in a year.

Calmly she replied, "Milton, I know that I said just that a year ago and I'm still not sure where this will even go, but I'm bored and ready to work again and this will require only a few days a week and Sunday mornings. The league is *non*-partisan, but Connie, Bonnie, and many of the women involved in the production, are Democrats. It has nothing to do with party choice. It's about women and another plea to get registered voters out to vote and get the unregistered ones registered. We're a focus group, dedicated to all sorts of women's issues, all leading back to political choice and how one's vote counts. They're going to pay me $2,000 a show. I thought you'd be excited about the shurrrprize?" Milton smiled as his wife held the long "Z."

"Meredith, I am surprised. Very surprised. A talk show, wow."

"Yep. A talk show. I saw Katherine today too. She's going to be part of my team. She, Connie, and Bonnie." She stood up to put her plate in the sink and opened the refrigerator, staring at the contents. Milton got up and walked behind her, wrapping his arms around her waist.

"How's Katherine?"

"She's sad, darling. It's been 6 years since they started trying and they've gone through every painful procedure known. She needs to occupy her mind with something else."

"And Connie?"

"Oh she's the same. Spry, brightly colored, and insatiable when it comes to issues about women and children. It's been really nice talking with her again. She sends hugs and kisses.

"And Bonnie?"

"Really?" Meredith chided.

"Nah. Just kidding."

"Bonnie's wonderful. Still a bit angry, but the brightest, hardest working teammate I've ever had. She and Karol have had their ups-and-downs but I think they've found a comfortable place."

"A place?"

"Yes, Milton. A place. Common, forgiving, sweet, place.

"Did she send her love?"

"Nah," Meredith chided.

He whispered, "I think it sounds wonderful, honey. I think you'll be a beautiful television host. Does this mean that we we'll be invited to the award shows and we can get all gussied up and mingle with the rich and famous?"

She turned around and faced him with an enormous strawberry protruding from her lips. "Darling," she whispered as she sucked on the fruit, "We won't be mingling with any bevy of beauties from Hollywood, I'm sorry to say. But lucky you! You get to mingle with this old 'Bevy' from Boston." She bit down and the pink juice ran down her chin. Milton kissed her and took her hand as he led her toward the stairs, just as she added, "And who knows, maybe one day you can call me Mrs. Governor?"

Milton shook his head and laughed.

CHAPTER 25

It was an unusually cold October morning in Alabama when Gerald Revo's mother passed away. She had taken ill back in Mississippi, diagnosed with a progressive cancer, and was quickly brought to a teaching facility in Birmingham where she could receive the best care. Gerald had arrived just the day before with an urgent call from his father ordering him home. He stood by his mother's bed alone and felt completely helpless. She had always been there, but in the shadows of his life. He wished it could be anyone's mother but his own. She was the only one that had ever been able to make him feel good. Feel loved.

"Gerry?"

"Yes Mom. I'm here."

"Gerry, is your father here?"

"He just went down to the nurse's station, Mom. He'll be right back."

"I want to speak with you alone, Gerry."

"OK Mom. We're alone." He held her hand carefully, avoiding the intravenous line.

"Gerry, do you hate me?"

Gerald stared down at his mother, shocked.

"Did you hear me, Son?"

"Yes, Mom. Mom, of course I don't hate you."

"Do you love me, Son?"

"Of course I love you, Mom."

"I just seemed at times that you didn't love me. You never married. You never gave me any grandchildren."

"Mom, what are you talking about? I love you and always have. Marriage and grandchildren have nothing to do with loving you."

"I thought you might've married that nice girl before I died."

"I'm sorry that didn't happen, Mom, but that doesn't mean I don't love you."

"Is it because...."

"Mother, no. Please, let things lie."

"Would you make me a promise, Gerry?"

He pondered this question for a moment then answered, "Of course, Mother, anything."

"I know your father's been hard on you at times. He's been hard with me at times, but we both love him, right?"

Gerry nodded, concerned his mother was delirious. She had never spoken an ill word about his father in his 41 years. She had never spoken an ill word about anyone for that matter.

"Gerry?" She pulled at his hand and he felt his heart tug. He put his arm around her slight frame and leaned toward her.

"Gerry? I'm sorry if I haven't been a good mother," She put her finger to his lips so she could continue. "I've loved you and your father the best that I could and I mean that." Gerald nodded, consciously holding back emotion. "Mom, you have been the best."

"I want you to be the best that you can be, Gerry. I don't want you to hold yourself back for anything. I want you to live life and love someone and I want you to see what I haven't allowed myself to see."

"What's that, Mom?"

"Do everything you want to do, because God intended it that way. Don't let life pass you by."

"Mom, I'm happy. Really happy. I don't understand." She looked at the hospital door; almost able to sense her husband was getting close.

"Gerry, you won't be happy until you have it all."

"Mom?"

"Keep taking your medicine. Darling. I saw it the last time you were here. I've prayed and I'm sure there will be a cure soon. You'll make a wonderful President."

"Mom?" *She knew*?

"Goodbye, Son." Her body felt limp in his arm. He reached quickly for the call button. He held her until the emergency team arrived with his father running behind them.

"Oh, Son, I'm so sorry I wasn't here. Did she say anything? Are you all right?"

Gerry looked at his father, his eyes glazed, "Yeah Dad, she said she loved us. And I'll be fine. Just fine."

On the first Sunday of Meredith's debut show in Boston, Gerald Revo sat in the back of the church in his hometown, his father by his side, and he made the decision. On Monday morning he announced to the right ears that he was throwing in the towel for the Republican Party and arrogantly declared his plan to bring morality and truth back into the presidency. He planned on winning.

"So, what do you think of this Revo guy?"

Meredith put down the newspaper she was reading and smiled at Bonnie, "You're late." It had been two days since the show and Meredith was anxious to prepare for the next one.

"Meredith, I'm sorry, but this was kind of impromptu, don't you think? I'm never late. Never. What a show!" Meredith nodded in agreement.

"Bonnie, I'm just kidding. Lighten up, OK? And yes it was a great show. I really felt an energy there. I hope the ratings prove it. Now what did you just ask me?"

Bonnie pulled out a chair beside her and tapped on the front page with her umbrella. "What do you think of this Revo guy? Oh and the ratings were excellent for Sunday morning's first."

Meredith glanced back at the page. "He's very conservative. I'm a little worried about him. I don't know, maybe I have a bad feeling about this one."

"Me too, Meredith. Me too. You know in just 24 hours I've read more dirt on this guy than I've read on all of the other 'hopefuls' combined that are trying to oust our party."

"What do you mean 'dirt', Bonnie?"

"This guy is scary. First of all, he's adamant that homosexuality should be banned, or even eliminated."

"Now Bonnie, aren't you being a bit dramatic?"

"I'm not kidding, Meredith. Karol even thinks he's backward. And you know how rare it is that she says a bad word about anyone. She called him a bigot at breakfast. That really made me think. He slams people with his morals and scruples crap. He believes in the Bible, literally."

"Wow. You're right about Karol. She is a darling. You're very lucky, Bonnie."

"Thanks, Meredith. I don't need to be reminded. I know. But what about a show slamming him just a little? Get the American people thinking."

Meredith put her hand on her chin and looked at Bonnie sweetly, "I think we need to arrange the next show on all of the candidates and get a perspective from all walks of life. Let the American people brandish him. Let them decide."

Bonnie nodded. Meredith was always right, but added for topic's sake, "Make sure you get a lesbian in there, OK?"

Meredith smiled and picked up the menu to order.

Meredith recruited Katherine immediately following her call to Bonnie. The pay was very little, but both were excited about the work. The premise of the show: women, speaking about women's causes, beliefs, and the need and responsibility of every woman to vote. They drew attention, which in turn slowly drew in more powerful guests, and Meredith was starting to be recognized again. She looked healthy, primarily from the sabbatical away from the stressful forum, and she had a new, fresh outlook. She spoke openly and expected frank answers from her guests. The second show was an exciting success with the ex-Governor of Massachusetts, also the first female, making an appearance. They shared their tales of being the first females in such prominent political positions and the aspect that both had been sworn in due to their decisions to seek a higher office. They ardently agreed that the percentage of women that got out to vote was discouraging, and that a change was necessary for the commonwealth as well as any political realm to be fairly represented. Women needed to speak to be heard.

"Do you think we should run again?" The Governor joked when the director was wrapping it up.

Meredith smiled sweetly and just nodded yes.

The camera faded out and both women burst into laughter. A photographer for the *Globe* had heard from David that Meredith would be doing the show live, and caught them leaving the set, thoroughly amused. It made the front cover of the *Boston Globe*. Great minds and publicity for a new show and Meredith answered every question the same, "Watch the show. You really ought to tune in."

"You know we come from a state that focuses on intellect but there are still so many women that have not had the opportunity to go to school or to watch us on Sunday. They are eligible voters and their voices need to be heard. We need to get out there and make sure they know we're here for them too." Meredith rallied her team and with the support of the League, they dispersed on Massachusetts and made plans for the rest of New England. They invited all types of women to visit the set, and they talked about their lives and their dilemmas and viewers were relating.

Men were joking about the show and women were tuning in. Victor Floramo, the current mayor of Boston, was quoted, saying, "Well she *is* a looker". He immediately retracted his statement but ratings were boosted 30 percent. *Women on Women* was referred to as, *Women on Top,* but Meredith ignored the jokes and stayed focused. Some people were starting to take her very seriously. The feeling was back and she was going for the ride.

"Come in."

Milton looked up from his desk, buried behind a hundred files, his eyes burning from the computer screen glare.

Professor Salinger popped his head in, "Got a minute, big guy?"

Milton immediately minimized the folder he was reading and motioned his boss to come in. He had been bombarded with "big guy" since the afternoon he accepted the job. He hated his "new friend."

"Dick, please sit."

"No, no, Milton, don't want to interrupt, just checking in to see how you're doing?"

"Fine, Professor, just fine."

"Milton, please. Call me Dick."

Oh if you only knew, thought Milton.

"Sure, sorry. Dick, everything's great. Thanks for asking."

"Absolutely big guy. We both know how important this project is. If you need anything, anything at all, you know you can count on me. Right?"

Milton nodded.

"Hey, big guy. How's your wife's show?"

Milton couldn't put his finger on it, but when Dickey Salinger mentioned his wife, his blood boiled, his skin burned, and his fingers curled into fists.

"Oh, seems to be going just fine, Dick."

"Great. That's great. Nice to see her back in action huh?"

"Excuse me?"

"You know, back to work. Must be nice having two money makers in the house."

Milton counted to 10 slowly. He had been practicing this new calming routine more frequently. Dick Salinger was a pig.

"Dick, it's really a great opportunity you've given me, and on that note, I have lots of work to do before the deadline next month. First quarter, right?"

He liked to remind Dick that it would be time for his bonus, since it had taken Milton only four weeks to develop a stronger serum than the one being currently tested and the lab rats were taking to it with excellent results. Milton thought about the new boat instead of the weasel in front of him.

"Oh sure, sure, big guy. Of course, I won't bother you anymore. Hope your afternoon goes well and please tell your wife I said congratulations." Salinger slipped out quietly.

"Dumb Ass," Milton stammered as he went to optimize his screen.

Salinger returned to his office and called the IS department to request the computer records of the entire science staff. He had been requesting this almost weekly and rumor had it for sure one of science geeks was more into Korean porn than boring lab work. But there was only one person Salinger was interested in, and he was viewing documents much more lethal than porn.

"It's pretty ugly stuff, huh, Son?" Milton's grandfather looked concerned through the rearview mirror.

"Pop, you scared the shit out of me," Milton tossed his briefcase in the front seat, "and why do you insist on the backseat now?"

"Well, Son, your driving is something to be desired and I think you need to pay more attention to the road. And what's with the cussing?" Milton wanted to say something but didn't.

"I know what you're thinking. You're thinking, 'Pop, wherever you're sitting it's deterring my full attention. I guess you're right. Honest, I like being in the backseat. Never had anyone drive me around before. Always was the one driving. Meredith must like that."

Milton smiled and pulled out of the parking lot, accustomed to the chatter without responding, until he was safely away from his office.

"She like her new job?"

"Yes, Pop, she seems really happy."

"Just 'seems'? Have you asked her? Does she like being driven around?"

"Pop, yes I've asked her, and she drives herself now. I've been busy too you know."

"She drives herself? Oh, I thought...well never mind...Do you know who her guest is this Sunday?"

Milton shook his head.

"Son, you've got to keep up on these things. Your wife is a popular, successful television star now. Do you want to know?"

"Yes, Pop."

"OK, then when you get home, you ask her again."

"Please Pop, just tell me. I promise I'll ask her when I get home."

"OK, OK, Son. It's the President's wife!"

"Who?"

"The President's wife!"

"The president of what?"

Milton's grandfather started laughing and coughing simultaneously. Milton's cell phone started ringing and he cursed again. He'd made a pact with Meredith that he wouldn't talk on it while driving, but he was expecting an important call.

"Pop. Please stop laughing."

"Son, you're really quite humorous sometimes. What president!"

"Well?"

"The President of our great country, Son. That President's wife. She told you last week."

Milton reached into his pocket as he looked in the rearview, hoping to catch his grandfather's twinkle that gave away his gag. He glanced down at the number and saw it was a Texas exchange.

"Pop, you're kidding right?"

"Son, you need to ask her again. And this time, be excited! Now who's that that called?"

"Just a call I've been waiting for in regards to work."

"Oh Yeah, back to that. Pretty ugly stuff huh?"

"Pretty ugly, Pop. Pretty ugly."

Chapter 26

On December 31st 1999, the world waited and watched with anticipation as midnight and the millennium approached. The fear of Nostradamus and the Y2K bug came in with little chaos. There was no Armageddon and the potentially disastrous computer bug was confined. The Stafford-Nicholson clan celebrated at home, like many, allowing children to stay up and count down with America's oldest teenager, watching the ball drop in Times Square. Meredith and Milton cuddled on the couch, reminiscing. They had both celebrated their 40th birthdays and their 16th wedding anniversary. Emily was a thriving 9 year old, excelling in every aspect at school and life and a pure joy for them all. She loved to wear dresses and perfume and whenever she got the chance she would follow one of her parents or Beatrice around the house, asking questions. Her handicap inhibited her very little, more often convincing them all that she could see more than anyone. Connor anxiously awaited his 14th birthday and the end of childhood. He would be a freshman at a New Hampshire prep school in the coming fall. He was tall for his age, with deep blue eyes. His wavy brown hair fell into his eyes often, but he refused to cut it short. Sending him away to school was their only option with the local schools unable to keep up with his mind. He was quiet and sensitive and Meredith was convinced he was just like Milton when he was a child. Milton would disagree, hoping his son more outgoing, but his grades proved his genius and his personality was almost identical. They were both seemingly happy introverts.

"Mom?"
"Yes, Emily."

"When exactly, I mean, what day do we get to get the dog?"

"Ugh, Em! Not again." Connor blurted, keeping his eyes on the Times Square revelers.

"Connor, I want to know the day. Don't you?"

"Not really, Em. The dog is for you, not me." Connor had been asking for a dog since the day he could pronounce "dog".

"Connor, come on buddy. You know that time just slipped away and we were all too busy to take care of a dog. Emily is getting a dog that will help her. You know that."

"Yeah, I know. Sorry, Em." Connor reached over and tickled his sister's side.

Giggling, she asked again, "When is it?"

"Summer," her parents said in unison.

"Emily, in the summer, after you're finished school." Connor added

She jumped up and went to her room, coming back with the new Braille calendar from school, and carefully she counted down the days until she hit the month of June.

"What day in June, Mom?"

Meredith, Milton, and Connor all smiled and Meredith answered, "The 19th, little lady."

"Only 170 days to go until Daisy is here!"

"Daisy?" Connor joked, holding his side in laughter.

"I think that's a very nice name, Miss Emily," Beatrice added as she came in the room with more popcorn and champagne.

"It's almost time, Dad. Turn it up."

Beatrice sat down beside Meredith, who wrapped her arms around her husband's and Beatrice's shoulders. The fire glowed in the fireplace while the blustery, winter wind off the sound pushed desperately to get inside.

"Ten…nine…eight…."

"HAPPY NEW YEAR!"

"Happy New Year, my love." Milton kissed Meredith sweetly, who then kissed Beatrice and they had a group hug. Emily and Connor jumped up, blowing horns and throwing streamers. Milton looked up and smiled at his grandfather, beaming, at the top of the stairs.

The phone rang and Milton got up to answer it in the kitchen.

"Meredith?"

"Hi, no it's Milton. Katherine?"

"Hi, Milton. Happy New Year!"

"To you too Katherine. You and David."

"I'm so excited I'm going to burst."

"Are you all right, Katherine?"

She was almost crying as she told him the news and he congratulated her several times before they said good night and he went back to the festivities, now winding down.

"Who was that?" Meredith asked as she and Connor collected some of the streamers.

Milton walked over to her and smiled.

"Honey?"

"It was Katherine, sweetie. She called to say Happy New Year."

"Oh that's nice. Did she sound good?'

"She sounded pregnant."

"She what? Oh my goodness!"

She squeezed him tightly, then grabbed both of her children for a bear hug!

"Aunt Katherine is going to have a baby, kids! Should auld acquaintance be forgot...."

2000 was starting perfectly!

Meredith went into the kitchen with the dishes, encouraging Beatrice to relax, and she stared at the wall phone in the doorway. She picked it up and dialed the number, remembering it like it was yesterday. A groggy, irritated voice answered the phone.

"Hello."

"Dad? It's me, Meredith."

Gerald Revo sat on the edge of the bed. He couldn't look at her. He grabbed the phone, dialing slowly. He looked at himself in the mirror and noticed a large scratch just above his nipple. She had put up quite a fight. He changed his mind and replaced the phone on the cradle. He went into the bathroom, helping himself to two pills from his jacket and a piss in the tub. He smiled at his reflection, but avoided looking at her as he went for the phone again, hesitating, then wisely reaching for his suit coat pocket where his cell phone would be. She deserved it, the bitch, laughing at him like that. At first she was sensitive, even sexy. She had whispered such sweet thoughts when he had told her his mother had just passed. Then she had undressed him and seen his deformity. He didn't have time to tell her, and she laughed. She screeched. He had to shut her up. He couldn't stand the sound. He had to shut her up. He shook his head. Only his mother had ever made him feel normal. His father had made him feel mutant, until he had proven himself in the war. There were no other women like his mother—caring, loving and understanding. There would never be a woman like his mother. He dialed the number, wiping his eyes with his handkerchief.

"Yes".

"Desmond, it's Revo."

"Yes, Gerald. I know. Are you calling to wish me a Happy New Year?"

"No, Desmond. Uh. I need your help. I'm, well, I did something stupid."

"Gerald, it's not a good time to be doing something stupid. Where are you?"

"I'm in Birmingham. At a hotel."

"All right. I'll be there tomorrow. What hotel?"

"No, I need you to come now."

"Gerald, what the hell is it?"

"I killed someone."

There was silence on the other end.

Desmond was at the hotel and had disposed of the body before the sun peeked over the horizon. He had Gerald Revo on an airplane to D.C. and back at his Capitol Hill condominium before the Monday morning commuters started pushing each other around.

Desmond was back in Houston and at his own desk before lunchtime and made only one call to Boston on his return. He appreciated the fact that Salinger was terrified of him. He was sure that Revo feared him a bit now too. He felt comfortable with the fact that his fortune was now completely secure. Revo's slip had confirmed that. Confirmed that his physical ailments would be his demise. A demise that would entail, only after Desmond had what he needed. He admired the city skyline through the 14-foot windows. It was just a matter of time. Just a matter of time.

CHAPTER 27

By the time "Super Tuesday" arrived, Revo had the Republican nomination wrapped. When all was said and done, Democrats had almost the lowest turnout in history while Republicans experienced high turnouts and a powerful candidate. The fact that both nominations were effectively settled so early depressed turnout in the remaining states. Revo cared little for the "Primary Process" proposed reform. It worked perfectly for him.

He was a military hero, a respected Senator, and now he was heading for the White House. As a devout Alabama Christian, whose mother had just passed, he had the south wrapped up. He also had most of the Bible belt and northwest in his palm, because of the last President's questionable family values. He was backed by some of the most powerful organizations and lobbyists and he appeared unstoppable.

The Democrats voted as predicted: the current Vice President would be their candidate. In one of the most important speeches of his career, he accepted the nomination focusing on environmental and healthcare issues, hoping not to be compared to anyone else's downfalls.

"We are a country witnessing great economic prosperity and I intend to keep it that way. But this is more than a popularity contest. The proposed tax cut is for the wealthy and I intend to be a President of all the people. One who fights day to day for everyone. I might not be popular with the big corporations, the huge polluters, or the HMOs but this is more than a popularity contest. I might not be the most exciting President, but I will never let you down!"

Gerald Revo watched the Democratic Convention from a private office that Damion Desmond had set up for him at the beginning of the campaign. Desmond had insisted on a more suburban location, less press and curiosity to contend with. Gerald had little to say either way. Since the unfortunate incident with the prostitute, his demeanor remained confident, yet he became more quiet. When he did speak, everyone listened. There was a light knock on the door. Gerald didn't acknowledge it. Desmond entered and sat in a club chair adjacent to the television. He stared at his new boss.

"Gerry?"

Gerald looked up at Desmond, smiling.

"How are you feeling?"

Gerald smiled again and replied, "Wonderful!"

"Are you enjoying the program?" Desmond leaned over as he asked, cocking his head to catch another glimpse of the enemy. Gerald ignored the question, but instead asked,

"Did you see his wife's little speech? All that crap about being a husband and a father! Yeah, that really helped this last schlep. Don't you think?"

"I saw her, Gerald."

"I can't stand that bitch. Can't stand her." Gerald's eyes glassed over.

"I think you need to get some rest, Gerald. It's been a long day."

Gerald looked once again at Damion and nodded in agreement.

"You're right as usual, Desmond. I am tired. Tired of the morons that think they can run this country by being nice and sweet and telling the American people that it's all about them."

Desmond smiled and nodded.

"You know already what's going to happen, huh, Desmond?"

Damion smiled and answered, "Of course."

Gerald sat back and lifted his teacup to salute the television.

"Yes. We know exactly what's going to happen."

Desmond stood and turned the television off.

"When you're Chief of Staff, someone will do that for you." Revo chided.

"Won't that be nice," Desmond mustered a smile.

Four days later, Meredith was fired.

She had been an advocate for the commonwealth of all women, but after the Republican Convention, became an advocate once again for the Democratic Party. The television program, sponsored by a bipartisan group, had no other choice. She had somehow contacted the Vice President's wife, who had cancelled numerous times, but finally agreed to detour her trip to the Midwest, for one small but very important interview. The cameras rolled and after the surprising entrance of the possible new first lady, everyone tuned in. The conversation aimed primarily at the concerns of women and the low turnout at the primary polls with just a hint of fear that the Republican Party's choice disliked them.

"I don't think you need to be married to be a good President though, do you?" Meredith asked, a twinkle in her eye.

"Absolutely not," her guest answered enthusiastically, "what I meant to stress before is that being a wonderful husband, father, and now grandfather isn't necessary at all to run this country. I don't think. But it can't hurt, right? I mean, having a strong family conviction. Having the opposite sex's opinion. Looking at humanity as a whole, not as a gender. I know that you've been focusing on women and voting now for sometime Meredith, right? Wouldn't it be nice if we focused on everyone voting? It is something everyone has the duty to do." Meredith smiled and, at the moment, on the air, Milton watched and saw something he hadn't seen in almost 3 years. He saw it in her eyes. She put down her notebook and looked directly at the first lady hopeful and tapped her on the knee.

"You are so right. So very right! It's been too long that not just women but men too have neglected their civic duty to vote. You know, it's kind of like the seatbelt law. It's one that is hard to enforce, but I see more people with a seatbelt on now than not. Remember when we were kids? We used to climb from the very back of the station wagon, to the backseat, to the front seat, all while one of my parents was driving and the other one was looking at a map. I even remember seeing as a child, a woman breastfeeding while driving on the interstate. That impression is still with me today. We would never be so negligent now. Our children are restrained in car seats and we're buckled tightly in the front. I think voting needs to be the same way. I think if year after year someone neglects or decides that voting is not for them, maybe they can fill out an application, relinquishing their right to vote. Just having to say that makes me sad. Everyone needs to take their right seriously and vote. We need to evaluate who and what is about to lead our country and make a conscious decision to choose. Please, take a look at your candidates; take a look at your country and you and your family's future. Get out and vote! Thank you, thank you so much for being with us."

The Vice President's wife looked confused as Meredith turned toward the camera, asking the cameraman to zoom in on her lapel then she smiled as Meredith Nicholson reached over and donned a huge "Vote Democrat" pin ending the show with, "Have a nice Sunday, everyone."

Milton sat back and watched the credits roll. He stood to catch a glimpse of his children outside playing and nonchalantly glanced at the untidy pile of sections to the Sunday paper. He was glad he hadn't called them in to watch. A thousand different headlines ran through his head for the Monday edition. He had waited since the day his grandfather had mentioned the surprise guest and now it had happened. His wife had just suggested that one's constitutional right be dissolved. The phone rang.

"Hello," Milton answered cautiously.

"Hey Milton, it's David.

"Oh, hey David. Did you watch?"

"Milton, it's Katherine. She's in labor. We're at Brigham and Women's.

"Oh, wow, OK then. I'll get the—never mind. We'll on our way."

Milton dialed the studio's phone and was told that Meredith was in a "do not interrupt" meeting.

"But it's an emergency. Please, get my wife."

"Is someone hurt or dying, Mr. Stafford?"

"You've got to be kidding? What's your name?"

"Mr. Stafford, my boss told me, unless someone was dead or dying, I was not to interrupt the meeting, so I'm sorry, I have to ask. Is someone dead or dying?"

Milton pulled the receiver away from his ear in disbelief. He wondered if having a baby constituted an emergency or if he reached through the phone and strangled her, she might go get his wife. He counted to ten.

"No one is dead or dying, what did you say your name was again? My wife's sister-in-law is about to have a baby and I think it's an emergency."

"I'm sorry Mr. Stafford. Please. As soon as she's out, I'll give her the message. Please, my job!"

Milton hung up the phone and grabbed is coat. He called for the kids and the dog to get in the car, leaving Beatrice a note in case she came home early on her day off. An hour and a half later, leaving the dog in the garage with the window cracked, he rushed into the labor and delivery unit, leaving Connor with Emily in the waiting room. The first person he saw was Charlie.

"Oh man. A sight for sore eyes!"

He put his head against his brother-in-law's shoulder and took a deep breath.

"How's she doing Charlie? Did you see Meredith this morning? Who's here? Oh my God, oops, sorry, God. My mind is racing. The dog's in the car and the kids are downstairs."

"Milton. Hey there, take a deep breath. Katherine and the baby are fine. She had a little girl. Samantha. They're both fine."

"Oh my God, oh, Charlie sorry. Did you see Meredith this morning?"

"Milton, please sit down. Come over here. You're making us all nervous. My parents are already here. Come on. They will be thrilled to see you."

"Charlie! Meredith?"

"Yes, Milton, I saw her this morning. She isn't here yet though."

"My God, Charlie, what was she thinking?"

Charlie shook his head and led Milton toward the private waiting area. He reached for Gertrude, his mother in law, and squeezed. He shook his father-in-law's hand and whispered, "Seems they've named her after you, Sam!" Samuel beamed, unable to speak since the stroke.

"Milton, where's Meredith?" Gertrude looked anxiously around him.

Milton looked down at his father-in-law and answered, "I'm sure she's on her way. I called her as soon as David called me. She was at the station." He didn't mention the morning show, but he didn't have to. He saw in their expressions that they had both seen the show.

"Hey Gertrude, the kids are downstairs. I wasn't sure if they could come up…."

His mother-in law interrupted before he could finish. "Oh, yes, yes. I'll go downstairs right now. Will you be all right, Samuel?" Samuel winked one eye and she was gone. Milton smiled and sat down beside Samuel, patting his hand on the couch. Charlie took the other side. They all watched the hospital shuffle, as gurneys and white coats flitted by. Then David was standing in front of them.

"Wow, nice welcoming group. Where are the women?"

Milton stood and hugged his dear friend and brother-in-law and said, "Meredith's not here yet, but she should be soon. Your mom went down to check on the kids."

David frowned, not interested in why, and took the seat open beside his father.

"Hey, Dad? Do you want to go and see her?"

Samuel nodded sporadically and Charlie reached over to get the wheelchair. The three of them slipped him in with ease and as they turned toward the nursery, Meredith was rushing down the hall with a tray of coffee. She saw all of the men in her life and started to cry.

"Here, here, Sis, let me take those," Charlie offered as Milton hugged her.

"They just told me at the station and I came right away. I saw Mom in the waiting room and she told me everything. They had just come in from walking Daisy. Oh David, a girl. A little girl!"

David beamed as his sister clung to him. The "Vote Democrat" still pinned to her lapel. He added, "Nice show this morning." She averted her husband's eyes, looking down at her father's head, hanging low.

"Dad? Hi Dad."

His head bobbed and she reached down and pecked him lightly on the cheek. He tried to look up at her, but couldn't, so she crouched down so he could see her face.

"A girl, Dad. Another granddaughter."

Samuel struggled to smile and focus on his daughter's face. She smiled back.

"All right then. Where are we off too? Anyone for coffee?" She straightened her suit jacket and reached for the tray, passing out the coffees, made just the way they liked them. She placed a bottle of water with a straw in her father's hand and helped him sip it.

"We were just about to go see Samantha, Meredith, but I know Katherine would love to see you. She's in room 1108." David pointed down the hall the other way.

Meredith squeezed Milton's hand tenderly and headed toward her best friend's room. All four of them watched her go.

"I'm here."

Katherine turned her head on the pillow to face the door and smiled.

"I'm so happy you're here."

"I'm so sorry I'm late. It's been a busy day for us all, I guess. How are you?"

"Did you see her yet, Meredith?"

"Not yet. Came in to see you first, girlfriend. You look fabulous!"

Katherine shook her head adding, "Yeah, a real beauty queen, don't you think?"

Meredith sat down beside her and wrapped her arms gently around her, whispering, "You've never looked more beautiful, Mrs. Nicholson. Never!"

The television was on but muted and Meredith saw that the local news was reporting. She averted her eyes back to her sister-in-law, who saw the concern.

"I heard."

"Already?"

"Word travels fast in this family. David told me while I was pushing."

"You're kidding?"

"Well, maybe in between pushes. He was trying to distract me. Hoping I wouldn't curse him for the pain.

They both giggled.

"Oh, Katherine, I'm so happy for the two of you. I can't think of two better parents."

"I can only think of two, "Katherine replied, yawning. "Is everything going to be all right with you, Meredith? I mean, with the show?"

Meredith looked back up at the television, then down at Katherine, smiling.

"Everything's going to be just fine, Katherine, just fine. Want me to go ask that nurse to bring the angel in?"

There were ten people in the room when the nurse announced that visiting hours were over. Everyone shuffled out, blowing kisses and saying goodbye, leaving David, Katherine, and Samantha to a quiet night.

Charlie and his parents were making plans to go to dinner, but Meredith and Milton decided to head back to the cape, with Daisy still in the car and two tired children to get home. They would see everyone in a week or so after Samantha came home and Gertrude reminded them again about Thanksgiving, even though it was months away. It had been over 20 years since they had been together for the holiday. Gertrude was not about to let anyone forget it. They bid their farewells, Emily whispered into her grandfather's ear a goodbye. Milton held Emily's hand while Meredith wrapped an arm around Connor's broad shoulders.

"I hope Daisy's not angry with us. Grandpa thinks she might be," Emily said sleepily.

Connor and Meredith looked at each other, not sure exactly how Emily heard words that were not spoken, but Connor added encouragingly, "I'm sure she slept for the most part, Em. She's a dog. She has that princess bed you brought for her. She likes to sleep almost 18 hours a day. Kind of like you."

"Oh, OK." Emily answered without argument.

Connor and Meredith followed Milton, weaving through the halls and she whispered, "I'm so happy you were home this weekend. So happy."

"Me too, Mom. Is everything OK at work?"

Milton didn't turn, so Meredith presumed he wasn't listening.

"Things are a bit hectic, but fine."

"Really Mom? I heard that you got in trouble on the show today. Grandma was talking with Aunt Katherine."

"No. Not really in trouble. Just had a very special, *surprise*, guest."

This time, Meredith was sure she saw a hesitation in her husband's step. She looked at her son, who was just about her height, and put her finger to her lips, whispering, "I need to talk about it with your father first, OK?" Connor understood.

The ride home was quiet. Both Connor and Emily fell asleep, with Daisy in the middle, snoring. Meredith stole a few glances at her husband in the rearview as he followed her home. She was relieved they had separate cars and felt a bit of anxiety when they finally reached their driveway. Their grandmother had stuffed them with cafeteria food, so both children gladly went upstairs to bed.

"Are you hungry?" Meredith asked Milton as he pulled Emily's door closed.

"A little, I guess." He answered tentatively.

He followed her down in the kitchen and watched as she made them two sandwiches. It was rare experience again, watching his wife in the kitchen. He missed her.

"What happened?" He asked as she placed the sandwich in front of him with a bottle of water.

"Milton. Eat first." He obliged her and his appetite by doing so slowly. When he took the last bite, he rested his hand on his chin and said, "Well?"

"They fired me." She looked down, dabbing at the crumbs on her plate.

"Meredith, I would imagine so. You were completely out of line."

"You think so, Milton? Really?" She stood to rinse the plates and he took her hand motioning for her to wait and finish.

"Yes, I do. It's a bipartisan show, sponsored by a nonprofit organization. It's not a pulpit for you to start preaching at."

"Tell me what you really think, Milton!" Meredith stood, pushing his hand away, as she grabbed the dishes and began to rinse.

"I mean it, Meredith. What happened today?"

She tuned the water off and turned toward him.

"If you really want to know, will you keep your opinions to yourself for a moment?" Milton felt the sting and sat back with his arms crossed.

She pulled her seat out, a little further from the table and him and sat down. She rubbed her temples and looked up at him. "I'm not really sure what happened today Milton." He opened his mouth, but no words came out.

"What I mean is I'm not really sure what came over me. I went with an impulse, a gut feeling I guess and I'm sorry. It was unprofessional and uncalled for. That is why they fired me I guess." She looked at her husband's exasperated expression and wanted to tell him everything, but she left it with, "They fired me Milton. Just as you would've." She stood up and went upstairs to the spare bedroom. Milton got up and turned the kitchen lights off then sat back down at the table in the dark. He wanted to hold her.

"So then go hold her, Son." His pop now sat in the chair where his wife had been

Without hesitation or response, Milton made his way upstairs to find her.

"Please forgive me, "he asked as he crawled into the small spare bed beside her.

"I'm sorry too darling. I just...."

"Never mind Meredith. It's all right. He wrapped himself around her as she whispered into his ear, "All that is necessary for evil people to come to power is that good people do nothing."

She fell asleep in his arms.

CHAPTER 28

Milton avoided unrolling the newspaper at the front door and set it on the bench inside. He would leave the headlines to his wife this morning. He thought about her body, wet with perspiration as she pulled him inside her. He could still taste the salt of her skin; smell the perfume in her hair. He was smitten, as always. He smirked, flooded with pleasure, as he heard the door handle turn and the sweet voice of his daughter say, "Mom? Dad? Why are you two in here?'

Meredith watched from the window as he backed down the driveway, still wrapped in her robe, and reminisced. She had closed all of her thoughts except for the pleasure of her husband's body and bathed in his love. She had intended to tell him the rest of the story, but the morning got away from them. Now he was on his way to work and she would have to wait and plan on how it would transpire. She could not feel badly. It was best sometimes to let one thing linger, before starting something new. The touch of Milton's fingers still lingered.

A rare moment alone, she intended to enjoy it. Connor had left early on the bus back to New Hampshire and Beatrice had already brought Emily to school, so she settled down on the chaise with a warm cup of coffee, the quiet, sun-filled room. Like a soft down comforter, draped around her. She opened the paper just as the phone rang, interrupting her euphoria. "What will become of Meredith Nicholson?" was the headline she read.

Meredith reluctantly picked up the phone.

"Are you sitting down?" Bonnie blurted out.

"Bonnie, yes, I'm sitting down." Meredith wrapped her legs underneath her on the couch and started to read the front page.

"Meredith, I need your full attention."

Meredith sighed and put the paper down. Bonnie knew her all too well.

"OK, OK. What do I need to be sitting for?"

"Two things. One, Darryl Rodriguez called me this morning."

"Really? Darryl? That's nice. How is he?"

"Oh cut the crap Meredith. You don't sound anything like a woman scorned."

Meredith chuckled into her coffee cup.

"No, really Bonnie, how is he?"

"He's doing very well. He's on the committee of course for the next President—but always has his fingers in the next bubbling brulee."

"The what?"

"Oh never mind. It's just a phrase I heard yesterday. You know, I thought it sounded funny when I heard it, but now? Never mind."

"Bonnie, please."

"He was returning my call."

"Your call? Why'd you call him?"

"I was very frustrated after yesterday's meeting and I wanted to bounce a few ideas off of him. He was returning my call."

"OK, cut to the chase Bonnie. I'm enjoying my first day of unemployment and want to get back to the paper."

"Did you read it yet?"

"No Bonnie, that's what I'm trying to do right now."

"Uh, good. Well, seems one of the national broadcasting stations wants to offer you a job. They've been in touch with Darryl too."

Meredith said nothing.

"Meredith?"

"Yes."

"Did you hear me?"

"Yes, Bonnie. I heard you."

"What do you think?"

"I was just thinking how nice it was that my husband and I made love this morning."

"Meredith! What the hell are you talking about?"

"No, really Bonnie. I mean it. I'm so happy that we had time together this morning. This beautiful morning. I'm afraid I'm going to be very busy for awhile."

Bonnie smiled on the other end.

"We meet with them tomorrow afternoon, at the studio. They want to make the pitch right away. OK?"

"OK."

"Meredith?"

"Yes, Bonnie."

"This is really big. You know that?"

"I know, Bonnie. I know."

Meredith hung up the phone and folded the paper, leaving it unread. She dialed his office number slowly.

"Hello. You've reached Milton Stafford's office. I'm not available to take your call right now. Please leave a message and I will return it soon." Beep.

"Hi darling, it's me. Sorry you're not there yet. I hope the traffic didn't dampen your memories of the morning. I just wanted to call and say I love you. Have a wonderful day." She hung up the phone and could imagine his smile as he listened to her voice.

"So, who the hell is she?"

"A public television talk show host in Boston. She had a short stint as the Mayor."

"And she said what?" Revo wrapped himself in a towel and sifted through his closet, pulling out a designer suit and tie.

"Desmond? She said what?" Revo looked into the bedroom, where Damion was reading the paper at a side table, the local television station muddling through the statistics of the local district winners and losers.

"She said nothing, Gerald. Nothing important. She may have hurt the enemy more than she, or even he knows. She's nobody. I've been waiting here for 45 minutes. We can talk about it in the car. We need to go. I'll get the driver."

Gerald Revo looked at himself closely in the mirror as he combed his hair back. He examined the slight scar from the last marking, but had seen no new symptoms in almost a month. He checked the supply in the small refrigerator and checked the trash container for any evidence of the night before. He hated to keep going back to that night. She was a nameless sinner. Not one thing about her in the paper. No one missed her. He felt no guilt. Then there was Desmond. Why hadn't he just taken care of it himself? Why involve Desmond? He had said nothing since that night. Nothing. Knowing that without him, he might possibly be in jail, not on his way to the White House. He missed the unlimited power he had before, but he would remain quiet. Practice patience. Desmond has proven his loyalty, in more ways than one. *Patience*, Gerald mouthed as he adjusted his tie, giving himself one last admiring look.

"One, two, three…." Milton counted slowly, as he listened to the message from Salinger. Never once had his voicemail been full when he arrived on Monday morning after a weekend. A scientist's life was usually quite dull. But after a hair-raising commute, an argument with his grandfather, and spilling his coffee once again on his shirt, he arrived to ten new messages. The first two were from Salinger, followed by three from Joyce Ridgefield, and then another from Salinger, the one that was elevating his blood pressure at the moment.

"Milton, I'm sorry to keep leaving messages, but each time I hang up, I realize I've forgotten to tell you something. The studies should be back tomorrow morning and I want to make sure we set up a meeting for lunch and oh, by the way, saw your wife this morning on television. Um, wow. We can talk about it sometime if you want?"

He pressed forward. Three more from techs, all different shifts, leaving messages about a certain shipment that was not protocol and then his wife's voice wishing him a wonderful day and reminding him of the perfect morning, lying beside her. He smiled, looking down at the stain in his shirt, and picked up the phone to call Houston, Texas. Joyce Ridgefield's voicemail went on.

"Ms. Ridgefield. I'm so sorry my cell phone was off this weekend. A little R&R with the family." *Hardly relaxing*, he thought to himself, remembering the new four legged baby in the family. "I'm back at work and hope to speak with you today. Thank you for your patience. I look forward to hearing from you when you get the chance. Of course if you need to reach me by my cell phone, please note I will have it on all day as well. Thank you."

He walked down to Shipping and Receiving.

"Hey, Isaac."

"Hello, Mr. Stafford. What can I do ya?"

"I got three messages over the weekends about a shipment that the techs were unsure about. They wanted me to check into it?"

"Hmm. Let me take a look. Yep, there were two as a matter of fact. Strange, them being delivered on Sunday, but it seems it's all set. They got their questions answered."

"Oh, OK then. Nice way to start a Monday. The right foot anyway."

"Yessiree. Short week next week though, with the holiday and all. Got to like that?"

"Oh, I keep forgetting that it's Labor Day. Let me get going so I don't get too far behind. Hey Isaac, just for my records, who signed off on the shipments?"

Isaac looked down at his records and grinned. "Seems Professor Salinger signed off on them early this morning. Nice guy, taking care of that for ya."

Milton thanked him with a wave and headed quickly back to his office. He had to call Salinger back right away to arrange that lunch date. It was bonus day. He got back to his desk just as his cell phone was ringing.

"Ms. Ridgefield! Thank you so much for getting back with me."

"Of course, Mr. Stafford. I was hoping to reach you on your cell phone."

"Well, either phone is fine Ms. Ridgefield. I'm so sorry about the telephone tag."

"Mr. Stafford?"

"Milton is fine."

"Thank you. My name's Joyce. And I think that it's best that we talk on the cell phone only."

"Um, OK. That's fine. I just don't want it to be costly for you."

"The cost is the least of my concerns. Please, do not stay in your office while you're speaking with me."

"Excuse me?"

"Please, if you don't mind. I'll call you back if necessary, but I don't think you should stay in your office. Please find a private place away from your office."

"All right then. Please call me back."

"I intend to, Mr. Stafford."

"Um," Milton stammered, but she had already hung up.

He went down the back stairwell and into the parking lot toward his car. "Hmm, I wonder if Pop will be joining us," he chortled as he huddled in the front seat, eyeing the building's thermostat. At ten o'clock in the morning it was already 93 degrees.

"So much for global warming," he said shivering right as the phone rang.

CHAPTER 29

The 2000 Presidential election in the United States was the closest race in the history of the country. The states were split on a their decision. Who would serve as a better leader? After a voting debacle in the Sunshine State and finally a Supreme Court ruling against the recount, Gerald Revo was handed the throne with controversy and suspicion. Hundreds of political jokes and parodies transpired the final weeks of the race, the two candidates sharing the butt end. Revo remained calm and collected, reassured by his committee, carefully voicing his plan to be a President of the people, not a party. Almost two weeks after the Thanksgiving holiday had past, the tallies were totaled and the Democrats conceded to the Republicans.

One hundred and ten million voters made the effort at the polls and the vote was so close that a recount in several states was necessary. The population of the United States at that time was 282 million and 74percent of that population was at or above the legal age to vote. Approximately one hundred million people that could have or should have voted declined to do so. If ever an apathetic absentee were heard to voice that their vote did not count or that their fundamental right proved fruitless, then this selection disclaimed them forever. Anyone that whined, yet didn't vote, could only be ignored.

With selections of his cabinet and other offices under the authority of the White House fully underway, Gerald Revo took a short break in the late afternoon to sit with Damion Desmond in the Oval Office. He instructed his assistant that he was not to be disturbed.

"Well, Desmond?" Gerald leaned back in the Queen Anne chair and crossed his legs.

"Well what?" Desmond sat across from him with a Cheshire grin.

"The plan worked, Desmond. You were right."

"Of course it did, Gerry. Did you ever doubt me?" Desmond's smile wavered.

"I have to admit, I was on the cusp a couple of times. Fucking Florida and California. Was hoping they would just break off the continent and cease to exist."

Damion looked directly at the new President and smiled again.

"That would've been too easy, don't you think, Gerry? I mean, a challenge is always so refreshing."

"When you win, of course it is."

"Gerry, that's not what I meant."

"I know. I get it. We should set up a meeting in the next couple of weeks. As soon as we can." Gerry stood and shifted a few papers on his new desk.

"Patience, Gerry. We have plenty of time for that. We need the rest of this year to get your house in order. Then we'll be able to proceed. Anyway, how are you feeling?"

Gerry now faced one of the portraits left on the wall by the last schlep. He planned to put several portraits of his mother and parents up as soon as they arrived with his other things. He turned and walked over, standing in front of Desmond. "I feel great. Really, the best I've felt in a long while."

"Good. It's imperative that you stay at the top of your form. We have a lot of work ahead of us. I mean *you* have a lot of work ahead of you, Mr. President." Damion said with slight sarcasm.

Gerry had heard the slip many times before. He never asked what he meant. He knew his intentions. Who wouldn't want to be the richest man in Texas? He also understood how being the President of the largest, most powerful country in the world was going to be able to help. He owed him that much. He had grown to depend on Desmond for so many things. Don't bite the hand that feeds you. It was time for payback.

"Now, Mr. Desmond. Did I hear a bit of animosity in your tone, maybe a lack of respect?"

Damion stood just inches from Revo, a much larger presence, and responded, "Absolutely not, your highness. I have the utmost respect for my boss." He leaned over and brushed his lips slightly on the cheek.

"Your highness!" Damion inched back and saluted then sauntered out of the room. Revo stood rigid, staring at the door as he left.

"Time for payback," he whispered.

The Television network painted an interesting, fly-by-the-seat-of-their-pants portrait, and Meredith waited until just before Thanksgiving to give them an answer. As she lay in bed with a mug of coffee, watching the Sunday morning news program the weekend before, Milton came in with a tray of waffles, strawberries, and cream. He fed her slowly, and she smiled, keeping one eye on the television, waiting for the flock of turkeys that they showed every year. At the end of the show, when the childhood memory and predicted gobble-gobble flooded the room, she smiled, put her mug on the end table, and climbed on top of her husband.

"You're taking the job, aren't you darling?" Milton asked, fingering a stray curl of her hair.

"I think so. I think so."

"I think you should if you want to."

"Do you?" she asked as she rolled onto her side, stroking the salt and pepper hair on his chest.

"Yes, I think you should if you want to." He buried his head in her neck, inhaling everything.

"No, I meant, do you think I should take it. What do you want me to do?"

"Gobble, gobble," he whispered and bent down to caress her breast with his lips.

The Presidential election drained Meredith and only the family gathering over the holiday rallied her spirits. Everyone, including Milton's mother, Katherine's family, and the Nicholson clan, emerged on Falmouth proceeding to take her mind off the recounts and Supreme Courts involvement with the final decision. Meredith was energized, watching Emily coddle the new grandchild, Samantha and Connor outwitting and outrunning Uncles and fathers in touch football. But mostly doting on her father, whose speech was slowly returning. He could say his wife's name, and his grandchildren's names. Meredith silently and childishly hoped he would be able to say her name next.

"He's so excited you're going to be back on television again, Mere." Gertrude boasted as she basted the turkey, while Beth Stafford held the pan of juices and Katherine's mother Roberta held the stove door.

"Oh, yes, we're all excited, Meredith," Beth added, "I tried relentlessly to see your program before. New Hampshire has got to get with it and their broadcasting. Bunch of country folk we are out there. This new program, well it's so much bigger. Even our networks will carry it. Thanks so much for the video-tapes though, that last program was really incredible."

A kitchen full of women suddenly went quiet. Gertrude finally piped in, "Ooh boy, it sure was!" Then she sighed.

Katherine snorted into her hot cider, then reached to tickle Meredith's side, who in turn tickled Emily and the matriarchs at the stove had to stop what they were doing to wipe the tears from their eyes with dishtowels.

"What's going on in here?" Charlie asked. His face flushed from the outdoor activities.

They all broke out in laughter that could be heard throughout the house and even down to the dock, where Milton was showing David the new boat, purchased with the quarterly bonus he had just received. He wrestled with his thoughts each time he stepped on the glistening new deck. He was going to make a difference, going to find this cure and going to save the lives of thousands. He wanted so badly to shout it from the rooftop, but he remembered Joyce Ridgefield's warning.

"Sounds like they're having fun?" David smiled, looking up from the steering column, towards the house.

"It sure does, "Milton added, "it's nice to hear. Really nice." He couldn't help but grin, as he wiped his hand along the teak dashboard.

"It's truly pathetic how it all ended," Bonnie winced as she watched Darryl pacing as he read the script.

"Bonnie, it's not something we can think about right now. We need to come up with the final draft for the show and we need to get it to the producers by noon."

Meredith walked in, dressed in a winter-white wool suit, her hair piled high in a twist, her face fresh and vibrant and tanned. Her eyes twinkled through her new birthday glasses that Emily had picked out herself. From the looks of it, Emily knew her face better than she did. She looked stunning.

"Whew, looks like that little Caribbean jaunt did wonders for someone?" Bonnie blurted out, envious and enamored.

Meredith grinned. "I promised him I would go, before this whole 'thing' began. I thought it would be nice for all of them. Turns out, I had a wonderful time. It was a lovely Christmas holiday."

"That's great, Meredith. Really wonderful! You should take a few days in the sun more often. You look absolutely radiant," Darryl exhorted with flirting charm and Meredith blushed.

"Well, thank you, you two. Thank you. Maybe once we get this going, the two of you can take a few days off?"

"I don't intend to take a day off until I see the current hoax ousted from the Capital and you on the throne."

"Jesus, Bonnie. Give it a rest." Darryl put his hands to his forehead and closed his eyes.

"I'm sorry. It's just a fresh wound. Sorry, Meredith, we need to get to work."

Meredith took her seat behind the desk and asked, "What exactly have you two been conjuring up, while I was away?"

Milton steadied his hand as he prematurely flipped the calendar over to the New Year. He counted the days. He had never intended or thought he would count down until their meeting. The vacation had been magical with his family, but the moment his office building loomed in front of him on his return, all he could think about was what she said. They had spoken only the one time.

"Most of my mother's work is public knowledge, Mr. Stafford. You can find it over the internet." It seemed the Ms. Ridgefield was more comfortable with formality.

"I know, Ms. Ridgefield. That's how I located you. But was there any information that your mother did not publish after her lecture in 1996? It may be helpful with my research and make her efforts less futile. I was hoping to speak with her. I am so sorry about your loss."

There was a pause and Milton thought he might have offended her. She had informed him at the beginning of her mother's untimely death and had also proclaimed that she was carrying on her legacy. He'd read the lectures and transcripts and he knew the controversial contents. It wasn't the first time the United States Government or any other government for that matter had been accused of covert actions, but he was here to help. He had been hired and was project manager of the operation to cure this bastard of a disease and he was sure that Joyce Ridgefield's mother would be happy to hear the news. She had asked him to secretly sneak in his car and take her call. He was positive she was paranoid with a few screws loose.

Joyce Ridgefield finally responded, "She has a few journals that she never made anyone aware of, including me, until I found them after her death. She was always very private, except when it came to her disease and her killers." Milton winced.

"Did you read them, Ms. Ridgefield?" He was getting a bit exasperated and uncomfortable as he crouched down in his car. He sat straight up, perturbed.

"Yes, yes I did. I think it's time to share them with someone and I've decided, after some investigation of my own, that someone is you. I've made preliminary arrangements to be on a plane to Boston the first week of January. Can you meet me at the terminal? I can give you them there."

"You're coming to Boston? Wouldn't you rather just send them to me? Of course I guarantee their safe return."

"Mr. Stafford, you don't seem to understand. I think my mother not only died from the syndrome, but she knew what the cure was and who was keeping it to themselves. I also think because she had this information, she and everyone that she knew was and still is in danger of their lives."

Milton swallowed. "Danger?"

"Yes. I must go now. This conversation has been long enough. I'll be in terminal B at gate 23 on January 4th. I'll be wearing a yellow hat. Please meet me there if you wish to have these."

"I will. Hard to explain what I look like, I guess you could say…."

"Mr. Stafford, I already know what you look like. Goodbye and Happy Holidays." The phone clicked off. Milton sat, perspiring through his suit as it stuck to the leather seats, and stared at himself in the rearview and said, "Now Pop, what would you think of all that?"

That had been three months ago and now he would be meeting this woman in six days. He had been working on the project alone for over a year now and was excited about the results and the money. He had enhanced an already existing antibody and in just a short period of time, developed a much more practical and systematic antidote that, once approved, he was sure would help many. But there was something that she said that he kept hearing over and over. *She knew what the cure was and who was keeping it to themselves.*

Did Joyce's mom know about the sample that he had been given to start with? Was it what she was referring to as the cure? Far from it he thought. The initial sample had been a weak link and barely could conceal a symptom, let alone redefine it and cure it. What was she referring to then? She had died two years earlier, so it was impossible she was privy to his work. He had never been given the information on the sample and its original developer. Keeping it to themselves.

Wasn't that exactly what he was doing?

A scientist asked many questions of himself but rarely of anyone else. Maybe it was time to ask some questions of his own.

CHAPTER 30

Meredith's debut and was an overnight success. It was a morning talk show, before the soap operas, with a dose of prime time thrown in. Her first guest, a controversial aging senator who held wide appeal throughout Massachusetts. Meredith steered clear of controversy, handed him a button that read "wouldn't you like to be me?" and settled in for a chat about the weather at the capitol and his mother's favorite recipe for clam chowder. Her second guest was a local boy, gone famous in Hollywood for an award-winning screenplay and a smile that lit up the big screen. She handed him a button—"single and very, very rich." He reminded Meredith of Connor and she said so, and he gingerly joked back, "Gosh, you don't look old enough to have a son in high school. I was hoping you could introduce me to some of your single girlfriends. Unless, of course, you're available?"

Just before they wrapped, a special guest walked on the stage and Meredith was caught off guard and giggled uncontrollably into her glass of water. The wife of the Democratic candidate strolled on the stage and gingerly handed Meredith, the actor, and senator each a button. They all donned the new button—"Bipartisan Bah Humbug" with a large red X across the front. It was a gimmick that everyone would want to be part of. Meredith shook all of their hands and hugged the cameraman.

The last guest, though her husband had lost, was especially good for Meredith. Let bygones be bygones, and a little humor healed. The local press latched on, but Meredith returned with national and entertainment news programs on alert and, without a lot of coaxing or kickback from upstairs, they introduced her to the world. Most who saw the program would blame only one person for its success. Meredith. She was intelligent, witty and beautiful with no apprehension speaking her mind and an innate ability to make even the squeamish comfortable. She mixed up celebrities, politicians, and working-class America all in one hour and entertained while she educated. She declined the comic style set up, with a backup band for support, and went for the more formal, face-to-face confrontation, usually found on cable or from certain pretentious radio personalities. She had her critics, but those critics had their own critics and the majority of the time she came out on top of the ratings. Her old program and notorious "Vote Democrat" button were always in the spotlight, with a different button customized daily, depending on the topic or guest. She and her guests wore them proudly and America watched with anticipation. No one was sure how the next day would measure up, but Meredith was in the spotlight now, her old cronies backing her up, and instead of politics as the main focus, the world was now her catalyst. She was suddenly a star.

"Meredith, I really think we need to do a show with maybe a famous lesbian. I think we can now." Bonnie squirmed in her chair, finding herself unsettled with her boss's newfound fame and formal attitude.

Meredith didn't look up from the script, but nodded her head as if she agreed.

"So you think we can pinpoint a date for it?" Bonnie crossed her fingers in her lap.

Meredith put the script down beside her desk and folded her hands. She looked straight into Bonnie's eyes.

"Bon? Why is it always something?"

Bonnie blinked her eyes, and didn't answer.

"Really," Meredith continued, "we've known each other for years, respect each other completely, and never once have I said no without a good reason. What exactly is it with you Bonnie?"

Bonnie looked down and uncrossed her fingers in her lap. "I'm not sure. I'm sorry. I know I'm one-sided sometimes, but the prejudice is not resolved. Civil union is still not available or legal, and the lesbian—I mean, homosexual community wants answers."

"And you speak for all of them?"

Bonnie fidgeted again, then relaxed. "Yes, I'm here to represent all of them."

Meredith rocked back in her chair and a smile came across her face. "It would be fun to poke at the President, wouldn't it?" They both knew how frail homosexual issues remained in the White House. Reality was, the President didn't believe nor could he even begin to acknowledge the idea that homosexuals even existed in "his" country. Every issue skirted off his desk and into the trashcan without discussion.

Bonnie had her hook where she wanted it. "Yes, it would really piss him off."

Meredith pondered the idea as Darryl Rodriguez knocked lightly then let himself in the opened office door.

"Hey. I just wanted to see what you thought of tomorrow's script"

"Darryl, what do you think of doing a show on homosexual rights and needs in our country?"

Darryl frowned. He had heard it before and knew Bonnie was the culprit but before he could answer Meredith added, "It would be a bit scandalous at the big house, don't you think?"

"Well, it would. But right now I think we need to stay on the roller coaster a bit longer. Really dig our feet deep before we attack the issues that may lose some of our audience."

"Good answer. Coming from my clear thinker. I don't know though. This guy is just enough to make me do something crazy. Kind of like before."

"Meredith, remember what happened before?"

"Oh, I know, but this wouldn't be live and it would be edited and in good taste and, lord knows we don't discriminate anyone else's views or ideas." She wondered what the button would say and grinned.

Bonnie smiled. She hadn't lost yet.

"Hey, I see that smile and I hope this isn't personal. You know we are big and you know we're also disposable. I'm afraid it might not be the right time."

"You never think it's the right time. Sometimes I think you might be a bit homophobic."

"All right you two. All right. We can chew on it for a while. I'm sure it will come up again. Let's keep an eye on the "big guy" and when he makes a stupid move, we'll react with our brilliant ploy." She picked up the script and pushed her glasses up the bridge of her nose.

Bonnie and Darryl looked at Meredith and they both knew something had changed. She was still Meredith Nicholson, but she was on a higher road, with bigger plans. She was grooming herself for the next step. They needed to swim a little faster in case they missed her boat.

"Enough you two, I have a few things I've got to do, then I need to head home. Emily's surgery is tomorrow and I want to spend some time with her tonight."

They both nodded and said good night. Darryl lagged behind as he watched Bonnie make her way to the elevator.

"Darryl, do you want me to hold it?'

"No thanks. I have a few things I need to get from my office. I'll see you in the morning."

"OK. Good night." He heard her say as the door closed.

He turned back toward Meredith's office and knocked again, this time waiting for her to acknowledge.

"Yes? Oh, hi Darryl. Did you forget something?"

"No. Um, yes I mean." He closed the door behind him and sat across from her.

"Yes?" Meredith asked curiously.

"Meredith, I just wanted a moment in private to say I'm really proud of where this program is going so far. I'm not sure any one of us would've thought it could happen so fast. I just wanted to say that."

"I agree with you one hundred percent and I owe so much of it to you. You negotiated the network's deal and you believed I—we—could do this."

He was flattered. He sometimes felt he was the sole reason it had all happened, but now he knew that he was losing some of the power and Meredith was truly in control.

"I also wanted you to know that I have always believed in you and trusted your judgment."

"Now Darryl, what is this ass-kissing? I know for a fact that when I was given the mayoral seat, you were the most concerned."

"Meredith, I didn't know you then, nor did I know your potential. I was a political prick and had to stay that way."

"I know, I know. Just kidding with you. Of course I didn't expect you to bow to the whole idea right away. You know how much I need you to make things work around here."

"That's just the point, Meredith. Things here are incredible right now, but a few people have been in touch just recently, wondering what next?"

"What next? Hmmm. We've just been hatched and now we have to start walking?"

"Meredith, people are talking about the potential for a political career again."

Meredith looked at him without reaction. She kept one hand under her chin and the other grasped the edge of her chair.

"Did you know that?"

"I don't think I'd ever get that information before you, Darryl. What are they saying?"

"You know this television show has not only boosted the ratings, but your name is becoming a household word."

She smiled.

"Is that what you want?" he asked needing to know her intentions.

"I'm not sure. Everything I've done in my life has somehow fallen into my lap. Every action resulted in a better reaction, even if at the time I didn't think it was a good thing. Moving to Boston, meeting my husband, my two children," she hesitated, "what I mean is, I've never had to work so hard that my fingers bled, yet I've never been completely satisfied. I've struggled with why since high school. Most people would feel completely satisfied with what I've become and accomplished, silently. But every day, I crave more. Something gnaws at me and has started to mold me into something I'm not even sure I want to be. I've put my finger on it, finally, but have told no one and don't intend to until I'm completely sure."

Darryl looked at her perplexed.

"Not even your Milton?"

"Not even my husband." She answered without hesitation. "Not yet."

"Good night, Meredith." Darryl stood to leave.

"Darryl?" He turned, "I don't mean to keep you in the dark, I just want us to enjoy the ride for a bit. It's fun—invigorating—don't you think?"

"You can say that again." He teased and waved good night.

Meredith looked into the empty hallway through the open door and thought about what she had had just shared.

Darryl took the stairs, ten floors to the lobby, convinced he knew exactly what her intentions were and at the moment he stepped out into the evening chill, he was adamant that if she chose the path, she quite possibly could win. There was just something about Meredith Nicholson.

Meredith picked up the phone and dialed.

"Hi Beatrice, is Emily close by?...Hi, darling. I'm leaving now...Yes, I know, I'll be home in an hour, I promise...Is Dad there?...No? Not home from work yet?".... She glanced at her watch and frowned. "Hmmm, OK, I'll call him from the car...You are?...Great! I don't think you need to pack too much though darling, they said you might be there for only one night...OK, OK...You're so organized...Oh Emily, I hope so too sweetheart. I hope so too. Let me get going, so I can get home...You too sweetheart. I love you too. Bye bye."

Maybe by this time tomorrow, her 11-year-old angel would be able to see. She put the next day's script in her briefcase and locked her office door. She dialed Milton's office as the elevator doors opened into the lobby. His voicemail was there to greet her. She hung up and scowled as her second call to his cell phone automatically was greeted by the same salutation, "Hello you've reached Milton Stafford. I can't take your call right now, but please leave a message and I will return it soon." Beep....

"Hi darling. I'm surprised you're not home. I'm leaving the office now and will have my cell phone on if you get this message in the next hour. Emily's excited about tomorrow and I hope we can all have dinner together. See you soon. Love you." She ended the call and made her way to her car in the deserted parking garage.

"Desmond, has everything been taken care of?"

"Gerald, I told you before, we have nothing to worry about. Everything will be taken care of."

"I know. I just find the subject and situation fascinating and want to be kept well informed."

Desmond had no intention of keeping him informed of everything but added, "As soon as it's done, I will let you know. Where's the Vice President now?"

"Oh Jesus! Back in Asia as we speak. Let's keep him there another six months. Good. Good. I'm glad everything's going to plan. Good work, Desmond." Revo disconnected the private line.

"Poor, pretty cunt," Revo chuckled, "she'll never know what hit her."

Milton sat frustrated and dazed at the same light he had just idled at five minutes prior. He missed the turn again to get on Route 93 South, the maze of construction from the airport almost impossible to navigate through. Joyce Ridgefield had called frantic that morning after canceling their initial visit almost three months before. She panicked and hung up when she realized she had called his work number and immediately called back on his cell phone, asking if he could meet her at the same terminal in a few hours. She didn't explain why she had cancelled or what the hurry was now, but Milton felt compelled to meet her, since he still wanted to read the documents her mother had left hidden. He had received his seventh quarterly bonus check from the company the same morning and an overwhelming congratulations from Salinger in regards to his work so far. He was also told that his work was almost through, since the antibody he had developed was an almost perfect correlation for a cure. Persian Gulf Syndrome was about to be halted for good. He had smiled with the compliment but couldn't help worrying about what was next for him and how long it would take the FDA to approve, so the hundreds of thousands that would benefit could finally find relief and live the lives they were born to live. He chastised his selfish thought and determined that with the results finally posted and the discoverer acknowledged, there would be no future issues and he could probably write his own ticket anywhere. Their meeting squelched that assumption. Their meeting was the biggest quagmire of his life.

He saw her first as she exited the airplane, wearing the yellow hat she had reminded him of. He had no real picture of what she might look like, just an image of someone extremely nervous and dramatic. She was neither. She was tall, even elegant, and as she glanced around the terminal looking for him, he felt a knot in his stomach. She was breathtaking. Everyone that walked past her glanced her way. When she spotted him, she smiled the most brilliant smile he had ever seen. His right knee quivered as she approached him.

"Milton. Thank you so much for coming on such short notice."

He smiled and nodded.

"Please, let's go somewhere a little more quiet."

"Not a lot of places like that in the airport, "He said as they passed the restrooms. He had the sudden need to splash cold water on his face. "Excuse me one minute," he mumbled, looking downward. She understood and said, "Oh of course. I could use the facilities myself. See you in a moment."

As he stared at himself through the soap-splashed mirror, he found himself counting backward. He checked both his shoes for toilet paper before he made his way out. She was waiting and still smiling.

"Do you want to go to one of the restaurants here in the terminal?" he barely squeaked out, embarrassed he was reacting this way.

"I was hoping we could possibly go to your car, Milton. I'm afraid the information, well, I was just hoping we could go to your car."

"Of course. Yes, that's a good idea" He was certain it was the worst idea.

They walked to the garage in silence and once they reached his car, he absently forgot to open her door. He jumped out his side to do just that, but she had already settled into the passenger seat, a leather carry-on, propped on her lap.

"I'm sorry. I would've opened…."

"No, no trouble. You have more important things on your mind right now, as I do. A little chivalry is not necessary at this time."

He watched as she shuffled through the folders, noticing her legs were bare under the dashboard. And tanned.

"It's warm in Houston today?" He asked filling the silence.

"Uh, I think it's in the seventies. I'm not sure though. I flew in from Miami and yes, it was very warm there." She reached under the dashboard as if she were searching for something.

"Oh," he added, as she brushed under the dashboard on his side.

"I'm sorry. I'm just a little paranoid. I think that we're safe here."

"Safe?"

"Mr. Stafford, I've been followed for the better part of the last six months. I've never been sure by whom, nor have I confronted anyone, but I can tell you that someone is very interested in every move I make."

Milton looked at her and didn't respond. The paranoid voice he was accustomed too was now in full view, emerging from a pouting, perfect mouth.

"Please. I know you must think I'm crazy but…."

"No, no. Not crazy. I just need you to explain what's been going on."

"Yes, I know. I was afraid I might find something, but it seems clean. I'm not really an expert at this."

Milton tried not to focus on her legs. He was having trouble looking at any part of her, so he concentrated on the digital clock. He was unsure of this meeting and this situation. He glanced out the window and Meredith came into his mind.

"Mr. Stafford, please don't take me for an imbecile which I promise you I'm not. I want you to know, you're the first and only person I'm sharing this information with."

"Ms. Ridgefield, what information? Please, it's been months. You cancelled before with no notice and I'm cold and want to get home." He said it with such sincerity, that even he believed it.

Joyce reached inside the leather bag and pulled out two generic, manila files and handed them to Milton.

"I'm sorry about January and the previous meeting we intended to have. I'm sorry I couldn't explain anything then, really. Here, I think this will explain everything." Her voice sounded aggravated and relieved.

"OK, what exactly is this?" Milton turned facing her, less confrontational.

"Those are the files that I found. The files that my mother hid from everyone. I found them only after she died and I think they have all the answers."

"You mean her theories about the distinction and reason for the syndrome as well as her ideas for a cure?"

"What I mean is, she pinpoints all of the distinction and reasons. Fact. And she painstakingly gives all the details for an antibody, the serum—basically, the cure."

"Really?" Milton asked unconvinced as he flipped through the pages, "and where does she painstakingly give this information?"

"Mr. Stafford. If you're not interested, I'm sure someone will be. I'll take that back now."

Milton looked at her, the pouting lips, the radiant green eyes, and realized his demeanor. "I'm sorry, Ms. Ridgefield. I'm sorry. I didn't mean to offend you or your deceased mother. I'm just so curious. I've been working only on this issue for so long and I'm just a hopeless romantic. I want this to be over in more ways than one."

Joyce looked at him and took the second folder from his hands and opened it to almost the last pages and handed it back. Milton accepted it graciously and started to read. After only one page all he could say was, "Shit."

It was almost an hour before either spoke again. Joyce Ridgefield had lit a cigarette and was blowing the smoke out the open window. Milton, under any other circumstances, would've never allowed this, but he was dumbstruck and terrified at the information laid before him. Joyce Ridgefield's mother, along with two Texas scientists, had labeled and instructed anyone that had their hands on the material, of the exact cure for Persian Gulf War Syndrome. The answers had been hidden in a box in a bedroom closet for years.

"Where are the Andersons? How can I get hold of them?" Milton asked, almost winded and scared.

"Milton, they're all dead. All of them. My mother and both Betty and Walter Anderson. They're all deceased. My mother died of extenuating circumstances definitely brought on by the syndrome. Betty and Walter died in a car crash, over a year ago, while they were driving home from their office in Houston. I'm sorry Milton. There's no one left to talk to. Only me."

Milton looked at the woman sitting inches from his side and wanted suddenly to be home. He needed his family. His cell phone rang and he reached in his pocket and turned it off without looking at the caller's ID.

"I'm sorry, Mr. Stafford, I really am. I know this is difficult and you're just absorbing it now, but I need you, I really do. I hope you understand why I've gotten you involved in this. I've been so alone with this information and I'm hoping I can trust you. I can, right?" She looked at the confused man innocently.

"Ms. Ridgefield, please, call me Milton."

"I have to go now." She glanced at her watch assuredly.

"I'm not sure what to say Ms. Ridgefield. I'm just not sure what to say."

"Just tell me you'll keep my mother's will in check. Make sure that everything she lived and died for is palpable and God help us, make sure that the world has access to the cure."

"Of course I will. Yes. Of course I will. Joyce, I don't know what to say?"

She leaned over and kissed him on the cheek. "You've already said it, Milton. Thank you. I'm not alone anymore. I have a plane to catch."

"Let me walk you to…." Milton added, grasping for the door handle.

"No, No. Please Milton. Let me go alone. I've already become quite good at this and, just to be on the safe side. I would hate to put you or anyone else in jeopardy."

"I don't think that walking you to the terminal could put anyone in jeopardy, Ms. Ridgefield. I insist."

She leaned over and took his arm away from the door. "Mr. Stafford, I insist. My life has been a living hell since my mother died. I've been more worried about my everyday existence than I want or could dream you would ever know. I have no intention of wishing that on anyone else. Please, for me. For your family." She released her hold and opened the passenger door.

"I'll be in touch," He added before he saw her smile and close the door. He watched as she disappeared onto the pedestrian walkway.

Milton started the car and fumbled for the ticket, pulling his cell phone out simultaneously. He turned it on and saw that Meredith had called twice. He left it on the passenger seat as he made his way out of the parking garage. He had to get out of the city and closer to home so he could breathe.

CHAPTER 31

The doctors were cautiously optimistic. Unlike the thousands of candidates that qualified for laser surgery to correct their vision, Emily's condition was much more complicated. With the rare form of infant glaucoma, no one could conclude whether Emily would ever really see. One thing was for certain: numerous studies listed her condition as incurable thus far and for any child born with this disease most learning and communication abilities were labeled mentally handicapped at best. Emily was completely the opposite. Apparently because of her disease, she was at a dramatically higher level of ability and knowledge through her other senses. It didn't matter that since birth she was blind. It was almost if she was never meant to see and never relied on it. She was an amazing child and both Milton and Meredith sat beside her bed, praying that when she recovered, she would be able to see them.

Their evening the night before had been melancholy and quiet. Milton had called Meredith as soon as he saw the first Cape Cod sign.

"Hi. Where are you?" She asked concerned.

"I have about 20 more minutes here then I'll wrap up and be right home."

"I'm sorry, sweetie. I didn't know you were going to be late. I would've left the office earlier."

"Oh, no, that's OK. Is Em all right?"

"She's fine. Excited...She's waiting for you. Beatrice fed her early because of the surgery, but she seems very at ease. Just fine."

"Good. Of course, our little girl, the one most at ease."

"Are you all right Milton?"

"Uh. Sure, yeah. Just tired. I'm sorry."

"No, no. Don't apologize. We'll see you soon. Yes?"

"Yes, Meredith. I'll be there as soon as I possibly can. I love you."

"I love you too, darling."

Milton powered down his phone and tossed it back on the passenger seat. Joyce had been paranoid about using it for any communication and here he was talking sweet nothings to his wife on it. Was it possible someone was listening to his conversations?

"Oh my God," he whispered, "What have I gotten myself and my family into?"

"Milton?"

Milton looked into the rearview, adjusted to keep the oncoming headlights diffused, and saw his grandfather gazing out the window,

"Yes, Pop?"

"I'm worried. Really worried."

"Me too. Me too." He felt his hands trembling, as he gripped the wheel.

"That woman's mother already had all the documentation. All the work that you've been so caught up in—useless, wasted time."

"Pop. Why would they pay me so much money?"

"I don't know, Son…I don't know. Maybe they didn't have the information that you have right now. Maybe they've been looking for it."

"Who? The government?"

"I don't know, maybe. You might be the sole recipient of that information and if so, I'm afraid when they find out they might not be very happy."

"Why would she keep it secret, Pop? Why?"

"That is something you're going to have to find out Milton. No matter what, you have to find that out."

"I'm scared, Pop. I'm really scared."

"Now you listen…." His grandfather was now sitting beside him, on top of the phone and folders. "You're a brilliant man. One that came up with a cure for this horrible disease. You're very capable of doing that with many more diseases. It's all right to be scared, but you need to remember, your brave actions, tackled and destroyed a lethal byproduct of poison. You're a hero and you need to remember that always."

"I wasn't the first." Milton said, his eyes getting moist.

"No, and who gives a hoot about that? You're the one that gets it out to the world. You'll be the one that carries on Ms. Ridgefield's mother's vision. It goes hand in hand, don't you see?"

Milton just nodded, keeping his eyes on the poorly lit two-lane highway.

"Do you know what your next step is?"

Milton shook his head downtrodden.

"Your next step is being with your daughter through her surgery. Your boss already knows about it, so there's nothing you can do to prevent that. You need to return to work afterwards and be an elite, Academy Award actor. You need to approach this as if you have never heard of nor seen Ms. Ridgefield or the information she has given you. As long as you can act that way, we have some time."

"We?"

"Milton, do you really think I'd leave you alone at a time like this?"

"Pop, you're a ghost, a hallucination. I really don't…."

"Milton, you can use all the support right now you can muster and you cannot tell a soul about any of this. So isn't a specter alongside you better than no one or nothing at all?"

Milton glanced at his grandfather, mustering a smile.

"Plus, I think I've got some pretty good ideas. I might be able to help."

Milton looked ahead at the approaching Bourne Bridge, the back entrance to the cape. He was almost home. Almost home.

"Oh, I can't stand that bitch!" Revo's hands gripped the newspaper tightly as his elbows dug into the desk in the Oval Office. He pounded on the speakerphone.

"Lynne, get in here now."

A pretty, twenty-something woman quickly came into the room with a notepad and pen in tow.

"I need to know exactly when that meeting is again today with the directors."

"Um, sir? Sorry, I'm not sure what meeting you're talking about."

"God damn it, why do I keep you working here?"

Lynne looked down at her feet, unable to answer.

"Well?" Revo barked.

"Sir, you have no meeting today with the directors. You are scheduled to meet with them tomorrow at 8:30 in the West Wing board room, but you're not scheduled today for any meeting with them."

Revo looked at her blankly then added, "Are you sure?" with a snarl.

"Yes sir. Positive."

"Good, then, that will be all. Oh and Lynne, make sure my tailor is here by three o'clock. I'm working so damn hard, I've lost a couple more pounds."

"Yes sir." She returned to the refuge of her desk just as Damion Desmond was entering her office. He saw that she was flushed, almost in tears.

"Lynne, is everything all right?"

She put away her compact and answered, "Yes, yes sir," as she threw the used tissues in the basket under her desk.

"Are you sure?" Desmond asked again, patting her hand. She smiled and nodded yes.

"Is he alone?"

"Yes, Mr. Desmond. He doesn't have another appointment until after one. I'm afraid he just got confused with his schedule, that's all."

"Ah, all right then, may I go in?"

"Of course, Mr. Desmond."

Damion smiled. "Give us a 15 without interruption."

"Of course, Mr. Desmond. Thank you."

Damion knocked lightly then let himself in, closing the door quietly behind him.

"Well, how is everything today, Gerald?"

Gerald looked up from the paper with a scowl.

"Hmm, not a good day."

"Fucking terrible. I don't know what it is. I was feeling great and now I'm just fucking agitated. I thought I forgot a meeting. I hate this fucking queen."

Damion glanced down at Gerald's finger, tapping on the Canadian Prime Minister's picture.

"Hmmm. I know."

"Desmond. What's wrong?"

"Nothing. Not a thing for you to worry about. I have something that will make you feel a whole lot better." He handed a small vial to the President.

"What's this?"

"It's the answer."

"Really?"

"Really."

"That one nerd scientist, married to that bimbo talk show host. He came up with this?"

"One and the same, and she's far from a bimbo"

"What now? Kill him? Can we kill her too?"

Desmond looked at Gerald's bloodshot eyes, then looked away.

"Well, Desmond?"

"I think I have a better plan than that."

"Really? What?"

"I think we need to keep him around. He has been the only one to tackle this almost effortlessly. His brain is worth keeping."

"Well, how are we going to keep his mouth shut though? His wife is fucking popular and God forbid she gets wind of this, if she hasn't already."

"I know for a fact that she's completely unaware of his project and study."

"How the hell would you know that?"

"Gerald, please. Give me some credit."

"You didn't answer the question about keeping his mouth shut."

"Already taken care of, Mr. President. Already taken care of."

Revo had to believe him. He excused himself and went into the adjoining bathroom with the vial. He had to believe him. He had to.

Desmond waited, doodling a dress and high heels on the Canadian prime Minister's picture. When Revo returned, he was smiling.

"Almost instant."

"I know. That's what I was told."

"Nice picture, Desmond." Revo smirked at the picture of his northern nemesis.

"We need to talk."

"Nope. It's all taken care of." He walked over to the portrait of his mother and removed it from the wall. He carefully entered the combination of the safe and extracted a large manila envelope.

"Is this all of it?"

"Those are cashier's checks, Desmond. Yes, it's all there."

Cashiers checks, Desmond thought. *Brilliant.*

"I doubt they're cosigned in your name?" Desmond smiled as he opened the envelope.

"No, as a matter of fact, I decided to have them drawn up in a few people's names. People that I know and love so dearly. As a matter of fact, I think this prima donna faggot signed a few." Gerald laughed again at the sketch.

Desmond stood to leave and Revo asked, "Leaving so soon, Desmond?"

Desmond grinned and before he opened the door added, "I'll be back by six for the state dinner."

"Of course you will, Desmond. Of course you will. Have a nice flight to the Caymans."

Damion nodded and winked.

Chapter 32

On the evening that Emily woke in her hospital room in Boston, Gerald Revo watched Damion Desmond enter the lobby with what appeared to be a lingerie model. He was slightly amused. Milton and Meredith waited beside Emily's bed with several family members, including Connor, in the waiting room, all saying the same prayer. Gerald Revo did his best at avoiding the Canadian Prime Minister and his wife and was successful until just a few minutes before the dinner announcement.

"President Revo. With all due respect sir, have you been avoiding us?"

"Excuse me? Of course not, Prime Minister. Of course not. It's just been busy and, well, work before play, don't you agree?"

"But President Revo, I was hoping we'd have some time to discuss the terrorist committee I've put together. I wanted to advise you—no warn you—of certain border situations that must be addressed immediately."

Gerald stared directly into his eyes. He focused on the black of his pupils and leaned in closely. "Prime Minister, I'm sorry if this seems a bit rude, but I dare say that a state dinner is neither the time nor the place to discuss such issues."

"But President Revo! I've tried numerous times to set up a meeting with you about this and…."

"Prime Minister, please, I'm going to ask you to please call my meeting specialist and arrange for this to be discussed in private tomorrow, all right?"

The Prime Minister seemed miffed but nodded in agreement as the meal was announced.

Saved by the fucking bell, Revo thought as he linked arms with Damion Desmond's escort and smiled, shaking anyone's extended hand, all clamoring to see who they would be sitting beside. Revo made it perfectly clear that he wanted to be as far away from the Prime Minister and his wife. He preferred they eat in the kitchen, but opted to not share this with his staff.

Emily's mouth moved but no noise came out. Meredith reached quickly for the water and put the straw to her lips. She started to drink and Milton and Meredith sighed in relief. The bandages would not be removed until the next morning, so they sat with her until she faded off to sleep, then retreated to the waiting area to let everyone know it was time to go home.

"We've got the spare rooms set up at our house Meredith. Everything is ready." Katherine reminded Meredith as she accepted her coat.

"Thank you, Katherine. Just for a few hours. I want to be back when she wakes up again."

"Meredith, I'm going to stay here," Milton said humbly, as if he were asking permission.

"Darling, don't you think you'd sleep better at David and Katherine's?"

"No. I doubt I'll sleep at all. I'd rather stay here. Really. You go and I'll see you in the morning."

"Are you sure?" she added, not convinced leaving was the best thing for herself either.

"Yes, really, I'm sure. You go and I'll call if she wakes before you get here. I know she'll be happy to have me here if she wakes up."

"All right Milton." She kissed him tenderly and walked with her arms linked through Katherine and Connor's.

Connor looked back and added, "Dad, I'll bring you a bagel in the morning."

"That would be nice, Son. Thanks. Good night. Sleep well."

Milton went back into Emily's room and made himself as comfortable as possible on the cot they had provided. He lay on his side and watched her sleeping, her eyes in heavy bandages, her hands lying peacefully on her chest. He intended to stay awake all night and make sure she would be fine. Make sure no one harmed her.

Revo rose early, refreshed and satisfied that the dinner was another success. He felt comfortable with the fact that most of the invites were staunch supporters and the few, like the Prime Minister, were nothing to worry or contend with. He called down to security, was met at the residence door, and set out for a five-mile sprint. He found great humor in tiring the youngest and strongest of his agents. *Marines,* he thought, *nothing like they used to be.* "Let's go kids!" he taunted as a few struggled to keep up with him. He liked the city early in the morning, before the indigents arose and pollution filled the air. He ran past the Lincoln Memorial and saluted, sarcastically. *Got to keep an eye out more closely for your enemy boy,* he thought, *or one of them might sneak up and shoot you.* The Secret Service in front of him, instructed that he would have to turn in 15 minutes back to the residence. He nodded and smiled, sprinting even faster.

When first light broke through the blinds of the hospital room window, Milton lifted his head. He looked over at his daughter and at first thought she was sleeping, but then he saw the smile and he reached over to squeeze her hand.

"Dad?"

"Yes, Em, I'm here. How are you feeling sweetheart?"

"OK, I guess. Kind of sore. What time is it?"

"It's 5:30 in the morning sweetheart. It's early."

"Dad, did you sleep here?"

"Yes, angel. I wanted to stay in case you woke in the middle of the night. Mom and Connor went to Aunt Katherine's but I'm sure they'll be here soon. I should call them."

"Yes, I know. But let's just wait a few minutes and you and I talk, OK?"

"Sure baby, anything. What would you like to talk about?"

"Dad, the other night, the night before the surgery, you were so quiet when you got home. I just knew something was wrong but I didn't want to alarm Mom. Are you all right Daddy?"

He leaned over and sat on the edge of her bed, still clutching her hand. Leave it to his blind daughter, just after a trying surgery, to sense something was bothering him."

"Darling, I'm fine. I was just worried about you."

"Now Dad, that's a load of bull and you know it."

"Em, watch your language. And no, it's not a load of anything. You know how worried I get with you kids and, well…."

"Dad. You don't need to tell me now, but I want you to know. I know when you're sad and I know when your worried and I know when something is eating you up inside. I know, Dad. I just know."

Tears came to Milton's eyes and he laid his head on her shoulder.

"I know, baby. I know you know. Everything's fine, sweetheart. I'm just hoping, really praying hard, that the operation worked."

Emily smiled and brushed back his thinning hair, "I know, Dad. I do too."

He lifted his head, "I love you sweet girl."

"I love you too, Dad. Now stop worrying."

Milton leaned over and dialed Katherine's number.

"Meredith, Hi…Yes, she's awake…Yes…She's smiling…."

Revo arrived back at the residence, showered, and donned one of his designer suits. He was greeted by Lynne, who was pleasantly surprised at his cheerful mood, and she quickly briefed him on the day's agenda.

He nodded and added, "Make the Prime Minister's meeting the first if we can. I want to get this over with." And then thought, *get the queen out of my country pronto.*

He poured himself a glass of fresh-squeezed grapefruit juice, to the dismay of his secretary, and entered the Oval Office, feeling powerful.

The bandages were removed slowly, to prevent injury as well as to allow increments of light to penetrate. Everyone stood back, holding hands, as the doctor exposed his handiwork. Emily remained quiet and calm. When they were completely off, the doctor asked her to blink. She did.

"Do you feel any pressure, any pain?"

"I feel a burning sensation."

"That's very common. Is it bearable?" Milton sighed when he heard this.

Emily answered, "It burns, but it's not the worst pain. I have a headache, Doctor Lisa."

"We'll get you some aspirin. Anything else?"

Emily took hold of the doctor's arm and squeezed. "Doctor Lisa? I think I just saw something!"

"Prime Minister, I understand the situation you have explained quite vividly and I will get a team in touch with you in the next month or two, to start investigating how we can proceed with these concern of yours."

"President Revo, it should be a concern of yours as well. They don't want anything or anyone in Canada. They want the United States and will find any way to get into your country. They have before and they will again."

"Well, all due respect Prime Minister, but don't you think it's wise that you work to prevent these people from entering our country? They're entering North America through your gateways, correct?"

"Mr. President, these people are not criminals yet. We can't detain them for crimes they haven't committed yet. I'm just here to warn you that we need to act now and act fast. Terrorists are a patient breed. But I'm afraid for the future."

"Patience, yes patience. Something all of us need to practice a bit more of. Prime Minister, I have another meeting I need to attend. Thank you for your time and insight into this matter. I will take it under advisement."

"Please do, Mr. President. Please do. It could be a matter of life and death."

"Hmm...." Gerald pondered as he showed the Prime Minister to the door, "Have a safe flight, Prime Minister."

"Thank you. I'm sure I will. Thank you for seeing me, sir."

"Of course, of course. I'm sorry there was a delay before. Good day."

President Revo shut the door behind him and mumbled, "Fucking queen".

There was a light tap at the door and Damion entered.

"I saw your favorite leader leaving. How did that go?"

"Oh that homo thinks that terrorists are looming at the border and constantly trying to penetrate our country, ready to strike at any minute."

"Well, Gerald, remember Seattle?"

"Of course I do, Desmond. I'm just not going to drop everything we're doing here and head up to the tundra to investigate his concerns."

"Yes, I know, he does seem a bit paranoid. But either way, you should assign at least one man to look into it."

"Yes, I guess you're right. He's probably got a legitimate point somewhere in all that flab. I just find it very hard to take the bitch seriously. Have you seen that third chin?"

"I try not to look, Mr. President."

"Yeah, seems you've taken to only looking at lookers."

"Gerald, it's time for the director's meeting and then we need to convey the Middle Eastern situation."

"No response to lookers?"

"You know exactly what I like Mr. President. I'll see you in the meeting, sir?"

"Yes, of course Desmond. I'm sorry, I was just...."

"None taken, sir. I'll be leaving now."

"Desmond. Thank you."

"Absolutely, Mr. President. Absolutely."

"Can you see us, Emily?"

"Oh my gosh, I see two fuzzy blobs. Mom, Dad, are you two fuzzy blobs?"

Everyone chuckled. Foe the first time in over 11 years, Emily could see light.

"Connor?" She asked looking around the room.

"Yes, Em. I'm right here." He reached over to hold her outstretched hand.

"Oh my gosh! Is that you? You're really fuzzy too, Connor, but I think I can make most of you out. Oh my gosh, you're not nearly as good looking as what you told me all these years."

He stifled his laughter and leaned in to whisper, "Doctor Lisa says it will be a few days before anything takes real shape, Emily, remember? Prepare yourself, I'm quite a hunk!" He wrapped an awkward arm around her shoulders and looked back at his parents, with tears in his eyes.

After another hour, Doctor Lisa insisted everyone take a break, so Emily could get some rest. She stepped outside and let them know it had been a good morning, but they needed to be patient and many more tests needed to be done. Meredith and Milton left Connor with his Uncles and arm in arm, found their way to the lobby, to use their phones and contact work. Meredith chatted quietly with Bonnie as Milton retrieved the two messages on his work phone, one the old message from Meredith the night before and a second one with no recording, just the sound of a loud engine, then silence. He looked at his phone and hit the repeat button, but there was nothing more to decipher, just a loud engine and silence. He made his way to a payphone with a pocketful of quarters from the gift shop and dialed Joyce Ridgefield's number. A man's voice answered, "Hello, Ridgefield residence".

"Yes, um, hello. Is Ms. Ridgefield available?"

"Who's calling?"

"This is a colleague. We spoke yesterday and…."

"I'm sorry, what did you say your name was? This is Detective Marino of the West Houston homicide division. Ms. Ridgefield has been involved an accident."

Milton's hands started shaking and he lost his balance falling forward into the booth, his forehead hitting the top of the payphone.

"Excuse me, sir? What did you say your name was again?"

Milton placed the receiver in the cradle, as he heard the voice on the other end calling out to him again and again. He could see his reflection in the grimy silver plated change box and saw a trickle of blood just above his right eye. He grabbed his handkerchief and held it to his head just as his wife was approaching him.

"Hi honey. I've been looking for you? Did your cell phone battery die? What happened to your head? Milton? You're bleeding." She reached up but he pulled his head away.

"Meredith, I'm fine. I just turned and hit my head. I'll be fine."

"Do you need to use my phone?" She asked as she reached up again to inspect the injury. This time he allowed her to look.

"No, no. I uh…I just need to get to work. It's really getting busy and, well, seems no one can do anything without me."

Meredith frowned. "But darling, what about Emily?"

"I know. I know, goddamn it. I'll be back early evening and everyone else will be here all day. The doctor says she needs some rest. I really need to go." He grabbed his briefcase and brushed her cheek lightly with his lips.

"Really? Right now? Right this minute?" she asked bewildered.

"Meredith, please tell her I'll be back later this afternoon. All right?"

"Sure, sweetheart, of course I will. Milton, is everything all right?"

"Yes, Meredith. Fine, just fine. I have to go. Bye."

She watched as he made his way swiftly through the double doors, almost colliding with a teenager on crutches. He didn't look back. He repeated over and over in his mind, *Joyce Ridgefield's accident was not an accident.*

CHAPTER 33

On a dazzling fall morning the world watched in horror as the United States fell prey to an enemy. The World Trade Center and Pentagon were attacked by air while a fourth plane, crashed into Pennsylvania farmland. Over 3000 innocent people perished and the finger was immediately pointed at Afghanistan and a terrorist regime. In shock and anger the world rallied, with the President thanking the courage of rescue workers and strangers coming to help. He praised countries from all over the world for their participation in the "striking back" cause and the outpouring of support. He was determined to "meet violence with the justice it deserved." And the world watched and prayed.

Meredith was interrupted just as she was about to sit down for the taping of her show. She sat frozen, staring with the staff; her hands to her face, as the horror unveiled on the morning news program.

Milton looked up, the incessant tapping on the lab window breaking his concentration. One of the child prodigies looked frantic, so he placed the specimen in its protective case and proceeded to the adjoining room where he could communicate without having to go through the sterilization process. He had hours of work ahead of him and hated the interruption. In panicked increments, his youngest colleague sputtered through the speakerphone that the world was coming to an end. He pointed to the television and through the glass Milton saw the South Tower crumble to the ground. He strained to read the words for the hearing impaired: "Terrorists attack the World Trade Center."

He stumbled to the door. The workday was over.

"Yes...Meredith, you're breaking up...Yes, I'm on my way now...She's fine. I just talked to Beatrice and she went and picked her up from school right away...Yes...It seems everyone was sent home...You did?...How's he doing?...We can go get him if you want...No?...I know...Call your mom, Meredith...Call her and mine, OK?...I'll be home shortly...Yes...I will...I will...Drive carefully...I love you too...."

"Hello, Son." Milton's grandfather sat beside him shaking his head.

"Hi, Pop. Nice to see you."

"Really bad day, huh, Son?"

"Yeah, Pop. Really bad day. They just evacuated the building. I'm not sure what's happening but everything we know today has been changed in one way or another."

His grandfather shook his head again and reached to turn up the radio. They listened, as the numbers of victims were still being predicted and the reports that the nation's entire air travel system was at a complete standstill. The President's plane was somewhere between Oklahoma and Georgia and the word "terrorists" rang over and over.

"Some of the planes came from here Milton?"

"I know, Pop. God bless all of those people." Milton was having trouble focusing on the road. He turned the radio down.

"Milton, does this have anything to do with...."

"I don't know. I don't think so, but I don't know." He glanced over at the sweet old man and saw tears in his eyes. He imagined the whole country was crying.

He held Meredith tightly when she opened the door. Emily looked at her father, her dark sunglasses wrapped around her head, and put her arms out. He sat with them as the grim pictures were repeated over and over again on the television. He looked down at his daughter and wished he could save her from this grim reality.

"Are we going to be all right, Dad?"

Milton wrapped his arm around her tightly and nodded.

"I think we need to get away from the television and go for a nice walk or something. Meredith?"

She glanced up at him as he put his sweatshirt on and whispered, "There's going to be a war now isn't there? There's going to be a war."

Milton squeezed her shoulder, but she didn't respond. He took his daughter's hand and put Daisy's leash on. He looked at the television one last time, as the plane ran through the South Tower, over and over again.

They walked along the water's edge, while Daisy chased the seagulls.

"Dad? What did Mom mean, there's going to be a war?"

Milton looked at his daughter and smiled.

"Now don't you worry. Your mom is just involved in so much with her show and she's just so sad about what happened today."

"But Dad, will the war be here? In Massachusetts?"

He got down on his knees and faced his daughter. She faced him and he swallowed hard, knowing now she could see as well as sense his fear.

"Emily, please believe me. The war won't be here. It will be far away but many people will be involved. War is a terrible thing, but it's possible after what happened today, the only way we can confront the enemy. The United States has soldiers that will protect us; protect Massachusetts."

"Are you sure, Dad?"

"I'm sure, Emily."

"I guess I just thought...How can they protect us if the two planes that hit the buildings came right from our airport? The same one that we were in when we went to Disney World."

Milton looked down at his daughter and squeezed her hand assuredly.

"They'll find a way. Don't you worry. They'll find a way. We need to trust that our government will protect us. They'll find a way."

A week later, with a very powerful State of the Union Address behind them, the American people returned to work and school with trepidation. The opening bell greeted the stockbrokers at the exchange and the United States waged war on Afghanistan and terrorism.

Milton had been handed his last bonus check almost six months before. His new assignment was a group project involving Alzheimer's and did his best to forget the last two years of work. The day his daughter saw light was also the day that Joyce Ridgefield died. He had read the details in the Houston paper. She'd been walking through the parking lot of the Houston airport when a speeding car hit her. The driver still had not been found or identified. The day he had met her was the day her life ended. Her return home would be her last hours. She had spent the last day of her life passionately passing her mother's legacy to him. And what had he done with it? Nothing. Absolutely nothing.

He acted as if "it" didn't exist, except for the fact that he made 50 exact copies, at a copy place on the cape, and put them in envelopes addressed to almost everyone he knew. He left them in a safety deposit box at his bank. He avoided Salinger, which became very easy since the end of the secret project—he was ignored like the rest of the science staff. He wondered occasionally when the Food and Drug Administration would approve the treatment he had perfected, but he kept his head to the grindstone and didn't dare ask the question. He became invisible again. The way he had been before everything had changed, before he became greedy. Milton was haunted with her memory though. Joyce Ridgefield's face, her eyes, her hair, everything about that day haunted him. There were days he was sufficiently convinced that he was not strong enough to handle the burden anymore. Of course, then he would return home and see his family, the people that he loved, and once again everything became bearable. For short spurts he would forget his dirty little secret. Two months after the September 11th tragedy, something happened, something clicked, that would forever change Milton Stafford.

It was early when he walked into shipping and receiving to check on the manufacturer's packages he was expecting. He had been assigned the task of making sure the product and ingredients were received and regulated for the Alzheimer's grant and he had secured an exemplary deal with a Dutch company and he was anxious to get the product in motion. He was comfortable being number two on the project, comfortable that someone else had to answer to Salinger. He knocked lightly and Isaac Washington looked up from his desk and waved him in.

"Well, well, Mr. Stafford. How are you, sir?" Isaac smiled and reached for the coffee being passed his way.

"I'm fine, Mr. Washington, thank you for asking. And yourself?"

"Oh just fine sir. Always happy to wake up in the morning. Wife's been harping a bit on when I might retire, but I just can't imagine not working sir. Just can't imagine it."

Milton looked around the office and noticed the pictures of his wife and children, one of them graduating college.

"Is that new, Isaac?"

"Yes, yes, Mr. Stafford. That's my middle boy, Dwayne Abraham. His middle name is after our 16th President. All my kids named after great Presidents and of course, the last name, well, Dwayne graduated from the University of Massachusetts this past May. We, as a family, we were gonna have a reunion this September, but after, well, you know, we've put off the reunion and celebration until after the holidays. He's a good boy, Mr. Stafford. We're all very proud of him."

"You must be, Isaac. You must be very proud. I had the nice lady add an extra sugar for you this morning Isaac. Is it right?"

"Oh, it's just fine, Mr. Stafford. Just fine. Thank you very much. Sometimes I think it's only you and me and Professor Salinger working the crazy hours." Milton winced slightly at his boss's name.

"Yes, I know what you mean Isaac. I know what you mean. Wondering if those packages came in overnight from Holland?"

"Hmm, let me check here. Sorry, I was still finishing up the paperwork for Professor Salinger. He's been down here almost every day. It's amazing, how he wears so many hats. In the lab late at night and in the office during the day. What a dedicated man he is." Milton listened, staring out into the loading dock.

"In the lab at night too?" he asked curiously.

"Yessiree. My night guys see him all the time, toiling and tired, working so hard. He just never stops. I told him he needs to take a vacation. No one body can handle all of that for too long."

"You're right. He's so busy upstairs, double-checking the big jobs, when does he find time to work in the lab? What would he be doing that one of us can't get done?"

"Oh, don't know that sir. But it's darn important. He's been shipping out boxes to D.C. and Houston, almost on a daily basis. I'm telling you, if there were more people like that, this world would be in a much better place."

"Yes, I think your right on the money there, Isaac. I'll check in with the Professor and see if there's anything I can help him with."

"Gosh, Mr. Stafford. You must be thinking the same thing as him. He's always talking about you with upstairs. You're very important too." Milton's ears burned.

"Yeah? I'll check in with him, Isaac. Thanks. Any luck with that shipment?"

"I'm sorry Mr. Stafford, it wasn't delivered last night. I'll flag it though and hopefully we can get it to you by tomorrow. I'm sorry about that. If I had control of."

"Never mind, Isaac. Not everyone can be as efficient as us."

Isaac laughed heartily and shook Milton's hand.

"You have a good day, Mr. Stafford."

"You too Isaac. You too."

Milton hurried back to the elevator. He glanced at his watch. He had less than an hour before his staff would arrive at the lab. There was something he needed to check.

He religiously followed the precautionary steps of sterilization but worked quickly. An "old pro," as some called him. He helped himself into the sterile suit and mask and rechecked the seals around his shoulders before he entered the refrigeration room. He went to the lock-down room and pressed the code, entering without hesitation. He knew exactly where to look. The supply looked exactly as he had left it, six months earlier. Four trays, each labeled exactly the same, except for the date of execution. He had been told that his work was commendable and that many suffering people would benefit from it as soon as it was FDA approved. He had believed that it was being reproduced in large amounts at one of the government's facilities, with test groups ready and waiting. He glanced over the trays and nothing appeared abnormal. He glanced up at the time. He pulled the second tray and scanned the data. Nothing. He carefully pushed the tray back into its allotted slot and just as he was about to shut the door, he saw it. The label on the edge of the tray was different. Whenever he had labeled the first trays, there was a basic, regulatory coding system that was used. Date, time, specimen, conclusion, and prognosis. It was all a very simple yet precise number system that anyone hired was trained proficiently on, even before they were allowed to enter the general lab, let alone the unit where deadly agents or virals were kept. Someone must have entered the code in error. The dates and times seemed accurate, but the specimen was labeled DCO with no numbers and the conclusion and prognosis were both coded 99, which stood for toxic or lethal. But the computer system should have ejected the data that was entered incorrectly? Somehow the information had been added? He placed the tray back and repeated the codes over in his head. He was sure it was just human error, but the correct way was embedded in his brain. He had entered the data thousands of times before. How could one project, so important, be labeled incorrectly and who would that benefit?

He followed the proverbial steps of lock-down and entered the other lab, relieving himself of the claustrophobic mask. He donned new surgical gloves and walked over to the computer, just as he heard his name being paged overhead. He grabbed a notepad and wrote down the numbers that he had been repeating over and over. He placed the code in his boot and went to answer the phone. It was Salinger.

"Yes?"

"Yes, Stafford. I thought you were here. I couldn't find you in the office. Are you in the lab?"

"Yes, sir. I thought I'd get started early. Was hoping the shipment from Holland had arrived. Really exciting stuff we're working on right now."

"Good, Stafford. Really good. I'm sorry to interrupt you, but I was hoping we could get together for lunch today, say about noon?"

Milton grew cold. His mouth was dry and he barely answered, "Um, sure Professor, but let me check my schedule."

"That's all right Stafford. I already had my secretary check the computer schedule and you rarely eat, let alone go to lunch. So noon it is, all right?" He wasn't taking no for an answer.

"Sure, Professor. I'll see you then."

Milton turned toward the computer and punched in the code quickly, his hands shaking. The computer responded with an error so he tried again. His secretary checked my electronic scheduler, he thought? They had access to everything and everyone he spoke to. The computer flashed the same error. The computer would only allow the lettered code version. Someone would have to override the code, to change the labeling. He picked up the phone and called the IS department.

"Hello, help desk."

"Hi. Who's this?" Milton asked assertively.

"Mike Wetzel. Who's this and how can I help you?"

"Hi. I'm in the lab and had just a quick troubleshooting question." Avoiding any introduction.

"Sure. What can I help you with?"

"Well, we were about to print a label for a generic placebo, but were hoping to change the coding for the tray, since it is generic."

"Oh, well, hmm. Let's see. Not sure if you want to do that. We have the code system for a reason and the only reason we would change or override a code would be for proprietary reasons approved by a V.P. or for sealed documents. Why would you want to change it anyway?"

"Oh, we were just hoping for a better way to document the generic trays. Sorry to bother you."

"No problem. Professor Salinger I'm sure would be available to hear your ideas and approve the override."

"Oh, he can do that?"

"Of course. He does it all the time."

"Thank you Mr. Wetzel."

"Any time. Glad to help."

Milton hung up the lab phone and glanced at the time. He had less than 5 minutes before staff would arrive. He grabbed his mask, sealed the seams and entered the lock-down again. He went over to the tray and ejected a vessel from the back, allowed one drop to hit the platelet and turned on the microscope. He looked through the lens and saw that the vial contained what appeared to look like a sugar solution. He replaced everything in its home, burned the specimen in the hazardous container, and exited the lockdown just as his young staff was arriving for a grueling, hopeful day of research.

He looked in the mirror as he removed the hood. His face was gaunt. Something had gone terribly wrong. His project, his cure, was being reproduced, but had been completely changed. He glanced at the lab door and through the glass he was sure he saw his grandfather's face. He was trembling as he greeted one of the scientists and excused himself to his office. It took every ounce of energy to get back to the office, finding refuge only as he closed the door. He had less than four hours before the lunch with Salinger. Less than four hours to find out who or what had sabotaged his project.

CHAPTER 34

Meredith beamed towards the camera and repeated, "Have a great day everyone." The director's hands rolled and then gave the thumbs up. They finished their 100th episode and the crew hooted and hollered in celebration. In just over a year, Meredith's face appeared everywhere on newsstands and checkout counters and everyone who was anyone and everyone who was no one wanted to be on her show. Meredith obliged them all. She took her popularity in stride, kept her ego in check, and when she went home at night, did her best to remain, "just mom" or "Milton's wife," but it was hard. She had been reviewed three times already with the contracts department and the studio boss and was now making five times the money her husband was making, with an expected bonus that might even put her in the millionaire category. She was rich and felt very powerful. More powerful than she had ever felt before. She thrived and very important people noticed.

"Wonderful show, Meredith. Just wonderful!" Darryl approached her with open arms. Meredith reciprocated.

"It was, wasn't it?" she added, squeezing him around the waist tightly.

"Are you kidding?" he joked, looking her over and laughing.

"It was a really good show." She repeated.

"Meredith, we need to set up that meeting with the execs soon. You've been receiving some very important offers and well…."

"Darryl, please. Let me wallow in my celebration for a few minutes, OK?" She smiled and jabbed his side.

"Of course, of course. I'm sorry. Always thinking a mile ahead."

Meredith grabbed two of the mimosas that were being passed around and handed him one adding, "Stop thinking for a minute and let's toast. Let's toast to another 100 episodes, since I'm sure you've already got a list of guests for every single one."

Darryl blushed and they tapped glasses.

"Meredith?"

"Yes, Darryl."

"Thanks."

"Thank you. We're a team. A great team." He stepped aside, letting a few more of the crew shake her hand or embrace her. Who would've thought they would be in this position at this moment. Whatever Meredith touched seemed to turn to platinum. He was the first to hear Bonnie's voice over the speaker.

"Meredith? Meredith, you have a phone call."

Darryl touched Meredith's shoulder and pointed to the control booth. Bonnie was waving frantically and had her hand over the microphone.

"Excuse me everyone, please keep the celebration going. I just need to grab this call."

Meredith walked quickly to the booth, expecting to hear her proud husband's voice. She needed to hear his voice, have his approval. She didn't ask, just accepted the receiver from Bonnie and answered, "Hello, darling."

"Excuse me?" was the woman's response on the other end.

"Oh my, I'm sorry. I thought it was my husband." She flashed Bonnie a glare, but Bonnie remained inches away, a worried expression on her face.

"Ms. Nicholson?"

"Yes, this is she. Who's calling?"

"Mrs. Nicholson, my name is Evelyn Bradshaw. I'm the dean of Exeter Prep School."

"Yes, Evelyn, we've met before. Is everything all right?"

"Ms. Nicholson, it's Connor. He's been injured and we need you to come here at once."

"Injured," Meredith caught her breath, "what do you mean 'injured,' Evelyn? What's happened? Where is he?"

"Ms. Nicholson, he was rushed to the emergency room just a few minutes ago. I don't know...."

"What? What happened?" Meredith reached for a chair and Bonnie rushed to get one underneath her before she fell.

"Ms. Nicholson, we're not exactly sure what happened. Some of the students' stories are conflicting. But what we do know is that he was found behind his dormitory, unclothed and bleeding badly."

Meredith's eyes filled with tears and she began to sob. "Evelyn, what hospital is he at?"

"He's at Memorial Hospital. We've contacted them and I can give you the number."

"Give it to my associate. I need to leave now. I'll be there in less than an hour."

"I'm sorry, Ms. Nicholson. Very sorry."

"I know. I'll be there soon. I need to call my husband now, here's my associate."

"Yes, of course, Ms. Nicholson. We did try him as well, but were unable to reach him."

Meredith handed Bonnie the phone, grabbed a different landline, and dialed Milton's work number. His machine answered. She then dialed the reception office and asked to have him paged. There was no response.

"I'm sorry, Ms. Nicholson, I believe he's left the building." The receptionist was called back.

"What? Do you know where?"

"He left with Professor Salinger for an early lunch. Professor Salinger left instructions that they would be unavailable for an hour."

"It's an emergency. Please get word to my husband that he needs to contact me as soon as he gets back."

"Yes, of course, Ms. Nicholson. Of course."

Meredith hung up and dialed Milton's cell phone, which automatically went into voicemail. She knew it would be turned off if he were with his boss at lunch. She looked down at her watch. It was fifteen minutes after noon. The lunch rush outside would be horrendous. She grabbed her trench coat and ran out of the booth. Darryl ran after her.

"Hey, Connor! Connor, can you hear me?"

Connor picked up his pace as he made his way on the path that led to his dormitory.

"Hey, Connor, lover boy. Are you queer?"

Connor's heart raced.

"Hey, Connor, do you like me near you? Do you want to lick my rear?"

He knew they would catch him if he tried to run. Maybe he should try to talk with them? Slowly, he turned around, trembling. For a brief moment he was sailing, his father at the helm, his mother and sister, huddled, faces smiling in the breeze. And then they attacked.

When she arrived at the hospital, there was heavy security at the entrance and several officers in the ICU where they were led. A physician introduced himself but she was too distraught to remember his name. She heard every other word, then started screaming, "Doctor, please! Just tell me what happened. Where's my son? Where is he?"

The physician took her elbow and steered her toward an open room and closed the door. Darryl stood outside the door in case she called for him.

The young physician asked her to please sit, which she obliged and he sat down beside her.

"Ms. Nicholson, I know you're confused and upset. Please let me tell you as much as I know."

"Thank you," she whimpered.

"Connor was brought into the emergency room over an hour ago with multiple contusions to the head and body. Someone hurt him very badly. We had to operate immediately to relieve some of the pressure. There was significant internal bleeding."

Meredith's head bowed, tears fell to her lap. "Why? Who would do such a thing?"

"Ms. Nicholson, it seems your son had one or several enemies. The authorities have questioned the students and several are being held. I have asked many questions myself, inquiring the same thing, trying to find out what kind of object was used to injure him."

"Doctor…."

"Adam Burns, Ms. Nicholson."

"Doctor Burns, please tell me everything quickly. I want to see my son." She wiped her eyes and nose again, and was handed a fresh box of tissues.

"Ms. Nicholson, as I said, he was beaten very badly with a blunt object, possibly a paddle from a boat."

Meredith head fell forward again. "Is he going to live?"

"Ms. Nicholson, is Connor's father here? It might be easier."

"No Dr. Burns, I haven't been able to reach him. Please, is he going to live?"

"Yes, Ms. Nicholson. He's alive and he's going to live. Thank goodness he was found when he was. Ms. Nicholson, the man outside?"

"That's my associate, Darryl Rodriguez."

"Would you like him to come inside?"

"No. No. Thank you. Please." She looked at him through swollen eyes.

"Ms. Nicholson, he has several teeth that were knocked out and he was sexually assaulted."

Meredith stared at the physician and cried, "What? Oh my God! Why, why, why? Why would someone hurt Connor like this? Why?" She put her hands to her head and rocked back and forth.

"Ms. Nicholson, I know this is terrible, but you need to take a deep breath. I can get you something to help the…."

"Dr. Burns, no! I need to hear the rest and I need to see my son."

"He was in the OR and has been brought to recovery. From there he'll be in the ICU until he's been cleared. Now, it's just time. I promise you, we did everything we could."

"Please, can I see him?"

"Yes, yes, of course. I'll bring you to him."

"Now!"

"Yes now."

Meredith could barely feel the tile under her feet as she walked behind Dr. Burns. She was unaware of Darryl's hand leading her through the maze of hospital employees trying to catch a glimpse of her and was oblivious to the armed police escorts. She was led into a private room, surrounded by glass walls and saw a body, covered in gauze and bandages, a head wrapped leaving only a few tufts of dirty blonde hair and a tracheal tube visible. Her legs buckled and Darryl caught her as she swayed, whispering, "Please, please. I need to get in touch with my husband." Then everything went dark.

Milton returned to his office and closed the door. He had spent the last hour with Salinger and couldn't fathom how something like this could happen. The solo project was back on and he had no choice but to accept the proposal. He was being forced to start all over. He had been informed that his earlier analysis had a weak link that enabled the drug to at first work its magic, then slowly, painfully, the syndrome would prevail. The FDA wouldn't think about passing it.

"How was the defect discovered?" Milton asked, embarrassed.

Salinger looked at him pitifully and answered, "I'm really not supposed to tell you this, but just to set the record straight, we had several volunteers who were given the doses designed for the level of illness and their symptoms, and at first a few felt almost 100% better, but then it happened. Something went wrong. Each volunteer is now at a worse stage of the syndrome than when they started the medication." Salinger looked down at the menu, shaking his head in shame.

Milton felt the burning in his cheeks and his head started to throb. His project had failed. If he didn't agree to start the project up again, he would have to pay all of his bonus money back and he would no longer be an employee of the company. Salinger's remark about Meredith's fame and fortune and it being a matter of pride made him feel small and pathetic. Of course he would start the project again, but not to retain his pride at home. He needed to retain his pride as a scientist. It was his intellect that had brought the project to fruition and it would be his intellect that would solve the weakened link and get things back in tow. He thought about Joyce Ridgefield's mother. It was time to review her data again, completely. Something was missing. Something he had to find. The phone rang and he reached to grab it, as he heard his name on the overhead page.

"Milton Stafford."

"Yes, Mr. Stafford. Your wife has been trying to reach you. She said it was an emergency."

"Thank you," Milton hung up, putting in his password to voicemail. He scrolled the caller IDs and saw that his wife's cell phone had called over a dozen times. He dialed her number and closed his eyes. "*An emergency,*" he whispered as it rang. Her voicemail answered. He listened to the first message. His heart started to pound.

Professor Salinger leaned against the window in his office, with a cup of tea in his hand, and watched as Milton drove out of the parking lot. He held back a smile.

CHAPTER 35

Meredith fidgeted in the green room, waiting for her cue. She wasn't used to being the interviewee, especially by someone as famous as the perky blonde host of the highly rated morning show and this would be the first time she would allow the questions that everyone had been asking for months. She kept glancing in the mirror, checking her lipstick, fiddling with her unruly curls. It was raining and heavy fog covered the city. The Statue of Liberty remained hidden. She watched the monitor as the weather forecast relayed the reason why her hair would remain unmanageable for the next few days.

She had spoken with Connor only minutes before and he had reminded her "Be not afraid of greatness, for some are born great, some achieve greatness and some have greatness thrust upon'em." She smiled thinking about her son quoting Shakespeare, now recovering at home. Their high school valedictorian pondered his college choices. He had been accepted to four of the Ivy League schools and all four wanted him on the roster soon. She hoped he would stay close in Cambridge. Since the incident, she couldn't bear thinking him too far away. Her nerves were still raw, her anger still steeped.

The investigation had led to two expulsions with probation and one jail sentence so far for the crimes against her son. The news story ran for weeks and Meredith finally returned to her own program, after a month of madness. She and Milton had been asked to testify, even though they had been unaware of their Son's sexual orientation, or that he had been having trouble with a certain group of students at school. He had been harassed several times before, but had not reported anything to the authorities nor to his parents.

The students that were finally found guilty also mentioned that they were paid for the crime and that they never would've done what they did had they not been paid well. The heinous things people, or children, would do for money. The investigation still had not led to any arrests in regards to the payment. The money was gone, spent on frivolous toys and keg parties off campus. Connor was still in the hospital when his class received their diplomas, but they had a special acknowledgement for him and one of his chess teammates gave a harrowing speech and praised Connor Stafford for his honor and bravery. Connor watched the tape and was clearly touched. He held his diploma tightly in his fist, his family around him, beaming.

The brutal exploitation and hatred that had been evoked by high school students shocked the country and sickened most. There were some who said maybe he deserved it, saying his sexual connotation was as sadistic and vicious as an animal, but they were few and far between. The prejudice against one boy's orientation, made the world wake up and take notice. His mother's notoriety and fame only added to the propaganda and the rally began against acts of violence like this, anywhere. Like the terrorists of September 11, this crime would not be tolerated.

Milton had arrived at the hospital, just as the officer had started the questions. He entered the room where his wife sat pale, breathing in a bag as she nodded her head to the investigator. Her associate's arm was wrapped around her for comfort. That day had had changed her husband. He looked down at her and fell to his knees, holding her tightly. It was hours before they could really talk to each other. They just sat closely and inhaled each other's air. Meredith stayed most of the time in New Hampshire, while Milton came back and forth, after a few days bringing Emily and Beatrice with him. Family members came and went and the shock started to soften. Milton stayed away from the office for two weeks, ignoring Salinger's calls. Their lives had been sliced open and each of them would mend in due time. Meredith saw the look on Milton's face when he had first seen their Son, wrapped like a mummy. His trampled body attached to tubes that in turn were attached to machines. Connor had survived, but the image would never disappear. Milton worried quietly now, but she sensed the strain.

And then of course there were the decisions that she had made for the future. Their relationship had been tested, many times, but he remained loyal, supportive and loving. She worried that there were times when she and the children took advantage of him, because he was so easily taken advantage of. His work was virtuous. He rarely spoke of it but she understood how important it was to him. He was the silent miracle worker. There would never be a time that she would ask him to leave his work. Then she saw Emily when she received her one-minute cue. Their angel at home with her convalescing brother, her Irish-tongued surrogate, her quiet worried father, and an absentee mother replaced by a cover of *People* magazine. Seeing Emily made everything all right.

"Are you ready, Meredith?" One of the directors leaned in the room.

"Ready as I'll ever be. Thanks." She stood poised and walked out of the room.

President Gerald Revo paced back and forth in the Oval Office, mumbling under his breath. He rubbed his knuckles incessantly, the pain in his joints almost intolerable. It had been almost 2 months since he had woken with the terrible aches and awful rashes that appeared in the most vulnerable places. Several physicians had been visiting on a regular basis, and no one could surmise or conclude what exactly could relieve his symptoms. One even had the nerve to bring up the fictitious syndrome that so many soldiers and civilians of the war he had been active in complained of. He looked at the physician and threatened his life and the lives of his loved ones if he ever breathed such blasphemy again. The physician never said another word. But somehow things were found out. There was a mole. A rat in his organization that had leaked information to the press and now the newspapers and the news stations were clamoring for the story. What was the President of their country suffering from and would it deter any of his ability or performance in the war on terrorism and the duties as Commander in Chief? Revo growled again at the idea that there were polls considering that his illness would demand too much of his energy, that his illness was a weakness that could not be ignored. And oh the illnesses that spawned through rumor! He heard everything from Epstein-Barr to tuberculosis and he was waiting for someone to point the finger at a possible sexually transmitted disease. When and if someone published something like that, he was going to have Desmond kill everyone that was part of the published lie. They would hang for their sins. Well maybe not kill all of them, but scare the shit out of them for sure.

His tense staff kept a watchful eye on all the propaganda, but Desmond was the only person he could really trust. There was a knock on the door and he shouted, "Who is it now?"

Desmond responded as he let himself in, "It's me, Gerald, just me." He looked around, as if someone else might be in the room, and he motioned for Gerald to leave the Oval Office and enter the secure room off the wing. Gerald didn't hesitate. He had been waiting too long.

"Well, do you have something for me?"

Desmond secured the second lock and motioned for Gerald to sit down.

"No, I don't want to sit. My fucking knees are killing me. It's best that I stay standing. So what do you have?"

Desmond took a seat beside the small end table and extracted a small file out of his briefcase. "I've got good news and I've got some bad news."

"Fuck! All right, the bad first."

"Seems the deadbeat authorities up in New Hampshire, along with a few New England FBI agents, have located the house where the money changed hands."

"Yeah, so?"

"They found some charred photographs in the house and one of them was the kid's father."

"Oh. Hmm. I don't think there's anything to worry about."

"Well, we just can't be too sure."

Revo walked toward the chair and sputtered, "Desmond, Jesus, don't you think we've got more important things to worry about right now? Like my fucking hands! Please, damn it, what's the good news?"

Desmond stood and touched both shoulders of the President. Revo looked into his eyes, pained and furious.

"Desmond?"

"I know, Gerald. I know. I'm working on it day and night. We've got a tail and a trace on the father every second. All of his phone conversations are tapped. He's working 18 hours days in the lab. He's struggling, but determined. He'll come up with the answer soon. One thing is for certain, this is better than anything you've had in awhile." He leaned down and reached into his briefcase, extracting a small container.

"Yeah, you sure?" Gerald grabbed the vial like an addict needing a fix.

"Yes, I'm sure. I'm sure. The last few months, the imbecile Professor's concoctions have been the sole source, but now that we have the expert working on it again, I'm sure things will improve."

"That bastard Salinger, why can't we just torture him?" Gerald asked, focused on the small bit of fluid in the vial.

"You know, I wish we could, but we need him still. He's ours and he knows that he doesn't have the ability to duplicate the medication. His shipments were a watered down version. He's a moron, yes, but he's the only one there right now who can keep us informed of the study and of the other situations."

"No sign of the Ridgefield papers?"

"No, not yet. We can't even confirm that Stafford has them, and possibly he's working with just the information that he was told by the daughter. Either way, we do know he is brilliant and that we need him."

"If we find those papers, I want them both dead."

"Yes, I know." Desmond watched as Revo tied a tourniquet around his arm, slapping the soft side for a vein.

"And the fucking wife, the talk show host. Anything on her?" Revo took a seat and closed his eyes, waiting for relief.

"Nothing really. The rumors have not been validated and it seems there's some pressure at home. Salinger has confirmed that the few conversations he's brought up Stafford's wife, Stafford seems uncomfortable, almost angry. We think there may be problems in the nest. It's doubtful he would ever say anything to her. He's worried sick for his family. Especially after Ridgefield and of course his kid"

"Hmm. He better stay that way. What was that idiot thinking, paying those kids anyway?"

"You can't get good help anymore, I guess. I took care of him."

"Of course you did. Don't worry about the stupid photograph. The guy's dead. Pictures don't talk. It was a brilliant idea anyway getting to the boy. Brilliant idea. The only thing more pleasurable would have been the little blind girl."

Desmond shifted in his chair. The idea had been Revo's. He let it slide.

"The girl's not blind anymore, Gerald. Don't you remember?"

"Oh, yeah. Shit! Maybe we could get her back to the way she was?"

Desmond saw the twinkle in his eye. He was definitely feeling better.

"It would be sweet if their marriage went south. It would be really nice knowing that they aren't together. That he's alone in this and hasn't said anything to her. What if that bitch decides to run?"

"We can't worry about that right now. We have a war to start and a country to disable. She's just a talk show host. Nothing that we should worry about. Plus you're at the top of your game sir. You're what the country needs and wants. Not a talk show host and definitely not a woman. Let's get to that war."

"You're right, Desmond. You're always right." Revo smiled, keeping his eyes closed. "One thing's for sure," he loosened his tied, "if she does run, I'd have a good old time rubbing up against her at a debate."

Desmond smirked. "Yeah, Gerald. I know what you mean. Would be ironic that her husband is the one that's keeping you alive and you're there, fucking his wife."

Revo chuckled, stretching his fingers out slowly. He felt good enough to start the proceedings. He was more than ready to start his war.

The studio lights went up and, on cue, Meredith grinned.

"Thank you so much for being with us today."

"Of course. Thank you for having me." Meredith nodded at the host. She folded her hands in her lap and relaxed.

"Well, we know the world has been waiting and I want to start by asking how your son is doing."

"Yes, of course. He, Connor our Son, is recovering. He's been through a lot and I'm so thankful that he's pulled through the worst of his physical injuries."

"How is he mentally, after such a trauma?"

"Oh, well, incredibly, better than ever. He is a kind, brave, young man, who survived a terrible attack. But I think, from the bottom of my heart, that no one can break his spirit."

"Oh that is such good news. Thank you for keeping us abreast of his situation. We're all rooting for him. I understand the one man has not been found that could lead to the whole truth about this incident."

"I'm sorry, I can't speak about the case, but I can tell you that the hatred some people hold in this country for someone's religion, color, sexual orientation, or even sex, cannot be endured. We are a country of freedom, a country with a constitution that protects one's right to choose. We are a country where being different doesn't mean right or wrong, good or bad. I invite the people of our country to look back at the vulgarity of prejudice and how far we've come. In the future there will be no separate water fountains for someone that is different. He is a true philanthropist. Isn't it ironic that that throughout out history and even today, the truly good are the ones who are persecuted. We need to put those persecutors on trial. We are all equal, each and every one of us and we are all mortal. Our son will be starting his higher education and he plans to follow in his father's footsteps. He wants to help protect our planet and help to discover cures of the awful things that plague the world. He wants to protect the very air that we breathe. He's a good man and I believe that justice will be served."

Bonnie and Darryl looked at each other and smiled.

"Well, thank you. Now if I may boldly ask about the rumors of you getting back into politics?" Meredith smiled and sighed.

"Of course. I know there has been a lot of speculation about my interest in politics and it is still very early, but yes, I have been considering it."

"Really? That's wonderful. I know that you were the Mayor for a short time in Boston years ago. At what capacity are you considering now?" The host uncrossed her legs and leaned in as if waiting for a secret to be told.

Meredith smiled and leaned toward her, "The futures of our families and the issues of the world can only be delegated by us. I am a person who cares very deeply for the rights and the situations of our country. I've thought long and hard about the possibility and am about to make an announcement soon. If I do decide to run, I'll be a candidate with a conscience. I believe there is hope and I believe in a safer world. A world that we can live in peacefully. I will continue to be truthful and I will avoid the stones that are thrown. I would lead our nation and we are a nation that desperately needs direction right now. I would not allow power to go to my head. I would serve and protect our country and people's right to choose. Yes, if I throw my hat in, well, that would be my platform."

The host sat up and put her hand to her mouth, "Oh my. Wow, this is an exclusive. But Meredith, it's almost two years until the election, isn't it early to be announcing this?"

Meredith smiled wide and responded, "I haven't announced anything yet really. I'm still the same person I've always been and just wanted to let you know. Oh, and really, my philosophy is it's never too early to make things happen." The director's eyes widened with delight and his hands rolled to wrap.

"Thank you very much for spending some time with us, Meredith. It was a real pleasure meeting you."

"The pleasure is all mine. I hope you can come and visit my show someday soon."

"Oh yes. I would love that."

They shook hands and the camera faded to commercial. Bonnie and Darryl embraced in the green room. The word was out and they were ready for the fall-out.

Milton watched from his office. His wife had just announced on national television that she might very well be entering the political world again and this time she would go national. Either way, whether Meredith knew it or not, it might be their only protection. Now the world new and everyone's eyes would be on them. That was their best protection right now. All three lines lit on his phone at once. He selected line one and Salinger's secretary almost yelled, "Mr. Stafford? Professor Salinger wants to see you at once."

Milton smirked and replied, "Tell the professor I'll be down in an hour."

"Uh, he wants to see you now, sir."

"Well, I'm tied up, but I will be up as soon as I can."

"Uh, all right sir, but please, as soon as possible. He seemed very serious."

"I'm sure he is, Marjorie. I'm sure he is." He hung up the phone and put his feet on his desk as he sipped his lukewarm coffee. The investigator's words kept repeating over and over in his head, "I can't figure out why someone would have photographs of you or any of your son's family or friends. Strange. Very strange. And then go and burn them, but not even take care to burn them completely. Why someone would pay the kids to do something so sadistic and cruel. Unless of course this attack was something much more designed than we can imagine. Do you have any enemies, Mr. Stafford? I know it's a hard question, but I have to ask. Do you, your wife, or any of your family members have any enemies?"

"Pop," Milton said out loud. "I really need to talk with you when we go home tonight. OK?"

The hissing from the vent under the window was the only response he heard.

CHAPTER 36

The economy suffered an enormous downward spiral after the 2001 attack. Unemployment was at its highest in 20 years and the national debt grew. Most people hoped, even prayed, for a brighter, more peaceful future, but were too busy worrying about getting food on their own table instead of someone else's. The United States had prospered during the previous administration's reign, but with the disaster in Manhattan and the Capitol and a dismal outlook on "catching the bad guy," they now sat apathetic, worried, waiting and watching.

The President of the free world's biggest decision was about to be unveiled. When plans to continue his war on terrorism and invade another country were announced, the world's core shook. Revo's stance, putting his faith in a higher power, fared best at putting the fear of Revo into the hearts of many. On command, thousands of troops were deployed daily, sent to a territory that he was all too familiar with from his own days of combat. He was called everything from a warmonger to a genius, but as he had started, few questioned his tactics directly. He was intimidating. He sugared the public with education and Medicare plans, to alleviate the regular Joe's bad view of him. His troops remained loyal, trained to do so, but eventually a large portion of the world clearly wanted him dethroned and the American people were being threatened to do so, or they too would pay for his decisions. Revo's admirers even became leery.

Meredith settled into the soft cotton sheets, her skin still tingling from the scalding bath. She glanced over at her nightstand, declining to pick up the best-selling autobiography that she had been struggling with for months. She dimmed the lights and listened. She heard bits of mumbled conversation and her daughter's laughter. She heard their son's voice on the telephone, a door close, his voice fading away. She heard the shuffle of slippers, tired feet dragging on the hall runner and watched the slow, quiet turn of the bedroom doorknob. She smiled at her husband as he focused in the low light. Instead of the nightly ritual in the bathroom with toothbrush and mouthwash, he dropped his clothes on the floor and crawled in beside his wife. They lay silently, holding each other, listening to the slight ticking from the overhead fan. Afraid he might sleep before she said what she had rehearsed over and over, she whispered, "Hey, what about that massage you promised?"

Milton lifted his head and looked at her and smiled. He was about to turn her over when she interrupted, "I was kidding, darling. You're tired. We can do that another night. I just want to make sure that you're all right before sleep prevails."

Milton chuckled into the sheets, his backside exposed to the cool current of the fan. Once again he lifted his head and smiled.

"Meredith, haven't I always been all right?'

"Um, I guess I would have to say yes to that question." She nestled down a little closer to him.

"I mean, haven't I always been OK, no matter what has happened or what decisions have been made about the next step in our lives?"

"Milton, yes, you have."

"Then why do you always ask?" He stared into her hazel eyes; tiny lines around them now, cheeks still freckled, but faded.

"I guess I always ask because I'm also asking myself. It makes me feel better asking."

Milton shook his head, the smile slowly fading. "Oh, I see, making sure you're all right, not really worried about me?"

"Milton, please. You know."

"I know. I know. Of course I know. Meredith, what you've decided, we have decided together, stands. I wish I knew how to explain how I feel right now, but I can't. You're just going to have to go with the answer. Yes I'm fine."

"I'm not asking you to change anything."

"Meredith," he looked at her and scowled, "you know everything is going to change and that's all right. I've accepted that. I accepted that 20 years ago when I married you. Nothing, I mean nothing, will ever be the same." He reached up and turned off the light.

Meredith looked at him, then past him out the window, hoping for a sign to end this conversation and a conclusion that everything would be all right. Milton watched her and waited. It had been 20 years since he had accepted the fact that his wife was beautiful, intelligent, loving, and selfish. In that order. Also in those twenty years he had learned to think before he spoke and he waited, knowing she would probably come up with the answer herself and hoping his well-being was included. She got out of the bed, her lean, naked torso silhouetted through the draped moonlight.

"Milton?"

"Yes Meredith." He rolled over and propped himself up on a pillow, facing her.

"I think that…I think that this decision is what it's all about. I mean, what I'm all about. I've wanted something like this since I was a child. I just couldn't put my finger on it, but I was destined to be in charge of something, I mean, other than just being a mother and a wife."

"And a talk show host," he added matter-of-factly.

She paced slowly back and forth as he watched her. Of course he knew she was different, special. Of course she was destined for something great. He had always been the cohesive one, standing away, allowing her to spread her wings, but holding her back, thinking that if he let go, she might be able to fly. Now she was about to take flight. He knew he had held her at arm's length, not worried she would leave, but worried she would crash and burn. Maybe his worries were something that he never had ultimatum or reason for? Maybe his concerns were really for himself and not really his wife's flight? Maybe it was his own paranoid conclusions that he in turn portrayed to his family, his wife, that disabled him from being the star. From taking flight himself.

"Milton?"

"Yes, Meredith?"

"I'm going to do this and more than anything I want your blessing. I want you to be proud."

"I know, Meredith, and yes, of course I'll be proud. We—Emily, Connor, and me—are all proud"

"Milton?'

"Yes, Meredith."

"I love you more than anything in the world and if you said no, then…."

"I could, I would never say no Meredith. I am with you till the bitter end, and bitter or not, I am with you."

"And?' She crawled up beside him and wrapped her body around him tightly.

"And I love you, Meredith, and I believe in you."

"I believe in you too, Milton. I believe in you too."

Milton laid his head back and saw the dance of tiny shadows on the ceiling. *She believes in me,* he thought. *She believes in me. I must believe in myself.*

"She's done it!"

"I know, Dick, Jesus, I know."

"What does that mean for us?"

Desmond walked back in the library from the office and selected the most comfortable club chair. "It means, Dickey that your job is going to be that much harder, that much more important and you'll have so many more chances to fuck up."

Dick Salinger stood at his desk, his hand trembling, as he listened to the voice on the other end.

"What I mean, Mr. Desmond, is what happens now? Do we need to cancel this project?"

Desmond grinned, knowing full well Salinger wanted out and that he was in it for good. He played with a letter opener between his fingers and answered calmly but with a deep growl, "I don't think canceling anything right now is part of the agenda. Your job is to keep an eye on everything he does, day and night. Anyone that you hire needs to be cleared through me and you know if he has said anything to her, anything, you will be the first one indicted."

Salinger swallowed hard and answered, "But I won't be the only one Mr. Desmond?" Desmond stood up. He breathed hard into the phone and calculated his next answer.

"Dickey, listen to me. Listen like you never have before. You, my friend, would be the first indicted. But I daresay, that would never happen."

Salinger exhaled, relieved.

"What I meant to say, Dickey, was no one will ever be indicted for anything that's been done so far. You would be the first they would point fingers at, but it's so sad, you would have already done the unspeakable."

"What? What are you talking about Mr. Desmond?"

"The unspeakable, Dickey. Isn't suicide against your religion?"

Dick Salinger sat down, a gleam of perspiration settled in the creases of his forehead.

"But Mr. Desmond, you promised."

"Dick, I did promise and I never break a promise. I promised to protect you and make sure that no one got in your way. And yes, I respect that I promised that, but Dickey, if this thing goes south because you're a pussy and can't handle the strain, then be aware, be very aware, that your suicide will occur and it will be most unpleasant."

Dick Salinger hung up the receiver and stared at the perspiration that dripped from his hand to the desk. He sat back in his leather swivel chair and put his clammy fingers to his face and cried.

Meredith stood, her brothers both sitting, ready for the bombardment. No one wanted to speak first. Meredith walked over to her desk and shuffled some files. She had known these two people longer than anyone in her life. She had loved and hated them, cried and laughed with them, and had become one of the team even before she had won the vote. She leaned against her desk and smiled.

"Well?" she said quietly.

David looked up from his folded hands and stretched his tired legs. He had been at the office for the past 48 hours, answering calls and knocks on the door with little more to say than, "Yep, it's true. My sister is running." Now he didn't know what to say but that. "Yep. I guess you're running."

"I am, David. I asked you both here to see how you felt about it now. I mean, we've talked about it before, but the two of you, well you know."

Charlie sat quietly; his legs crossed at the ankles, watching his siblings react.

"What I mean, Meredith, is I really was never convinced you would try."

"David, I'm sorry if I deceived you in any way, but even thinking about doing it, usually means that I will try."

"I know. I know. I guess I'm just surprised. I'm, well, worried."

"Is Katherine worried?"

"No. No, Katherine is proud. She's really very excited. She's one of your loyalists for sure, but that doesn't mean…."

"That doesn't mean that you are?"

"That doesn't mean that it's the right thing to do Meredith. Do you have any idea what this means?"

Meredith walked up to her oldest brother and looked down at him answering, "Of course I know what this means. It means that I might win the democratic nomination. It means that I might be running for the President of the United States. It means I might run this country."

"Meredith! Run the country! Do you really want to do that? I mean really?"

Charlie uncrossed his legs and leaned forward, facing the two of them. "Of course she does, David. Of course she does. That's why she's announced what she has. I sincerely doubt that our sister has not thought this thing through so many times. That she's made the idea old. She has a gift, David. She has a gift and she needs to pursue it. She has the need, the desire, and the ability to lead people and she has the utmost belief in peace. You and I both have known this for a very long time. I can't think of anything wrong with it. Can you?"

"Charlie, please. Of course peace is a good persuasion, but that's not how someone can run or rule the most powerful country in the world, on the option of peace."

"Why not?" Charlie asked, leaning back again content.

"Because, Charlie, it's not like your job, where you're here to make people feel good about themselves and about other people. Where you forgive people of their ill-doings and preach the word of the Lord. Charlie running a country isn't like running a church."

"Why not?" he asked again and Meredith interrupted.

"Listen both of you, I understand exactly where you're both coming from and it's the two of you combined that makes me me! David I know the world and our country's existence doesn't revolve around hugs and kisses and peace on earth, but I can tell you this. I know that we could use more of it to get our power or persuasion across. There's no harm in trying it a different way, with a different style."

"But Meredith they'll eat you alive."

Meredith turned back toward her desk and breathed deeply. She sat down and waited a few more seconds before responding.

"David, they will try but I'm telling you now I'm ready. I've been thrown to the wolves before and I have won—in court, in politics, in life—and I will defend my country and my decision the best way I know how. I will tell the truth, I will focus on the good and I will let the public decide the outcome."

Charlie smiled and stood, walking over to his sister. He put both hands on her shoulders and said, "You're the only one that needs to believe in this right now, Meredith. The only one. When you believe in something, things happen. I support your decision fully and I can tell you now that the people of my church, any church, are more than willing to listen to someone who preaches a little more peace than turmoil. You have my blessing." He leaned over and kissed her on the cheek. Tears welled in her eyes and she looked over at David.

"Well?"

David pushed himself up from the chair and limped over to where they stood.

"If there is any way that you can win, any way at all, then all due respect sister, you have my love and my vote. Damn though, the next year and a half they should just put me in the entertainment section of the paper." Meredith giggled and held him tightly.

"You know I am me because of you two. You know that, don't you?" They both hugged her and laughed.

Revo sat alone, one of very few breaks in the last few weeks. He glanced at the crushed headlines, peeking from the pile of trash in the waste can. He could see her hair and the side of her body, her right hand raised as if she were swearing on the Bible. *It was nothing*, he thought, *nothing*. She would have to win the party decision before he would ever have the opportunity of eating her alive and he was completely confident she didn't have it in her. He knew who and what she was up against and doubted any woman could get through even the first few months of campaigning without breaking down and making a fool of herself. She was a fucking talk show host, not a politician. He pulled the paper out of the trash and looked for a sign, something significant that might change his mind. He scanned the photo from left to right, up and down and then he saw it. Hidden in the back, barely visible, was the face that held the secret. The man who held the cure that could save his life. A man more powerful than any of them. Revo stabbed a ballpoint pen into his face and made him go away.

Chapter 37

With her announcement public, Meredith's audience mourned. They were her biggest advocates, yet the show could not go on. She received thousands of e-mails and letters asking her to reconsider her options and more than once was told, "You're doing a fantastic job where you are. Why change?" She had given very little notice, possibly with the notion that she would be talked out of the idea. Bonnie and Darryl had known only days before and their reactions were much brighter. They would stand beside her all the way—to New Hampshire, to the convention, and, last stop, the White House. Darryl also confirmed that there were backers and had been for sometime, waiting with millions to donate. That meant not having to rely on government funding. That meant the decisions she made would be her own.

Her last episode, viewed by millions, would be the pinnacle. The station stood proud, even though its bipartisan reputation would be under surveillance. They would allow a last show for Meredith to say goodbye and a last chance for the record-breaking ratings she entailed. She promised with utmost grace and sincerity that it was not intended for votes, but truly to close a chapter in her life. She sat alone on the stage, dressed in the same winter-white suit that she had started in. She took a sip of her water from the now famous mug, a deep breath, and smiled.

"Hello, America."

The audience stood and applauded.

"No, no, please sit. Please."

They slowly obliged.

She hesitated until the room grew quiet, then continued.

"I wanted to start by saying thank you. Thank you to all of you here and you," she pointed toward the camera, "all of you, the viewers, who have made this an unforgettable experience. Thank you for the encouragement, support, and true friendship I have felt."

Applause erupted again, but she quickly quieted them with a raised hand.

"It is with great reverence and apprehension that I am about to say goodbye today. But before I do, I wanted to spend the next 50 minutes, give or take a few for our advertisers," Bonnie and Darryl smiled, "and remember some of the wonderful people that have joined me on this stage. Without these people, this show would've never continued, let alone existed. Please take a moment to admire just some of the people that make this a world a better place."

The clip rolled and everyone watched as Meredith joked with the oldest living senator and the youngest philanthropist. Tears welled as the 12-year-old old leukemia victim danced and sang in the Oncology ward and the grandmother knocked on doors, peddling her home-made potholders to raise money for the local fire department. The focus changed to laughter as Meredith gave out signature buttons to small-town heroes and illustrious movie stars and she treated them all with the same respect and notoriety. At the end she sat, just outside of ground zero with tears in her eyes, and hugged one of the many canines involved in the search for survivors.

Meredith smiled and the audience stood again to applaud. She stood with them.

"That was wonderful. Thank you to the staff. The extremely, talented people who worked so hard on that clip as well as every show we aired."

"Now, goodness, where to start." She fell back into her chair.

The audience giggled.

"It's been a whirlwind and I wouldn't change a thing since the day we went on the air. When I was young, I was a bit of a loner and I was lonely. When I attended high school, my self-esteem and all-over attitude blossomed when a teacher of mine took an interest in my future. He, to this day, is still one of the most important people in my life. Without him, without teachers, we would be dog paddling. Thank you, Coach Mack Murphy. Thank you for showing me the way and letting me believe that I found it on my own. You are a tribute to your profession. Teachers are heroes and we need to let them know it." She beckoned for applause.

"College brought more than academic fulfillment and challenge. I met my husband, my life-long partner, while in college. He is my backbone, my torch, and I love him with all my heart."

Bonnie rolled her eyes jokingly.

"My family and my children have brought me so much joy. Their smiles are my inner strength. I love all of you."

"I've poured coffee and served bagels, worked in the judicial system, and had a part-time gig as Mayor of this city," The audience giggled and clapped, "then I was offered this chair and a chance to meet a small part of the rest of the world. My eyes are open wide. I have learned more in the last few years than in a lifetime. I was given the opportunity to meet and introduce people from all walks of life. Those who move and shake this great country. The heartbeat of America. If everyone gave just a little bit more, cared a little bit more and whined a little bit less. We are blessed to live in the greatest free country in the world yet we take it for granted at times. A country we need to remain proud of. It's not just a landmass. It's 258 million human beings all trying to survive. Once you feel the pride, it's hard to forget. Once you feel the need, it's hard to ignore."

"Volunteer for a good cause. Help your neighbor. Help yourself. My goodness, get out and vote. Participate in this wonderful country's freedom. The world and this country are only as vulnerable as we allow them to be. War, terrorism, hatred are only brought on by people and only can be stopped by people. Be aware of who you are and what you are capable of. Get educated. Get informed. Realize your dreams and reach for them."

"When our son was hurt this past year, my first reaction was bitter anger. When he became conscious, he looked me in the eye and said, 'Everything is going to be all right, Mom.' Here was someone that just experienced unbearable pain and always listened to me preach, and there I was feeling just the opposite. When our daughter's eyesight was restored after 10 years of darkness, her first reaction was 'everything's just the way I saw it before—perfect.' They saw the good before the bad. I had to find the good in the bad. I had to change the bad to good. My children gave me the inspiration to live my life to the fullest."

"Today we've invited 20 of the hundreds of guests that have graced this stage with their lives and hopes. Please join me in thanking them for their incredible achievements and selfless lives."

The stage filled and Meredith introduced and embraced each person individually. She then stood in front of the group and added, "These people, along with so many more, have helped me make a decision to do more with my life. I want to be all that I can be. I am so proud to be able to stand in the midst of these people and I am so proud to be an American. Goodbye for now, America. Thank you. Oh, and please remember, get out and vote. Your country demands very little, so do yourself a favor and give back a little of what this country gives to you. The world will be a better place."

The lights dimmed and the audience called out her name. The emotional reverence that hailed in the studio and across America was a breath of fresh air. The horror that America and the world seemed to be teetering on daily was put aside and a less grim outlook took its place. The world would never be the same after September 11th 2001 or any other horrible attack, but the realization that there were billions more good people than bad made life seem less complicated. Meredith gave people hope. She was ready for her next challenge, ready to make a difference. America was ready to stand by her. She said goodbye to one job and hello to what so many perceived as unattainable.

Revo glanced over at Desmond, busy doodling over the completed morning's crossword.

"Well?"

"Well what, Gerald?"

"Do you think we have anything to worry about, Desmond?"

"No, Gerald, I don't."

"I had no idea she had brass balls, Desmond. No idea."

"She's just another pawn, Gerald. No one will take her seriously. Really, she's just a fucking talk show host. We, you, have nothing to worry about."

Gerald scraped lightly at the rash beneath his Italian silk tie, careful not to open the wound.

"She's not something I want to deal with right now, Desmond."

"Don't waste your energy on her, Gerald. She will be taken care of."

"That's what I like to hear Desmond."

"Yes, Gerald."

"Desmond, make sure that fucking station is fined."

"Already done, Gerald. It's already been taken care of."

Revo smirked, catching the last glimpse of Meredith, waving goodbye.

"Son?" Milton looked up from the cage of small white mice enjoying their evening meal. He looked around, confirming as always that he was alone.

"Hi Pop. You never come in here."

"I know. I don't really like it, Son. It's, well, it's not a really nice place. I feel sorry for the little guys."

Milton digested the statement but did not agree.

"Well it's not a bad place either, Pop. It's where some of the world's worst enemies are fought. Some of the world's worst enemies are found out and trampled.

"I know, Son. I know it's necessary." He leaned over, peering into the small cage and smiled. "Did you know your grandmother hated those little critters? Hated them!"

"Yes, Pop, you've told me before. I don't know how anyone could hate them, but I know a lady who just announced she's running for President, who isn't too keen on them either."

They both chuckled.

"Funny how they can be so brave in some ways and so afraid in others. I mean, how could you be afraid of these little guys?" Milton tapped the cage and offered a crumb to the closest rodent. He took it gingerly from his fingers.

Milton's grandfather stood, considering his grandson, and took a seat at the end of the table. He watched as his grandson documented a chart, and then started tidying up.

"Are you done for the night?"

Milton glanced up at the wall clock and nodded his head. "Yep. I'm done."

He picked up the cage, taking a closer look before he covered it and put it back with the others behind him. He washed his hands and looked back to see if his grandfather was still there. He was.

"Are you coming, Pop?"

"I guess so. Not much to really talk about tonight, Son, is there?"

"No, not really. I'm tired. Worn out really. Just not sure where this is all going and I'm frustrated. Frustrated and tired."

His grandfather looked around and whispered. "Did you read the file again?"

Milton turned towards him and nodded. "Yes Pop, I read the file, again"

"All of it?"

"Yes, all of it."

"Hmm. Thought for sure that something might be in there that would help with this mess."

"Me too."

"You should read it again."

"Pop, I've gone over it with a fine-tooth comb. It's always with me. Thought it better to just keep it with me." He leaned over and pulled the folded sheets from his boot.

"Ah. Smart thinking, Son. Do you still have the others addressed and ready to mail?"

"Yes, Pop, but I doubt it would help me now. There's nothing in there that I don't already know."

"Can I see them?" His grandfather was reaching for them when Milton hesitated. Not only was he talking with his apparition on a regular basis, now he was going to allow the apparition to read the papers that were saving his and his family's lives.

"I don't know, Pop. You wouldn't really understand them."

He kept his arm outstretched and finally Milton obliged. He took a seat close to him and watched as he read.

"What does this mean, Son?" he asked as he pointed to a paragraph on the third page.

Milton leaned over and said, "That means that she and the physicians were testing without funding and their conclusions would be deemed unreliable."

"You mean they did this all on their own? No help from anyone—financially I mean?"

Milton looked at his grandfather and answered monotone, "Yes, Pop, I assume that's what that means." He leaned back and stretched his aching back.

"Son? What's this?"

Milton reluctantly leaned over again and looked at what his grandfather was pointing at. The initials were DDC and were captioned beside one of the formulas. He answered, "I'm not sure. I thought maybe it was their coding system. Now, I don't think it means anything, or anything important."

"You're not sure?'

"No, Pop. I'm not sure. I don't think it has anything to do with the formula or what they discovered. Much of the introduction is just hearsay now. It means nothing."

"Really?" His grandfather glanced at him perplexed.

"Yes. Really. Come on now, I need to lock up and get home. Let me put those back in my boot for safe keeping." He took the papers and carefully hid them in the lining of his boot. "Are you coming?"

His grandfather sat quietly, contemplating.

"Pop, are you coming?"

"Milton, for your information, I'm not nearly as tired as you and I think I might stay here awhile with the little guys. Make sure they get settled in."

Milton regarded him with a look, wondering if his apparition could disturb his little furry friends, then conceded he couldn't stop him from doing so anyway.

"All right then, goodnight. It's always nice to see you Pop."

"You too, Son. You too. By the way, I think I know what that DDC stands for."

Milton turned, just as he was about to shut down the lights. "You do?"

"Hmm. I think I do. I think it's a company that was started in the 80's in Houston. A company that's been noted for large donations in medical research and silent with government grants."

"Really? How would you know that?"

"Oh, Son, you always doubt me. I read. I read a lot. Not much else to do up there, you know."

Milton pondered the thought for a moment, but his head felt heavy so he declined to fuel the comment. "Well, thank you for your insight. Good night, Pop." Milton shut down the lights and the lab fell to black.

"Don't you want to know what it stands for?" his grandfather's voice echoed through the darkness.

"Oh all right, what does it stand for?" He held the door open a crack, the key already in the lock.

"Son, I think it stands for Damion Desmond Corporation. I think that's it. Good night, Son."

Milton quickly switched on the lights but the lab was empty.

CHAPTER 38

"I need you with me tomorrow night." Meredith held her chin on her hand and gazed across the table at her husband. The ride to the restaurant had been quiet. The whole week had been quiet. She slipped off her shoes and touched his leg with her manicured toes. They had been seated in a dark corner, but Milton still felt like he was under a microscope, anticipating another camera flash. Meredith's flirting only enhanced his anxiety.

"I know, Meredith." He answered calmly, moving his leg out of her reach.

She sat up and leaned across, closer to him. "I also know that your work has consumed so much of your time lately and I don't intend to interrupt that."

"I know, Meredith." He answered again.

"Milton, please. I'm learning to balance this situation too. What I'm sure of is that this is our anniversary and I'm hoping we can enjoy one another's company."

"Meredith, I'm sorry. Of course I'll be wherever you need me to be tonight, tomorrow, or the next day. My work is, well, just my work."

"It's not just your work, but Darryl says...."

"Meredith, please, spare me what Darryl or Bonnie has to say. It's all been said. I've heard it all. You are the leader, the top candidate, and I'm not surprised. You beckoned millions on a daily basis at three in the afternoon to your show and they watched and they listened and they did what you asked them to do. They love you, Meredith, and rightly so. Now they have a chance to make things happen. I've never said this to you, but tonight's as good a time as any. I've never thought for a moment that you would be any less than perfect as the President of the United States. Yet unlike your fans, I, on a daily basis, have to live with the fact that, very possibly, I'm not cut out to be by your side. What don't you think I understand?"

Meredith hesitated, adjusting her demeanor. This was not a grass-roots backer, nor an influential advisor. This was her husband, the man she had loved and lived with for 20 years and they needed to celebrate that.

"Milton, without you by my side, I wouldn't be here today. You know this and I have always known this. Please darling, please be by my side. Happy Anniversary." She handed him the small blue box tied with a silver bow. He smiled and accepted it.

"Well, yes, this is nice." He displayed the sterling silver button with the words "The First Gentleman" engraved on the front. He shook his head and chuckled, then quickly put it back in the velvet envelope, before a photographer could anonymously catch the shot.

"Thank you, darling." He said unconvincingly.

"You didn't read the card."

"Oh, no I didn't. Sorry."

He opened it slowly, and pulled out the small, generic card with only his name in Meredith's beautiful script. He glanced up at her before he opened it, and she smiled.

Then he read.

From the day I met you I could not forget you. I had no idea how important you would be in my life, or how much I would love you, but years have solidified that. You're my best friend, my confidant, and I only hope that I can spend another 50 years with you doing what we do. Because it works and it's right. I thrive because of you. Thank you for everything you've given me and everything you've helped me attain. Your choices have been valiant, your love unconditional and your friendship everlasting. Nothing could be better, ever. Thank God you chose me. I love you, Milton, with all my heart. Meredith

P.S. When this is all over and if I have won, thank you for your love and support. And I promise it will not be forever before we can go on vacation, just you and me and the Caribbean. And I will make passionate love with you the entire time.

P.S.S. When this ends and if I have not won, I thank you for your love and support and I promise that we will go on vacation right after, just you and me and the Caribbean. And I will make passionate love with you the entire time.

P.S.S. You are my love and my life. Happy Anniversary, Darling. Forever.

He blinked back tears. It had been sometime since he had felt her passion, months since he had felt her at all, and the card emphasized that it didn't matter. The traveling, the paparazzi, the six nights a week in a hotel. Nothing mattered more than this moment to both of them. She was the disheveled angel that he got the nerve to approach, as she scrambled to sign up for freshman classes. The girl he watched and waited for until the perfect day sat at the coffee shop. The girl he loved completely and married. The woman who gave him the two most beautiful children anyone could ask for. She was everything and he would do anything for her.

"Meredith, the card. It's beautiful." He slipped his shoe off and rubbed the inside of her calf.

She giggled into her napkin and caressed his hand. "I'm so happy you like it."

"I feel terrible, Meredith. I only got you a card. I couldn't think of anything else to get you, so I wrote it down. Your gift I mean."

"Darling, that's all right. It's perfectly fine."

He handed it to her and she opened it carefully.

"To my wife on our anniversary," she read. She smiled and inside read her husband's slanted scrawl.

You, my darling wife, have no idea just how much I love you. There is and never will be a greater love. No matter what happens, please know that I have loved you with everything in my soul. I know right now your life is consumed, but in the end I will always be there. I know what you need and what you want and I will help you make that happen. You will win and I will be there when you do. I will be there when you win. I will help you win."

"All my love forever. Milton

She looked down at her closed menu, her hand still on his, and she sighed.

"I mean that, Meredith."

"I know, Milton. I know. Thank you," she sniffled, looking up into his eyes. "Thank you for everything. I know it hasn't been easy at times. I know I haven't been…."

Milton put his finger to her lips and shook his head slightly.

"Meredith, I wouldn't change a thing about you. I wouldn't change a thing. Unless of course you'd like to drop everything, pack up the kids, the dog, and Beatrice and move up to Canada, where we can grown our own food, breathe clean air, live a peaceful, simple life?"

She smiled and shook her head no.

Damion Desmond's head was throbbing. After nine hours in the war room and another three behind closed doors with the 9/11 commission, he was determined to get home and have the masseuse work her miracles.

His pager went off and he answered, "Yes?"

"Mr. Desmond. The President would like to see you right now."

Damion sighed. "I'll be there in a moment." He had to go to Houston in the morning and he looked at his watch and made his way down the hall. The President's office door was open.

"Mr. President?"

"Ah yes, Damion. Come in and please close the door."

Desmond closed the door and helped himself to an overstuffed chair.

"No, no, Desmond. Come sit over here."

Desmond sat where the President pointed, crossed his legs and said, "Well?"

"Well. It's been a long day huh?"

More familiar with the door closed he answered, "Yes, Gerald. A bitch of a day."

"You going home to that Asian broad tonight?" Gerald teased, pouring two heavy scotches.

Damion declined to answer.

Gerald handed him one of the tumblers and sipped hungrily on his own.

"Hmm. I can't believe how much I like this stuff. Really wish I had discovered it earlier."

Damion frowned and placed his drink on a side table.

"Not thirsty, Desmond?"

"No, Gerald. Not thirsty. Is there something you needed me for?"

Revo leaned back, taking another large gulp of his drink. "Yes, there is. I wanted to make sure the day went accordingly. I haven't seen you all day."

"The day went fine, Gerald."

"And the commission?"

"I'd think you'd be more concerned about the war room negotiations."

"Nah. Not really my priority right now. I have good people taking care of that."

"But Gerald. The body count seems to be endless. We need to reevaluate our positions daily."

"Of course. I know. Just so many things to reevaluate right now. I was wondering what you'd think if I picked a new Vice President for the election?"

"Excuse me? What?" Desmond asked perplexed.

"A new Vice President. Dump Williams and go with, oh I don't know, maybe a woman?"

"Gerald, you've got to be kidding?"

"No. No, I'm not kidding. I would like your opinion on the matter."

"Gerald. Williams has been a perfect Vice President. The best kind. He's kept a low profile, very little bitching, and has done an exceptional job over in Asia."

Revo nodded. "Yes, yes he has, but I was just thinking a change might be what we need."

"Gerald, stop worrying about Nicholson. She's not significant at all. Sure she's got the party wrapped, but Jesus, Gerald, she's a talk show host, not a politician. She's a broad with brains and that's about it. Stop worrying about things that don't matter right now and let's focus on this fucking war, this goddamned commission and what we really need to get done before the election. You're a shoo-in for the next four years. Knock off the scotch though, it makes you stupid."

Revo glared at Desmond, but placed the half empty glass on the table beside him.

"And once again, how are you feeling? I mean before the scotch hits your brain."

Revo placed his hands on his thighs and massaged his legs. "I'm feeling great. Almost perfect."

"Almost?" Desmond asked.

"Well, yeah, almost. Most of the time I feel euphoric, like there's been a positive ion boost added to the vial, then for a second or two, it might happen."

"What happens?'

"I'm not sure. It's a blip. A sudden stop in time. I can't explain it. Really, it's nothing. I'm feeling really good. Really good. That fucking husband of hers is a genius. A real fucking genius. I wish we could do without him, but for now, he's really fucking good."

"I know there were issues with the dosage and strength before. I think he's licked it on his own, even without the Ridgefield file."

"Fucking file."

"I know, fucking file. I am sure now that she just burned all the evidence, somewhere. With all the man power and hours looking for something that doesn't exist."

"Well, thank God we didn't take him out too. Really. He's the answer."

"Yeah and his wife is just a blip in time."

"Just a fucking blip. Should have a final count by next week. The convention will be hers and then she's mine."

"We'll see about that. We'll see. Anything else?"

Revo stood, "No, no, nothing else. Go home to that chink, Desmond. Have some fun."

Damion stepped closer to him and said, "Lay off the scotch. It makes you fucking stupid and I hate stupid people."

"Bastard," Revo grumbled as Desmond left the office, knowing full well that he was right. He was always right.

"Aren't we really on the same team?" Meredith whined, dropping her briefcase loudly on her desk.

Darryl closed the door and opened the refrigerator, taking two bottles of water out. Handing one to Meredith he responded, "Meredith, no one is really on the same team and you know that. Listen we have three more days until Illinois and then his ass will be packed, heading for home. He's mortified that you've done so well. He's thoroughly convinced that his qualifications are better and is acting like a kid that was once popular but has lost his edge. It sucks for him, but that's the way the game is played and you've known that since the beginning. I'm hoping for an endorsement by May."

"Ugh. I know. We need the endorsement. I just hope we can come up with a better candidate for Vice President. It's bogus and has absolutely nothing to do with my endeavors or ability now. I was a kid—oh and about the kids, I'll not be bringing them in just to be campaign props."

Darryl shook his head and sat down. "Meredith, the kids need to be with you because you are a solid, capable, loving mother. They're not props. They're reminders. Your enemy is not a Democrat, but a Republican and I need you to remember that. He may be the very best choice for V.P. and we'll get to that when the time is right. About Mr. Curtis, whether you like it or not, it does reflect what you may do in the future. We need the African-American vote. We need the Hispanic vote. We need all the minority's votes. I'm not taking anything lightly and we need to make sure this is not going to be a problem."

"Darryl, I told you twice now, I haven't seen nor heard from him in 27 years."

"How about your parents?"

"Oh God, please let's keep them out of this. Dad and Mom don't need this and I hate the idea of opening healed wounds. There are scars that have faded. It's unnecessary. I was 17."

Bonnie knocked lightly and waited for Meredith's response. She walks deliberately and helps herself to a bottle of water as well.

"Well?" Darryl asks impatiently.

"Um, Meredith. We found him."

Meredith looks at Bonnie, then Darryl, and replies, "Wow!" That was fast."

"It really wasn't that hard. He's in Boston and has been for the last twenty years. He lives on the north shore with his family."

"His family?"

"Yes. He's married and has three children."

"Wow! Three?"

"Yes."

"OK, Darryl what next?"

"Bon, have you spoken with him?"

"I have."

"And?"

"He was very nice. He seemed very understanding."

"Good."

"Does Meredith need to do anything on this end?"

"Um, no I don't think so, but he would like to see her."

Meredith's eyes widened.

"For what reason?" Darryl asked defensively.

"Just to say hello and wish her luck."

Darryl shook his head and added, "Is that really necessary?"

"It's all right, Darryl. It's not a problem at all. I think it would be good." Meredith added pensively, "I think it will be good for a lot of reasons. Bonnie, when can we set this up?"

"Um, how about right now? He's downstairs in the lobby, waiting."

Meredith shook her head and laughed.

"Are you OK with this?" Darryl asked leaning closer to his boss.

"Yes, I'm fine. I'm fine." She straightened her hair with her hands self-consciously.

"All right then, let's get this over with," Darryl pressed the intercom, "Harmony, are you still there?"

"Yes, Mr. Rodriguez. I'm still here."

"Can you please go down to the lobby and escort Mr. Curtis up to the office?"

"Yes, Mr. Rodriguez. Of course."

The three looked at each other and smiled and Meredith remarked, "I'm going to do this alone, OK?"

Darryl opened his mouth to protest and Meredith raised her hand slightly. "Alone, Darryl. Alone."

Bonnie held the door open for Darryl and smiled back at Meredith, "Good luck."

"Thanks, Bonnie. Please call me when he's upstairs."

"I will." She replied, closing the door.

Meredith sat and waited the last few minutes for something she had anticipated since the day she boarded a bus for Boston. The waiting would finally be over.

Chapter 39

There was a hint of lilac in the air. Meredith made her way gingerly around the water's edge. She could see the house in the distance and noticed a few shingles had blown off around the chimney from the harsh winter. She thought of waiting for the call inside, but elected to have the message left instead. A rare moment to be alone, still conscious of the armed escorts lurking around the perimeter.

The past seven months were over and she was about to win the Democratic nomination. Who would've thought? Her loyal fans proved all polls significantly lopsided. She swept every primary but Illinois and the tabloids drooled with celebrity rumors. Her style, weight, marital status, maternal status, and all over qualifications were laid out and dissected and in an internet frenzy. She remained calm, as did her family—determined, without hesitation.

Not only would she be the third-youngest-President if elected, just a bit older than Roosevelt and Kennedy, but also the first female to hold the post. She was the news in the summer of 2004. The United States was at war in the Middle East and thousands of soldiers' lives were tested daily. There was a constant threat of terrorist hatred, and the economy, deficit, and stock market were at an all-time low. Still, Meredith Nicholson was on the cover of every reputable and not-so-reputable newspaper and magazines clamored for her cover shot.

She returned from D.C. after saying goodbye to their son, who had moved into his first apartment near school. Their daughter had been accepted into an elite prep school, and her eyesight was nearly perfect. Beatrice had retired and Daisy was now a calm, 5 year old Labrador. They celebrated aunts, uncles, and grandparents' birthdays and anniversaries and she and Milton celebrated their own 20th anniversary. They praised David on his promotion to senior editor at the paper and they watched as Charlie was made pastor of his own church. Connie and Katherine were still her closest girlfriends and her father now used e-mail daily to communicate with her. She'd spent an afternoon a month prior, cooking dinner with her mother, closing the chapter on a very old grudge. She went back to high school to see Coach Mack Murphy, was blessed by the now Monsignor Dennis, and visited Amy's grave. And yes, finally, she saw Jerome again.

When he walked into her office, she was already standing. He smiled and she smiled back. He was soft-spoken and polite. He stood confident and poised and he wished her the very best luck. He said he was very proud of her, yet not surprised. He said he always knew she was special. She blushed and said thank you and he stretched his hand out to shake hers. She accepted and pulled herself closer to give him a quick hug.

"It's good to see you, Jerome." She took a few steps back and let go of his hand.

"You too, Meredith. It's good to see you. Thank you for your time. I know you must be very busy."

"Yes, I am, but it's good to see you. Maybe we can…I mean, my goodness, this is strange. It's been a lot of years. A lot of water under the bridge."

"Meredith, I wanted to call. I wanted to explain."

"Then why didn't you?" She said sadly.

He sat and looked up at her, "Every day that went by, I became more afraid. Afraid you hated me, that you wouldn't speak with me. I know it's absurd, but as the weeks went by, I became paralyzed. I loved you more than you'll ever know."

"It was terrible for me, Jerome. But, what else can we say. It's been so many years. A lot has happened." She refused to cry.

"My wife and I will be voting for you."

"Oh, yes, of course. Thank you." Meredith looked out the window.

"She was very fond of your show."

"Oh, well, that's nice to know. I miss it sometimes."

"We'll watch the convention."

"Good. That'll be quite a day in Boston."

"Quite a day in the United States. Well, I know you're busy. I'll keep refusing to talk with the papers, OK?"

"Thank you, Jerome. We appreciate that."

"Goodbye, Meredith, and good luck. Have a nice evening."

"You too, Jerome. You too. Thank you for coming into the city. It was nice to see you."

"I wouldn't have missed it. Thank you."

Meredith blushed again and waved childishly as he opened the office door to leave. Then he hesitated, leaned back inside, and said, "Meredith?"

"Yes?"

"Meredith, I just wanted to say I'm sorry."

Meredith looked him in the eyes and said, "I know, Jerome. I know."

And then he was gone.

Meredith made her way back to the porch and inside, ignoring the flashing red light of the answering machine for a few more seconds. She poured herself a glass of wine, even though it was only mid morning and sat on the kitchen counter. She took a sip of the deep red cabernet and reaches over to press the play button.

"Meredith?...Hmmm, I wish you were there...It's Darryl and Bonnie. Yep it's official. Should be announced on the network tonight. We're declaring victory. Congratulations. Call us back when you get this and I'll try your cell."

Meredith enjoyed the rest of her glass of wine, grabbed the bottle to bring upstairs, and decided she would save the message on her cell phone for several years.

Milton was just about to settle back at the lab table, when Professor Salinger tapped on the window. Milton rolled his eyes and stepped outside the door.

"Milton, I just heard the news on NPR."

"The news?"

"Yes. Your wife. She's won."

"Yes, We've been expecting that for weeks. She's been the front runner for sometime."

"Yes, I know, but it's official. Unbelievable. A talk show host might be our next President. Do you think she can do it?"

"Yes, Dickey, I do. She's extremely popular. Did you really ask me that again? Is that all you needed?"

"Well I just wanted to let you know that I talked with the boss upstairs and he's agreed. We'd like to give you a personal day today. A day to spend with your wife and your family, to celebrate."

"Really?" Milton responded sarcastically.

"Yes, Milton. *Of course you are,* Milton thought. His wife's popularity and his affiliation with her and the company We're all very excited here."

Of had considerably raised the value of their stock.

"Yes sir. We're very excited too."

"I'm hoping you'll be staying on." Salinger shifted his gangly physique from side to side.

"I have no plans to go anywhere. I like it here."

Salinger slapped him on the back. "That's great news, buddy. That's great. Now go and have a nice day with your wife."

Milton didn't argue. "Thank you, sir. Should I call the President and thank him?"

Salinger stuttered, "Oh, no, no. No worries. I'll let him know you're grateful."

Sure you will maggot, Milton contemplated as he removed his lab coat. *I'm sure this is all your idea. Don't include anyone in your game, Dickey boy. I know exactly what's going on.*

"OK then. We'll see you tomorrow. Early, right Milton?"

"Yes, Dickey. Oh and thank you."

"Absolutely. Outstanding employees need to be rewarded.

"How fucking generous of you, prick," Milton mumbled as he headed back to his office for his car keys.

Salinger rushed back upstairs and waited to see Milton leave the parking lot before he called Desmond.

"Everything's status quo, Mr. Desmond."

"Good, Salinger. Good. No qualms about his attitude?"

"Oh, no. He's as dull as a butter knife and absolutely clueless."

"Good. I expect it to stay that way."

"Of course, Mr. Desmond. Of course. I think we may have this locked up in the next few months. Locked up for good."

"Really?" Desmond's ears perked.

"Yes, I think so. Stafford seems to have contained the original problem and expanded the solution."

"I seem to remember the original problem was you?"

"Sir? No, no, it was much more complicated than that."

"Of course it was, Dick. Of course it was. I expect you to keep me informed."

"Yes, of course. I gave him the day off to celebrate with his wife."

"Who's idea was that?"

"Mine, Mr. Desmond." Salinger fidgeted in his chair.

"Really? Good idea, Dick. That was a very good idea. I'm impressed. Keep the enemy happy and they'll never expect a thing."

"My thoughts exactly, sir."

"Maybe we can talk about a bonus soon."

"That would be nice, sir."

"Good day, Salinger. Good work."

"Thank you, Mr. Desmond. Thank you very much."

Dick Salinger hung up the phone and grinned. He had the White House eating out of his hand now. His wife was visiting her mother, so he could reward himself later with one of the new dancers at the club. He would be rolling in money soon.

"It's about time," he said out loud, "about fucking time."

Desmond closed his phone and replaced it inside his blazer. He watched as a jet's contrail evaporated in the morning heat. He was happy to be out of the capital for a few days. He missed Houston. He missed Texas. All he needed was confirmation that the serum was foolproof, a complete cure. Then he would do away with the moron Salinger and the idiot savant scientist. That in turn would destroy the Nicholson broad and in turn the President would easily be reelected. How fucking ironic, that the man in charge of keeping the President alive, was also the husband of his now arch-nemesis. It would be easy to do away with all of them, but her status now would not allow for that, so he would have to rely on her husband's tragic death to bring her to her knees and end this freak show.

He would have himself replaced as Chief of Staff, and he would be able to collect his due. He would miss Texas, but sacrifices had to be made for a billion dollars.

"I hope you're right, Dickey boy. If this is almost over, I promise you, I'll be the one to pull the trigger. Open wide, fucker!"

Desmond cocked his fingers and pretended to pull a trigger. The look on his face was satisfied until his private line rang. He hesitated, then answered, "Yes…Of course…No, I don't think that will be necessary…Of course I will take care of it…Yes…Yes…Of course…Soon…I'm not exactly certain, but…No…No, sir…Of course…Good evening…." Closing the phone once again, he leaned back in his chair, steadying his still cocked finger.

Milton pulled into the garage after being interrogated at the driveway entrance. It was unusual for him to be home mid-day and the secret service had not been informed. They'd been busy keeping curious passersby at a distance and they didn't like surprises.

"Ms. Nicholson is inside, sir," the agent finally added, looking about the same age as Connor. He walked into the kitchen and hears music coming from upstairs. His daughter's bedroom door was pulled closed but the bass vibrated the hallway floor under his feet. He recognized the Nine Inch Nails song that he has spoken with Emily about several times. He still wasn't convinced the lyrics were suitable. He pushed the door open a crack, slapped by the decibels blaring from the speakers. His wife, nude, her wet hair flailing, was singing, "Head like a hole. Black as your soul. I'd rather die, than give you control," Her arms raised, she bent, with her eyes closed, "Bow down before the one you serve. You're going to get what you deserve." Milton walked toward her and tapped her on the shoulder. She screamed.

"Oh my Gosh, Milton!" She jumped to get the volume control, but Milton had the remote and did the honor for her. He smiled.

"Milton, goddamn it. You scared the bejesus out of me."

"I'm sorry, my sweet. I'm home to celebrate your victory and I tried calling twice, but there was no answer on either of the phones. Hmmm. I guess you couldn't hear the ringing? Glad one of the agents wasn't trying to find you," he chuckled and brushed her breast.

She bent over again, this time to grab her towel. Embarrassed, she added, "Sorry. I guess I haven't had time to myself in so long. I must look pretty silly. I got a little carried away." She pointed to the bottle of wine.

"I see that." He added, nodding toward their daughter's bureau, where the half empty bottle sat. "I could use a little of that. Shall we?" He bowed to his wife, beckoning her to leave first and whispered as she passed, "Love the nude dancing thing, but darling, the choice of songs is, well, not the best."

She paused and dropped her towel, dragging it behind her. "I beg to differ, darling. I love that song."

Milton shut Emily's door and followed the towel to their bedroom.

CHAPTER 40

Darryl growled impatiently, waiting for the elevator. Under his arm he carried a stack of daily newspapers. "Damn thing must be stuck on seven," he grumbled to the two women waiting alongside him. As he turned toward the stairwell, they giggled. He was a regular celebrity in the press now. With no time or patience to chitchat, he elected the stairwell disgruntled, and admonished the 14-flight ascent, repeating to himself over and over, "Be smart, Darryl. Be smart." When he reached the floor he knocked loudly to alert security and went directly to her office to wait. Moments later, she arrived.

"Good morning, Darryl."

"Meredith," he acknowledged, then he stood and closed the door behind her.

"It is a good one, isn't it, Darryl?"

"If you mean the weather, it is, Meredith."

"OK, what's up?" she asked, pulling the chair out from behind her desk.

"I had a rude awakening this morning."

"Yes? What was that?"

"Talk radio was slamming you for prejudice."

"I know. I heard." She looked at him, despondent.

"I just wish I had known." He said as he crossed his arms.

Calmly she replied, "Would you not be here right now if you had known, Darryl?"

"Of course I'd be here, Meredith. But as your campaign manager I need to know everything. Everything, period."

"I understand, Darryl. And I'm sorry that I kept it from you—from everyone, but I was 17 and, well," she paused, sick of repeating herself.

"Meredith, it's important. It's imperative. I need to know everything to get where we need to go."

"All right, Darryl. I understand. Anything else?"

He walked over to the window and answered, "OK then. I intend to call a small press conference this afternoon, so you can address the questions again, about Jerome and the marriage. OK?"

Meredith pondered his idea and knew they had no other choice. "Is that all they want to talk about?"

"That and your marital woes." Darryl said begrudgingly.

"Marital woes again?" She rolled her eyes.

"Well, the public wants to see more of Milton. They want to see the two of you cozy and secure. The minorities want you to apologize and the Middle Americans want a love story. Fucking ridiculous."

"You know I'm not going to ask him to leave his position?"

"I know, but can he take a few more days off? Can he be with us the week before the debate? He'll be joining us on the campaign trip, right?"

"I'll talk with him again."

"Good. I'm not saying his work is not important, but I'm sure someone can cover while he supports his wife. We need him too, Meredith. We need everything we can get right now. This is far from over and not going to be easy. I'm stockpiling our ammunition now so we're prepared. Meredith, what exactly does Milton do anyway?"

"What? Darryl, I've told you before. He's a scientist that develops pharmaceutical drugs."

"What drug is he working on? I'm sure they'll ask that at some point."

Meredith pondered this question and said, "I have absolutely no idea."

"You two don't talk about it?" Darryl asked, as he poured himself a cup of coffee that Harmony had just brewed.

"No. As a matter of fact we don't. I'm the only one that brings my work home with me."

"Well you should ask. I'm sure *they'll* be asking. I've got to get to the polls committee and set up the press conference. I'll be back in about an hour to go over the related questions."

"Good. Thank you, Darryl. Have we heard from Bonnie this morning?"

"Yes. I spoke with her earlier. No one can get into the naval hospital, as you know, but she did say they keep having him wave out the window and one rumor is that he had an appendicitis attack."

"Ow! Hmm. OK, well. Poor President Revo. Keep me posted"

Darryl stepped into the hall and heard her call his name.

"Yes? Forget something?"

"Darryl, do you think he'll cancel the debate."

"Highly unlikely, Meredith. He wants to chew you up and spit you out in front of everyone."

"Nice. As Emily says, bring it on."

"That's the spirit. We may ask Mr. Curtis to be at the Convention. It couldn't hurt." He glanced at Meredith and she's relieved he's joking. "See you in an hour." He closed the door and smiled.

Meredith stared at the closed door, dumbstruck. *All the ammunition we can muster*, she considered as she picked up the phone to call her husband.

"Darling, sorry to bother you at work, but if you get a chance can you give me a call? Just a couple of things. You're going to think I'm silly, and I'm sorry I haven't asked in a really long time, but what medicine or research are you working on now? Also, just a reminder to pick up your suit this week. Saturday, hehe, well, Saturday you may need it. Give me a call back when you can. Love you. Bye." Hanging up the phone, she starts to shuffle through the pile of newspapers. The cover of a tabloid read, "Nicholson's Love Child Found by Prior Husband."

"Ridiculous," she sputtered, "fucking ridiculous."

"Desmond, good, you're here." President Revo pulled down his shirt.

"Good morning, Gerald. How are you feeling?"

A pretty blonde nurse finished taking his vitals.

"Never better, especially with Sheila here to take care of me." Sheila suppressed a smile as she documented the chart and quietly left the room. Gerald watched and smirked, "Nice ass, don't you think?"

"Gerald, you must be feeling better. But I thought you preferred redheads?" Desmond jokes back, pulling up a chair.

"No. I think I like blondes now. All types of blondes. Hmmm, OK then, what have you got for me?"

"Has the room been swept?"

"Of course the fucking room has been swept. I apologize, just a bit fidgety. Yes, yes. Just before you got here. Well?"

"She doesn't know anything."

Gerald looked at Damion unconvinced. "How is that really possible, Desmond?"

"I know. It sounds impossible, but she doesn't know a thing. We just traced a call she put into him just 20 minutes ago and she clearly knows nothing. She wouldn't be fool enough to leave the message she did. She's clueless."

"Yeah? What did she say?"

"She asked him what he was working on. Her campaign must need to know since she has never really showed interest before. And also said she was sorry they hadn't really focused on him in awhile. She sounded pathetic."

"And the nigger story?"

"We're being careful, but hinting about it as often as possible."

"I think we should hint everywhere and as often as possible."

"Yes, Gerald, that's what we're doing?"

"Will he talk?"

"Who, sir?"

"The fucking husband, Desmond. Jesus, what's gotten into you?"

Desmond shifted in his chair and looked down at the ground. He wished he could strangle the jackass in front him. He wished he could scream at the top of his lungs that he didn't give a fuck about anyone but himself, and if he didn't come up with some answers soon, well, fuck that, he would come up with answers. Looking directly at the President he answered, "Gerald. Absolutely not. He's a goddamn coward, afraid of his own fucking shadow. Salinger's convinced that he talks to himself more than anyone else. Says he's seen him having conversations with himself in his car. They're bugging the car again anyway. Just in case. The first one malfunctioned. Fucking brilliant psycho he is."

Desmond twirled his finger on the side of his head. "Everything is going according to plan."

"OK, let's just say that's fucking possible. What about the project?"

"He's been working 18 hour days. Hardly ever sleeps. He's as obsessed as you are."

"Me? You mean *we*, correct?"

"Of course, Gerald. Of course, *we*. He's had a good run for the last eight months. Salinger was almost sure that he was on the brink. There's been no downturn for eight months and then, damn."

"Damn is right. Damn the son of a bitch. The fucking pain was brutal. Felt like a bullet in my gut. They already drew blood. Give it to me." Desmond handed Gerald the vial and stood against the door as Revo gave himself the injection.

"It's fucking amazing. They were stumped with the tests. I need this shit to work for good. Do you understand, Desmond?"

"Yes, I understand, Gerald."

"I fucking mean it, Desmond. I need this shit to work. I'm not the only one going down if it doesn't." Damion wished to look out the window, but for security purposes, the blinds were pulled. He despised the threat but remained composed.

"Gerald, I'm sure it will be soon."

"Good, Desmond. I mean it. What are we sticking with?"

"Indigestion."

"Fuck! Fucking ridiculous. Not food poisoning?"

"No sir. We don't want the public to think that you've been poisoned."

"Yeah, good point. Thanks, Desmond." Damion took the bag, carrying the empty vial and syringe, and put it back in his briefcase.

"Anything else?"

"Twelve more of ours dead in Baghdad."

"I need to get out of here today."

"Yes sir. I believe that you do."

The Democratic Convention convened in Boston in July 2004. With 1,331 electoral votes, Meredith was nominated on the first ballot. To the chagrin of the party and with much deliberation and recognition, she picked her running mate, the Governor of Indiana, who in the end had been her toughest competition. She had been the first to declare her candidacy and was the last standing on the stage. Governor Davis had at first denied the prospect of vice presidency, steadfast of his victory, refusing to concede. With Meredith the certain victor, he then realized that it would be better to be in the White House as Vice President, than not in the White House at all. Meredith had a private meeting with him before the offer was accepted and most of her staff rumored that when he left her office, he looked as if he had been witness to either a miracle or a terrible secret. Either way, now they were a team. With the conventional wisdom and Davis's regional balance, they were as strong as they were going to be. They were ready to take on Revo!

"Milton? Son? I wish you'd talk with me." His grandfather leaned over the lab table, hoping for a response.

Milton ignored the question.

"Milton? Please!"

Milton then looked up through his goggles and could barely see the outline of anyone.

"Milton? Son?"

Milton bent his head and went back to the microscope.

"All right then. You don't have to talk with me. Your father and I are worried though."

Nothing.

"Milton, Son. You've been acting very strange lately and we're worried. Do you hear me?"

Milton nodded.

"Good, I'm glad you can at least hear me. Now listen, I'm not sure what you're up to but I'm afraid it's not something any of us on this side would agree with."

Silence.

"OK. I understand this has gotten out of hand. Completely out of hand. But I'm worried for you. I'm worried for the grandkids and for Meredith. I'm worried for the whole lot of you. Do you understand?"

Milton took the chart on the table and began to write.

"Milton? I'm not saying that this guy or his pals are not candidates for, well, let's just say the 'warm ground' beneath you, but really! I'm not sure that you're the one to make that decision. Please, Milton, do you understand anything that I'm saying?"

Milton pushed the tablet a few inches towards his grandfather. On it he wrote,

"Pop, I'm about to cure one form of cancer. Many more to conquer, but one will be eliminated—for good! Good night."

His grandfather's look was all that was necessary.

"Good night, Son. I have to go now. I may not be seeing you for a while."

Milton sadly bowed his head.

"Nicholson, Stafford, what the hell does she go by?"

"Nicholson. Stafford is her husband"

"Nicholson and Davis are in for a very rude awakening."

"Yes, Gerald, they are."

"Isn't it ironic?"

"Yes it is."

"Dumb pussy, signing on with her."

"Yes, he is."

"We need another four years to accomplish our goals."

"We do."

"Desmond, are you all right? You seem a little, well, nonchalant. Ever since my last visit to Bethesda. Come on boy, we've got a winner for sure."

Damion Desmond looked at his boss and shook his head. "No sir, I'm fine. Just have to make sure that we get those next four years. Just need to make sure."

Gerald Revo stood and walked over to his best soldier. "Desmond, you know that she won't win, right?"

Desmond didn't respond.

"Desmond?"

"Mr. President?"

"Well?"

"Yes sir. I am sure she has no chance of winning. Absolutely sure."

"Good answer. Good answer. For a moment I thought we were going to have to do something drastic to confirm what I thought was obvious."

"Drastic? Well that's always possible. Hmm."

"Desmond, you know what I mean."

"Yes, Mr. President. I know exactly what you mean."

PART III

Chapter 41

And In The End

This was the most unusual campaign of modern times. Nothing could just boil down to simple referendum, even though Revo's war and the handling of the economy were of great consequence. This was no ordinary election year.

Two hundred and fifteen years of leadership of the free world and never had there been a woman candidate facing the possibility of such a seat. And never had there been such a popular incumbent President falling so fast with absence of personal scandal. There were no independent runners to speak of and there was nothing that either could hide behind.

Revo was slow to react to the Democratic momentum. Busy with his war in the Middle East and bouts of illness, the President's arrogance was losing status at the polls. Even as he accepted the nomination to run for a second term, he seemed despondent about the grassroots pursuit and the successful bus trip across America that took Meredith and her family along with Governor Davis and his, solidifying more and more votes daily. Meredith Nicholson was a television star and nothing seemed to underscore the current President more than her ability to win votes just because she was who she was. A celebrity.

The first scheduled debate was cancelled just weeks after the Republican convention. President Revo was too busy due to delicate negotiations with the United Nations. The second, scheduled for October, was threatened by another Presidential trip to the hospital. Meredith's undaunted popularity started spawning all over the world. On October 10th, 2004, just six weeks before the election, they finally would meet, face to face, and the nation, along with the world, would watch.

Meredith sat watching Milton pace back and forth.

"Milton, are you all right?"

He looked back at her and nodded yes.

"Are you sure?"

"Yes darling, I'm fine. I need to get back to work. It's been almost two weeks and well.

"Darling, you told me the Alzheimer's research could be held down for the two weeks and this is really important too." Meredith's demeanor seemed slightly shaken.

He walked over to her and touched her shoulder. She reached up to touch his hand but he walked away before she could.

"Milton?"

He turned and tears were in his eyes.

She rushed to him. "Milton, what is it?"

"Oh Meredith, I just want this to be over."

"Over?"

"I mean, I just want this to be done. I want you to win and be on with the rest of our lives."

"Oh, all right, I thought you meant…."

"Lord no, Meredith. No, no, darling. I'm so proud of you. I'm so proud. I just need to get back to work."

"I know, sweetheart, and you will. Tomorrow or at least by the next day, you will, all right?'

"Yes. I know. Good luck tonight. I love you."

"Oh, I love you too. I love you so much."

They embraced, then kissed, and Milton closed his eyes.

Darryl Rodriguez knocked on the door and poked his head in. "OK. Sorry to bother you both but Meredith, they're ready."

Milton gave her a nudge.

Bonnie waited outside and embraced her as she left.

"I'm so proud of you, Meredith."

"Thank you, Bonnie. I'm so proud of you too. Thank you."

Bonnie didn't look at Milton as he walked towards her.

"Bonnie?"

"Yes, Milton?"

"Thank you Bonnie. For everything."

"Thank your wife, Milton. She's the one you should be thanking."

"Of course. Of course." He excused himself into a quiet office to make the call and Bonnie shook her head.

"You'll be back tomorrow?" Salinger begged.

"Yes, by Monday at the latest. I'll be there and ready to finish up the project."

Salinger's shoulders relaxed. "Finished?"

"I think so, Professor."

"Really? Well, that's a wonderful thing to hear."

Milton's stomach turned.

"All right then. I expect to see you back here Monday. Good luck to your beautiful wife, Milton. Politician or not, she sure is a looker."

Milton hung up the phone and was directed on where to join his wife and children.

The debate would be delegated by a prominent newsperson, and the rules were quite simple. Each candidate would have five minutes for an opening statement, followed by comments or answers to questions put together by a panel of correspondents. Statements would close the end of the debate from each, no longer than five minutes in duration. Meredith immediately felt de ja vu. She took her husband's advice and breathed deeply, counting to ten She had to remind herself that she had won that debate. For a moment she was in awe as she stood within a few feet of the leader of the free world as they were introduced. He smiled as she stood poised with intentions to dethrone him. Then she thought of his leadership. His inability to respond to the people and neglect in interpreting and explaining his reasons, doing exactly what his country did not want him to do. His guiding light was God, but his actions were evil. He was evil and he needed to be replaced, kicking and screaming if necessary. Her job was to make sure that he did. Revo's smile perpetuated as the red light went on the prompter alerting everyone to be silent.

"Good evening and welcome to the 2004 Presidential debate. I would like to start the evening by welcoming Republican candidate President Gerald Revo and Democratic candidate Ms. Meredith Nicholson to the podiums. Please note that I intend the rules to be strictly followed. On that note, time is short so let's begin. Ms. Nicholson, would you oblige?"

President Revo turned and smiled. Fit and tanned, he nodded toward Meredith and said, "Yes, please, ladies first." The world chuckled.

Meredith held both sides of the podium and faced the camera.

"Thank you, Mr. Olsen, Mr. Revo." She ignored Revo's comment.

"I am honored to stand before the American people today. I would like to ask each and every citizen one question quoting President Kennedy in 1960. 'Are we doing as much as we can?' I want to start with that premise because I propose that with the help of the American people I, as President, will be doing as much as I can to bring this country back to peace. Some may think the government can do this alone, but I don't believe that. I want individuals, the fifty states, and the nation to accept this challenge and responsibility. I want us once again to be the greatest, freest country in the world."

Milton watched as his wife addressed the economy and education. Her hand lightly tapped the podium as she pounced on the $480 billion deficit and the soldiers that were in danger even as she spoke. She stood tall and confident and he wondered if she had pictured Revo in his underwear. He watched as his wife finished and the President was introduced.

"President Gerald Revo." The moderator added.

"Mr. Olsen, Ms. Nicholson. Well it seems that I have a comparison to make. First let me say that my record proves that I know the way. Ms. Nicholson pokes easily at the situations at hand, with no experience whatsoever. I disagree completely with her goals because each goal much have a resolution and she has only brought out the guns and shown us what needs to be addressed with absolutely no idea of how she can resolve these things. I imagine right now what our people would've endured, had someone as inexperienced and naïve as herself been Commander in Chief when the terrorists invaded our country." Milton turned quietly, looking for an escape. He remained glued to his chair as Revo's voice rose, accusing his wife of everything but adultery. The moderator gave the time sign and Revo thanked the American people for their support.

"All right, Ms. Nicholson?" He turned toward Meredith's podium where she remained poised and self-assured. Now would be her chance to prove her ability.

"I would like to start by asking about your views on foreign policy. What exactly is your agenda on that matter?"

Milton watched from the prompter and held his daughter's hand. Connor stood just behind them with his uncles. Everyone was tense.

"I see more government intervention, to stimulate growth and opportunity for us all. I don't believe as a country we can go it alone. We are currently in a grave status among many of our neighbors and allies. I intend to make a strong forum to rectify what has been severed in the past three years with the world. I intend to have the world's respect again."

"President Revo, comment?"

"Of course I disagree with Ms. Nicholson once again, in-so-far as to her suggestions that this administration has put our country at a greater risk. You'd have to be ignorant not to see that we are in a different position now that terrorists have murdered on our soil. Ms. Nicholson once again acts as if we are a few decades younger and that everything is coming up roses. Well I am here to say that it is not and I am able to oppose the idea that we just sit back and let the world fall apart around us. We are the strongest, the greatest, and the freest country in the world and I intend to keep it that way. Not by apathy but by action."

"Next question will be for President Revo. President Revo, programs for our educational and healthcare bills are at a standstill. Can you please tell us what you intend to do about these issues?"

Milton quietly turned to leave the room.

"Hey Milton, are you all right?" Darryl asked concerned as he watched him leave.

"I'm fine, Darryl. Just need some air."

"Gotcha. Want me to join you?"

Milton hesitated "No. No, that's all right."

Darryl had already turned back toward the teleprompter.

Milton could barely hear the voices of his wife or the President as he stood against the wall in the adjoining room. The air was stale and he wished he could just leave the building, look up at the sky, and breathe. It took all his energy to return and he slipped back without being noticed. Everyone was mesmerized, just waiting for something to sway the swing vote.

"Now for the summation time please. The questions and comments are complete. Five minutes for each candidate. President Revo, will you make the first summation?"

The camera turned toward the President, who glanced down at his watch.

"Oh yes. Thank you, Mr. Olsen. I understand Ms. Nicholson's attempt to solve all the problems in one blow, but honestly, the picture is much bigger than that. As a qualified politician and leader, I can attest that foreign policy, though important, cannot and will not solve all of our problems. We need to act, not react. Terrorism is our number-one foe and foreign policy needs to be designed around our act to end this violence. If we don't have compliance, then we don't deal. I'm afraid Ms. Nicholson's ideas, though sweet, are not realistic. She talks the talk, but I doubt she can walk the walk."

Milton stared at the enemy as he promised and bragged and poked fun at his wife's ignorance. He watched the clock as the second hand ended his charade.

"Ms. Nicholson, your summation please."

Meredith started to speak and Milton felt delirious. He watched her lips move, her gestures, the curve of her shoulders, but he could barely make out the words. He put his hands to his ears and looked down at the ground and focused.

"And I believe that if I'm elected, not only will I follow through on such a policy, but it will permeate the other problems we sorely attest to. The economy, the deficit, our relations with other foreign governments and, in the end, our safety, because where we are now, exceeds all dilemmas of where we have ever been." She exhaled slowly.

"Thank you, Ms. Nicholson and Mr. President. This hour has gone by quickly. Thank you for allowing us your insight and letting us present the next President of the United States. This is Benjamin Olsen from Chicago. Thank you and good night."

The candidates shook hands and the cameras zoomed in on their faces. Both candidates looked relieved and tired but Milton noticed one other thing. Revo's makeup had separated just slightly from perspiration and revealed a slight abrasion just below his right ear. Milton couldn't take his eyes off of it.

"Thank goodness you're back, Milton. Thank goodness. We're in desperate need of production and I was hoping, well…." Salinger pitied the man.

"Professor Salinger, I've been back for two days and haven't been home since."

"Oh well, I know Milton. I know, I just…"

"Professor Salinger. I need to meet with you tomorrow. I think that I've done it. It will need to monitored of course, but yes, I think that we've won the war."

"Oh my. Really? That's wonderful. Just wonderful, Milton. You really are a hero you know. A hero! When tomorrow?"

"Late. Let's say after everyone goes home, since this is so hush-hush. I have some very particular steps you'll need to take. It would be conspicuous if you were in here with me when the lab was open"

"Of course, of course. All right. That sounds perfect. Tomorrow night at six. Good night, Milton and good work."

"Hmm. Thank you."

CHAPTER 42

"Well? What should we do?"

Meredith sat in the all too familiar office with Bonnie and Darryl directly across from her. She was tired. She was ready for the election.

Bonnie shrugged. "At times I think we should soak it for all it's worth."

Darryl smiled and turned toward his belligerent, ruthless partner. "You know, Bon, for the first time, without hesitation, I think you're right on the money."

Bonnie smiled, satisfied, then turned to her boss for affirmation.

Meredith put her chin on her hand and concurred. "His health is in question and so secretive. There are days when I think he may burst with energy. Days when I think he should stay the President. Powerful. Really powerful! He's truly an amazing politician. But there are also days when his whole demeanor seems trapped by an affliction. Trapped in another person's body. OK, what are the polls today?"

"40 percent, Meredith." Darryl rattled off.

"Hmm. I don't know anyone that's won with forty percent of the vote, ever!"

Bonnie pleaded, "Meredith, we need to press. We need to get to the bottom of his health, if nothing else, to prove he's unable to lead another four years."

"I know you're both right. It's hard. It's just not something I would have wanted to pursue. I despised when anyone brought up my daughter's handicap. I hate when a handicap is the only hindrance, or the one to secure the vote."

"Meredith, please," Bonnie responded. "Emily was born blind and now has sight. She has overcome great odds, but she is not about to lead our country. She's not about to take all of our lives into her hands and make decisions that could mean insufferable damage in the end."

"I know, Bonnie. Jesus, what the hell is wrong with him?"

Darryl shifted uncomfortably, and then stood. "Meredith, the guy has some kind of illness that's being kept secret only because it's debilitating in some way. They have not and won't come clean. His staff is as secretive and probably more capable of running the White House without him, but honestly, it's time. Let's get this done. We have two more weeks. We're at 40 percent and honestly I'm not comfortable with that at all. Neither of you should be."

Meredith and Bonnie looked at him and both nodded.

"OK. Let's do it. When will it run?"

"Tomorrow if we get down there now."

"OK then, let's go."

Darryl leaned out of the office and said, "Harmony, have the car pick us up in the back."

"Yes, Mr. Rodriguez. Where will I say you're going?"

Darryl looked at Meredith then back out into the hall "The studio. We need to do some final checks before next week."

"Yes sir."

Meredith reached for the script and shook her head.

Milton watched the clock. At 5:58, Salinger knocked.

"Come in, come in." Milton ushered him to a chair.

"Am I early?"

"No, Professor, this is fine. You're right on time. Now please sit here so I can go over some things with you and here, put these on." He handed him a lab coat and goggles, which Salinger clumsily fit on his head.

"Professor, put them on your eyes please."

"Oh, yes, of course." He fit them snugly on his eyes and Milton averted his stare.

"Now please, here is a status sheet. I have coded it very simply. There are two weeks of injections, but only ten days are necessary. I believe if someone ill starts with the first and follows the directions precisely, they will be rid of the virus within ten days."

"You're kidding?" Salinger asked, his eyes bulging through the plastic.

"No Professor, I'm not. I've worked over a thousand hours on this and I believe I have finally succeeded in neutralizing the growth of the virus as well as killing its existence. Literally obliterated it."

Salinger stared at him, grinning.

"Now please, you must listen. This is the order that it needs to be administered. It's imperative that it is done this way. It is a cocktail and cocktails can kill if not followed precisely. Do you understand?"

Salinger's head bobbed up and down.

"All right then. Here it is. It needs to be kept refrigerated and used immediately. Once your patient uses the ten doses, we can evaluate and make any necessary changes, but I think we've done it. This can be reproduced easily and I think many people will respond to the cocktail. This will save thousands of lives."

Salinger sat back, arms folded, and continued to nod.

"Here it is. Each day is labeled. Nothing more. Please take them and get them to your patient now. I am very anxious to get this started."

"I am as well, Milton. I am as well. I will have shipping get them out tonight. Amazing. Just amazing. You are truly a hero, Milton. You will be remembered, honored as much."

"If this works, I expect nothing but a full account of the prognosis. I understand how proprietary this has been and I have done my work here. Take it and thank you for the opportunity." He reached for Salinger's hand, who grasped his roughly.

"Oh, Mr. Stafford, you will be acknowledged, I promise. What a good day, a good year. Unbelievable really. You're a hero in medicine and your wife a Presidential candidate. Really unbelievable."

"Yes, we are truly blessed. Now I need to get home to my children. Meredith won't be home now until the election. I'll need some time off in the next two weeks."

"Of course, of course, Milton. Take the next two weeks, really. If we need you in an emergency, I'll call you personally, but good luck to your wife. No matter what happens, we'll always have a place here for you."

"Thank you, sir. I really enjoy it here. I'm sure I'll be back."

"Amazing, truly amazing," Salinger murmured, as he clung to the tray, carrying it into the hall.

"Now get it out quickly, please."

"Yes, yes. I'm going now. Good night, Milton."

"Good bye, Professor Salinger."

Salinger hurried down the hall and Milton ran up, two steps at a time, to his office, where he had packed his personal belongings. He went down the back stairwell and put the box in his trunk before anyone could see him. He didn't look back as he pulled out of the parking lot for the last time.

"I'm here for you."

Meredith smiled. "You took the next two weeks off?"

"Yes, and if necessary, the rest of my life off for you."

"Milton, I wish I could hold you."

"I know Meredith, soon. Very soon."

"They're running the ad tomorrow."

"Really?"

"Yes. The polls are holding at 40 percent. His health is wavering. It may be the last chance I have to sway them."

Milton exhaled.

"Are you all right?" She asked, hearing his sigh.

"Yes. I'm fine. I really don't think that you needed it, but I understand that it's a dirty game. I'm sorry that you had to partake."

"Me too. Me too. Milton?"

"Yes, Meredith."

"Please hug the kids for me tonight. I miss them."

"Of course I will, Meredith. Of course."

"Milton?"

"Yes darling."

"I love you."

"I love you more than you know, Meredith Nicholson. Good night and I'll see you Wednesday."

"Good night, my love."

Milton, Connor, Emily, Beatrice, Daisy, and two agents went out on the sailboat the next morning. It was an unusually mild temperature for the end of October and all but the two agents were excited. They caught the wind in the sails and no one spoke, except for Daisy barking at the gulls, all contemplating what their lives would be like if she won. When they docked after almost two hours, Emily reached for her father's hand and said, "Thanks Dad. I think we all needed that."

Milton wrapped an arm around her, smelling the salt in her hair and whispered, "I think you're right, Em. We did, didn't we?"

He made one call when he got back to the house from his cell phone. His mind raced as the operator picked up the phone and transferred him to Salinger's assistant Marjorie who indifferent as usual.

"Yes?'

"Hello, Marjorie, Good morning. May I speak to Professor Salinger?"

"He's not in today, Mr. Stafford."

"Oh, hmm, he told me to check in with him this morning."

"Well, he's not in today and I'm not sure when he'll be in."

"Oh, all right. Is everything all right, Marjorie?"

"Everything's not all right. I've got four days of work piled on my desk just for today and the man who needs to sign off on most of this is playing hooky."

Milton smirked. "OK then, please, if he does come in, let him know that I called."

"If he calls, I will. I'll have him do a lot more than that."

"Try to have a good day, Marjorie."

"Humph," she added with disdain.

Damion Desmond listened to the message again as he opened the package the courier delivered. "I think this is it. He says this is it. Ten days. Ten days, Desmond, that's all. I've included the instructions. They need to be followed exactly, please! He stressed that emphatically. Ten days. I'll wait for your call."

"Dumb fuck," Desmond said softly as he admired the package. He placed it carefully in his briefcase and called for his car. Revo was going to be just fine. Salinger and the scientist would be dead in eleven days. Damion murmured, "You'll be very, very dead. Both of you."

The initial reaction to the campaign advertisement was shock. There were questions that needed to be answered and the President was dodging each one. His health was fine, concluded his campaign manager, and the Chief of Staff finally spoke to the public and the press, labeling Meredith as inexperienced and grasping. The United States people hunkered down for the election. Meredith campaigned tirelessly until three days before the election when Darryl took her aside and managed to say, "We need to talk now." He shuffled her into an empty office and asked her to sit.

"What is it? Darryl, what's happened?"

"The President has been admitted to Bethesda Naval Hospital again."

"What? What for now?"

"No one knows, but our people there are solemn. I don't think he's doing well."

"Darryl, spit it out. What is it?"

"He went into cardiac arrest about an hour ago. They revived him, but I don't think—from the information I'm receiving—It doesn't sound like he's going to make it."

"Oh my God," she stammered, crossing her arms and holding herself tightly. "Darryl, what does this mean? I mean, what happens if...."

"The Republican Party will convene. I believe they are at this moment. What this means is, the Vice President will step into his place."

"You mean the election will take place?"

"Yes, Absolutely That's why you both have a running mate. The election will take place and their ticket will read 'Williams'. Arthur Williams."

Meredith had met the man only once and she was in the heart of politics. He was subdued and banished to the Orient or the Middle East for most of Revo's four years. He was kind, quiet, rumored to be a genius and black. She was at a loss for words.

"Meredith, are you all right?"

"Darryl, what does this mean?"

"Um, I think it means our chances have improved greatly on moving into the White House in January."

Meredith inhaled slowly. "All right. Please keep me posted and let's get the polls run immediately, even before the next announcement. I need to talk with my husband. Please have Harmony get him on the phone."

"Yes sir, Mrs. President." Darryl saluted sweetly as he jumped at her command.

"Oh and Darryl?"

"Yes, Meredith?"

"Thank you. My goodness. This is something."

"This is politics Ms. Nicholson. Welcome back to the crazy world of politics."

"I need to talk to that fuck right now!" Desmond screamed into the phone.

"I'm sorry sir, but he's not here. He's hasn't been here all week, or last week for that matter, and I will not listen to that kind of language."

"You fucking—" Marjorie slammed the phone in his ear.

"That goddamned son of a bitch is about to, oh shit—" He looked at his watch and secured a private line again.

A heavy accent answered, "Yes?"

"It's me."

"You're late."

"I'm sorry. The dumb fuck from Massachusetts hasn't returned my calls."

"That's too bad for you, Mr. Desmond. Too bad."

"But I'm sure if I get up there...."

"I'm afraid it's too late, Mr. Desmond. It's too late."

"No, really. I can take care of this."

"It seems you cannot, Mr. Desmond and because of this you are not needed anymore."

Damion Desmond wiped the perspiration from his forehead.

"Please, sir. Please. I've been working so hard on this. I know that I'm capable. I know that I can have this for you soon."

"I hate to hear you beg, Mr. Desmond. It's very unbecoming. Good evening."

"No, wait!" There was silence on the other end.

Damion Desmond paced the room. He didn't hear the intruder. He was grabbed from behind and bound and gagged. He was pushed toward the bathroom and shoved up against the shower door. He didn't try to run. He knew that he would be killed if he made any false movement. He closed his eyes when he caught a glimpse of the steel blade and for a fleeting moment wished he were a praying man. Then the lights went out.

When he was found the next morning, his head was crushed against the tile and two of his fingers had been severed. The act had been so vicious that even his shoes had traces of flesh and bone. But he was alive.

At the naval hospital, after desperate attempts to revive him, Gerald Revo was pronounced dead the next afternoon. Cause of death would be documented as heart failure. His autopsy would reveal alcohol and narcotic abuse, but the information would remain sealed that the President was a drug addict. The Republican Vice President was sworn in at the dead man's bedside. The country was in a panic as their government's stability wavered. With no time for grieving, the names were changed on the ballots and the election would go on.

Just before they joined their families, Meredith asked what Connor meant about Milton's boss tragedy.

"What?" Milton asked surprised.

"Connor said he overheard you talking about your boss. Is he all right? My God, after so much violence and death I hope that he's all right."

"Oh, Meredith, I'm sorry. I didn't want to add to everything else. No, he's not all right. Seems he's developed a terrible viral infection and has no use of his hands or his mouth."

"His hands or his mouth? Oh my goodness that's terrible. How? What is it?"

"From what I've been told, he contracted a flesh-eating virus on his hands and at some point, touched his mouth, so the virus spread there. He's lucky he didn't...."

"Milton!"

"I'm sorry. Just trying to make light under the circumstances. I know it's a terrible thing."

"Will he be back soon?"

"I have no idea Meredith. No idea. I guess it comes in threes—bad things I mean. I know one thing though; we have a lot of important good things to think about right now. You agree?" He tenderly put a hand on her backside and she blushed.

"Come on, Mrs. President. I'm feeling pretty good right now, pretty good. Let's get this thing over with."

"Milton, thank you."

"Of course, darling."

"You'll be 'The First Gentleman', won't you?"

"I've been preparing for that for almost twenty-one years, Mrs. President."

"You'll be the very best."

"Not a lot to compare to, but I'll try."

"Ready for the Caribbean?"

"Really?"

Meredith smiled and sauntered out of the room. Milton watched with wonder.

The families were together, as the states' electoral votes were calculated. Meredith stood most of the time, quietly pacing. Gertrude and Samuel sat side by side on a couch, their hands entwined. The shock of the President's death and Chief of Staff's brutal dismemberment scared the populace straight, and the polls overflowed with the largest turnout in United States history. When the outcome was assured, they joined the thousands waiting to celebrate her victory. Meredith Nicholson would honor the title as the 44th President of the United States.

10 weeks later

"Are you ready?" She glanced back at her family

"Yep," Milton nodded as he looked over at Connor and Emily. "I think we're ready."

They ascended the stage at the Kennedy Performance Center, together.

0-595-33193-9